"Watase has a gift for involving characterization. Though she sometimes uses Miaka for laughs, she also lets us see her heroine's compassion and courage. The Emperor Hotohori is not quite as noble as he seems, nor is the wily Tamahome as self-centered as he would have others believe him to be. Even treacherous empress-candidate Nuriko has many levels. Watase's storytelling is an engaging one. She paces her story well and knows when to pump up the energy."

—Tony Isabella

"One of the best manga ever, it can be enjoyed by female and male readers alike."

—Protoculture Addicts

"There are two points in Fushigi Yugi's favor. The first is Watase herself, who has written margin notes for the compilation. Unlike many creators who rabbit on about trivia, she wants to talk about her craft, and has interesting points to make about research and the creative process. The second is that the strip succeeds in being quite charming; in spite of its derivative storyline—at one point a character admits the similarities to an RPG! But any comic that leaves me wanting to know what happens next definitely delivers value for money."

—Manga Max

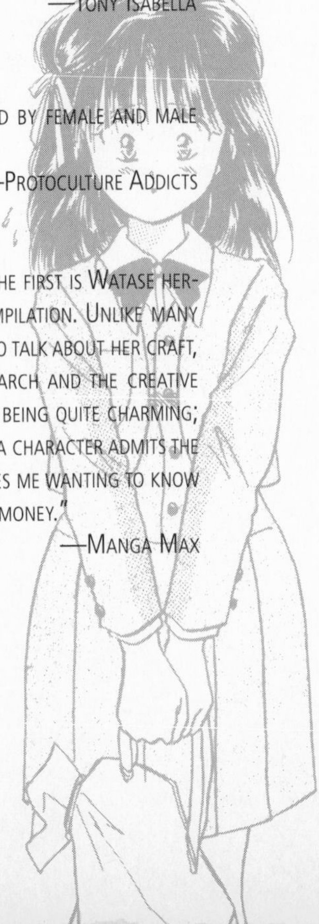

ANIMERICA EXTRA GRAPHIC NOVEL

fushigi yûgi™

The Mysterious Play
VOL. 4: BANDIT

This volume contains the FUSHIGI YÛGI installments from ANIMERICA EXTRA
Vol. 3, No. 5 through No. 10 in their entirety.

STORY & ART BY YÛ WATASE

English Adaptation/Yuji Oniki
Touch-Up Art & Lettering/Bill Spicer
Cover Design/Hidemi Sahara
Layout & Graphics/Carolina Ugalde
Editor/William Flanagan

Managing Editor/Annette Roman
Director of Sales & Marketing/Dallas Middaugh
Marketing Manager/Renée Solberg
Sales Representative/Mike Roberson
Editor-in-Chief/Hyoe Narita
Publisher/Seiji Horibuchi

Printed in Canada

Published by Viz Communications, Inc.
P.O. Box 77010, San Francisco, CA 94107

10 9 8 7 6 5 4 3 2
First printing, February 2001
Second printing, August 2001

- get your own vizmail.net email account
- register for the weekly email newsletter
- sign up for your free catalog
- voice 1-800-394-3042   fax 415-384-8936

ANIMERICA EXTRA GRAPHIC NOVEL

fushigi yûgi™

The Mysterious Play
VOL. 4: BANDIT

Story & Art By
YÛ WATASE

CONTENTS

STORY THUS FAR

Chipper junior-high-school girl Miaka and her best friend Yui are physically drawn into the world of a strange book—*The Universe of the Four Gods*. Miaka is offered the role of the lead character, the Priestess of the god Suzaku, and is charged with gathering the seven Celestial Warriors of Suzaku who will help her complete a quest to save the nation of Hong-Nan, and in the process grant her any wish she wants. She has already found four warriors: dashing-but-greedy Tamahome, the noble emperor Hotohori, cross-dressing and impossibly strong Nuriko, and the mysterious monk Chichiri.

Yui's fate was much crueler than Miaka's. Upon entering the book, Yui suffered rape and manipulation, and she attempted suicide. Now, Yui has become the Priestess of the god Seiryu, the enemy of Suzaku and Miaka.

Before Miaka can go on another journey to find the three remaining Celestial Warriors, Seiryu's country of Qu-Dong invades the weaker Hong-Nan. Qu-Dong demands that if Hong-Nan surrenders one item, they will retreat peacefully, but the item they demand is Miaka's love, Tamahome!

THE UNIVERSE OF THE FOUR GODS *is based on ancient China, but Japanese pronunciation of Chinese names differs slightly from their Chinese equivalents. Here is a short glossary of the Japanese pronunciation of the Chinese names in this graphic novel:*

CHINESE	JAPANESE	PERSON OR PLACE	MEANING
Hong-Nan	Konan	Southern kingdom	Crimson South
Qu-Dong	Kutô	Eastern kingdom	Gathered East
Tai Yi-Jun	Tai Itsukun	An oracle	Preeminent Person
Shou-Shuang	Jusô	A province	Lasting Frost
Ligé-San	Reikakuzan	A mountain	Strength Tower
Knei-Gong	Kôji	A bandit	Young Victor
Rui-Ni	Eiken	A bandit	Imperial Likeness
Huan-Lang	Genrô	A bandit leader	Phantom Wolf
Changhung	Chôkô	A northern town	Expansive Place
Shao-Huan	Shôka	A mystical person	Small Flower
Miao Nioh-An	Myo Ju-An	A hermit	Miracle Peaceful Life

No da: *An emphatic. A verbal exclamation point placed at the end of a sentence or phrase.*

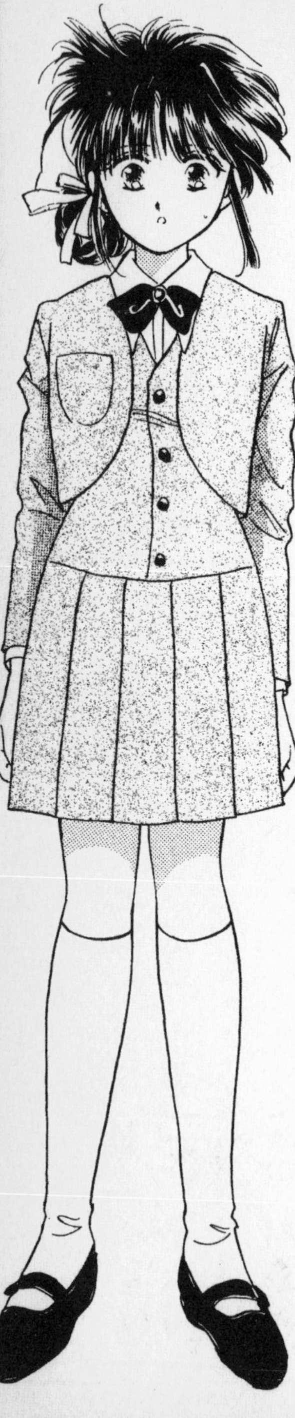

MIAKA
A chipper junior-high-school glutton who has become the Priestess of Suzaku.

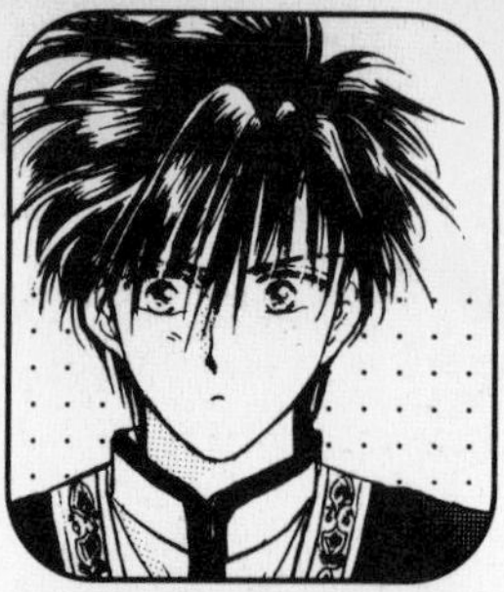

TAMAHOME
A dashing miser and a Celestial Warrior of Suzaku.

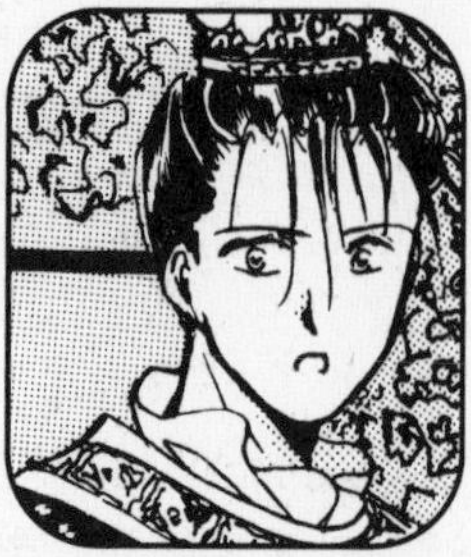

HOTOHORI
The beautiful emperor of Hong-Nan, and a Celestial Warrior of Suzaku.

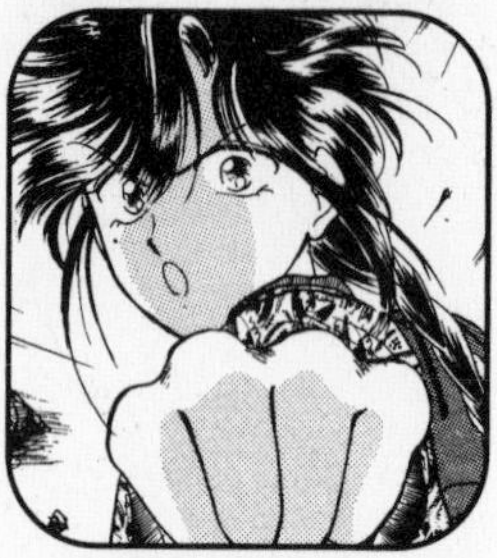

NURIKO
An amazingly strong cross-dresser and a Celestial Warrior of Suzaku.

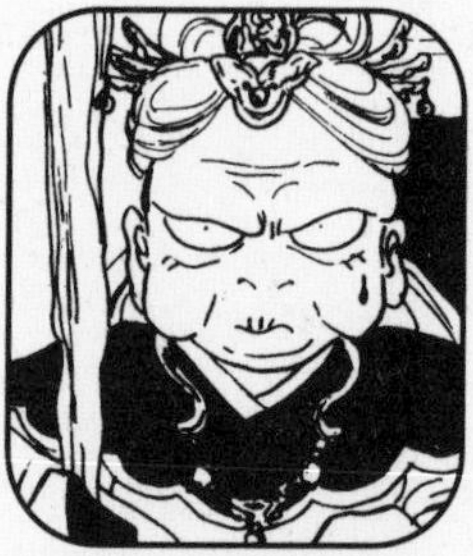

TAI YI-JUN
An aged oracle who gave the scroll *The Universe of the Four Gods* to Hotohori's ancestors.

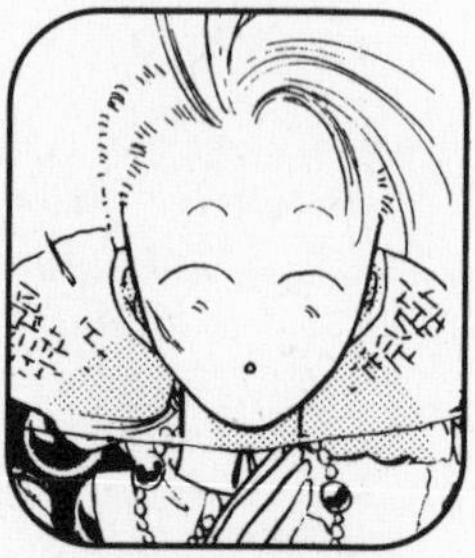

CHICHIRI
Former disciple of Tai Yi-Jun and a Celestial Warrior of Suzaku.

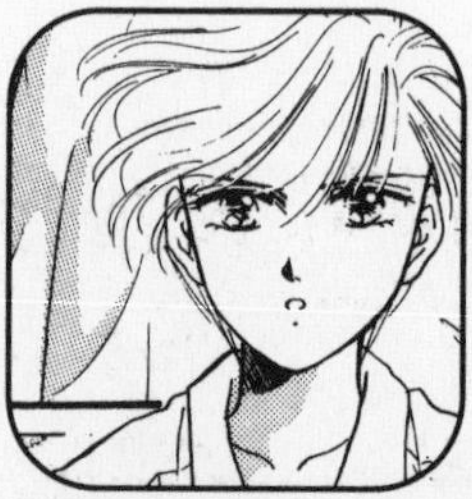

YUI
Miaka's former best friend, but now her enemy and the Priestess of Seiryu.

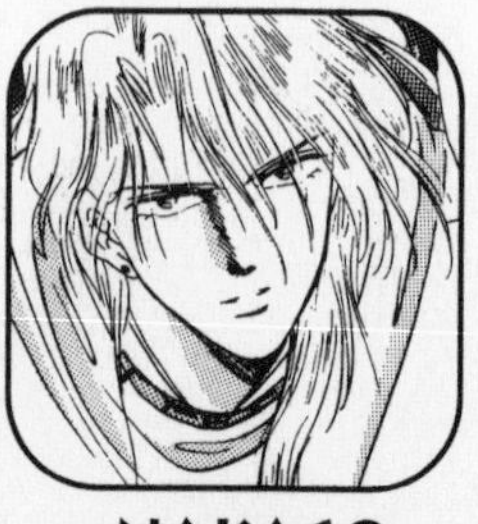

NAKAGO
A general of Qu-Dong and a Celestial Warrior of Seiryu.

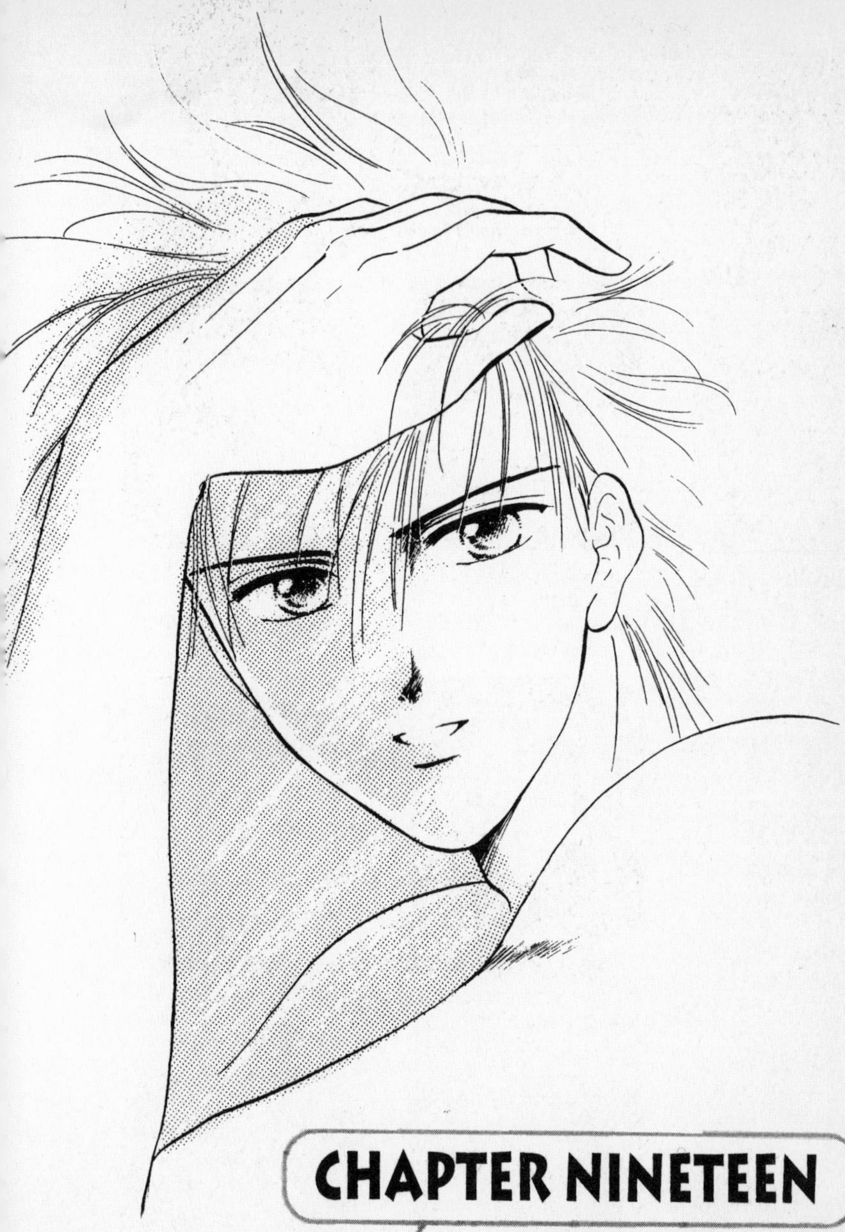

CHAPTER NINETEEN

WO AI NI
我愛你

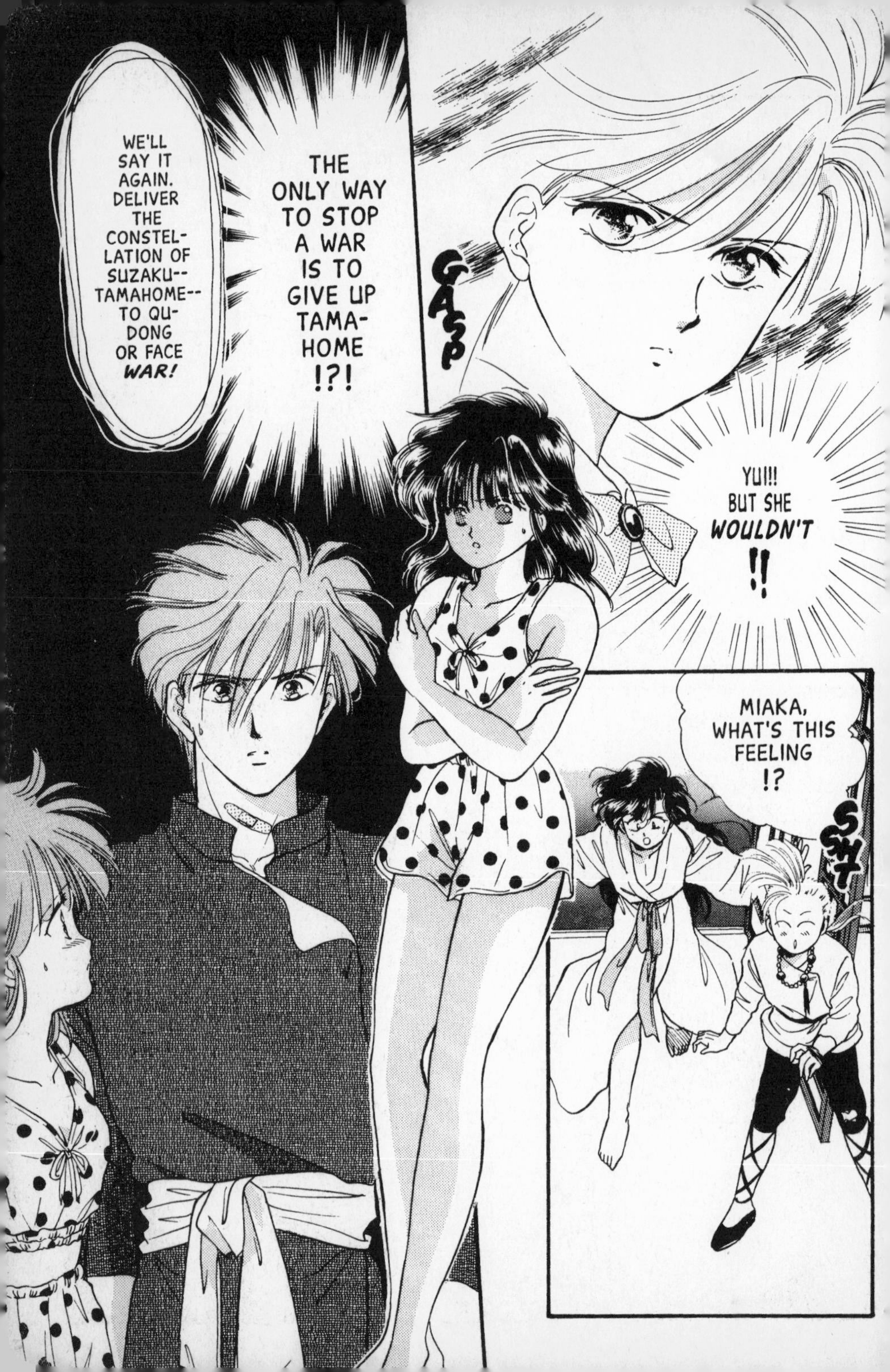
WE'LL SAY IT AGAIN. DELIVER THE CONSTELLATION OF SUZAKU--TAMAHOME--TO QU-DONG OR FACE WAR!
THE ONLY WAY TO STOP A WAR IS TO GIVE UP TAMAHOME !?!
GASP
YUI!! BUT SHE WOULDN'T !!
MIAKA, WHAT'S THIS FEELING !?
SSHT

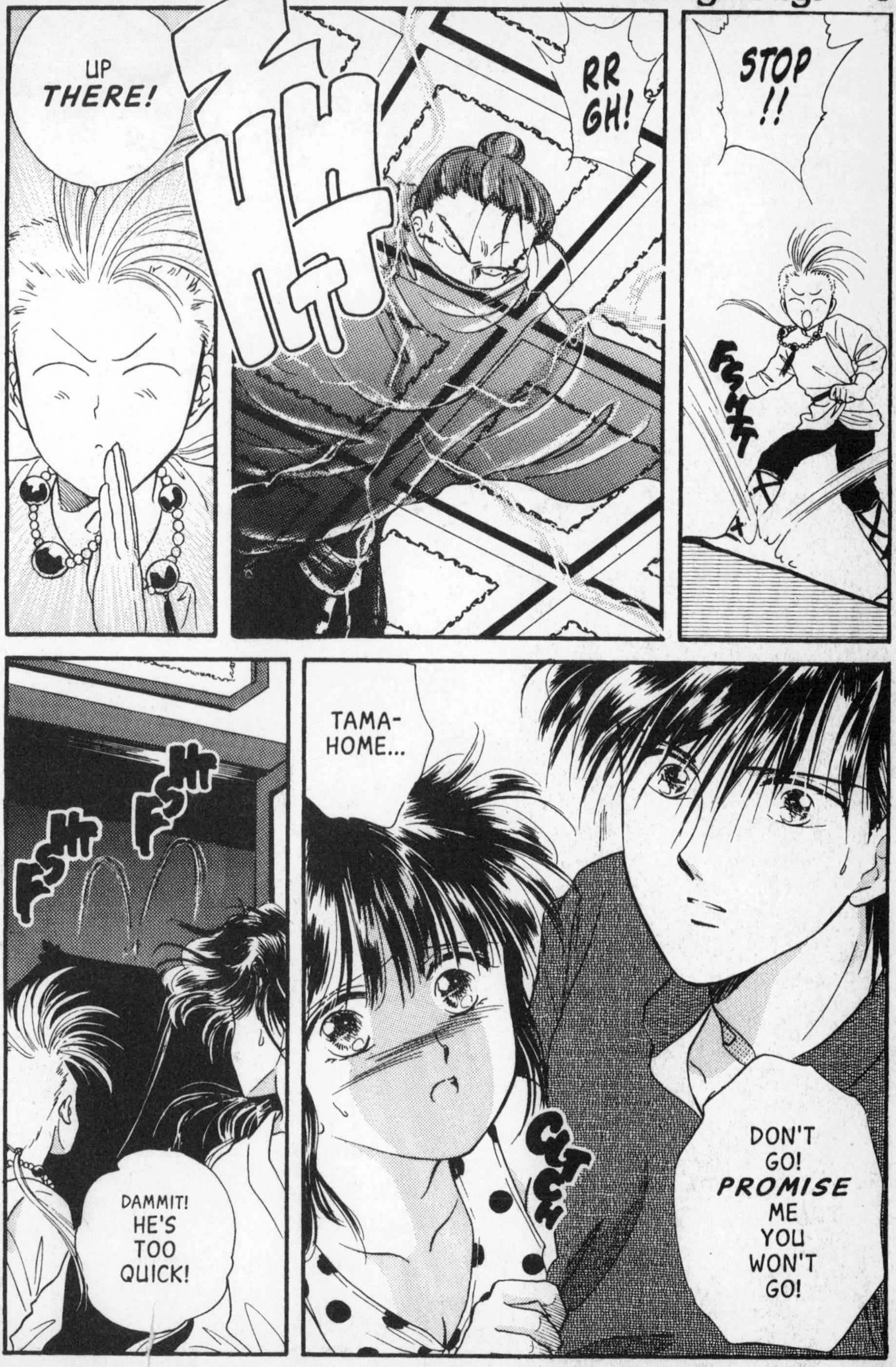
UP THERE!
RR GH!
STOP !!
FSHT
FSHT
DAMMIT! HE'S TOO QUICK!
TAMA-HOME...
CLUTCH
DON'T GO! PROMISE ME YOU WON'T GO!

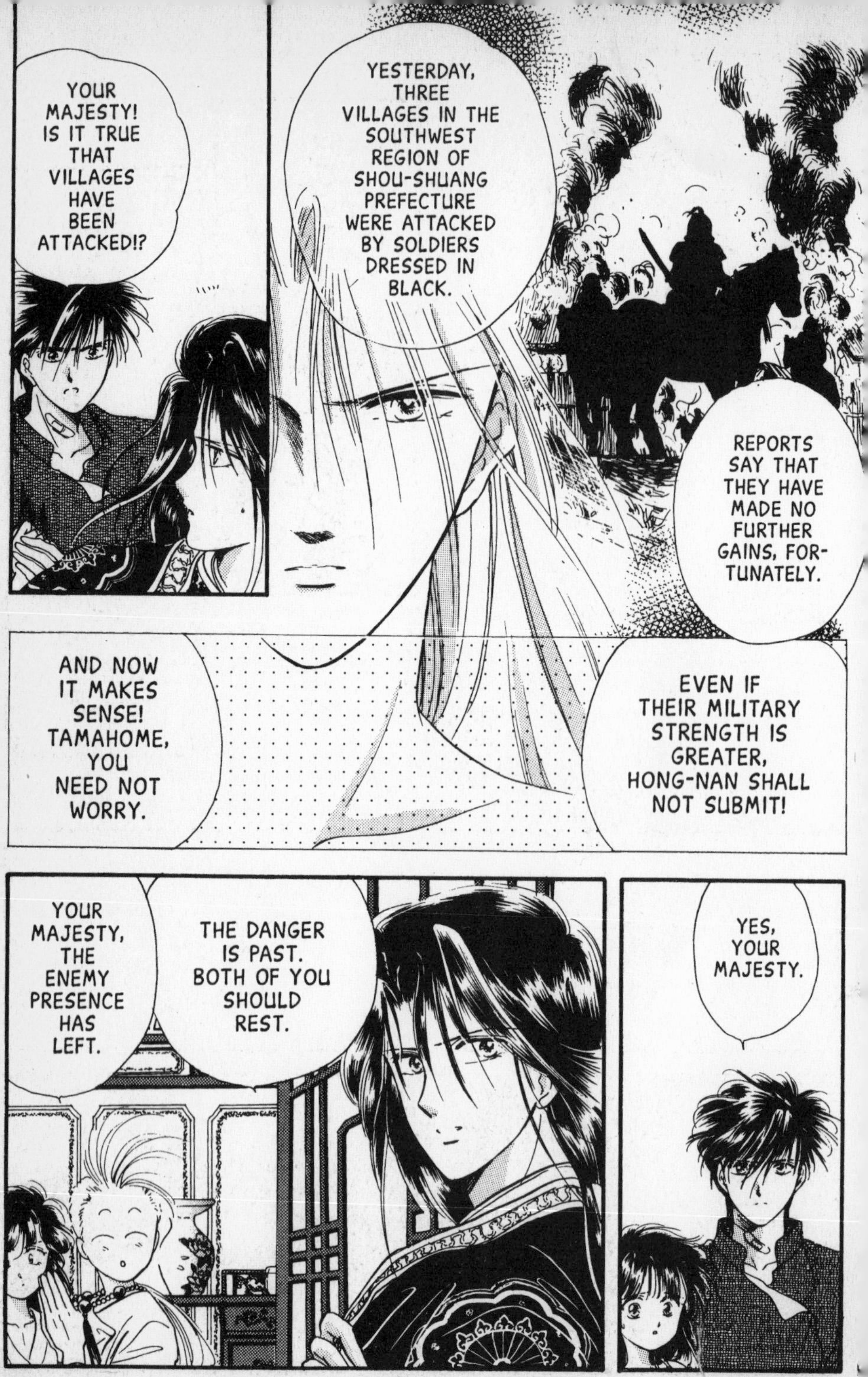
YOUR MAJESTY! IS IT TRUE THAT VILLAGES HAVE BEEN ATTACKED!?
YESTERDAY, THREE VILLAGES IN THE SOUTHWEST REGION OF SHOU-SHUANG PREFECTURE WERE ATTACKED BY SOLDIERS DRESSED IN BLACK.
REPORTS SAY THAT THEY HAVE MADE NO FURTHER GAINS, FOR-TUNATELY.
AND NOW IT MAKES SENSE! TAMAHOME, YOU NEED NOT WORRY.
EVEN IF THEIR MILITARY STRENGTH IS GREATER, HONG-NAN SHALL NOT SUBMIT!
YOUR MAJESTY, THE ENEMY PRESENCE HAS LEFT.
THE DANGER IS PAST. BOTH OF YOU SHOULD REST.
YES, YOUR MAJESTY.

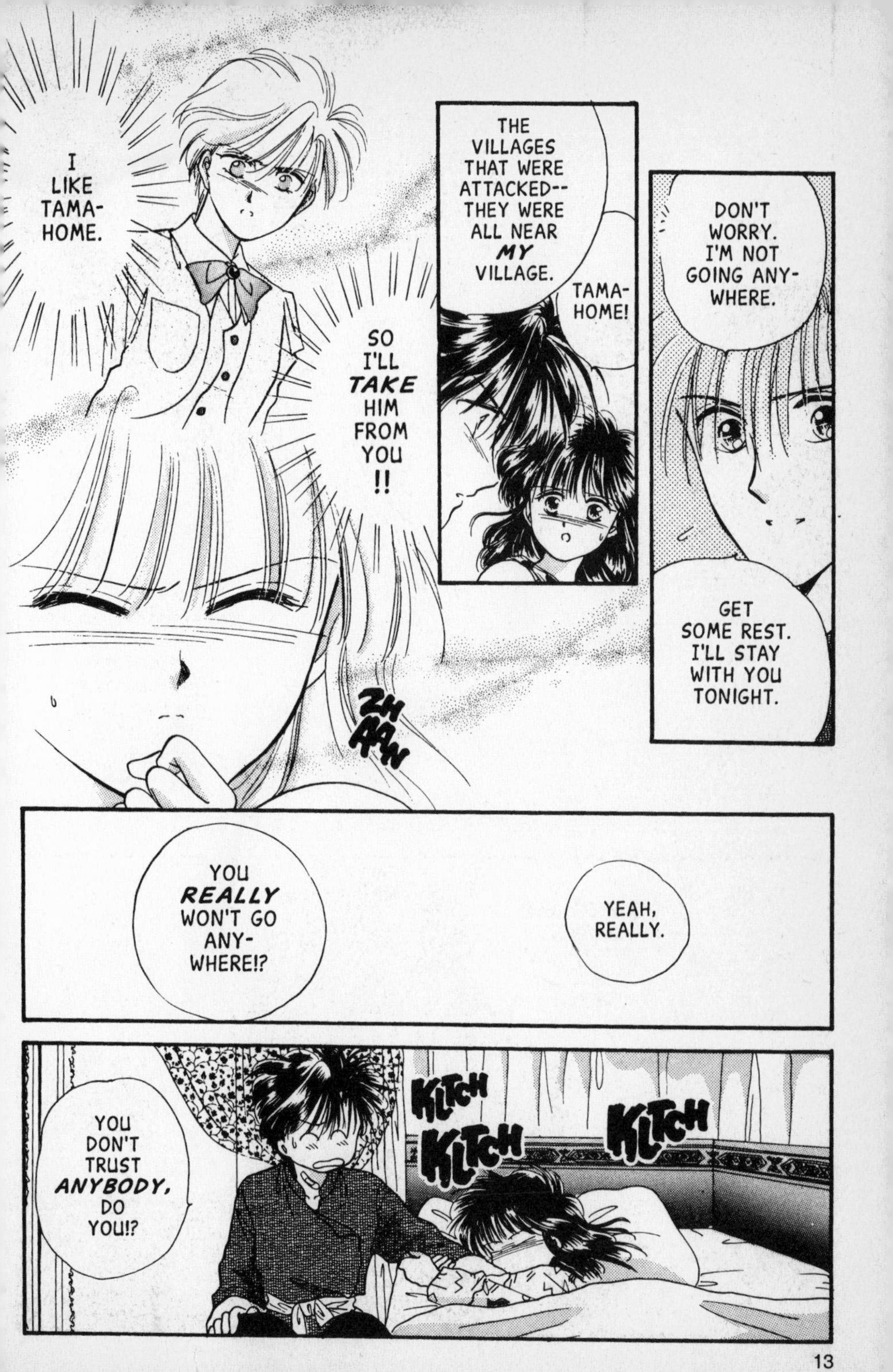
I LIKE TAMA-HOME.
SO I'LL *TAKE* HIM FROM YOU!!
ZHAAN
THE VILLAGES THAT WERE ATTACKED-- THEY WERE ALL NEAR *MY* VILLAGE.
TAMA-HOME!
DON'T WORRY. I'M NOT GOING ANYWHERE.
GET SOME REST. I'LL STAY WITH YOU TONIGHT.
YOU *REALLY* WON'T GO ANYWHERE!?
YEAH, REALLY.
YOU DON'T TRUST *ANYBODY,* DO YOU!?
KLITCH
KLITCH
KLITCH

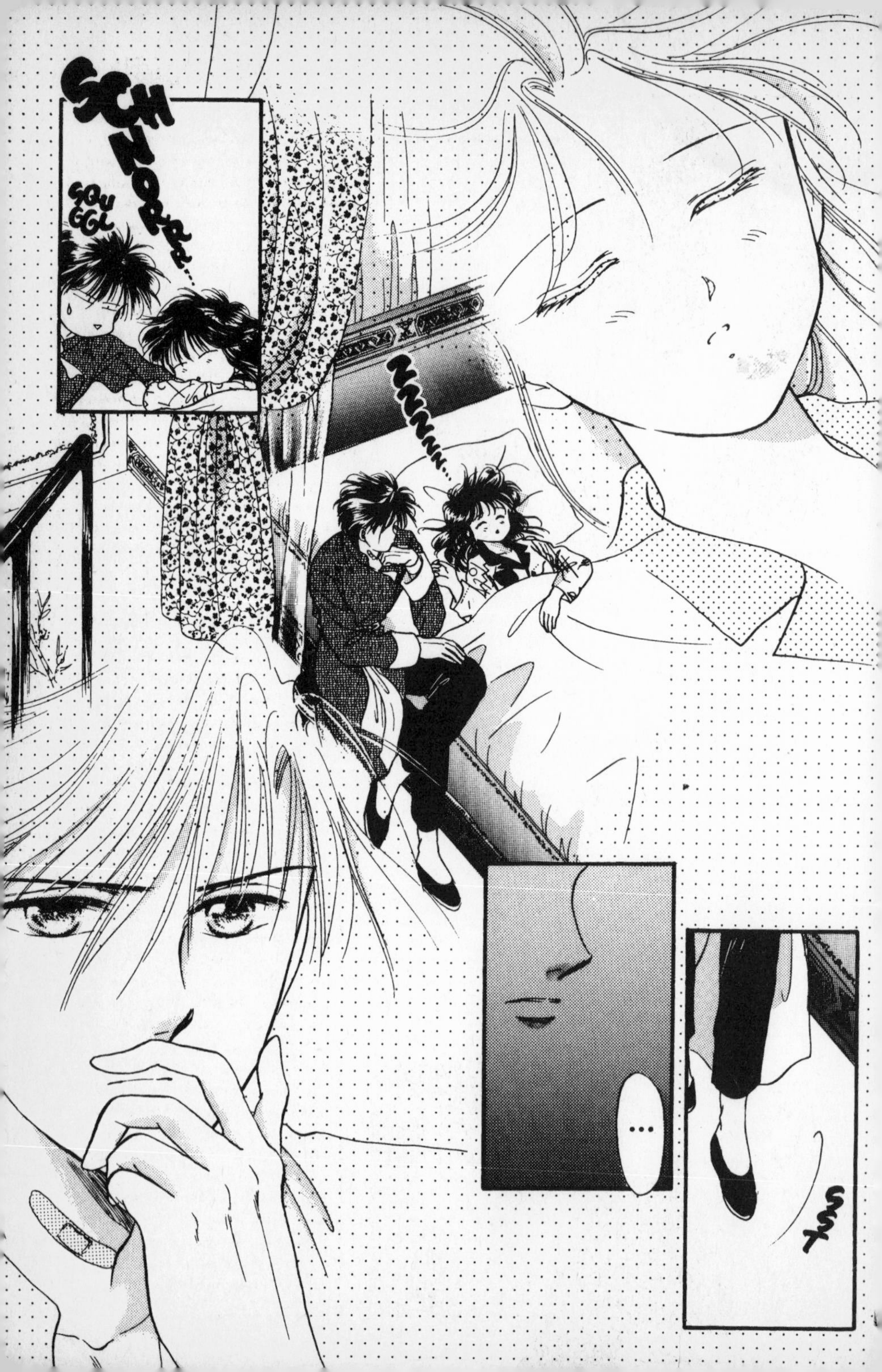
SCHNORRR...
SQUGGL
ZZZZZNN...
...
SST

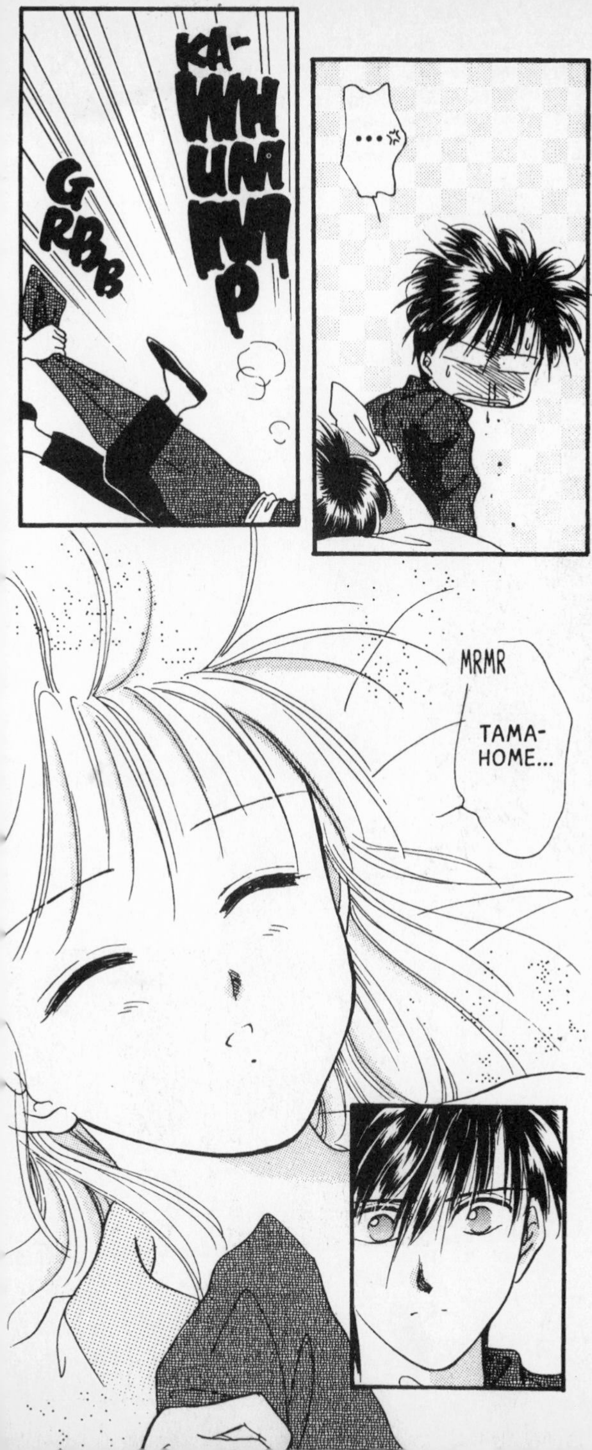
KA-WHUMMMP
GRBBB
...
MRMR
TAMA-HOME...

Bandit

Tah-ta-dahhh! (the curtain rises) (applause) Thank you, thank you, thank you. Thank you for your warm reception as you read this. Thank you. Soooo-- (adjusts the microphone) Winter's really hit us hard, hasn't it? My hands are so cold, it's making a mess of my handwriting. What's that? "What else is new?" Usually my hand measures 5 on the Richter scale! That's a good one! (a roar of laughter and applause) Enough with the standup routine! It's so cold, my hands are like ice. I don't have much time either, so I'll have to write this in my usual Speed Racer quickness. It reminds me of when I began writing this column in volume 1, I had all these opinions crowding themselves into the column... Ahh, I'm driving myself nuts! I can't write properly at this speed with these numb fingers. But don't worry, when I fill out important documents, I write very prim and proper. Every day I take my medicine for my muscle pains (fortified with vitamins), and then I set down to work. If I don't, my arm is just...
I take antacids, vitamins, health drinks, and herbal medicine. So even though I don't get much sleep, I'm still feeling energetic. I'm grateful! I've heard of experienced manga artists who're carted off by an ambulance after they've finished their pages. They're hospitalized with the IV needle inserted in one arm, menthol patches on the other, and a pen taped to their fingers as they draw more manga. Who knows, I might be next. It brings tears to your eyes. Sometimes, while working, I start to worry about it. Mmmm...this hot Calpis tastes great!
I've done quite a few columns now and when I reread them I'm really shocked!! My mental state at the time I was writing is so obvious!!
I have to start remembering what I've written every chapter!!
One thing I'm certain of--everyone must think I'm weird!! Bonkers!! "She's a total weirdo!!" Read the next chapter to find out how that's a complete misconception.

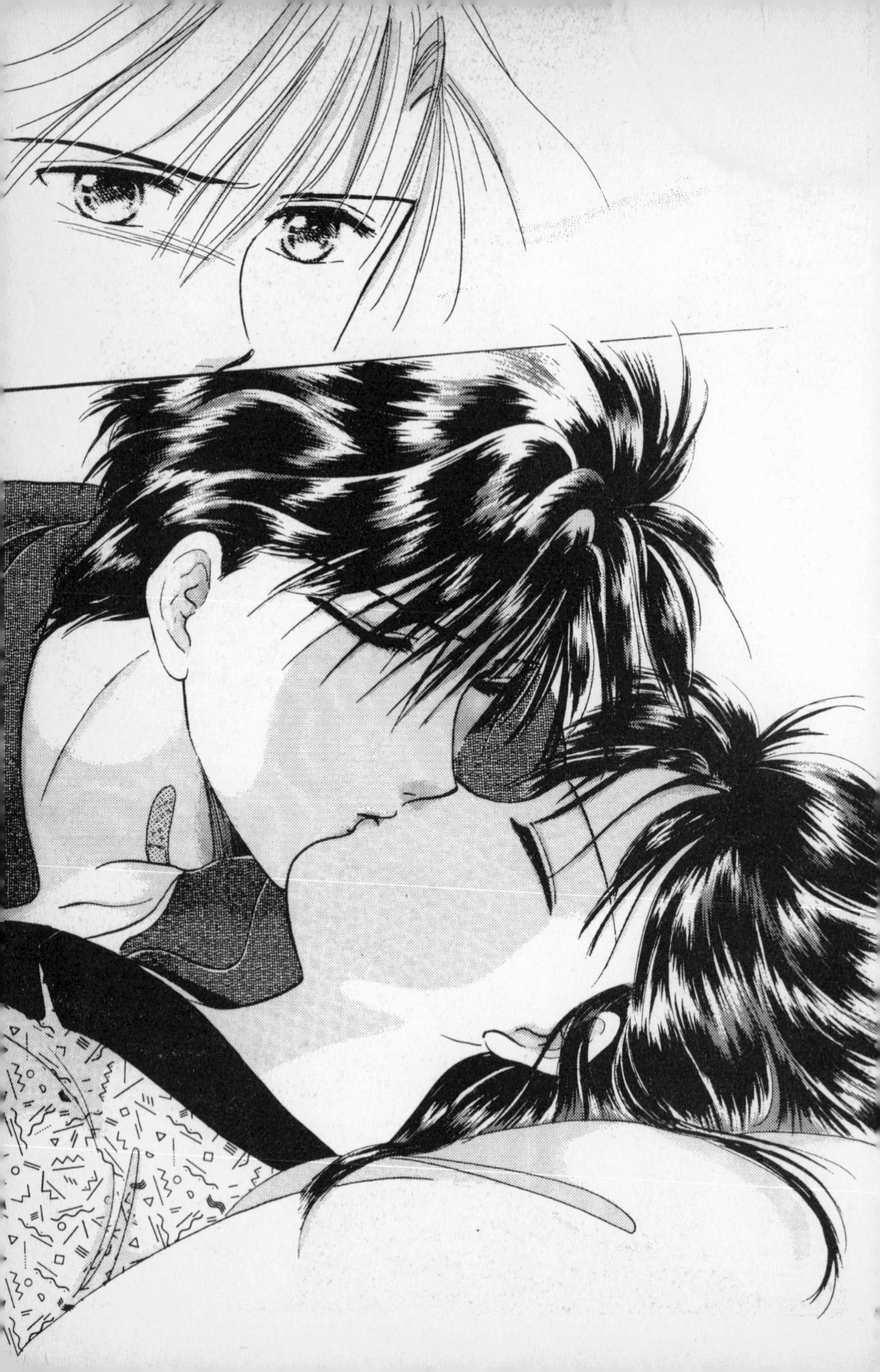

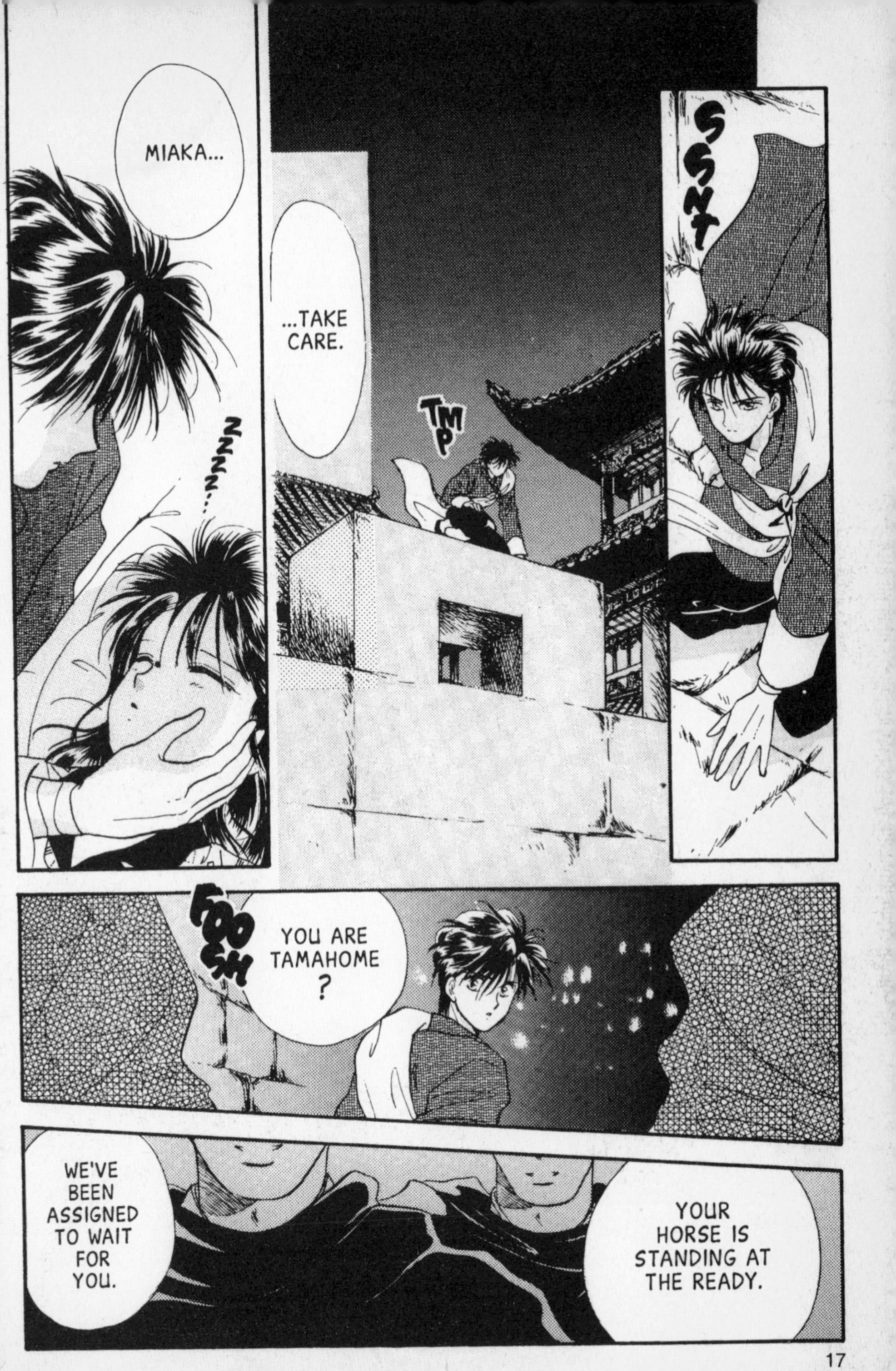
MIAKA...
ZZZZZ...
...TAKE CARE.
TMP
SSNT
FOOSH
YOU ARE TAMAHOME ?
WE'VE BEEN ASSIGNED TO WAIT FOR YOU.
YOUR HORSE IS STANDING AT THE READY.

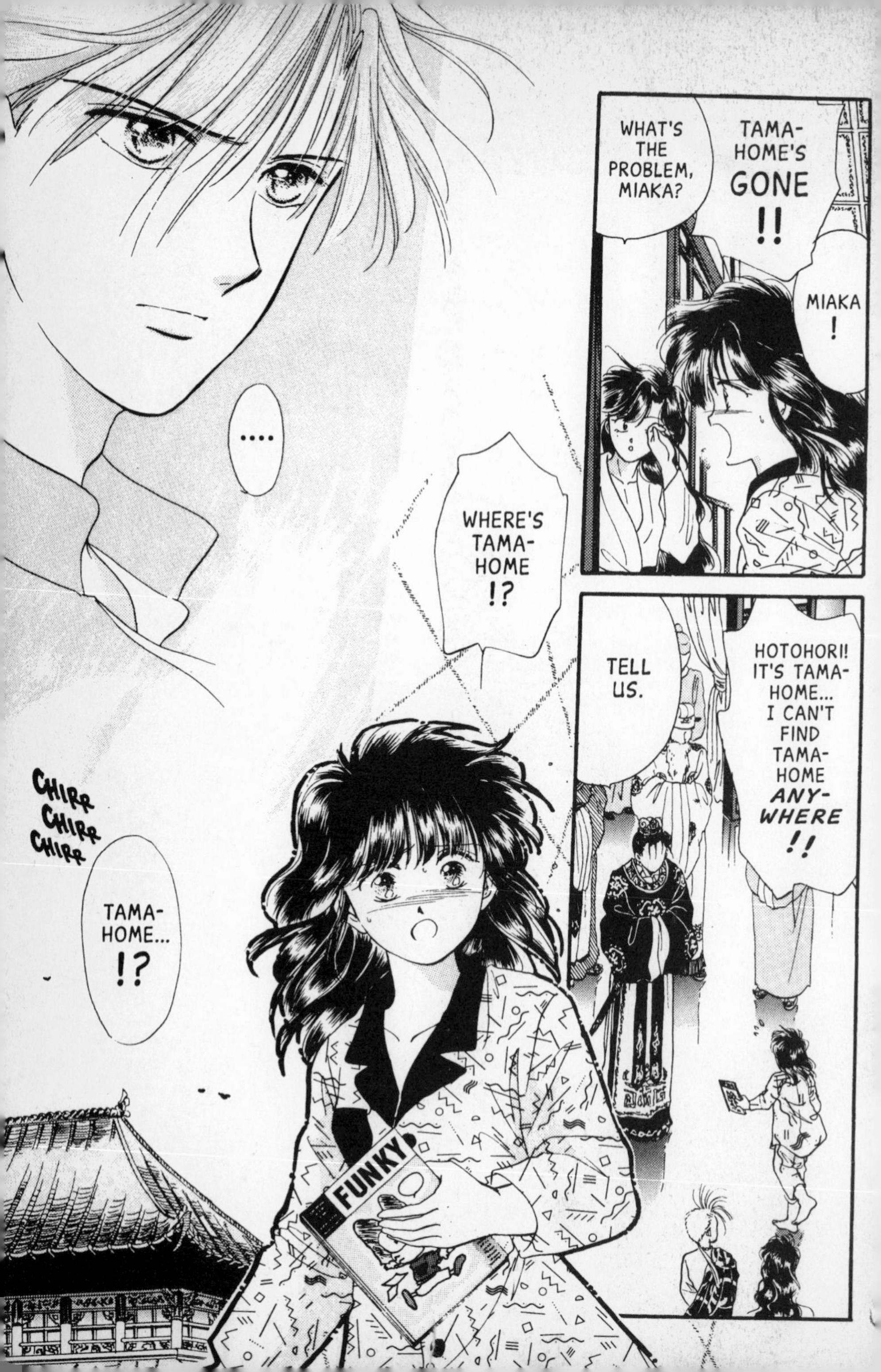
....
WHERE'S TAMA-HOME !?
CHIRR CHIRR CHIRR
TAMA-HOME... !?
FUNKY
WHAT'S THE PROBLEM, MIAKA?
TAMA-HOME'S GONE !!
MIAKA !
TELL US.
HOTOHORI! IT'S TAMA-HOME... I CAN'T FIND TAMA-HOME ANY-WHERE !!

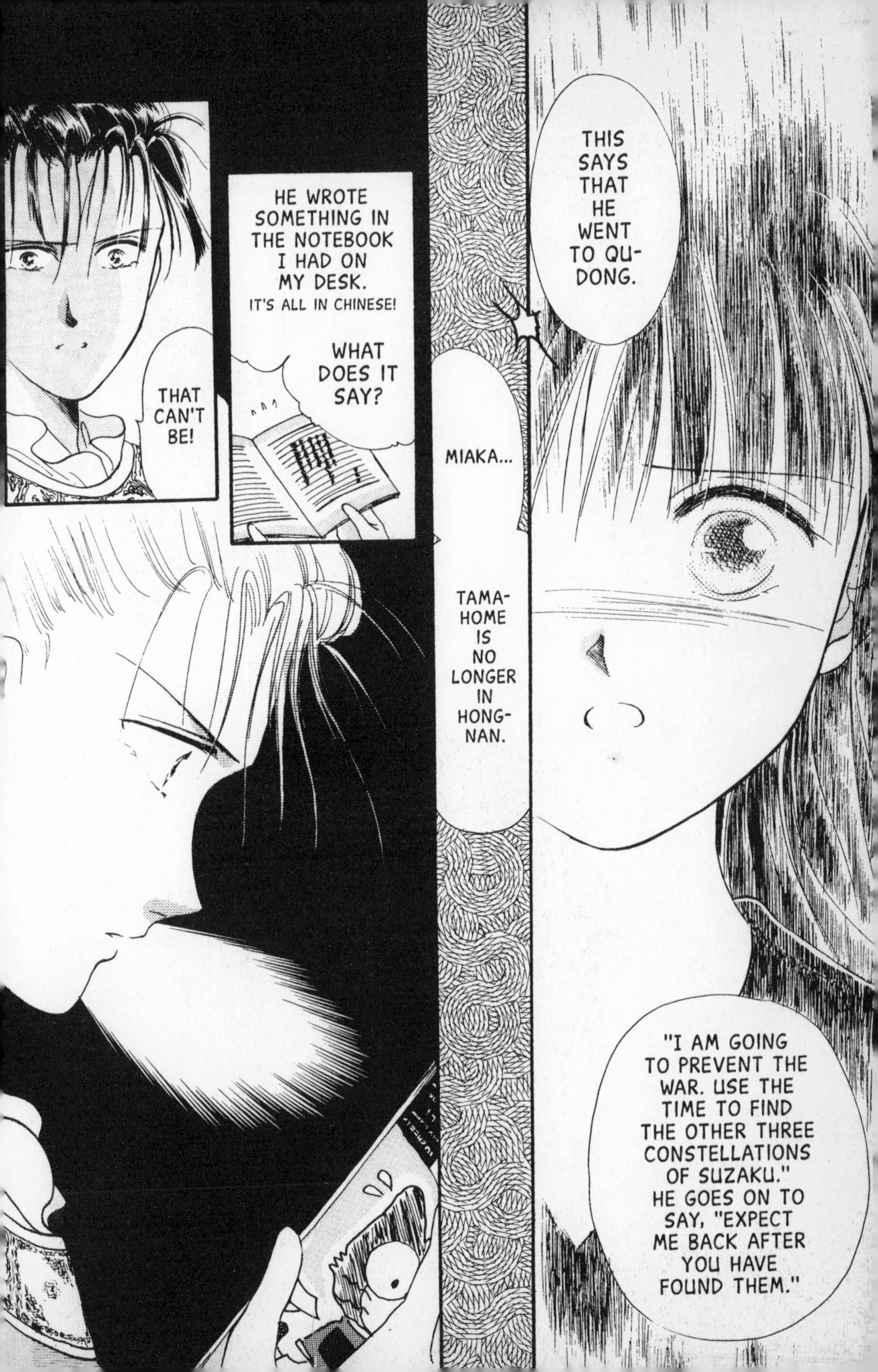
THAT CAN'T BE!
HE WROTE SOMETHING IN THE NOTEBOOK I HAD ON MY DESK.
IT'S ALL IN CHINESE!
WHAT DOES IT SAY?
MIAKA...
TAMA-HOME IS NO LONGER IN HONG-NAN.
THIS SAYS THAT HE WENT TO QU-DONG.
"I AM GOING TO PREVENT THE WAR. USE THE TIME TO FIND THE OTHER THREE CONSTELLATIONS OF SUZAKU." HE GOES ON TO SAY, "EXPECT ME BACK AFTER YOU HAVE FOUND THEM."

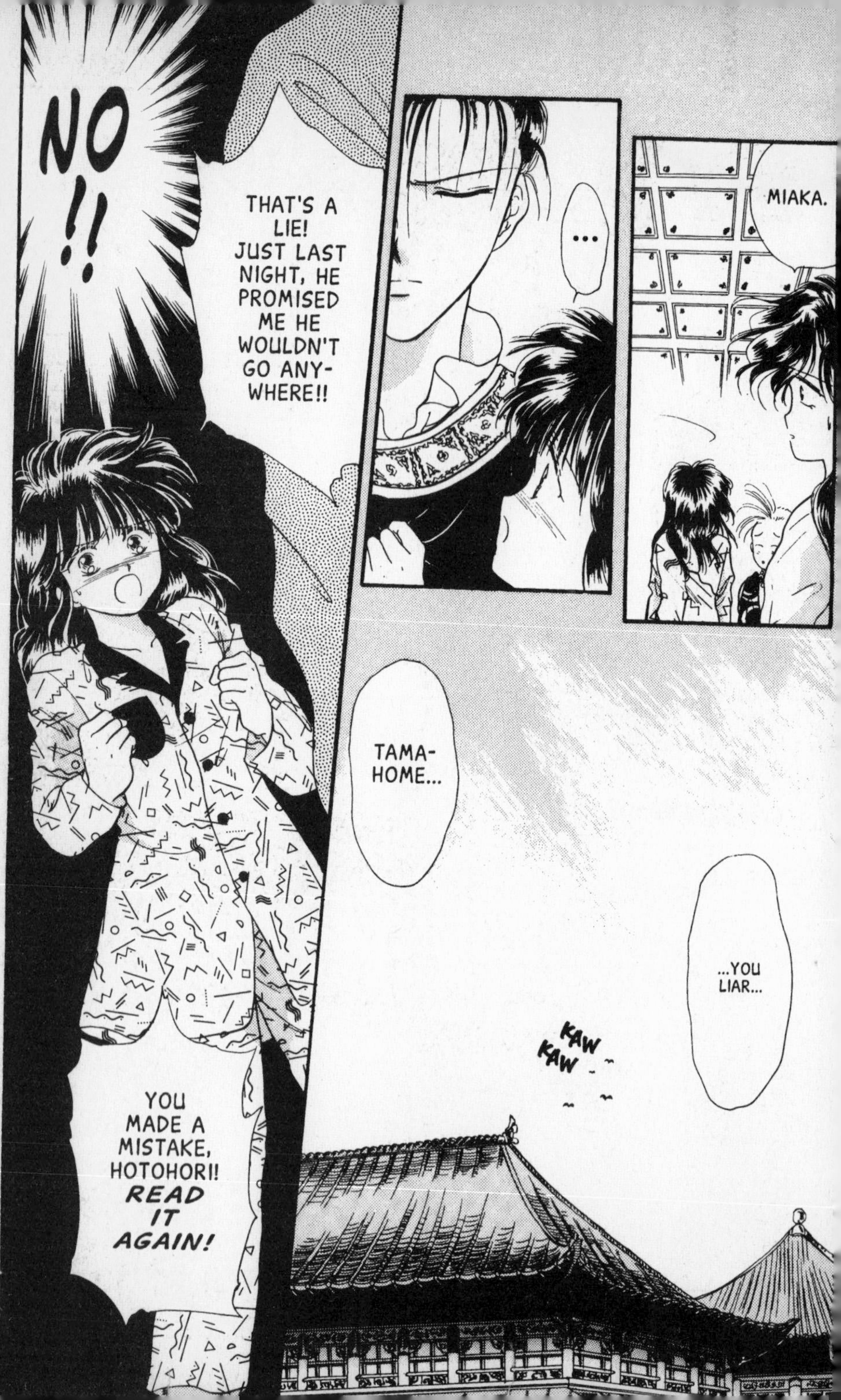
NO!!
THAT'S A LIE! JUST LAST NIGHT, HE PROMISED ME HE WOULDN'T GO ANY-WHERE!!
YOU MADE A MISTAKE, HOTOHORI! *READ IT AGAIN!*
...
MIAKA.
TAMA-HOME...
KAW KAW
...YOU LIAR...

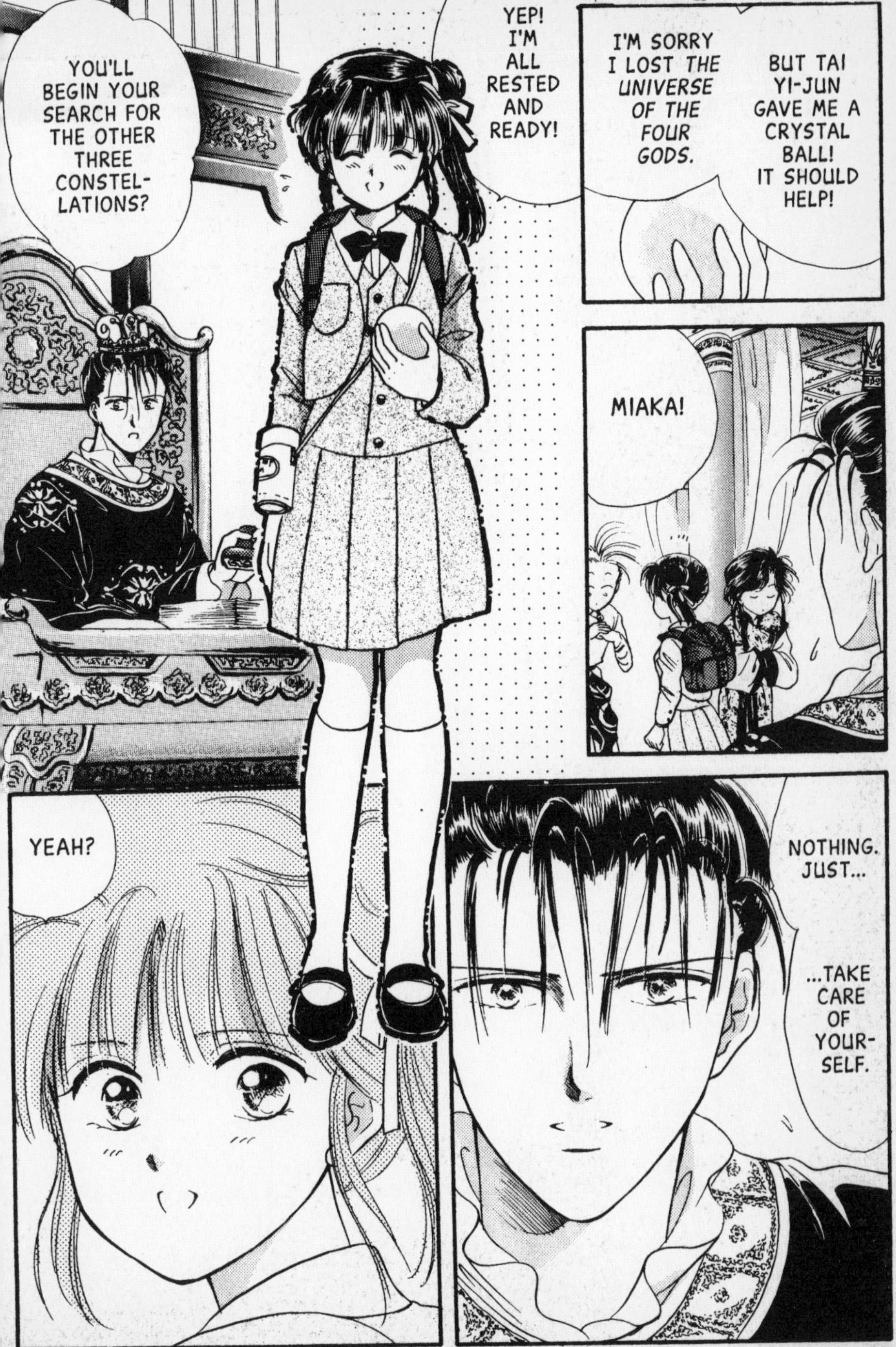
YOU'LL BEGIN YOUR SEARCH FOR THE OTHER THREE CONSTEL-LATIONS?
YEP! I'M ALL RESTED AND READY!
I'M SORRY I LOST THE UNIVERSE OF THE FOUR GODS.
BUT TAI YI-JUN GAVE ME A CRYSTAL BALL! IT SHOULD HELP!
MIAKA!
YEAH?
NOTHING. JUST...
...TAKE CARE OF YOUR-SELF.

HMMM. THIS IS SUPPOSED TO DO SOMETHING WHEN WE GET NEAR A PLACE WITH A CELESTIAL WARRIOR. IT DIDN'T DO NOTHIN' IN TOWN.

KLOP KLOP

...

MIAKA... ABOUT TAMA-HOME...

HEY!!

HYUOOO

THERE'S A CHARACTER FLOATING INSIDE !!

MOUN-TAIN...?

LIGÉ-SAN MOUNTAIN IS CLOSE. THERE'S SUPPOSED TO BE A BAND OF MOUNTAIN BANDITS THERE.

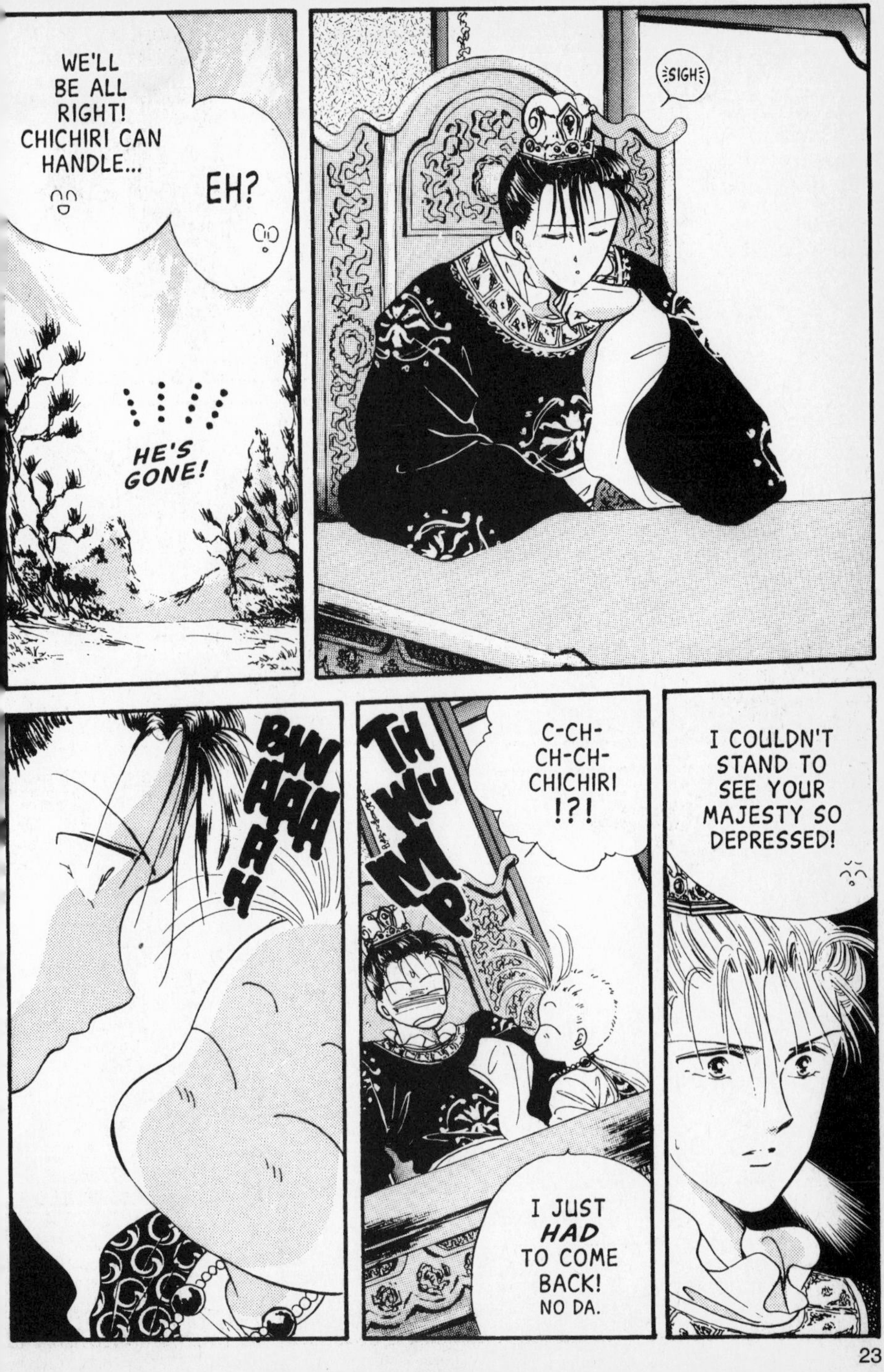
WE'LL BE ALL RIGHT! CHICHIRI CAN HANDLE...
EH?
HE'S GONE!
SIGH
BWAAAAAH
THWUMP
C-CH-CH-CH-CHICHIRI !?!
I JUST HAD TO COME BACK! NO DA.
I COULDN'T STAND TO SEE YOUR MAJESTY SO DEPRESSED!

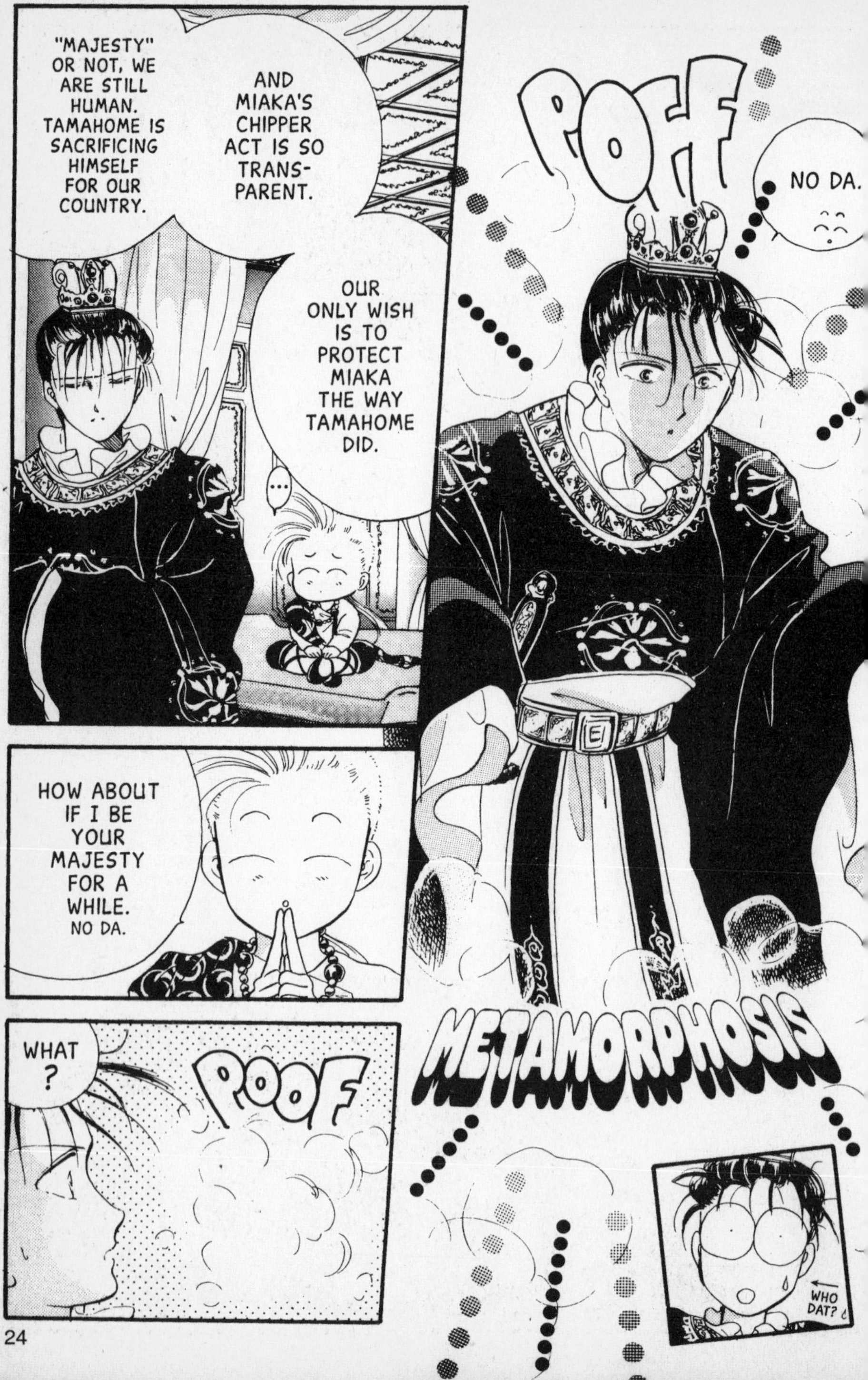
"MAJESTY" OR NOT, WE ARE STILL HUMAN. TAMAHOME IS SACRIFICING HIMSELF FOR OUR COUNTRY.
AND MIAKA'S CHIPPER ACT IS SO TRANS- PARENT.
OUR ONLY WISH IS TO PROTECT MIAKA THE WAY TAMAHOME DID.
...
HOW ABOUT IF I BE YOUR MAJESTY FOR A WHILE. NO DA.
WHAT ?
POOF
POOF
NO DA.
METAMORPHOSIS
WHO DAT?

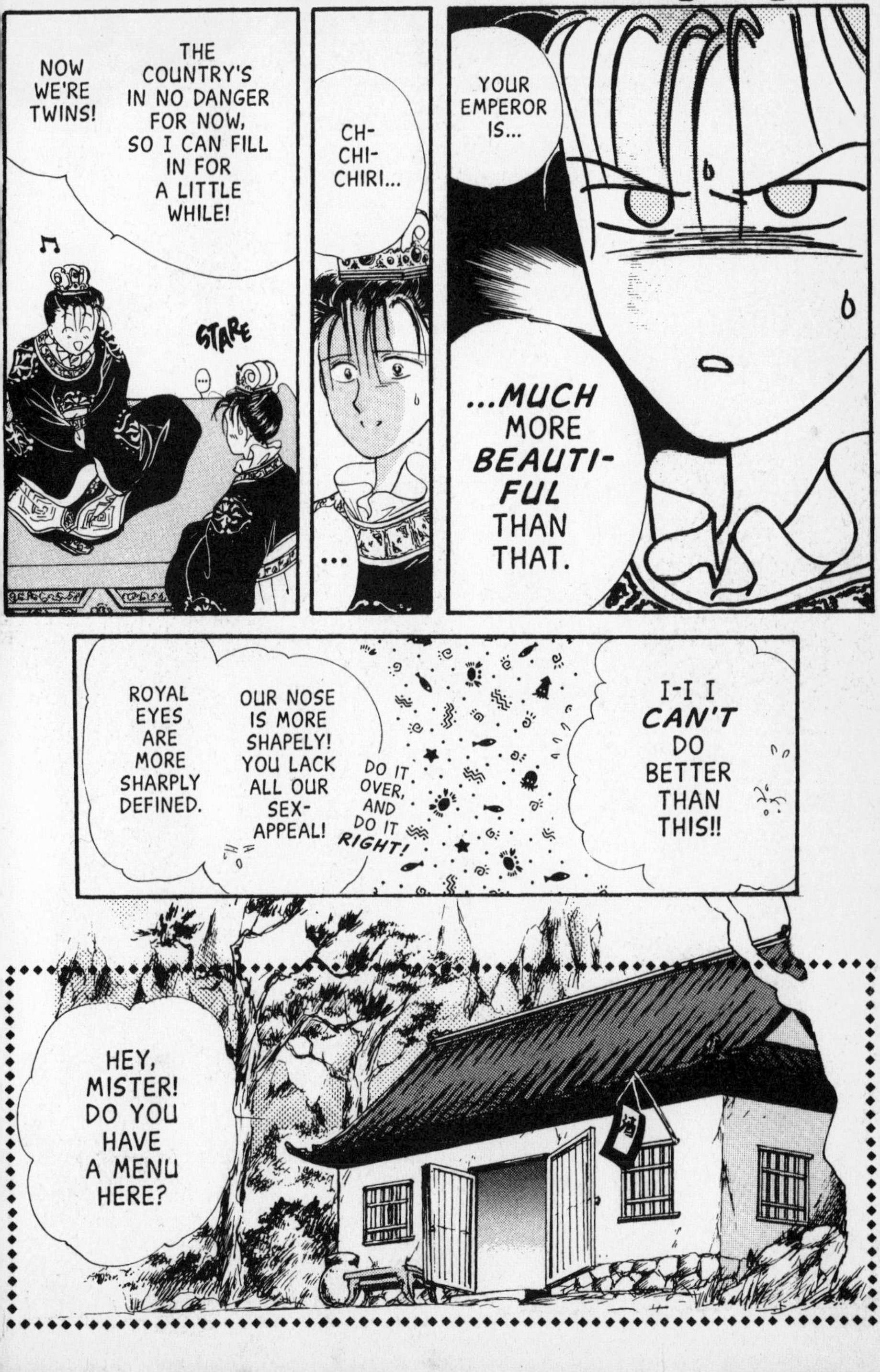
NOW WE'RE TWINS!
THE COUNTRY'S IN NO DANGER FOR NOW, SO I CAN FILL IN FOR A LITTLE WHILE!
STARE
...
CH-CHI-CHIRI...
...
YOUR EMPEROR IS...
...MUCH MORE BEAUTIFUL THAN THAT.
ROYAL EYES ARE MORE SHARPLY DEFINED.
OUR NOSE IS MORE SHAPELY! YOU LACK ALL OUR SEX-APPEAL!
DO IT OVER, AND DO IT RIGHT!
I-I I CAN'T DO BETTER THAN THIS!!
HEY, MISTER! DO YOU HAVE A MENU HERE?

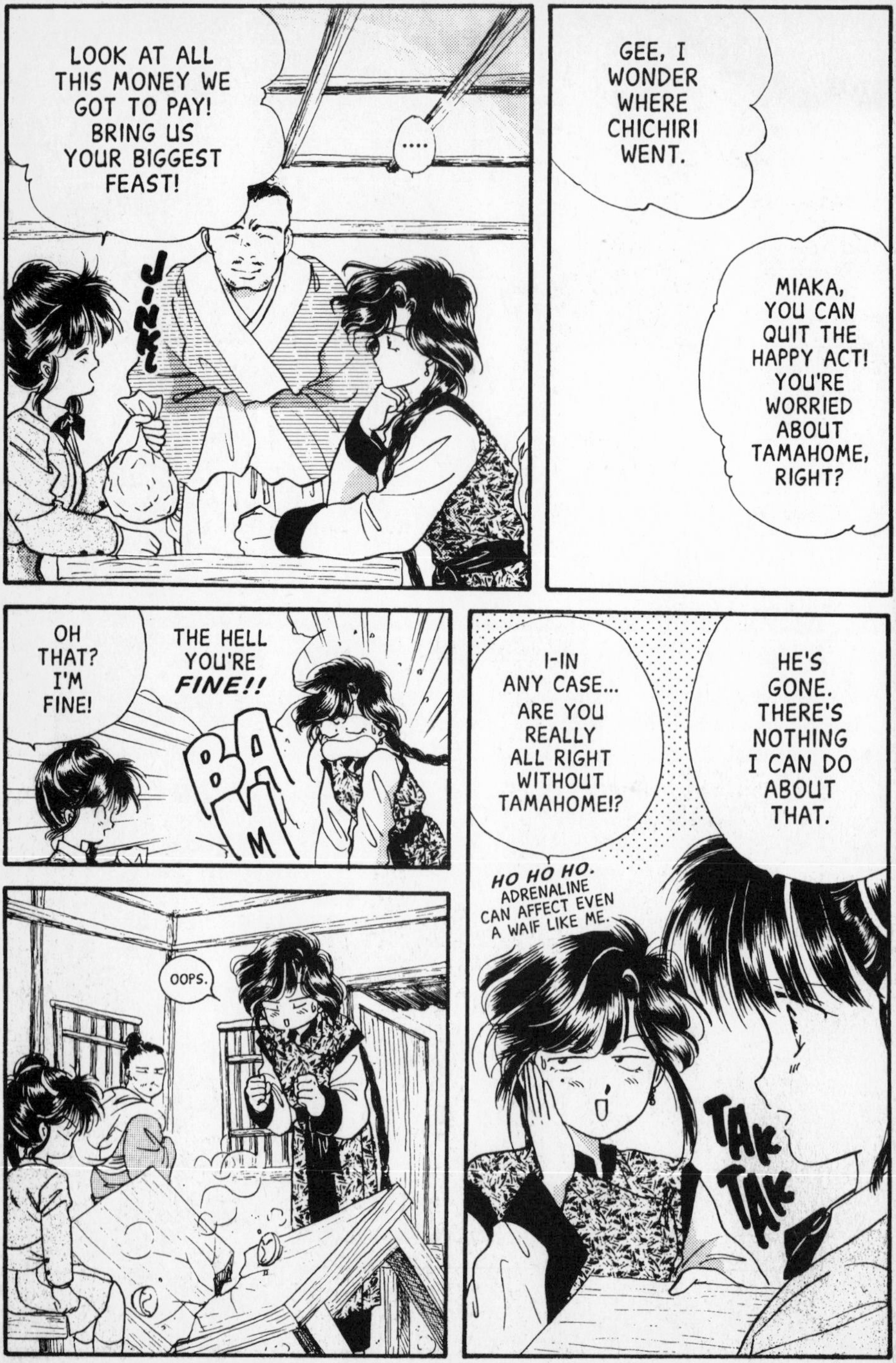
LOOK AT ALL THIS MONEY WE GOT TO PAY! BRING US YOUR BIGGEST FEAST!
JINK!
....
GEE, I WONDER WHERE CHICHIRI WENT.
MIAKA, YOU CAN QUIT THE HAPPY ACT! YOU'RE WORRIED ABOUT TAMAHOME, RIGHT?
OH THAT? I'M FINE!
THE HELL YOU'RE *FINE!!*
BAM
I-IN ANY CASE... ARE YOU REALLY ALL RIGHT WITHOUT TAMAHOME!?
HE'S GONE. THERE'S NOTHING I CAN DO ABOUT THAT.
OOPS.
HO HO HO. ADRENALINE CAN AFFECT EVEN A WAIF LIKE ME.
TAK TAK

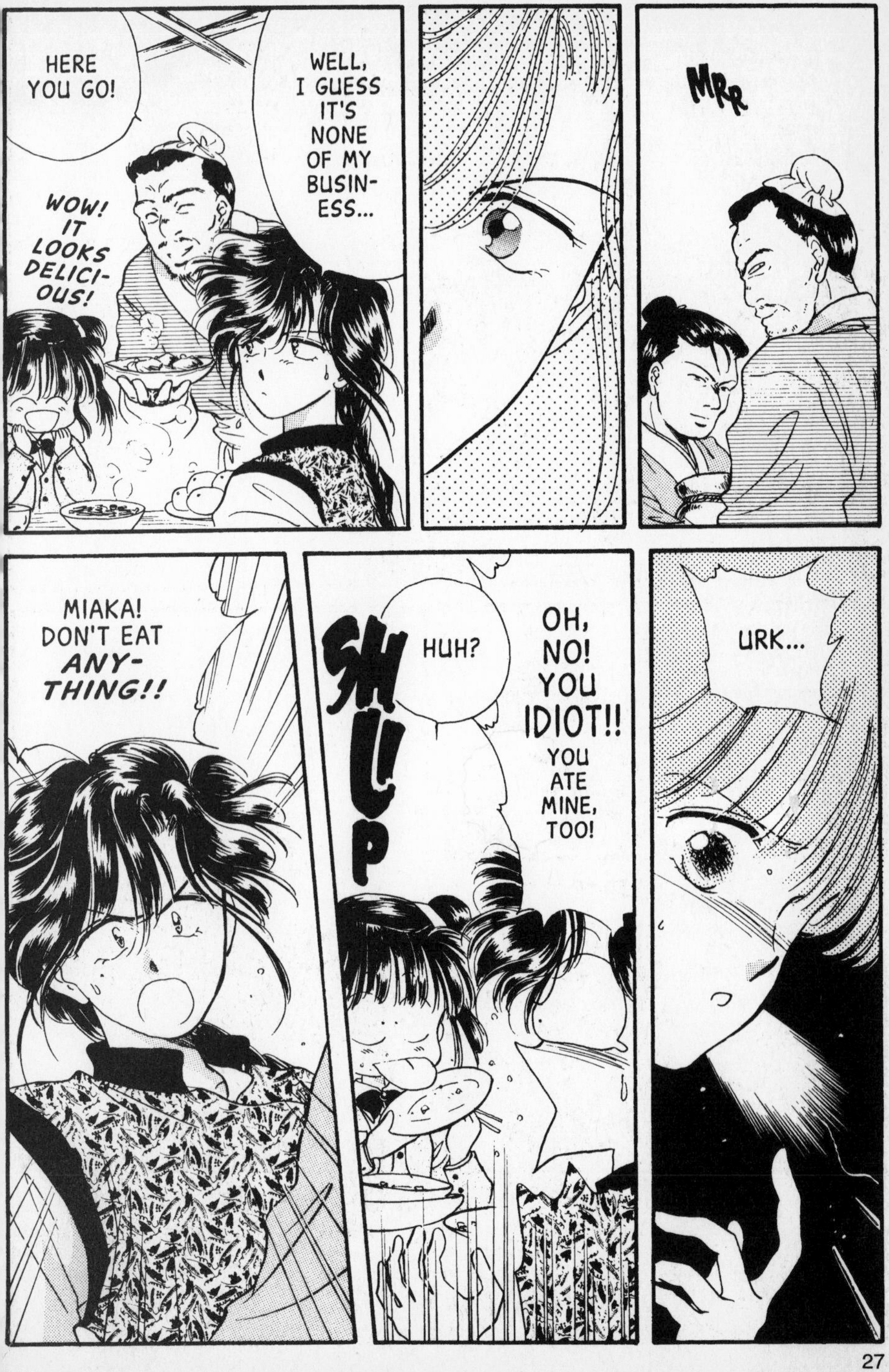
HERE YOU GO!
WELL, I GUESS IT'S NONE OF MY BUSIN-ESS...
WOW! IT LOOKS DELICI-OUS!
MRR
MIAKA! DON'T EAT ANY-THING!!
SHLUP
HUH?
OH, NO! YOU IDIOT!!
YOU ATE MINE, TOO!
URK...

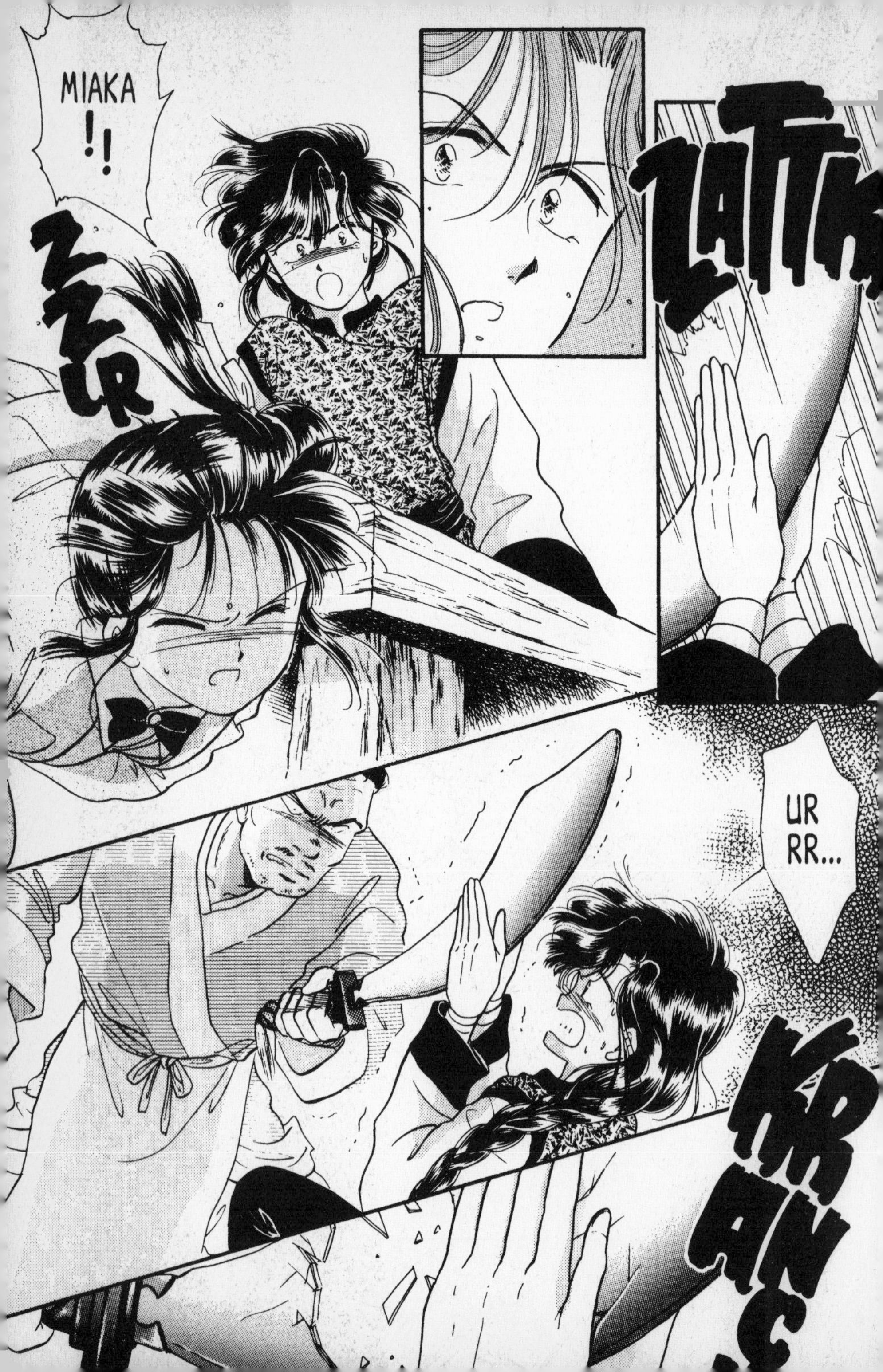
MIAKA
!!
UR
RR...

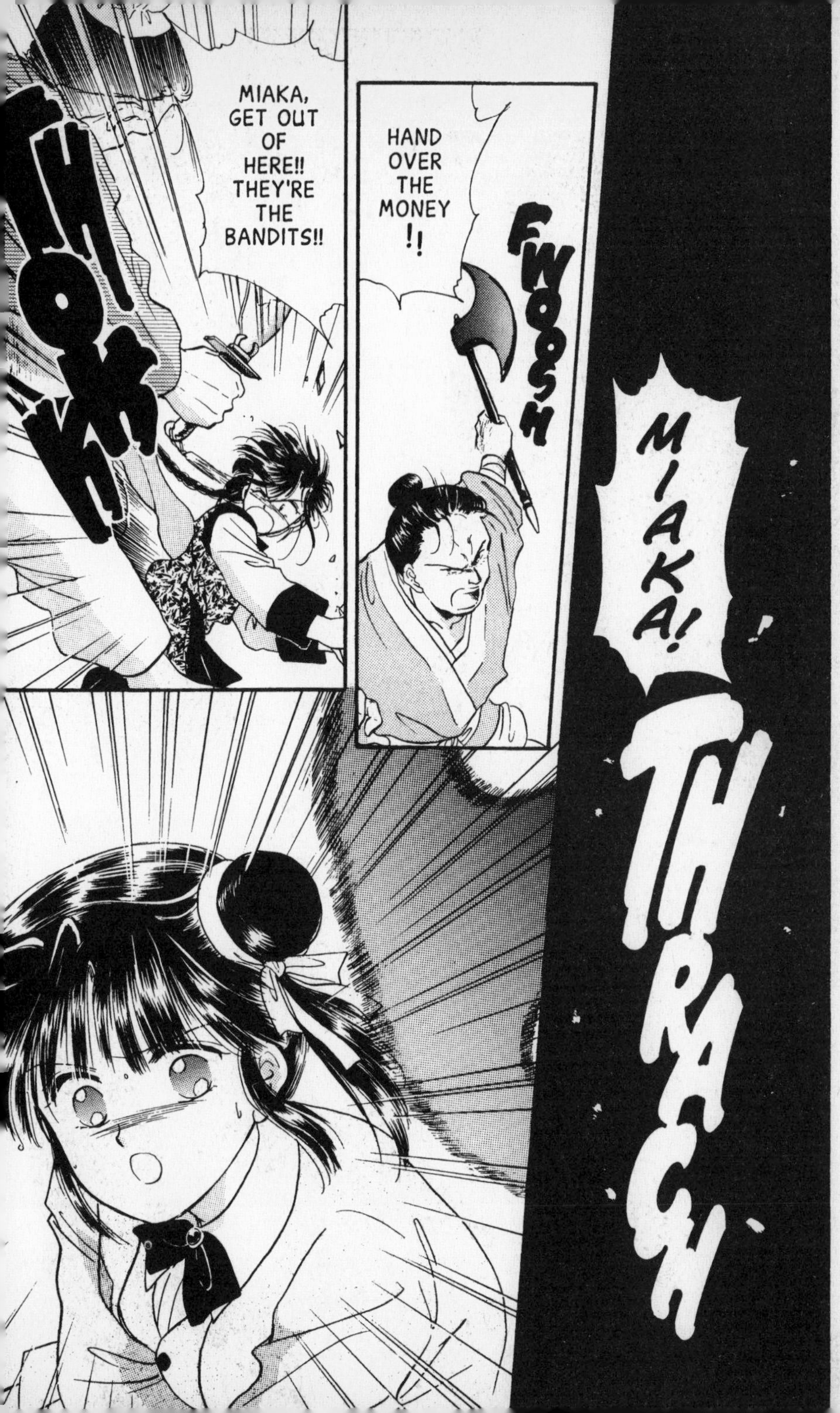
MIAKA, GET OUT OF HERE!! THEY'RE THE BANDITS!!
HAND OVER THE MONEY!!
FWOOSH
MIAKA!
THRACH

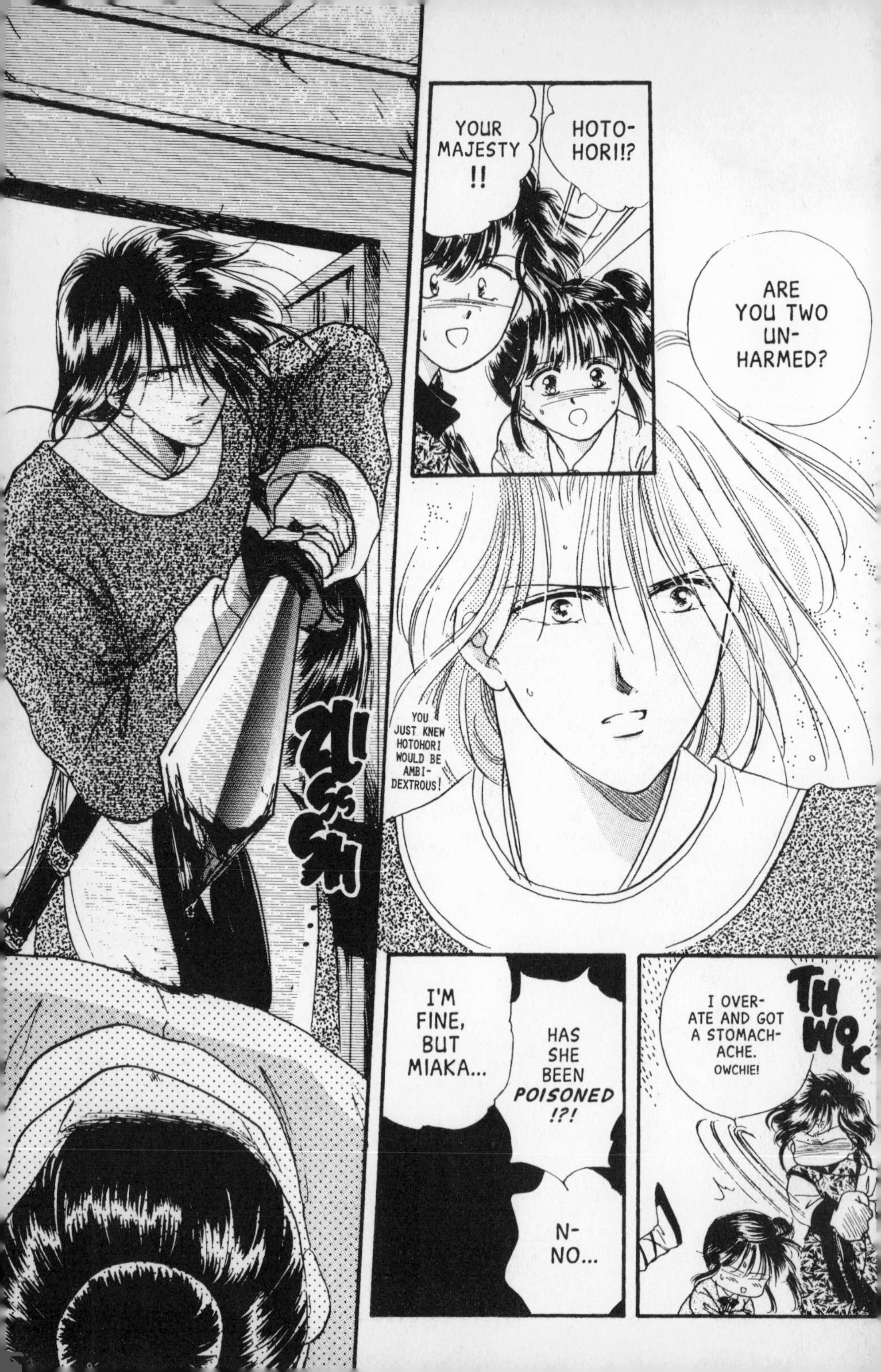
YOUR MAJESTY !!
HOTO-HORI!?
ARE YOU TWO UN-HARMED?
YOU JUST KNEW HOTOHORI WOULD BE AMBI-DEXTROUS!
I'M FINE, BUT MIAKA...
HAS SHE BEEN POISONED !?!
N-NO...
THWOK
I OVER-ATE AND GOT A STOMACH-ACHE. OWCHIE!

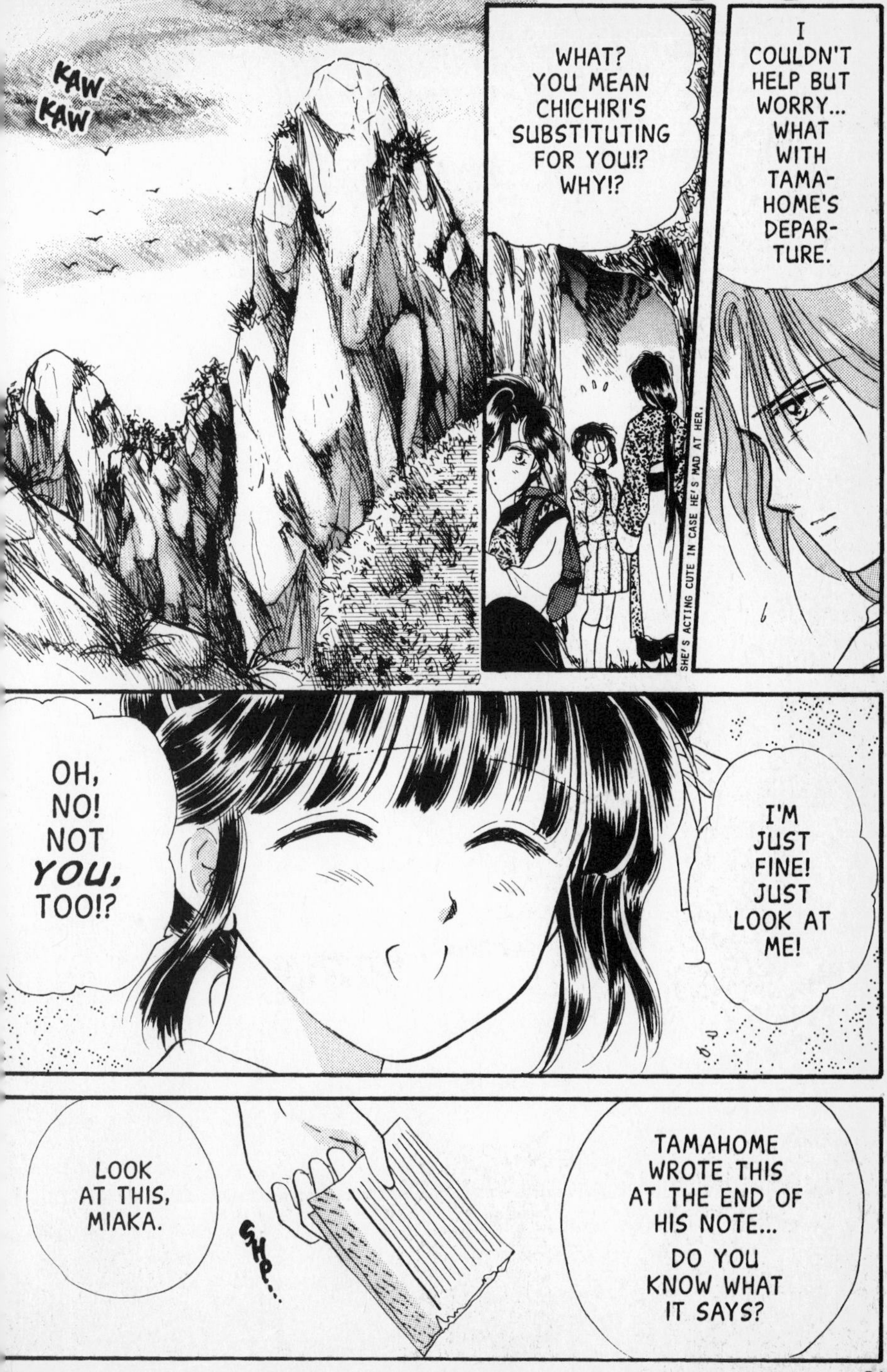
KAW KAW
WHAT? YOU MEAN CHICHIRI'S SUBSTITUTING FOR YOU!? WHY!?
SHE'S ACTING CUTE IN CASE HE'S MAD AT HER.
I COULDN'T HELP BUT WORRY... WHAT WITH TAMA-HOME'S DEPAR-TURE.
OH, NO! NOT YOU, TOO!?
I'M JUST FINE! JUST LOOK AT ME!
LOOK AT THIS, MIAKA.
SHP...
TAMAHOME WROTE THIS AT THE END OF HIS NOTE...
DO YOU KNOW WHAT IT SAYS?

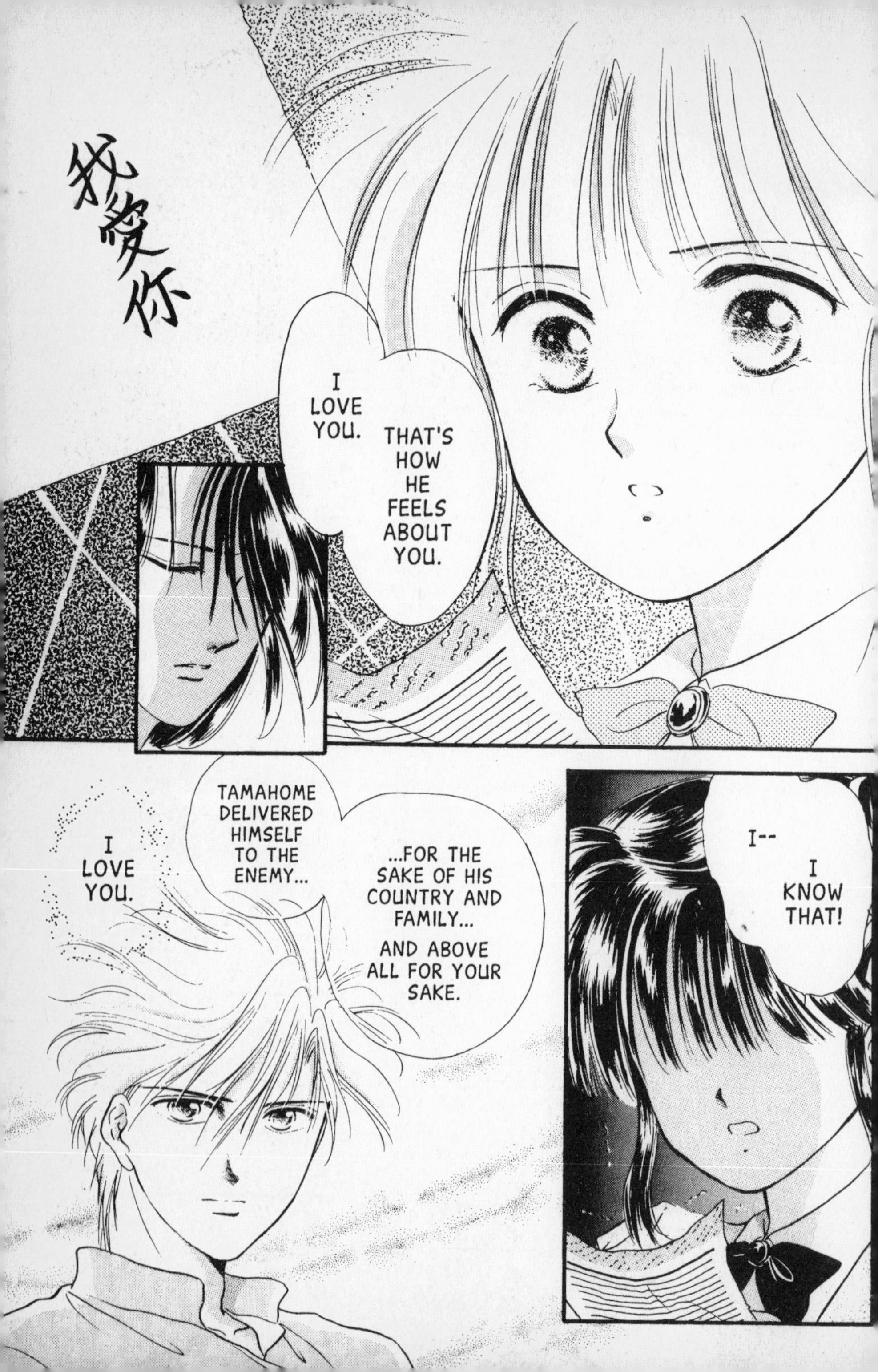

我爱你
I LOVE YOU.
THAT'S HOW HE FEELS ABOUT YOU.
I LOVE YOU.
TAMAHOME DELIVERED HIMSELF TO THE ENEMY...
...FOR THE SAKE OF HIS COUNTRY AND FAMILY...
AND ABOVE ALL FOR YOUR SAKE.
I--
I KNOW THAT!

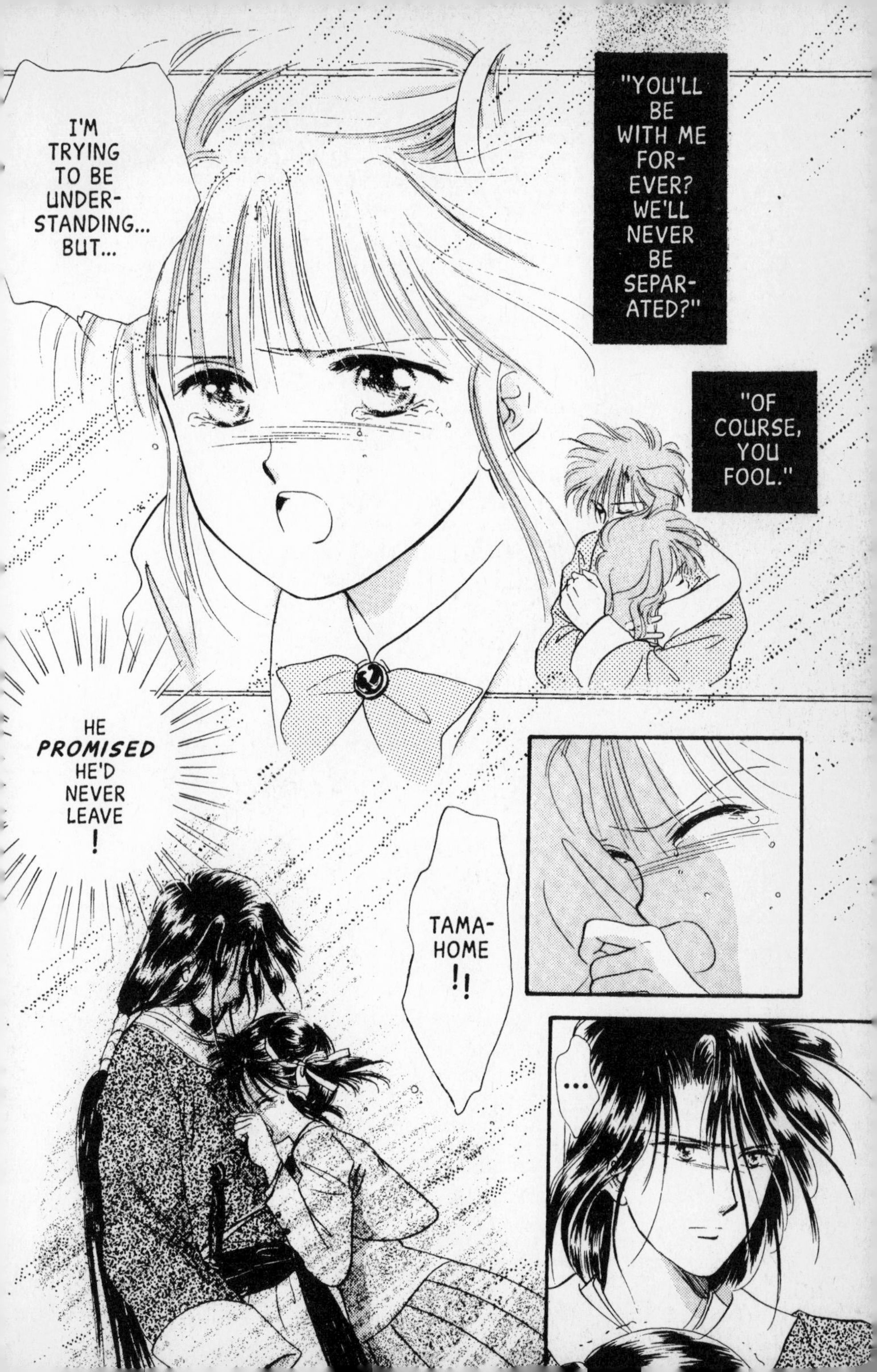
I'M TRYING TO BE UNDER-STANDING... BUT...
"YOU'LL BE WITH ME FOR-EVER? WE'LL NEVER BE SEPAR-ATED?"
"OF COURSE, YOU FOOL."
HE *PROMISED* HE'D NEVER LEAVE!
TAMA-HOME!!
...

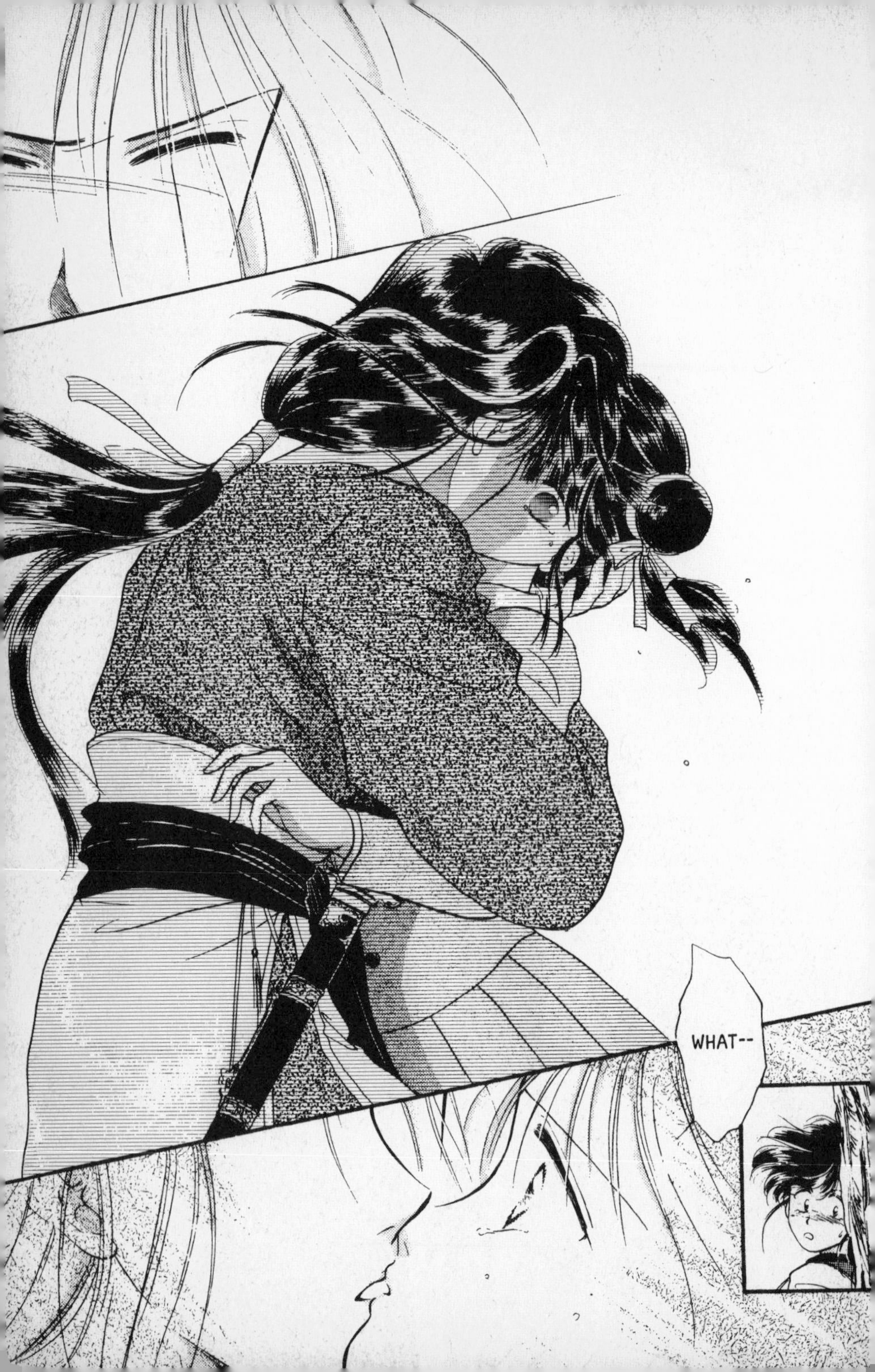
WHAT--

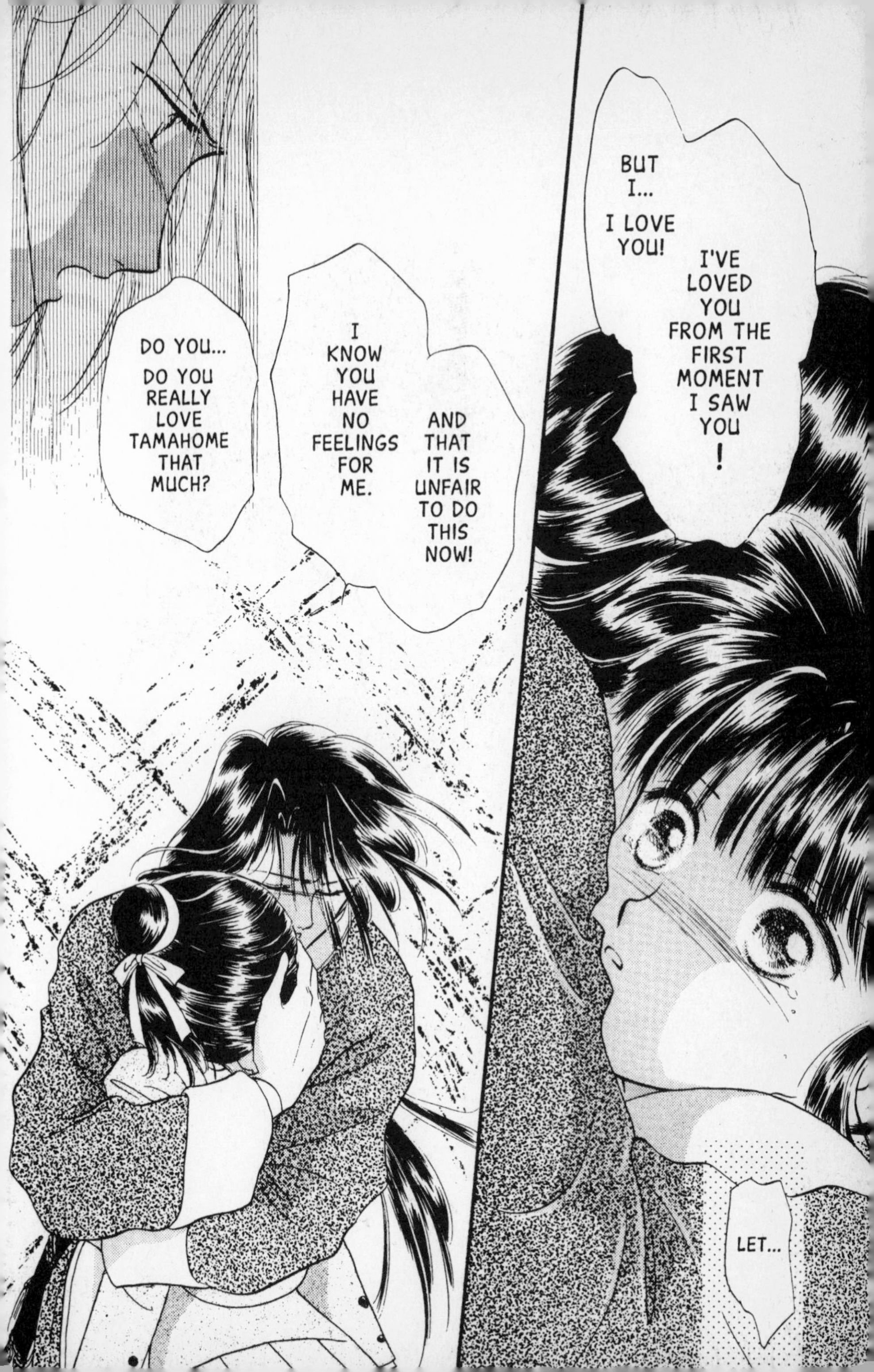
DO YOU... DO YOU REALLY LOVE TAMAHOME THAT MUCH?
I KNOW YOU HAVE NO FEELINGS FOR ME.
AND THAT IT IS UNFAIR TO DO THIS NOW!
BUT I... I LOVE YOU!
I'VE LOVED YOU FROM THE FIRST MOMENT I SAW YOU!
LET...

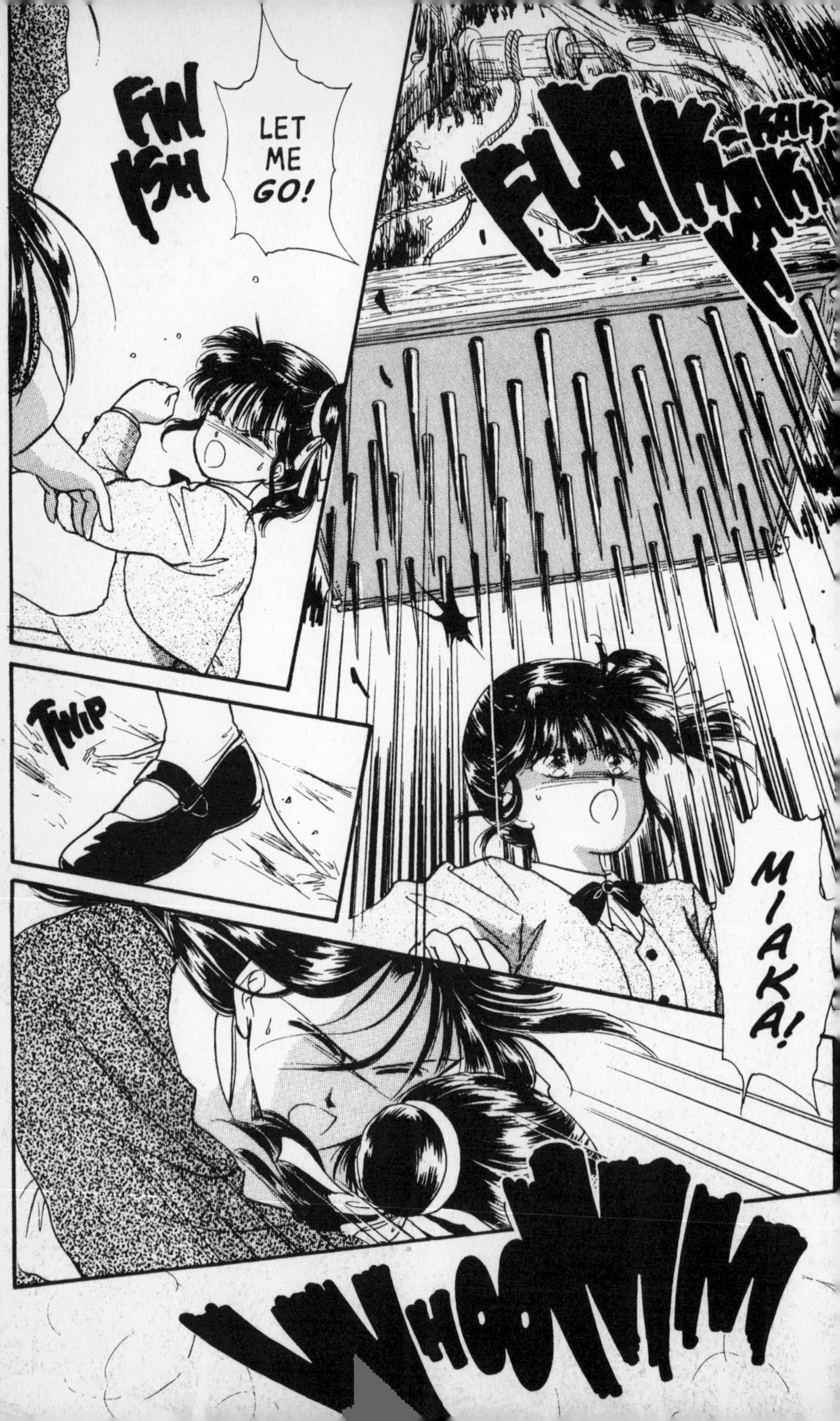
FWISH
LET ME GO!
FLAK-KAK-KAK!!
TWIP
MIAKA!
WHOOMMM

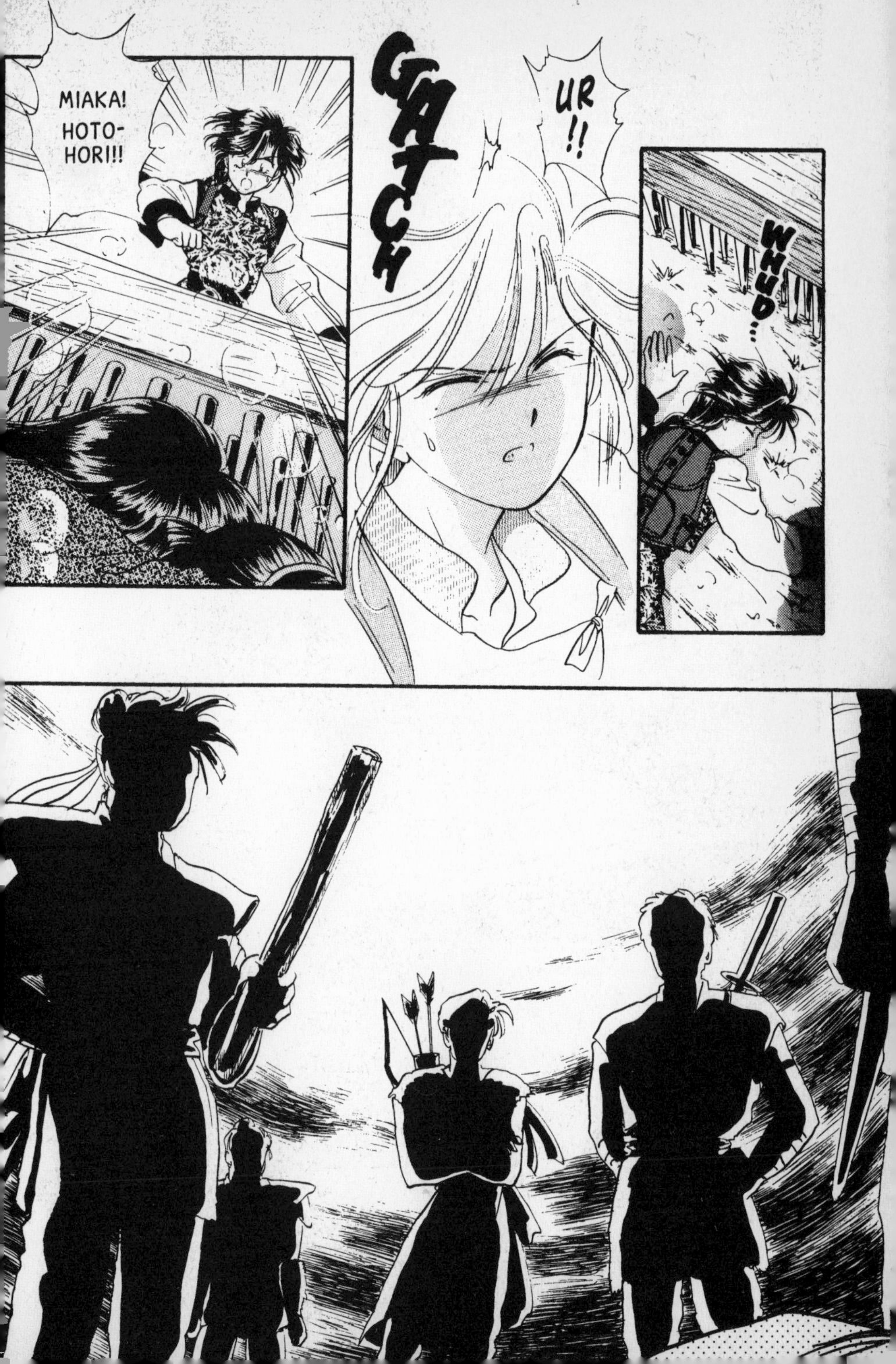
MIAKA! HOTO-HORI!!
GATCH
UR!!
WHUD...

Fushigi Akugi has been canceled for this volume!
(I don't have the originals to copy from) I spaced out.
I can use any interesting ideas. Send any suggestions you
may have my way. I'll give you credit!
But will this series go on if the story gets any more serious?
We may get canceled here...

→ You'll have to be reading it in the (Japanese) anthology magazine to get
your idea to me in time to be included.

To readers of the English version: Sorry! As much as we would love to have
some of your suggestions to be made into comics, it's too late!

TAMAHOME
(10 years old)

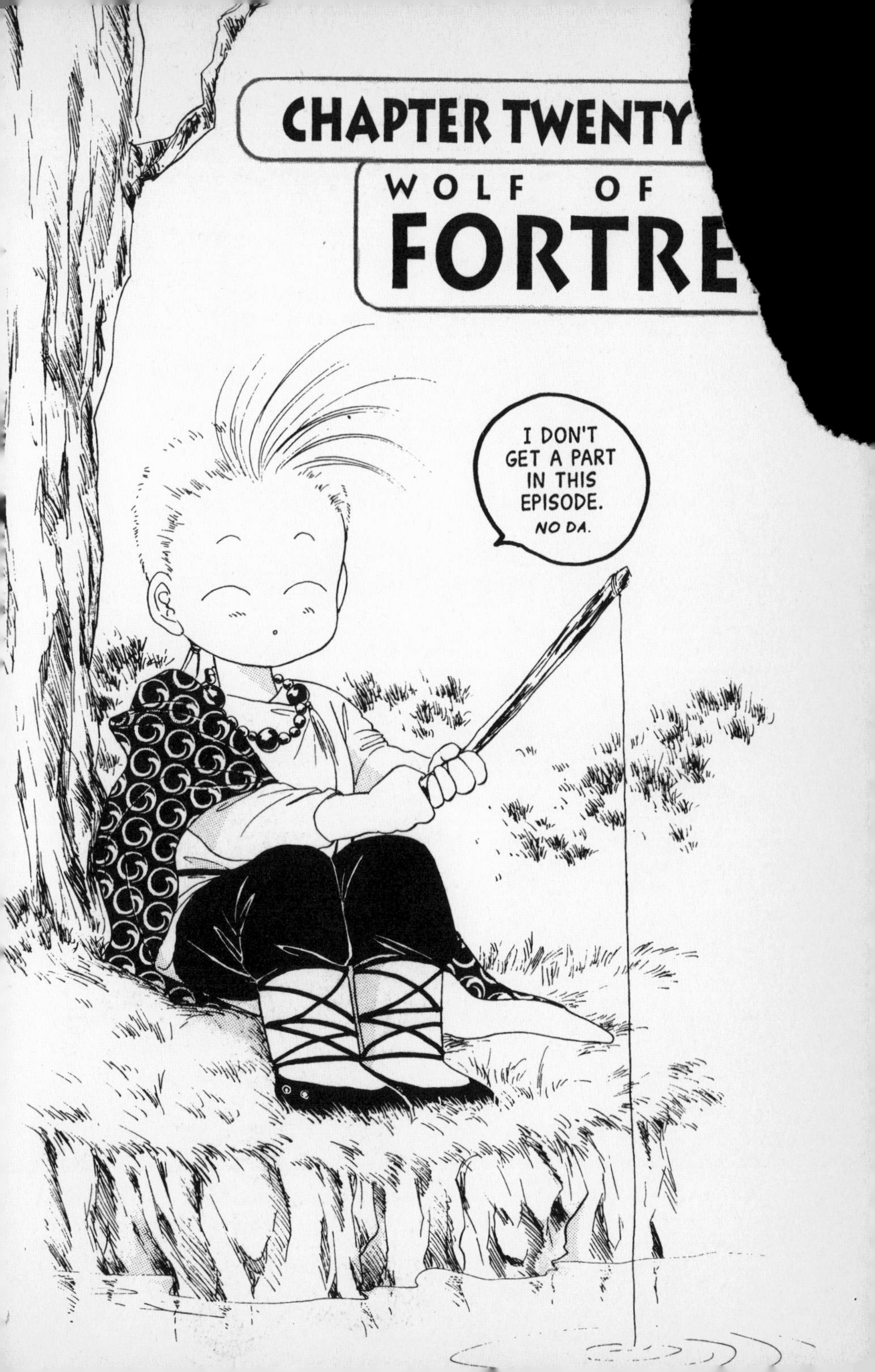
CHAPTER TWENTY
WOLF OF
FORTRE
I DON'T GET A PART IN THIS EPISODE. NO DA.

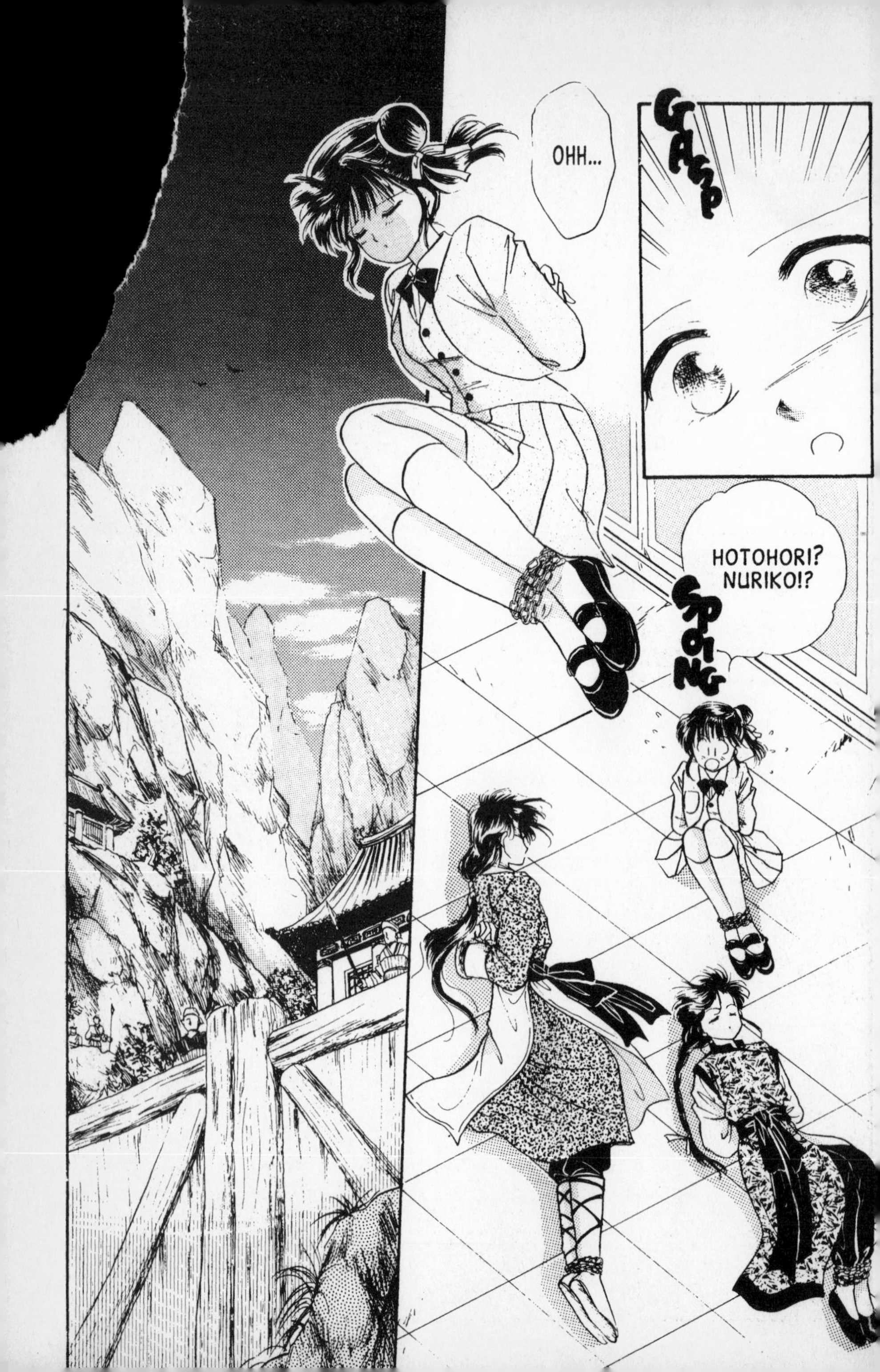
OHH...
GASP
HOTOHORI? NURIKO!?
SPOING

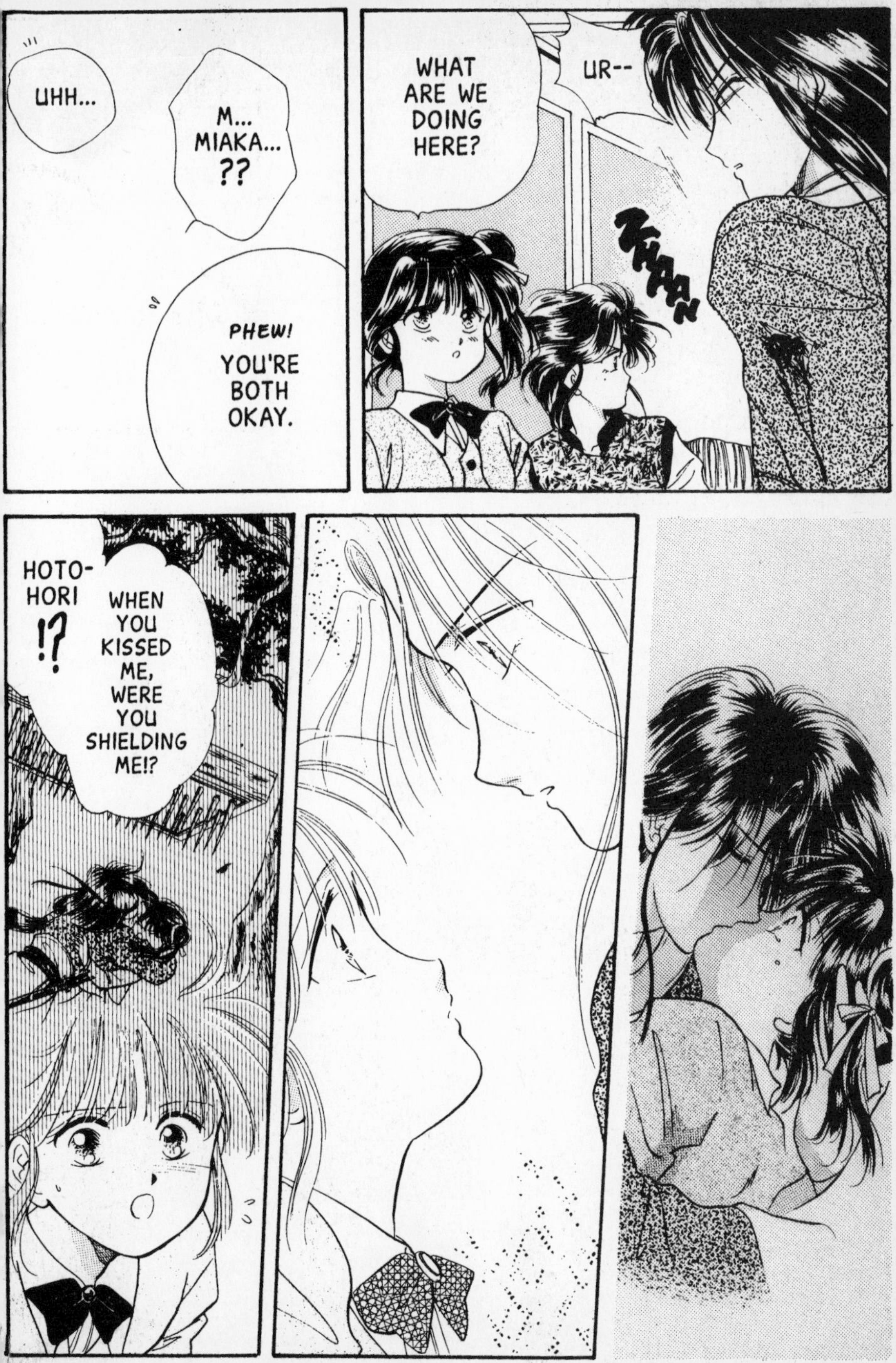
UHH...
M... MIAKA... ??
PHEW! YOU'RE BOTH OKAY.
WHAT ARE WE DOING HERE?
UR--
ZHAAAN
HOTO-HORI !?
WHEN YOU KISSED ME, WERE YOU SHIELDING ME!?

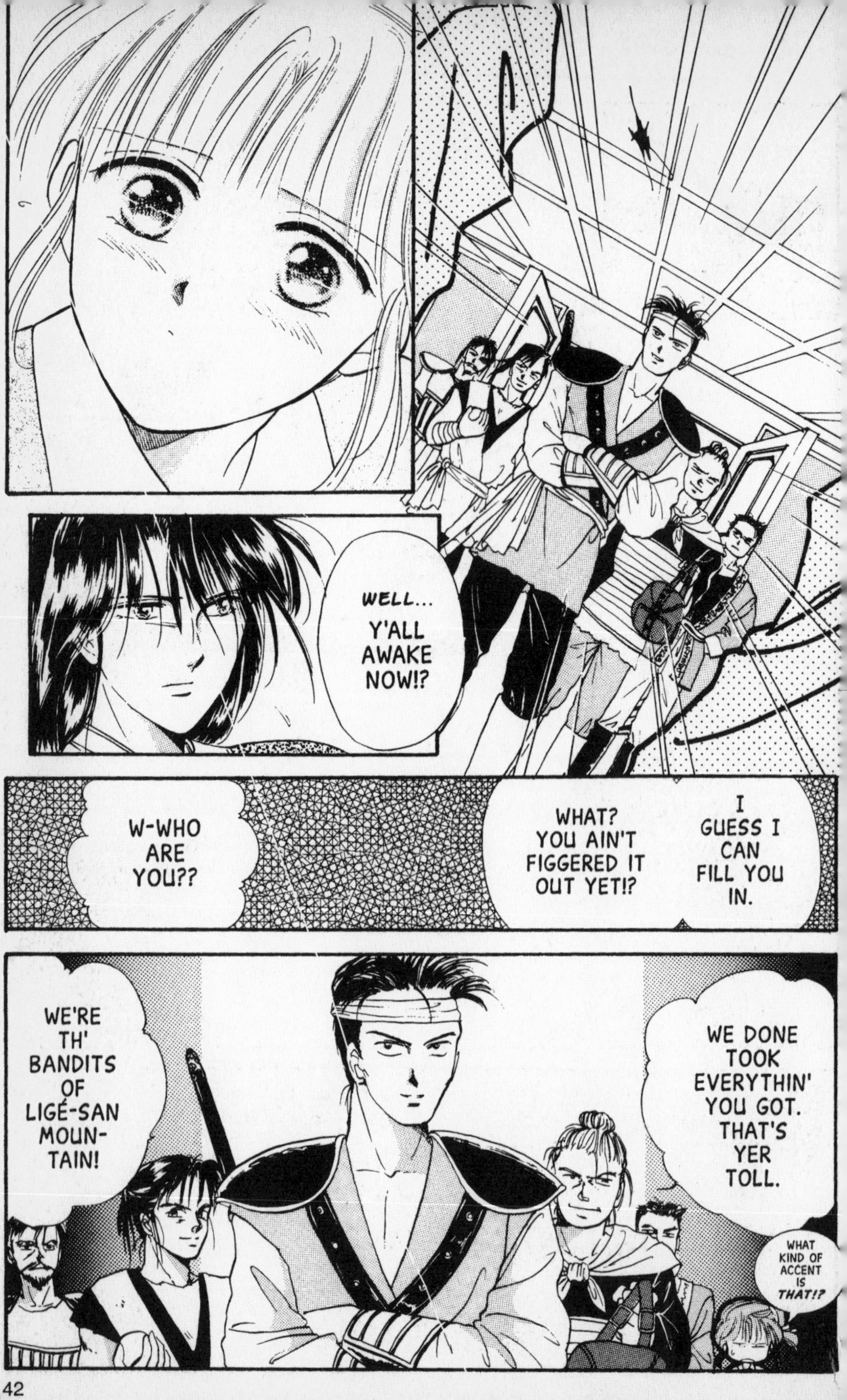
WELL... Y'ALL AWAKE NOW!?
W-WHO ARE YOU??
WHAT? YOU AIN'T FIGGERED IT OUT YET!?
I GUESS I CAN FILL YOU IN.
WE'RE TH' BANDITS OF LIGÉ-SAN MOUN-TAIN!
WE DONE TOOK EVERYTHIN' YOU GOT. THAT'S YER TOLL.
WHAT KIND OF ACCENT IS *THAT!?*

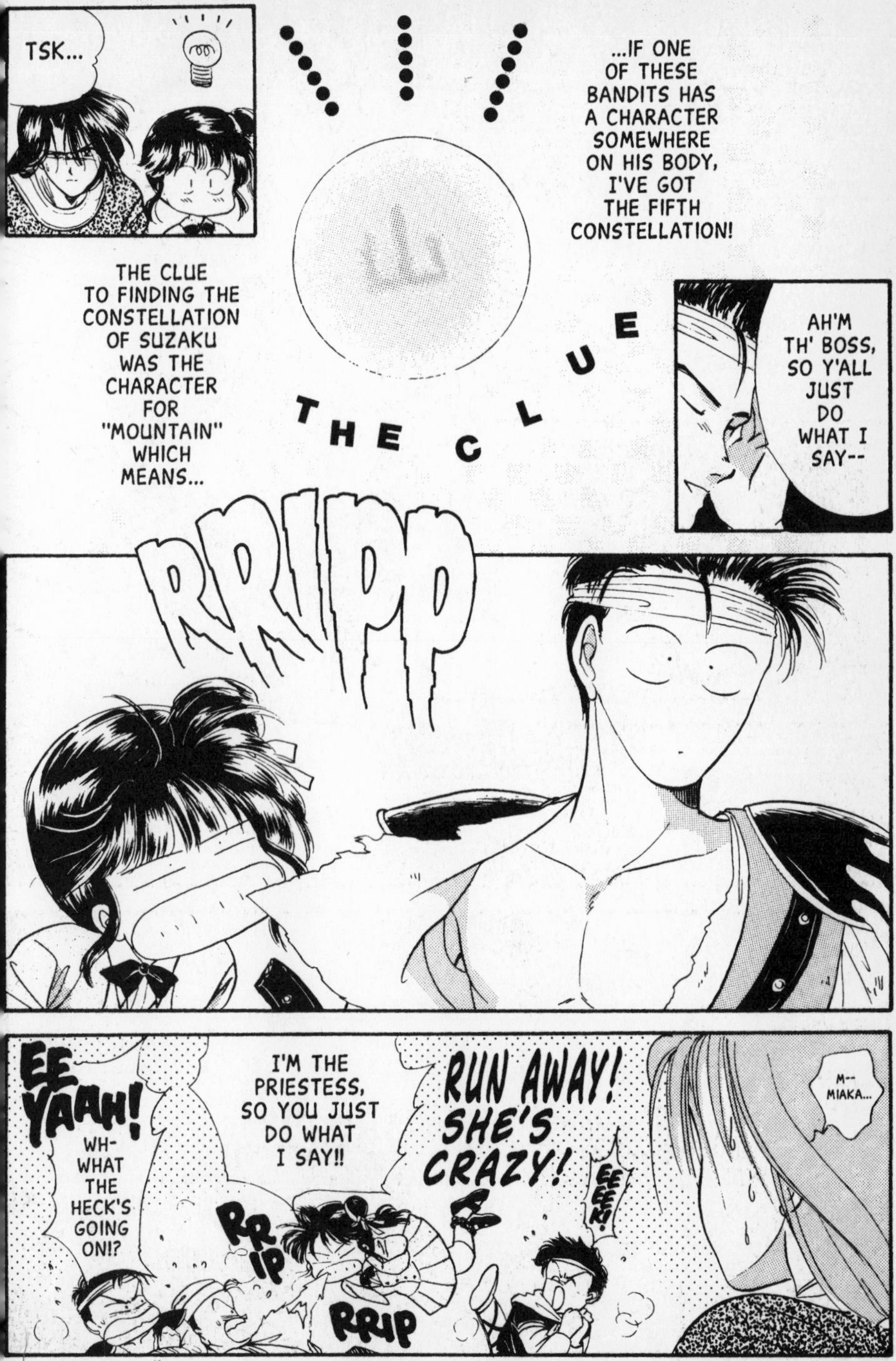
TSK...
...IF ONE OF THESE BANDITS HAS A CHARACTER SOMEWHERE ON HIS BODY, I'VE GOT THE FIFTH CONSTELLATION!
THE CLUE TO FINDING THE CONSTELLATION OF SUZAKU WAS THE CHARACTER FOR "MOUNTAIN" WHICH MEANS...
THE CLUE
AH'M TH' BOSS, SO Y'ALL JUST DO WHAT I SAY--
RRIPP
EE YAAH!
WH-WHAT THE HECK'S GOING ON!?
I'M THE PRIESTESS, SO YOU JUST DO WHAT I SAY!!
RUN AWAY! SHE'S CRAZY!
EEEEK!
M--MIAKA...
RRIP
RRIP

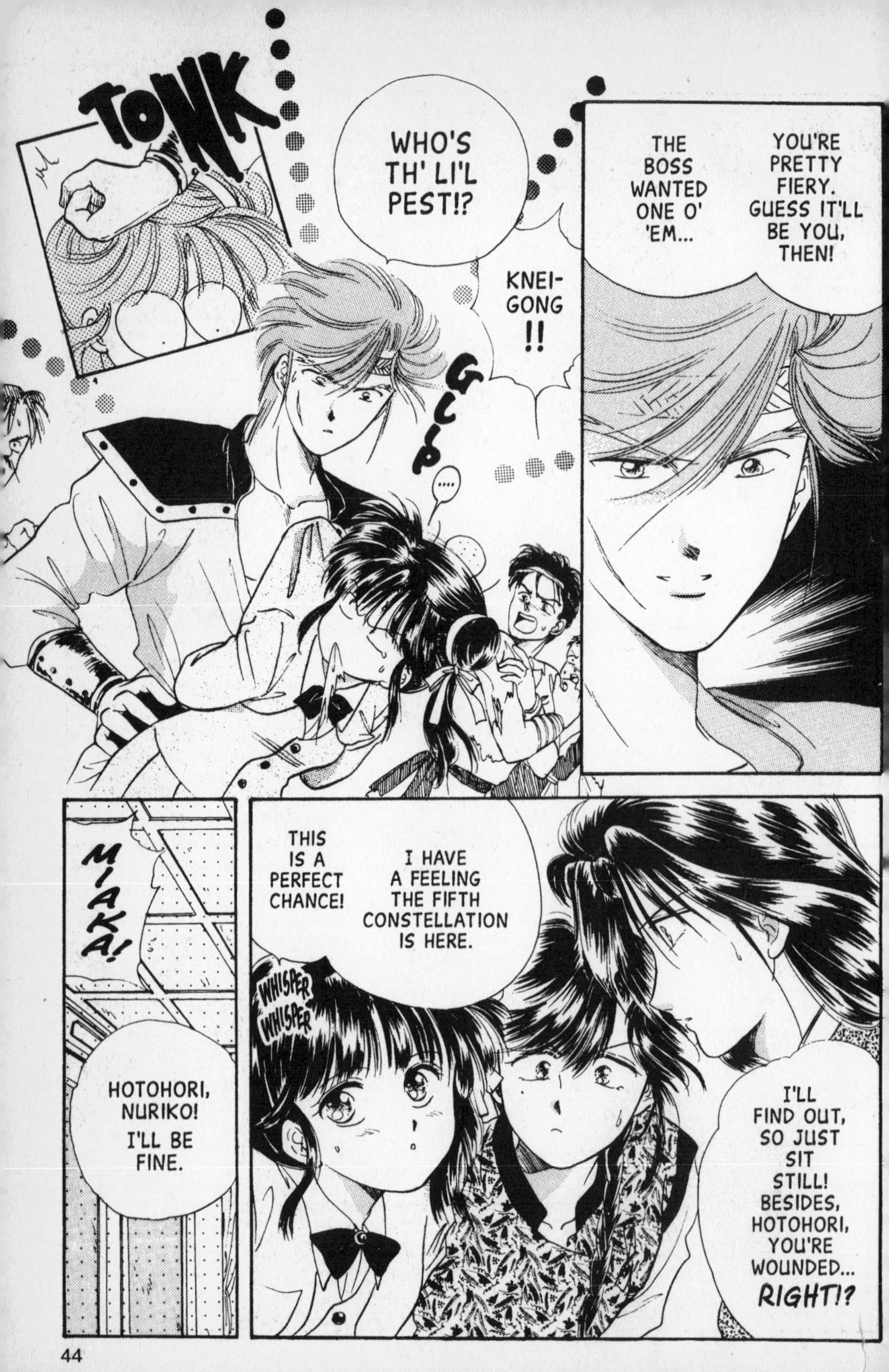
TONK
WHO'S TH' LI'L PEST!?
KNEI-GONG!!
GULP
....
THE BOSS WANTED ONE O' 'EM...
YOU'RE PRETTY FIERY. GUESS IT'LL BE YOU, THEN!
MIAKA!
HOTOHORI, NURIKO! I'LL BE FINE.
THIS IS A PERFECT CHANCE!
I HAVE A FEELING THE FIFTH CONSTELLATION IS HERE.
WHISPER WHISPER
I'LL FIND OUT, SO JUST SIT STILL! BESIDES, HOTOHORI, YOU'RE WOUNDED... RIGHT!?

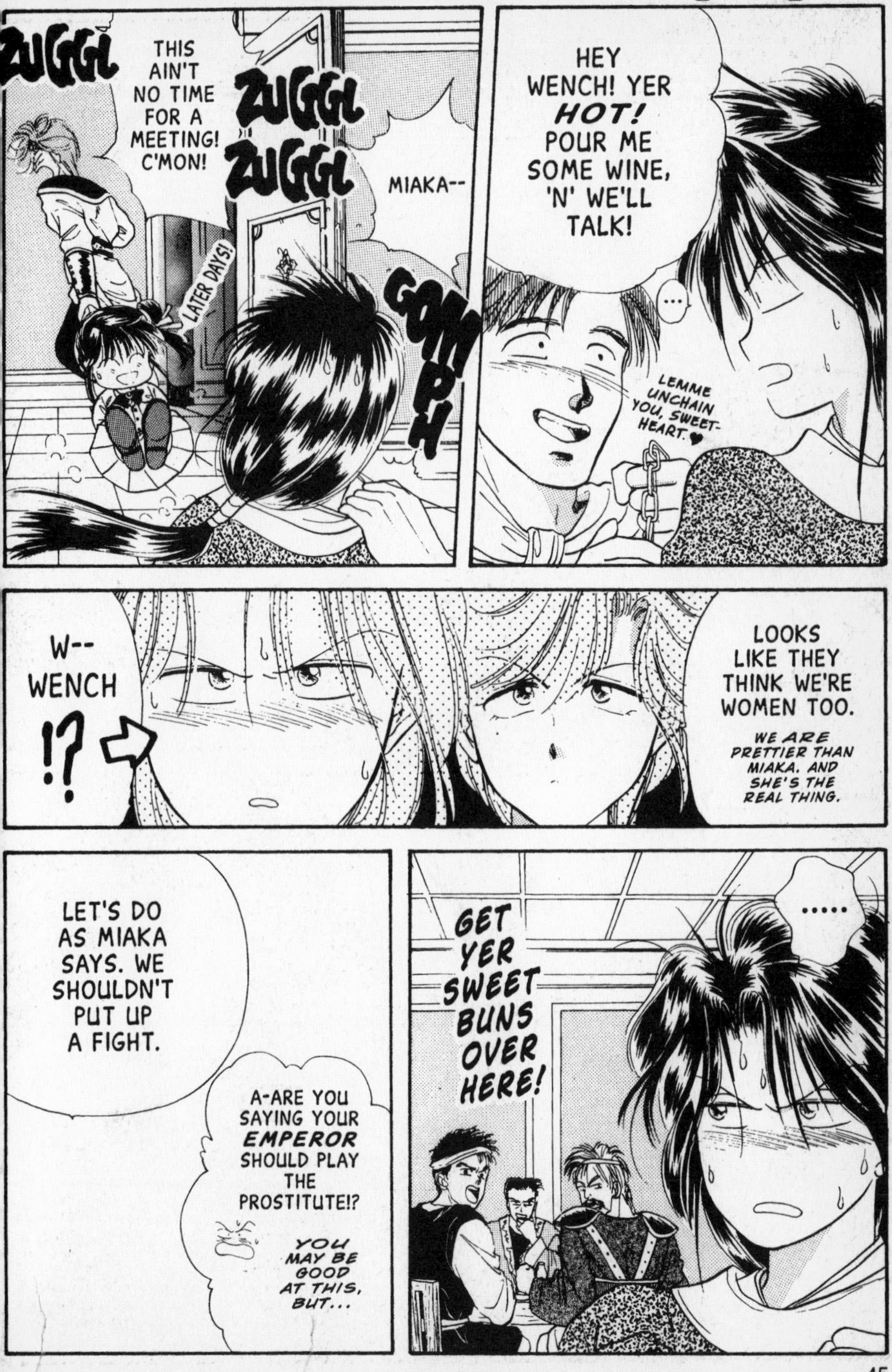
ZUGGI
THIS AIN'T NO TIME FOR A MEETING! C'MON!
LATER DAYS!
ZUGGI
ZUGGI
MIAKA--
GOMPH
HEY WENCH! YER *HOT!* POUR ME SOME WINE, 'N' WE'LL TALK!
...
LEMME UNCHAIN YOU, SWEET-HEART.♥
W-- WENCH !?
LOOKS LIKE THEY THINK WE'RE WOMEN TOO.
WE ARE PRETTIER THAN MIAKA. AND SHE'S THE REAL THING.
LET'S DO AS MIAKA SAYS. WE SHOULDN'T PUT UP A FIGHT.
A-ARE YOU SAYING YOUR *EMPEROR* SHOULD PLAY THE PROSTITUTE!?
YOU MAY BE GOOD AT THIS, BUT...
GET YER SWEET BUNS OVER HERE!
.....

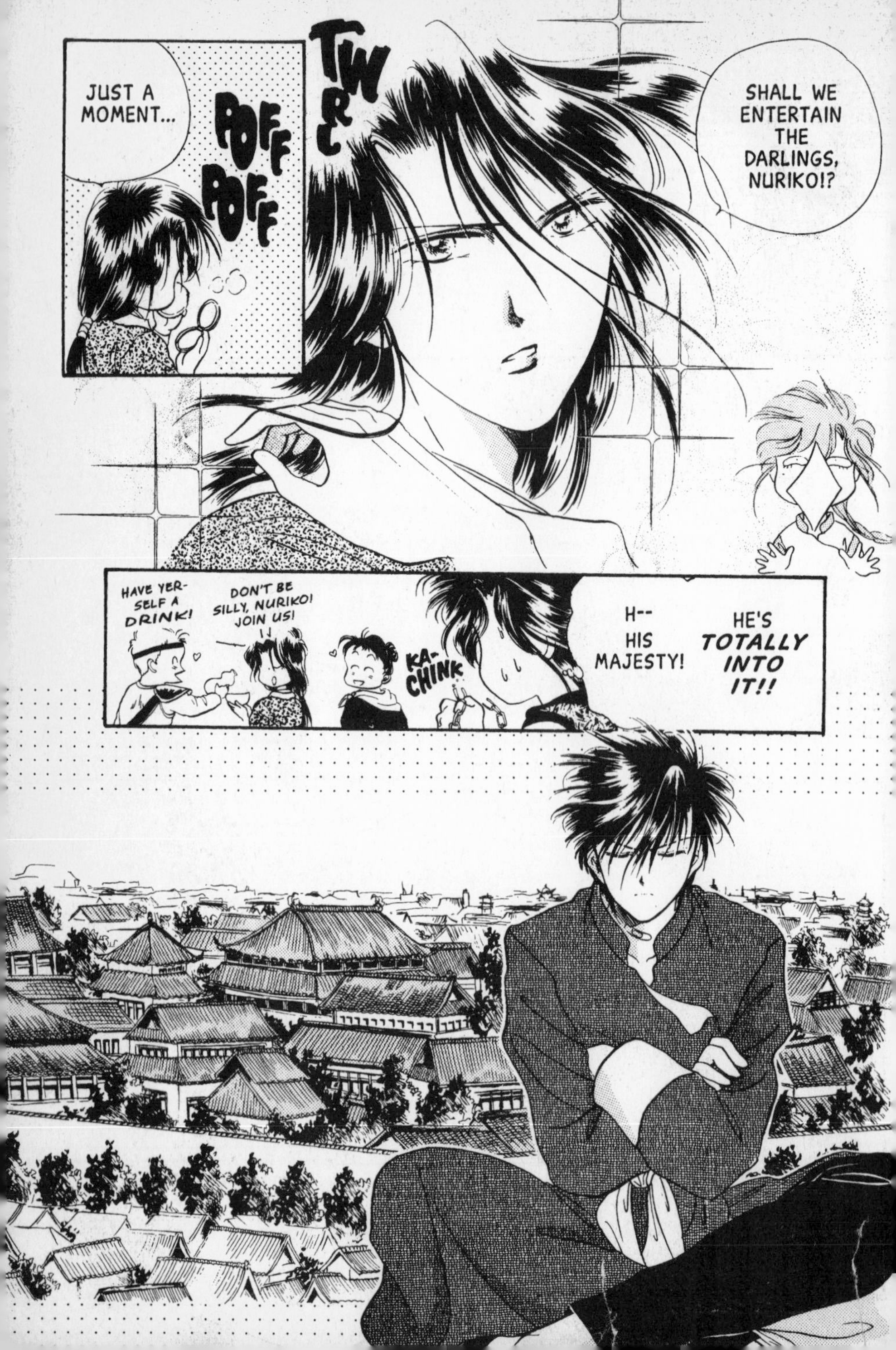
JUST A MOMENT...
POFF POFF
TWIRL
SHALL WE ENTERTAIN THE DARLINGS, NURIKO!?
HAVE YER-SELF A DRINK!
DON'T BE SILLY, NURIKO! JOIN US!
KA-CHINK
H-- HIS MAJESTY!
HE'S TOTALLY INTO IT!!

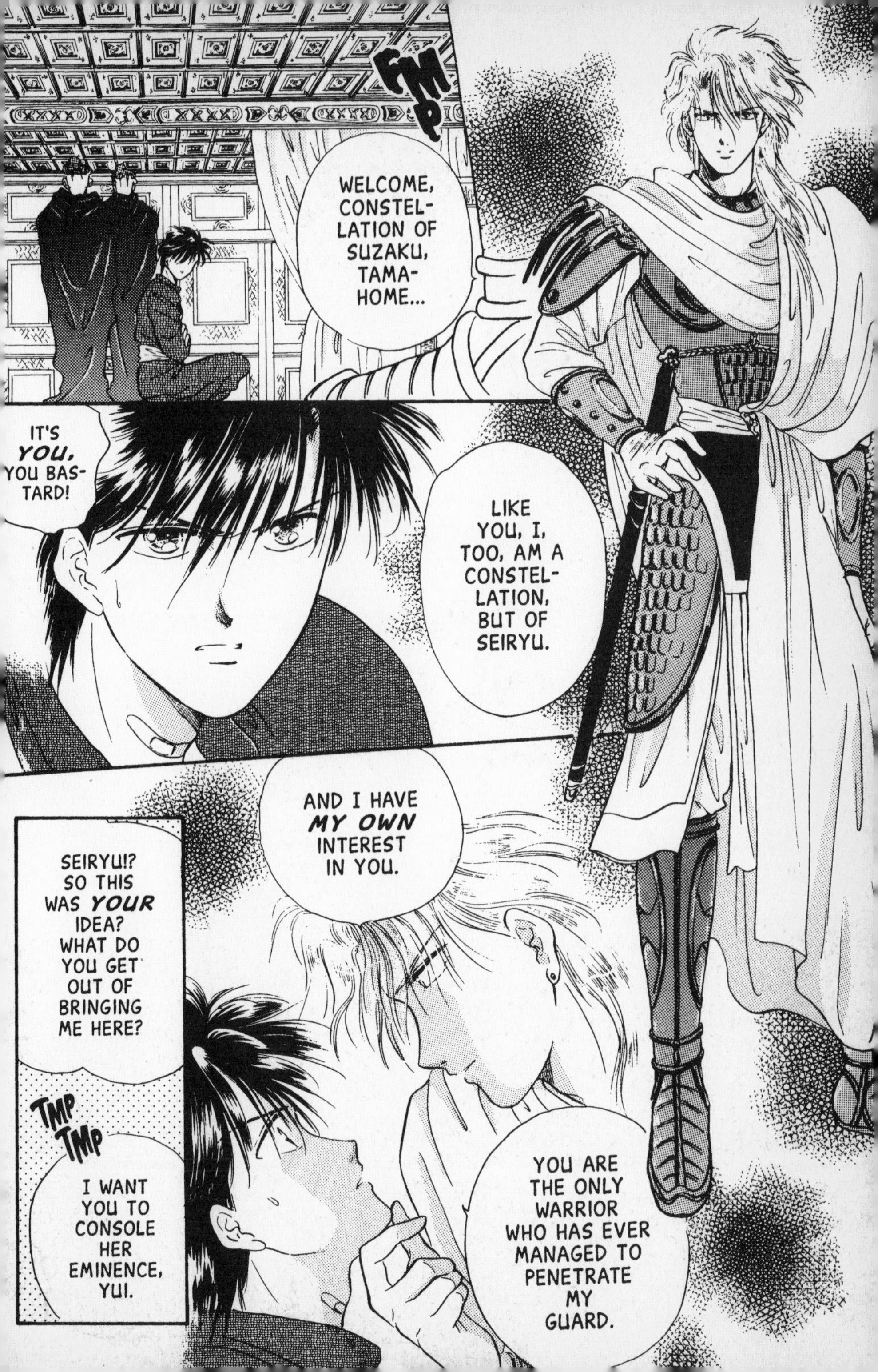
FMP
WELCOME, CONSTELLATION OF SUZAKU, TAMAHOME...
IT'S *YOU,* YOU BASTARD!
LIKE YOU, I, TOO, AM A CONSTELLATION, BUT OF SEIRYU.
AND I HAVE *MY OWN* INTEREST IN YOU.
SEIRYU!? SO THIS WAS *YOUR* IDEA? WHAT DO YOU GET OUT OF BRINGING ME HERE?
TMP TMP
I WANT YOU TO CONSOLE HER EMINENCE, YUI.
YOU ARE THE ONLY WARRIOR WHO HAS EVER MANAGED TO PENETRATE MY GUARD.

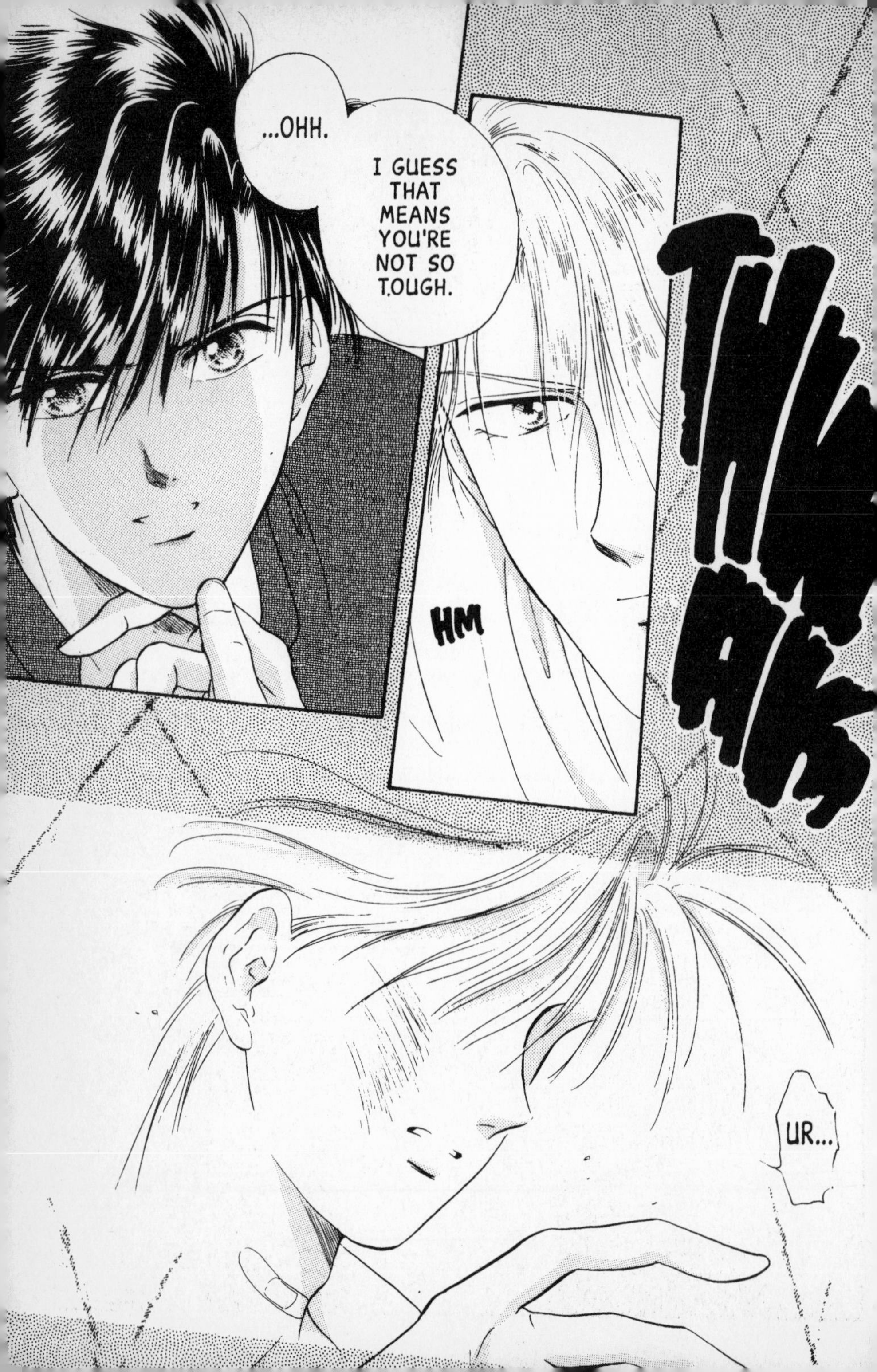

...OHH.
I GUESS THAT MEANS YOU'RE NOT SO TOUGH.
HM
THWAK
UR...

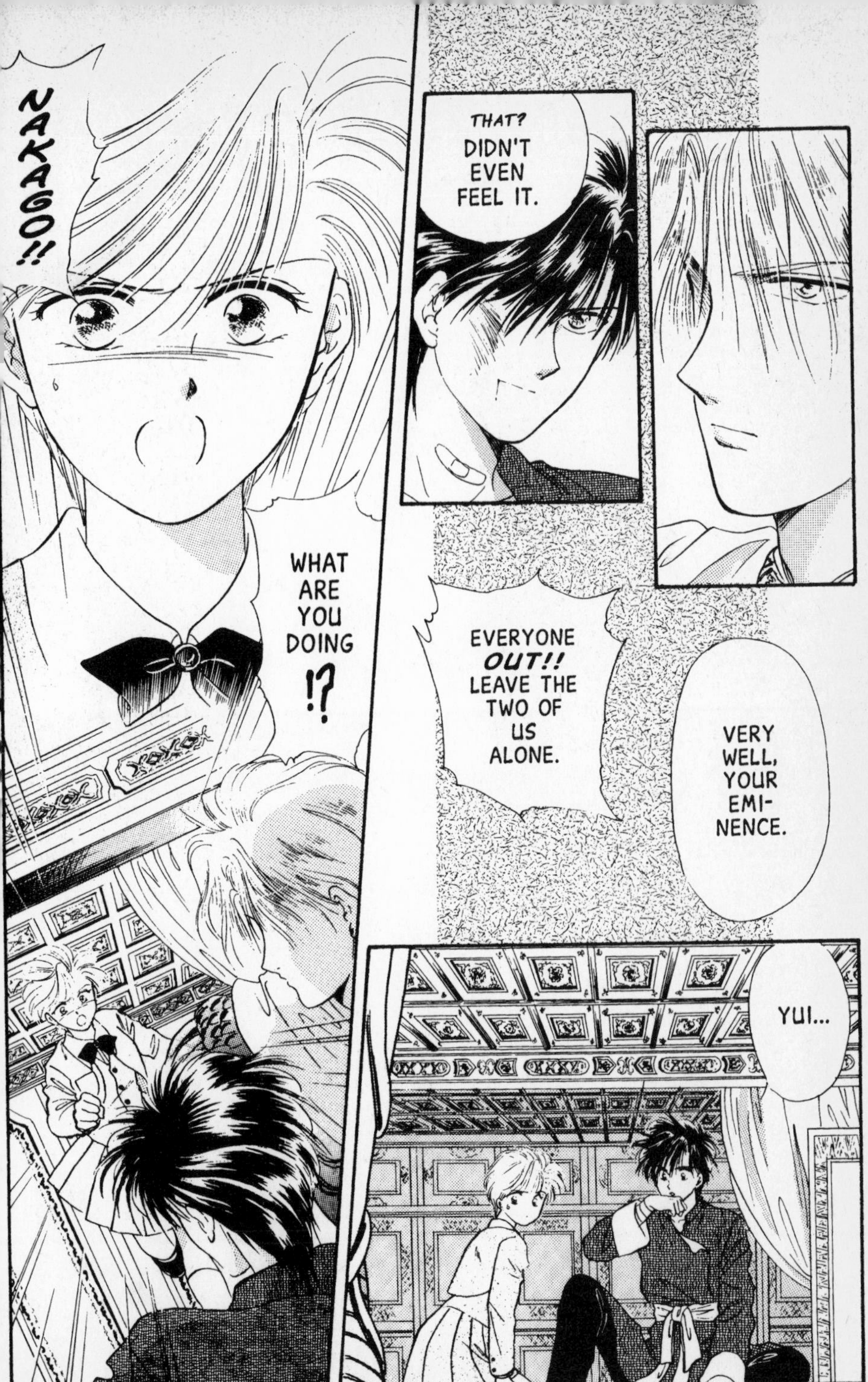
NAKAGO!!
WHAT ARE YOU DOING !?
THAT? DIDN'T EVEN FEEL IT.
EVERYONE OUT!! LEAVE THE TWO OF US ALONE.
VERY WELL, YOUR EMI- NENCE.
YUI...

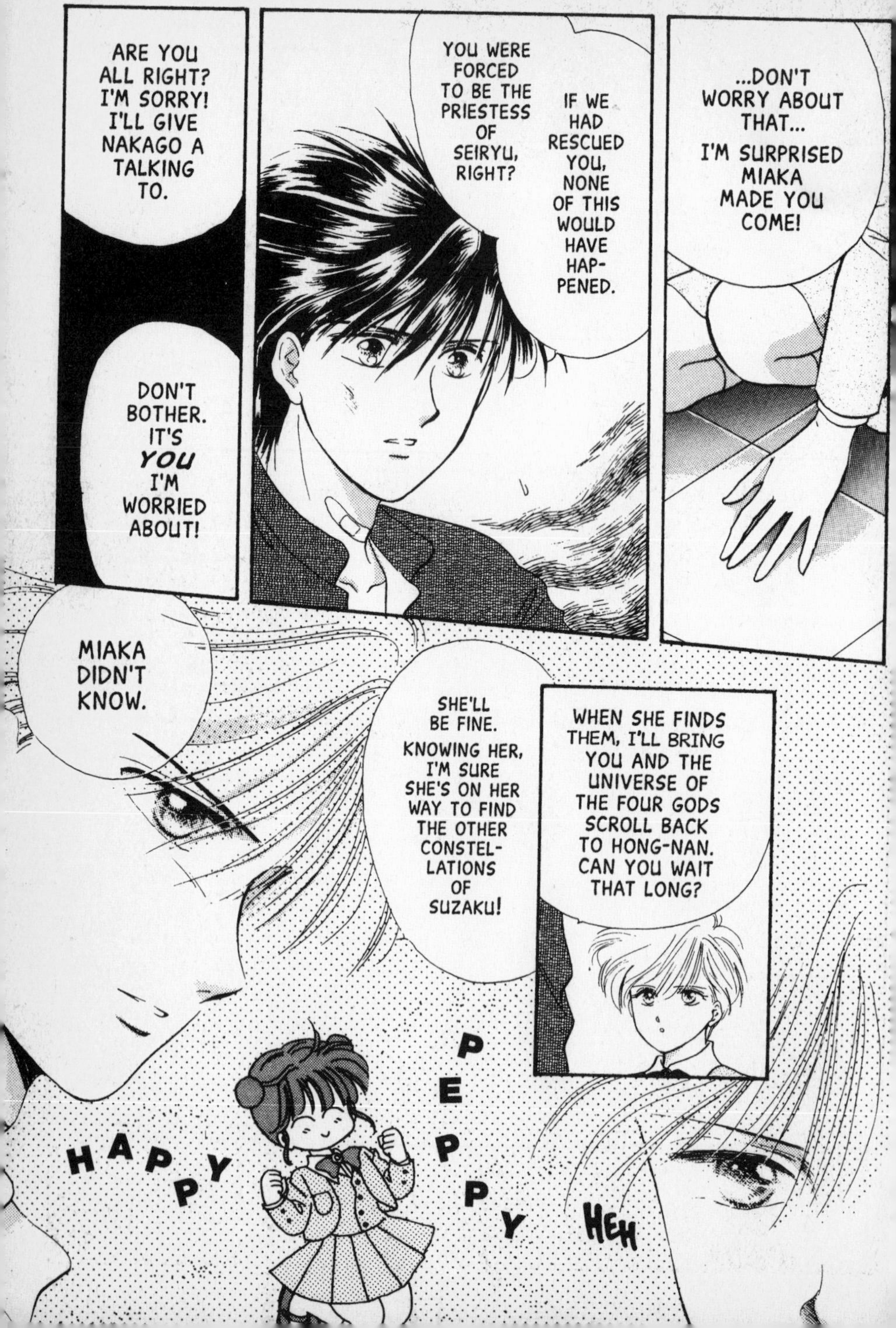
ARE YOU ALL RIGHT? I'M SORRY! I'LL GIVE NAKAGO A TALKING TO.
DON'T BOTHER. IT'S *YOU* I'M WORRIED ABOUT!
YOU WERE FORCED TO BE THE PRIESTESS OF SEIRYU, RIGHT?
IF WE HAD RESCUED YOU, NONE OF THIS WOULD HAVE HAP-PENED.
...DON'T WORRY ABOUT THAT...
I'M SURPRISED MIAKA MADE YOU COME!
MIAKA DIDN'T KNOW.
SHE'LL BE FINE.
KNOWING HER, I'M SURE SHE'S ON HER WAY TO FIND THE OTHER CONSTEL-LATIONS OF SUZAKU!
WHEN SHE FINDS THEM, I'LL BRING YOU AND THE UNIVERSE OF THE FOUR GODS SCROLL BACK TO HONG-NAN. CAN YOU WAIT THAT LONG?
HAPPY
PEPPY
HEH

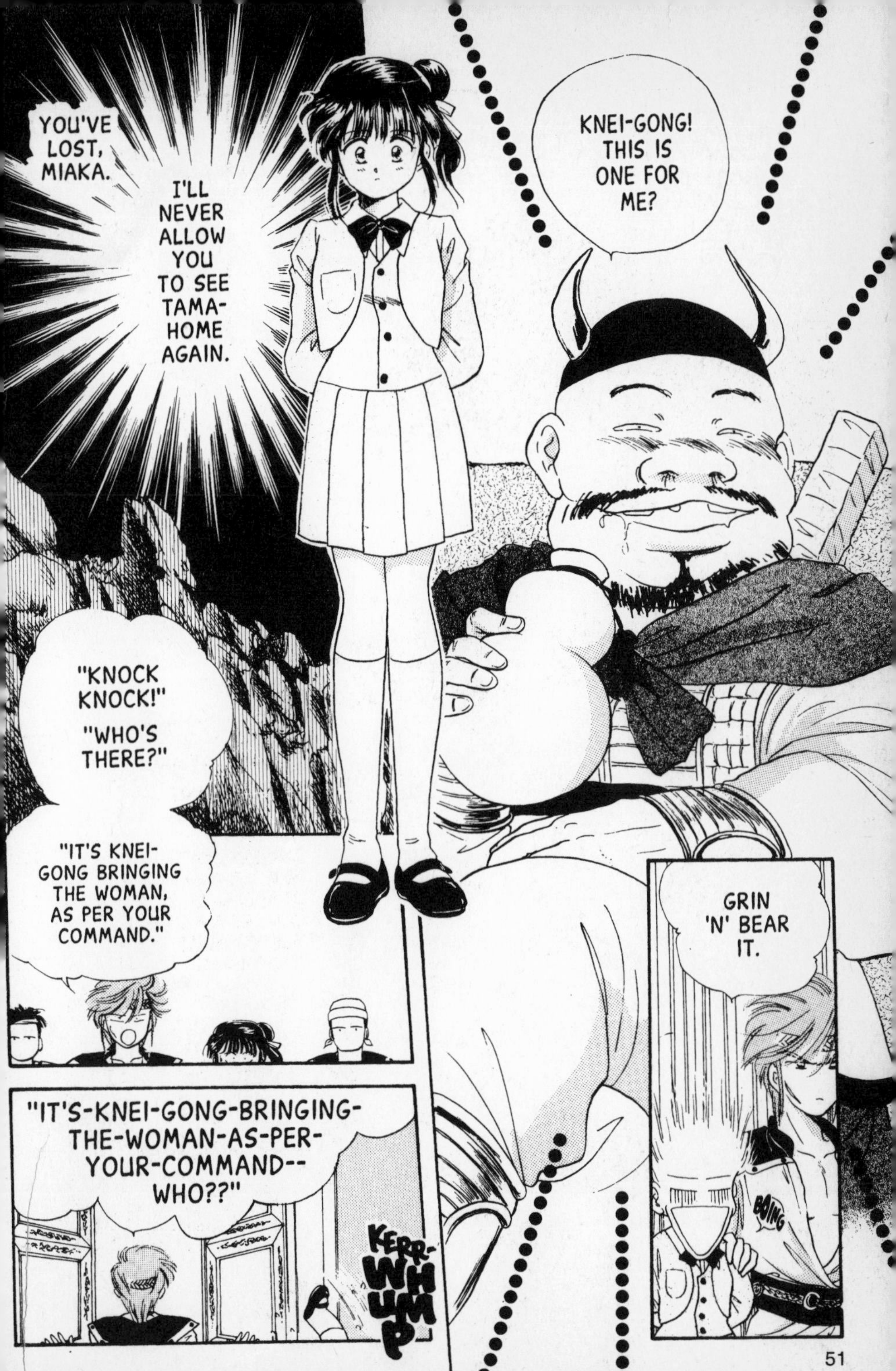
YOU'VE LOST, MIAKA.
I'LL NEVER ALLOW YOU TO SEE TAMA-HOME AGAIN.
KNEI-GONG! THIS IS ONE FOR ME?
"KNOCK KNOCK!"
"WHO'S THERE?"
"IT'S KNEI-GONG BRINGING THE WOMAN, AS PER YOUR COMMAND."
GRIN 'N' BEAR IT.
"IT'S-KNEI-GONG-BRINGING-THE-WOMAN-AS-PER-YOUR-COMMAND--WHO??"
KERR-WHUMP
BOING

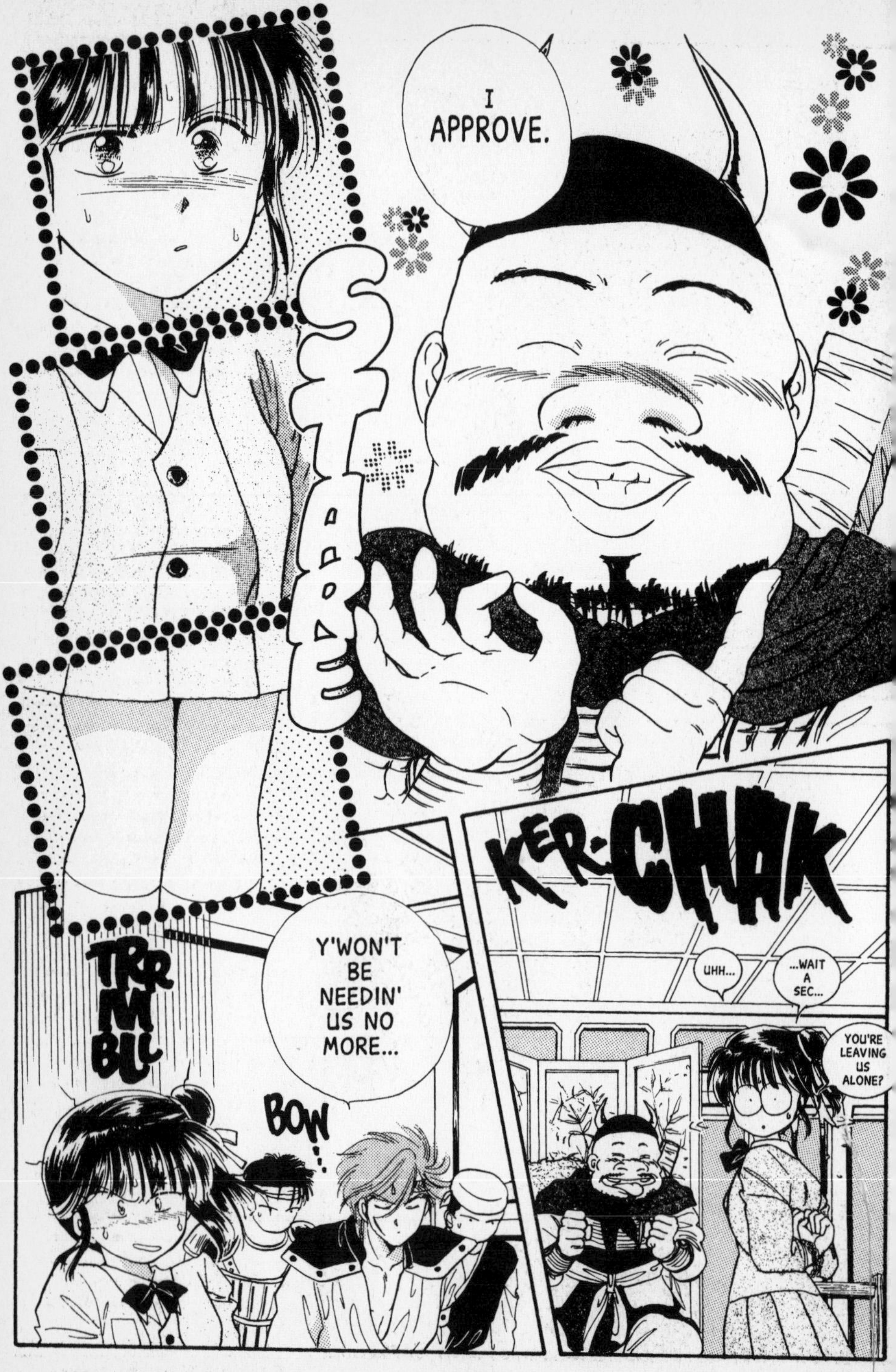
I APPROVE.
TRRMBL
Y'WON'T BE NEEDIN' US NO MORE...
BOW
KER-CHAK
UHH...
...WAIT A SEC...
YOU'RE LEAVING US ALONE?

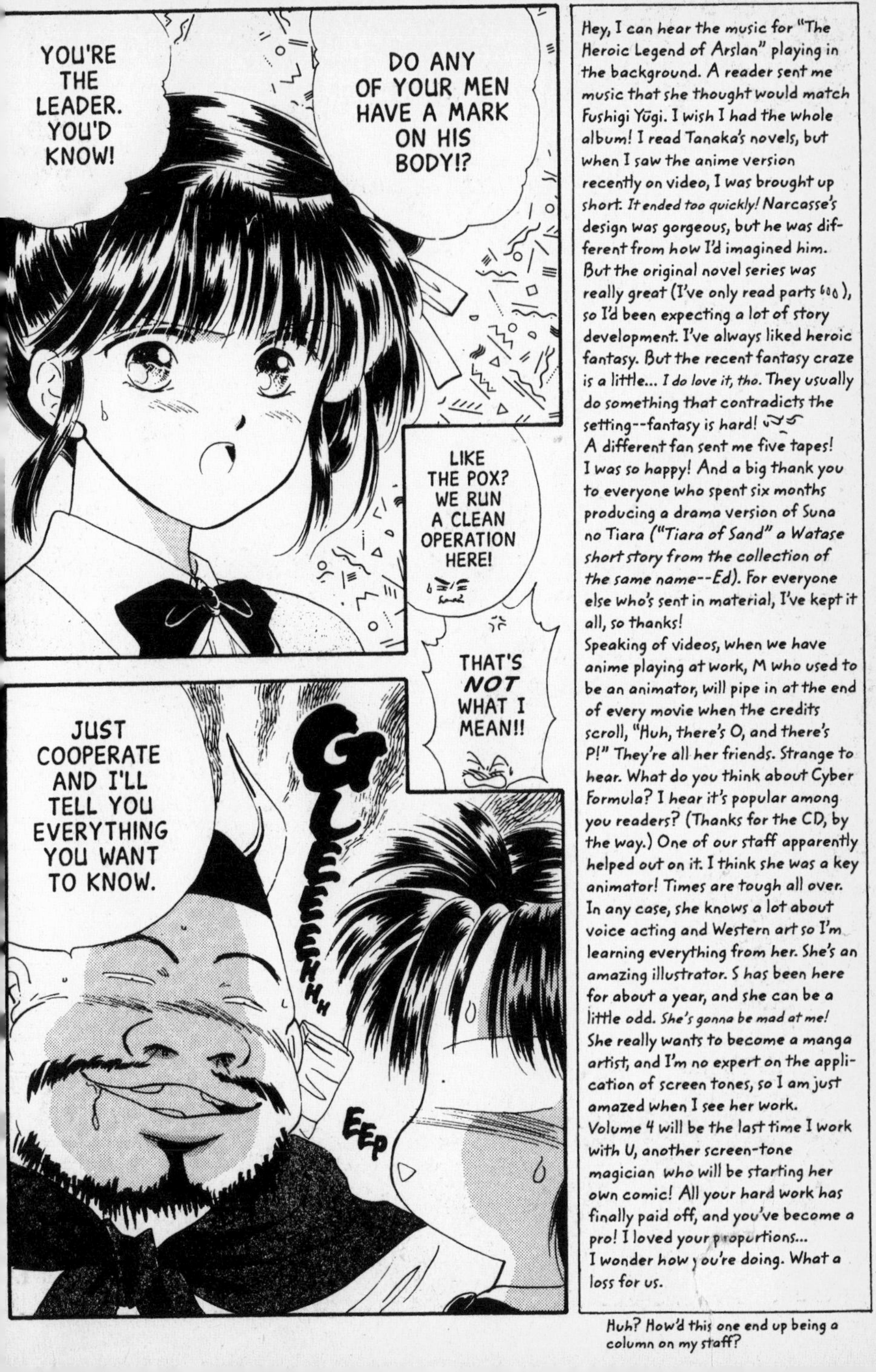
YOU'RE THE LEADER. YOU'D KNOW!
DO ANY OF YOUR MEN HAVE A MARK ON HIS BODY!?
LIKE THE POX? WE RUN A CLEAN OPERATION HERE!
THAT'S *NOT* WHAT I MEAN!!
JUST COOPERATE AND I'LL TELL YOU EVERYTHING YOU WANT TO KNOW.
GLEEEEEHHH
EEP

Hey, I can hear the music for "The Heroic Legend of Arslan" playing in the background. A reader sent me music that she thought would match Fushigi Yūgi. I wish I had the whole album! I read Tanaka's novels, but when I saw the anime version recently on video, I was brought up short. *It ended too quickly!* Narcasse's design was gorgeous, but he was different from how I'd imagined him. But the original novel series was really great (I've only read parts 600), so I'd been expecting a lot of story development. I've always liked heroic fantasy. But the recent fantasy craze is a little... *I do love it, tho.* They usually do something that contradicts the setting--fantasy is hard!
A different fan sent me five tapes! I was so happy! And a big thank you to everyone who spent six months producing a drama version of Suna no Tiara (*"Tiara of Sand" a Watase short story from the collection of the same name--Ed*). For everyone else who's sent in material, I've kept it all, so thanks!
Speaking of videos, when we have anime playing at work, M who used to be an animator, will pipe in at the end of every movie when the credits scroll, "Huh, there's O, and there's P!" They're all her friends. Strange to hear. What do you think about Cyber Formula? I hear it's popular among you readers? (Thanks for the CD, by the way.) One of our staff apparently helped out on it. I think she was a key animator! Times are tough all over. In any case, she knows a lot about voice acting and Western art so I'm learning everything from her. She's an amazing illustrator. S has been here for about a year, and she can be a little odd. *She's gonna be mad at me!* She really wants to become a manga artist, and I'm no expert on the application of screen tones, so I am just amazed when I see her work.
Volume 4 will be the last time I work with U, another screen-tone magician who will be starting her own comic! All your hard work has finally paid off, and you've become a pro! I loved your proportions... I wonder how you're doing. What a loss for us.

Huh? How'd this one end up being a column on my staff?

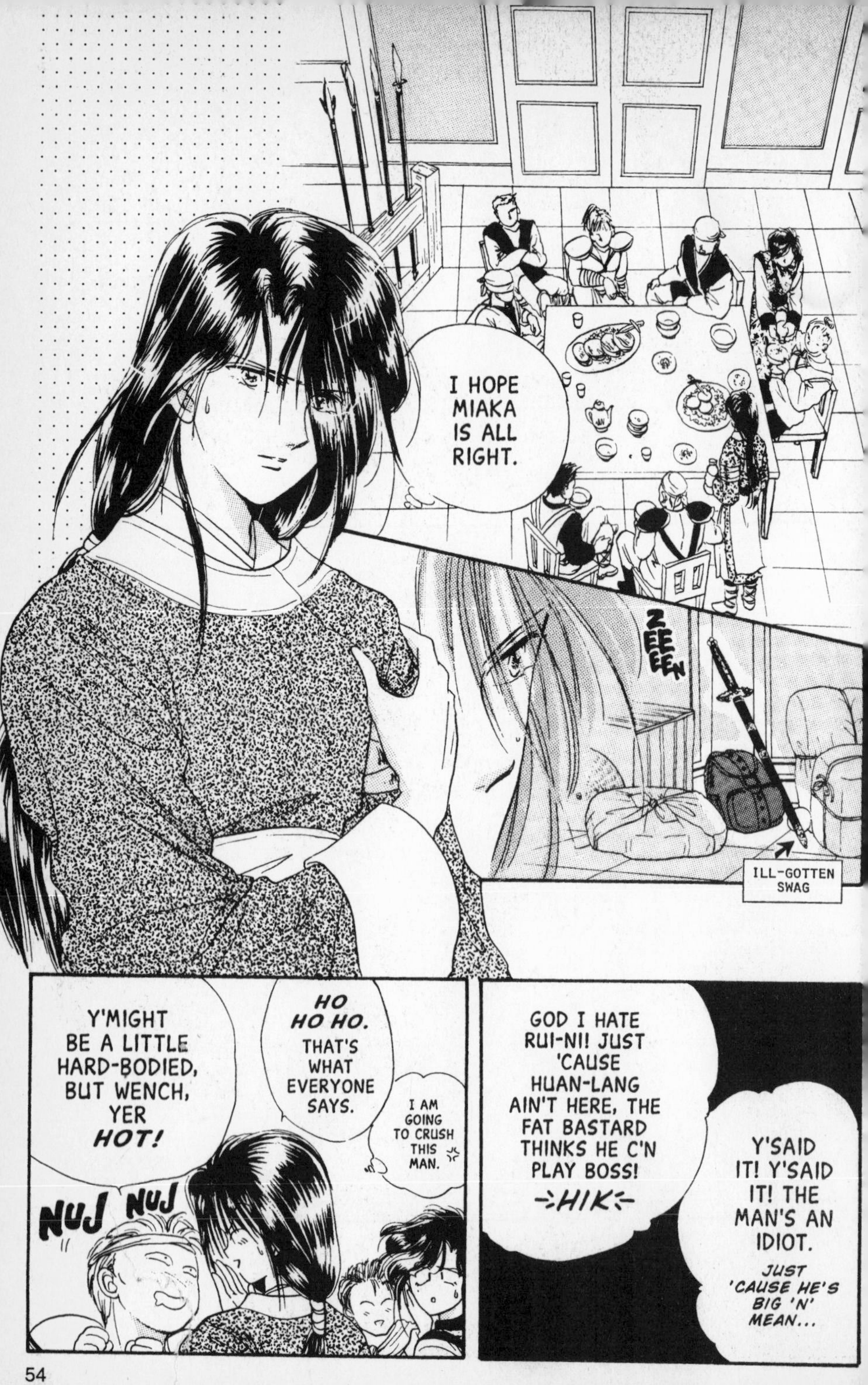
I HOPE MIAKA IS ALL RIGHT.
ZEEEEN
ILL-GOTTEN SWAG
Y'MIGHT BE A LITTLE HARD-BODIED, BUT WENCH, YER HOT!
HO HO HO. THAT'S WHAT EVERYONE SAYS.
I AM GOING TO CRUSH THIS MAN.
NUJ NUJ
GOD I HATE RUI-NI! JUST 'CAUSE HUAN-LANG AIN'T HERE, THE FAT BASTARD THINKS HE C'N PLAY BOSS!
HIK
Y'SAID IT! Y'SAID IT! THE MAN'S AN IDIOT.
JUST 'CAUSE HE'S BIG 'N' MEAN...

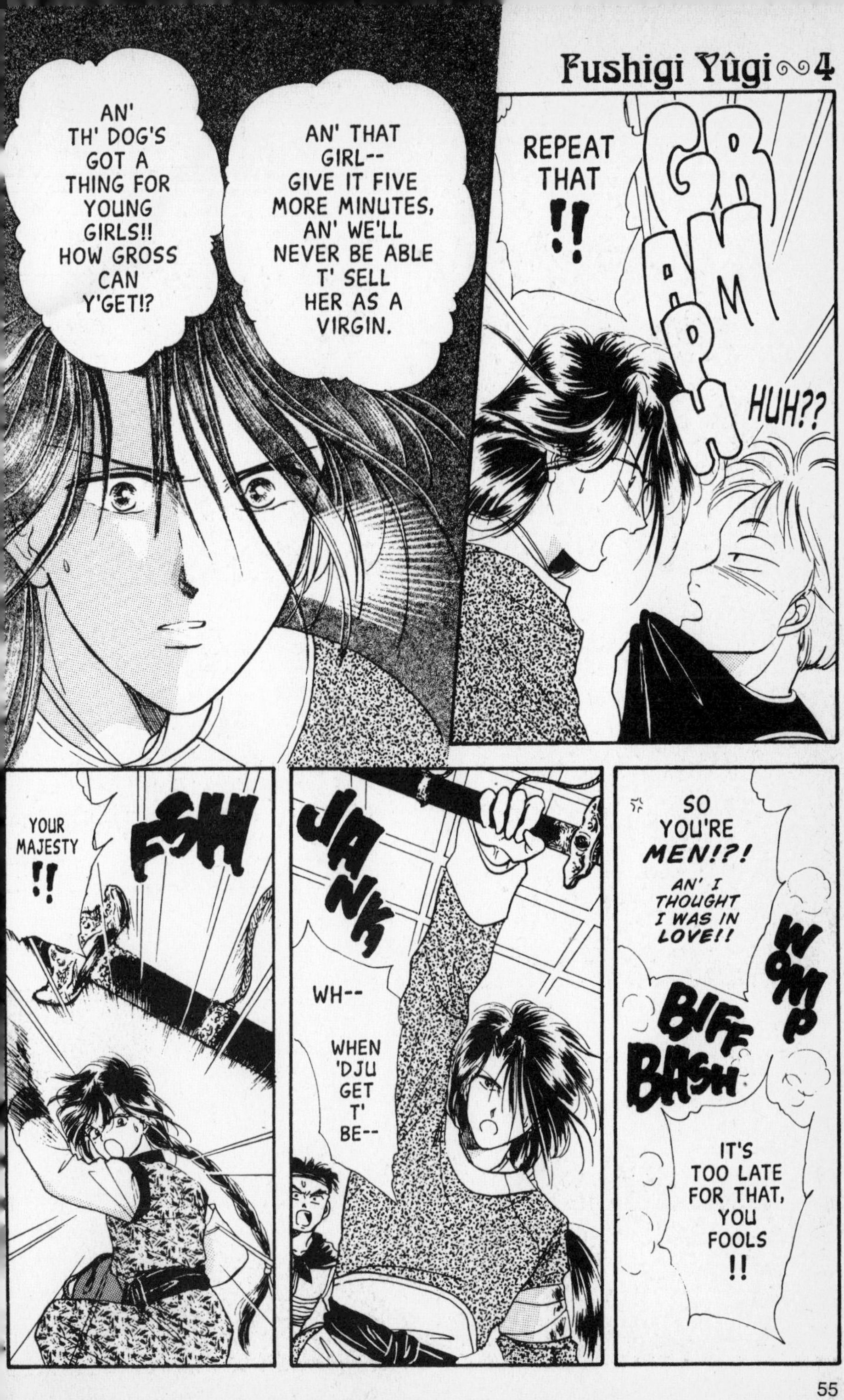
AN' TH' DOG'S GOT A THING FOR YOUNG GIRLS!! HOW GROSS CAN Y'GET!?
AN' THAT GIRL-- GIVE IT FIVE MORE MINUTES, AN' WE'LL NEVER BE ABLE T' SELL HER AS A VIRGIN.
REPEAT THAT !!
GRAMPH
HUH??
YOUR MAJESTY !!
FSH
JANK
WH--
WHEN 'DJU GET T' BE--
SO YOU'RE MEN!?!
AN' I THOUGHT I WAS IN LOVE!!
WOMP
BIFF
BASH
IT'S TOO LATE FOR THAT, YOU FOOLS !!

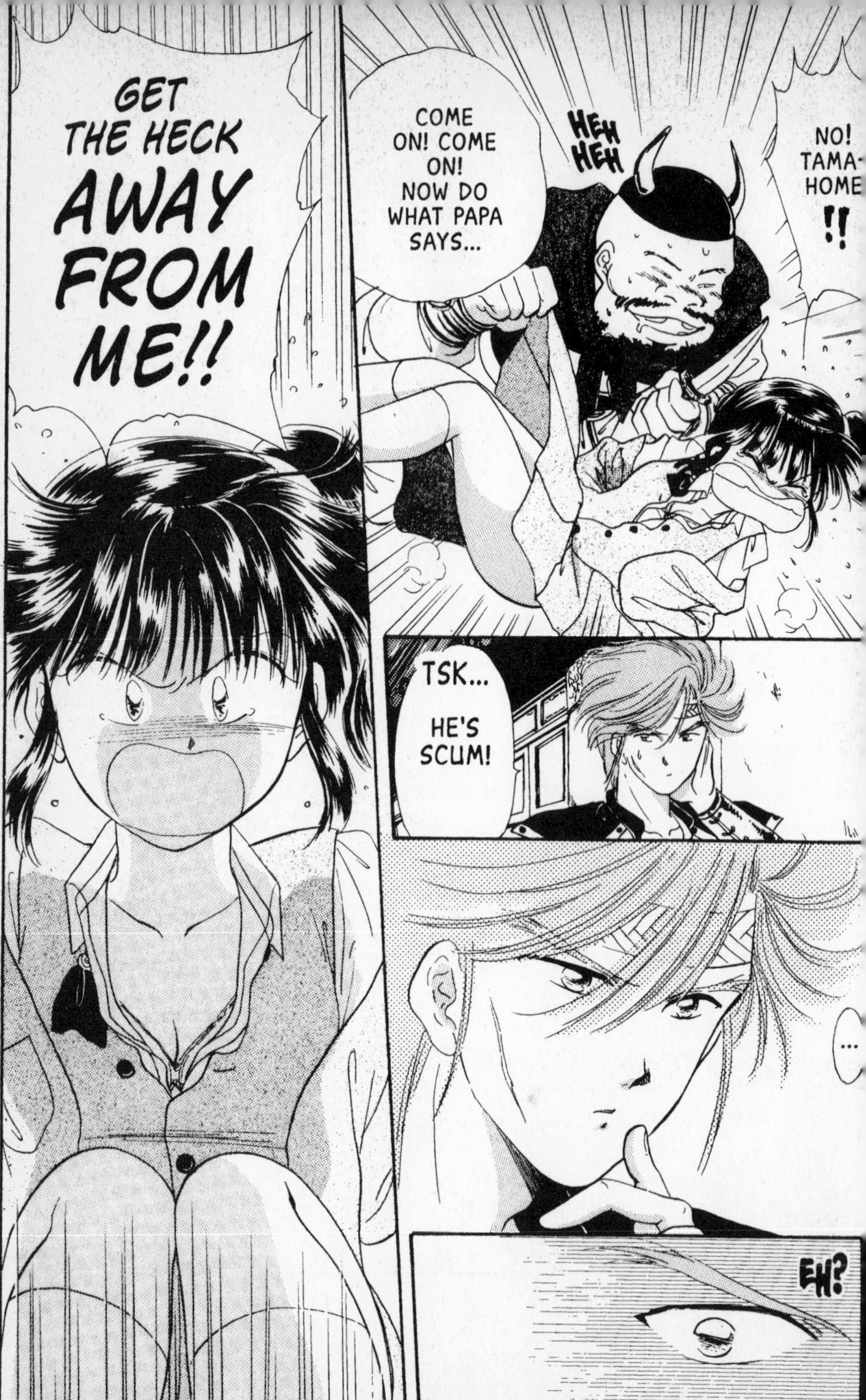
GET THE HECK AWAY FROM ME!!
COME ON! COME ON! NOW DO WHAT PAPA SAYS...
HEH HEH
NO! TAMA-HOME!!
TSK...
HE'S SCUM!
...
EH?

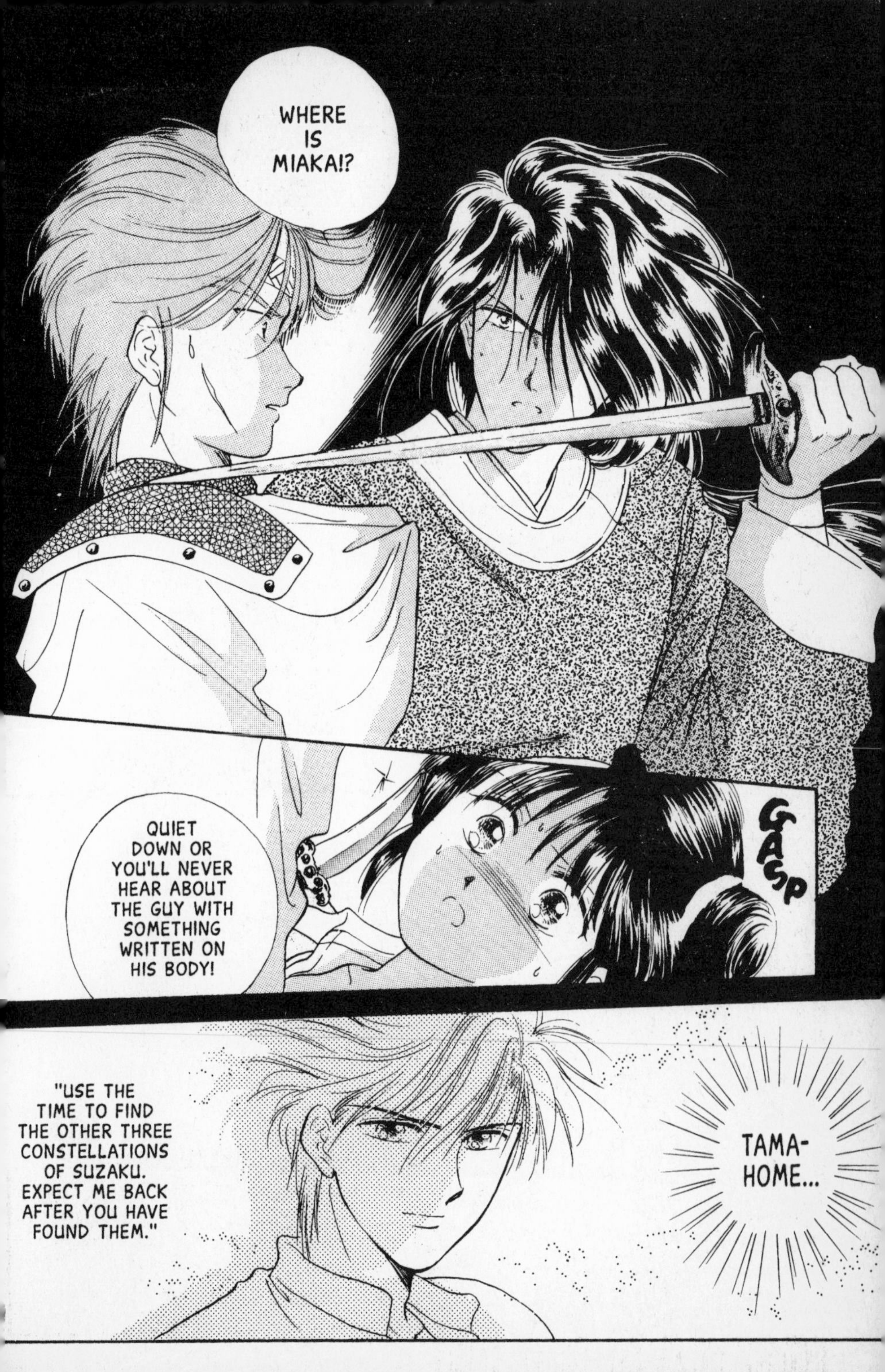
WHERE IS MIAKA!?
QUIET DOWN OR YOU'LL NEVER HEAR ABOUT THE GUY WITH SOMETHING WRITTEN ON HIS BODY!
GASP
"USE THE TIME TO FIND THE OTHER THREE CONSTELLATIONS OF SUZAKU. EXPECT ME BACK AFTER YOU HAVE FOUND THEM."
TAMA-HOME...

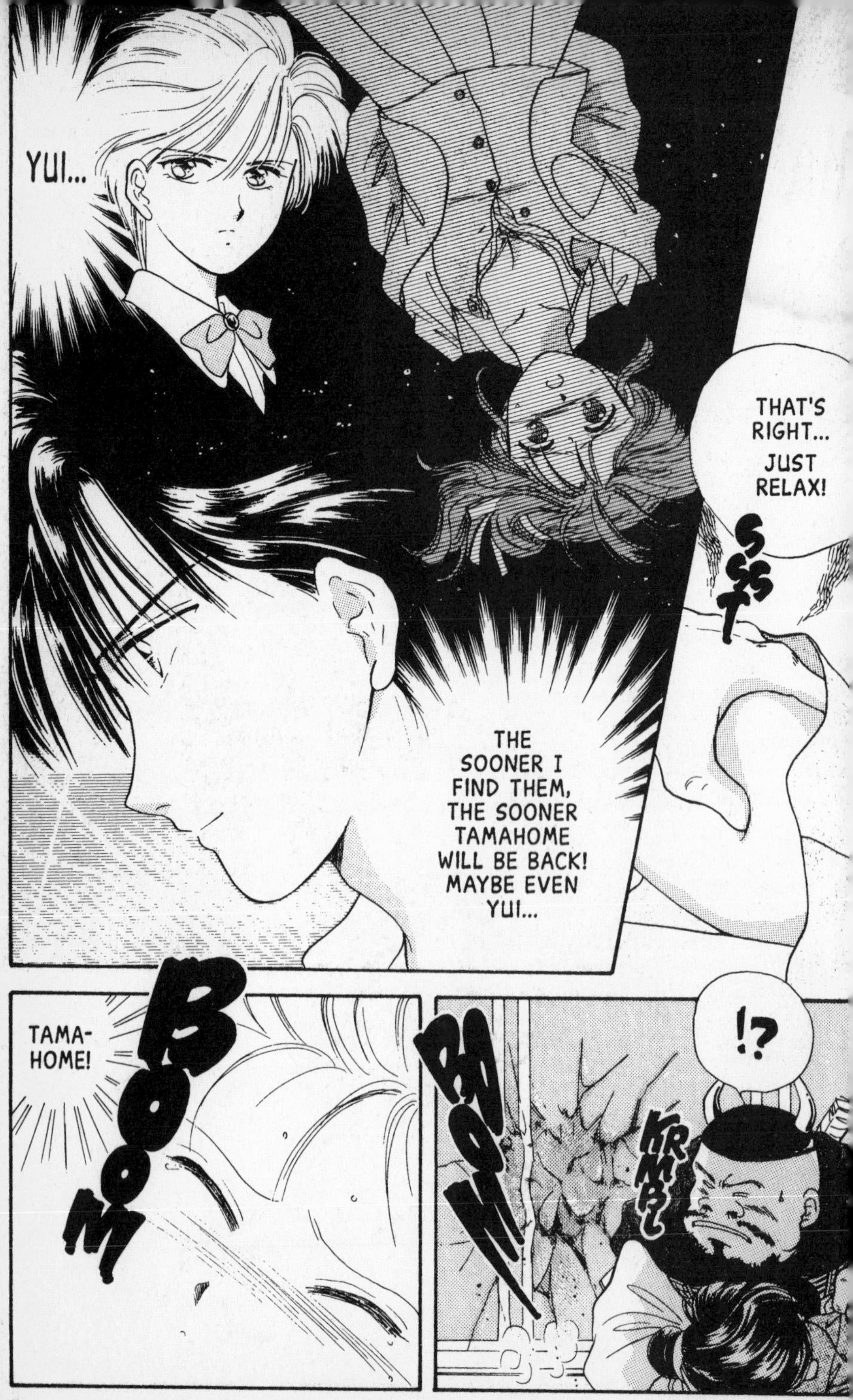
YUI...
THAT'S RIGHT... JUST RELAX!
SSST
THE SOONER I FIND THEM, THE SOONER TAMAHOME WILL BE BACK! MAYBE EVEN YUI...
TAMA-HOME!
BOOM
!?
KRMBL

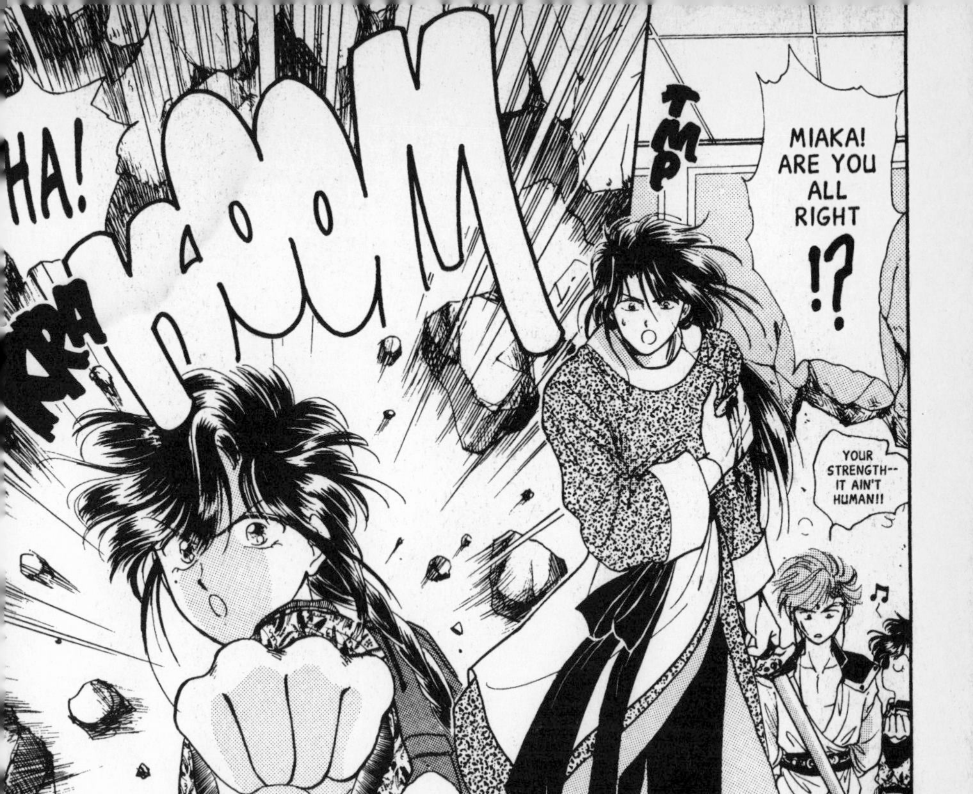
HA!
KRA
KRAAOOM
TMP
MIAKA! ARE YOU ALL RIGHT !?
YOUR STRENGTH-- IT AIN'T HUMAN!!
NURIKO !!
BOINK

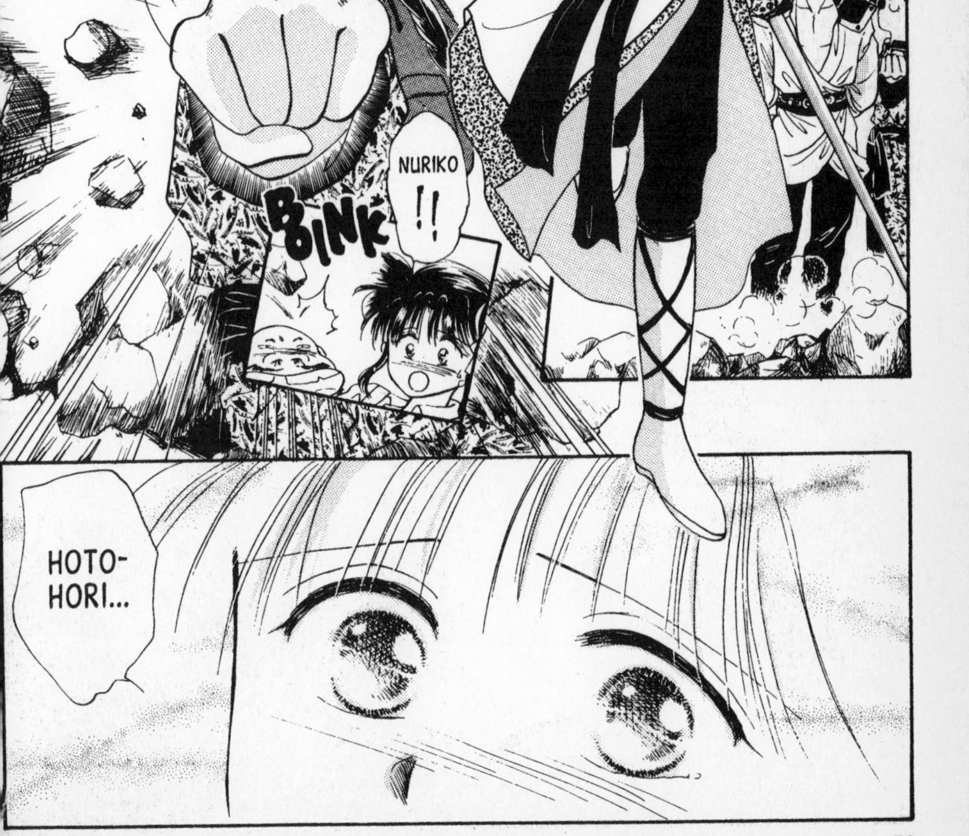
HOTO-HORI...

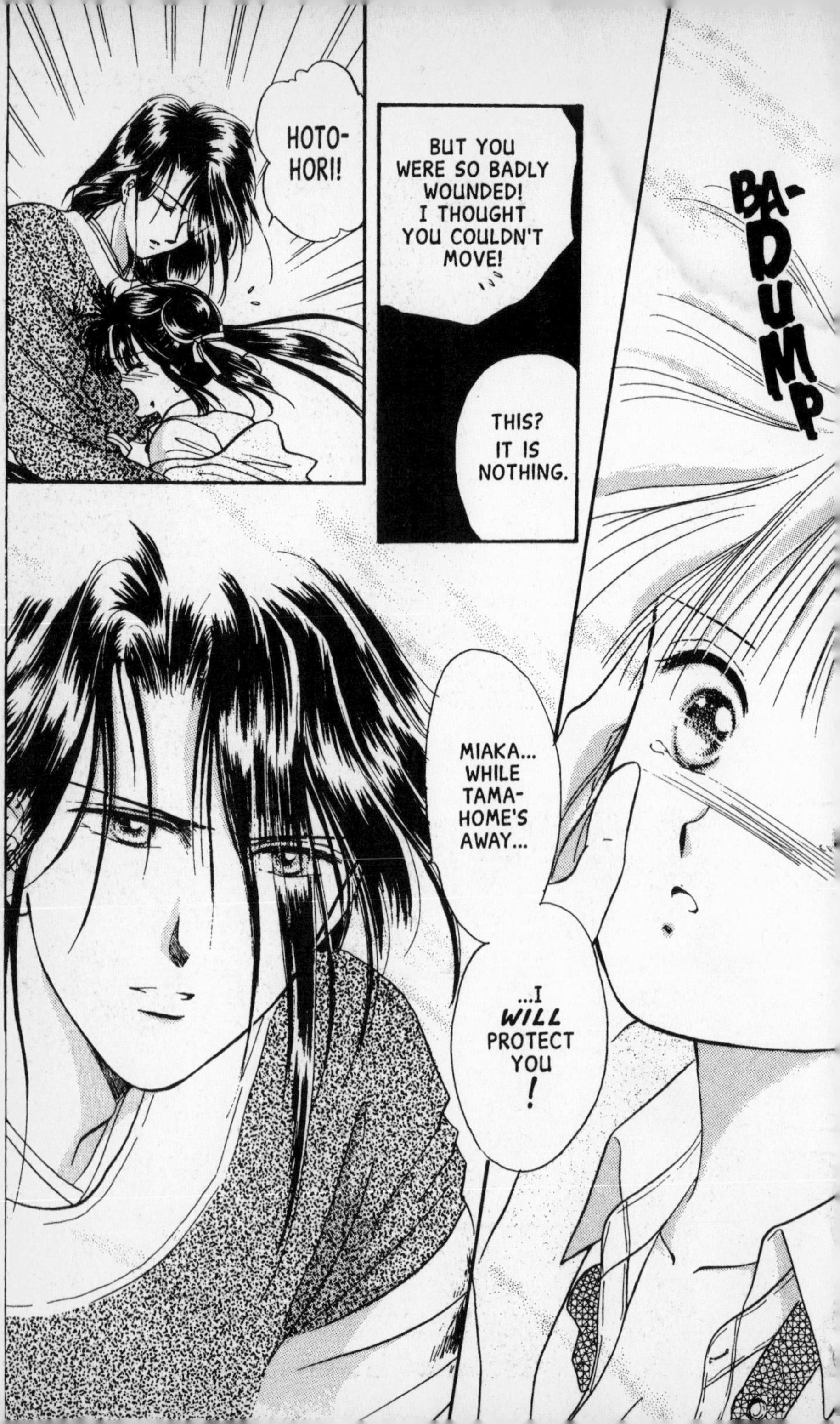
HOTO-HORI!
BUT YOU WERE SO BADLY WOUNDED! I THOUGHT YOU COULDN'T MOVE!
THIS? IT IS NOTHING.
MIAKA... WHILE TAMA-HOME'S AWAY...
...I WILL PROTECT YOU!
BA-DUMP

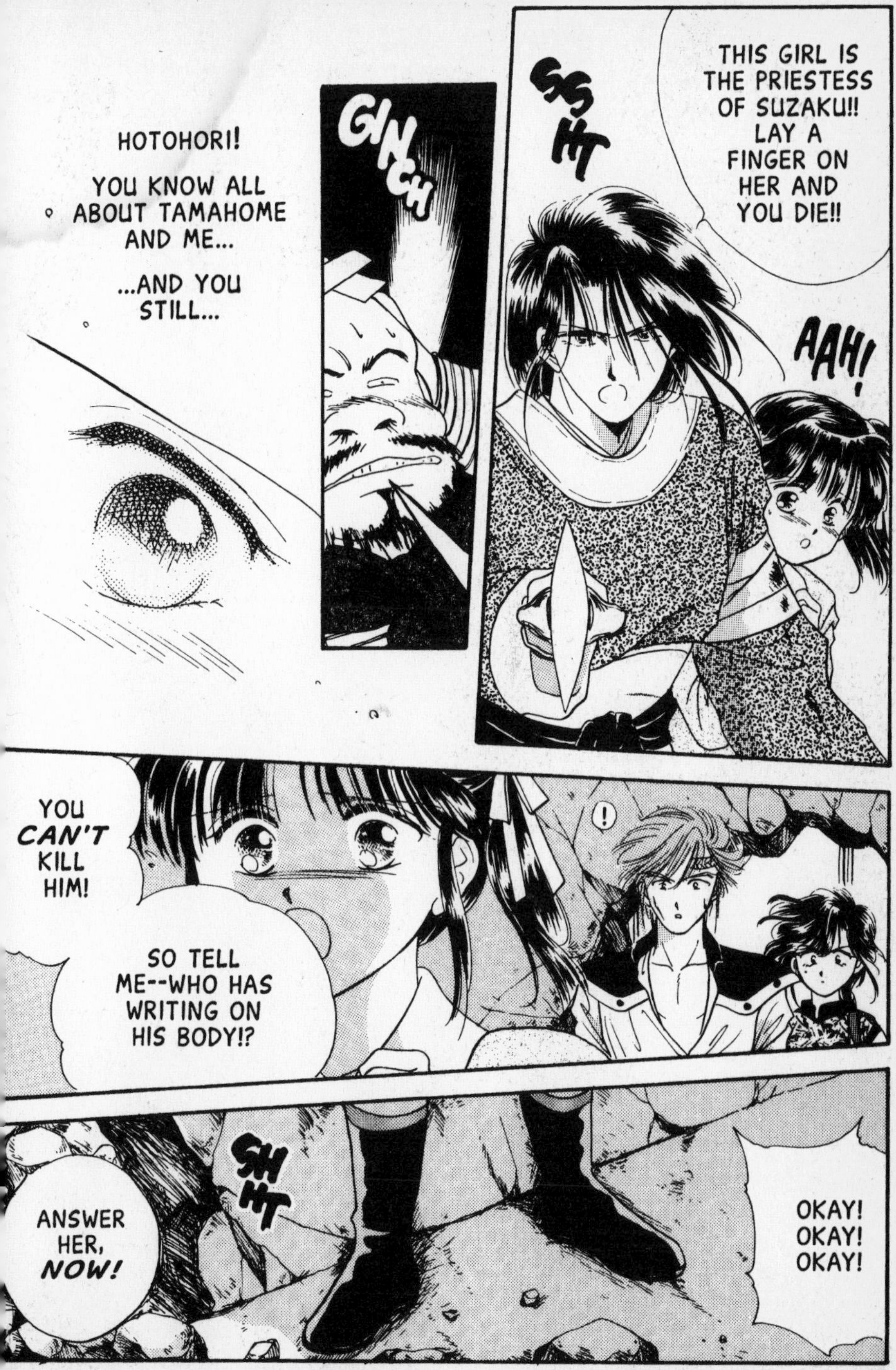
HOTOHORI!
YOU KNOW ALL ABOUT TAMAHOME AND ME...
...AND YOU STILL...
GINCH
SSSHT
THIS GIRL IS THE PRIESTESS OF SUZAKU!! LAY A FINGER ON HER AND YOU DIE!!
AAH!
YOU *CAN'T* KILL HIM!
SO TELL ME--WHO HAS WRITING ON HIS BODY!?
!
ANSWER HER, *NOW!*
SHHT
OKAY! OKAY! OKAY!

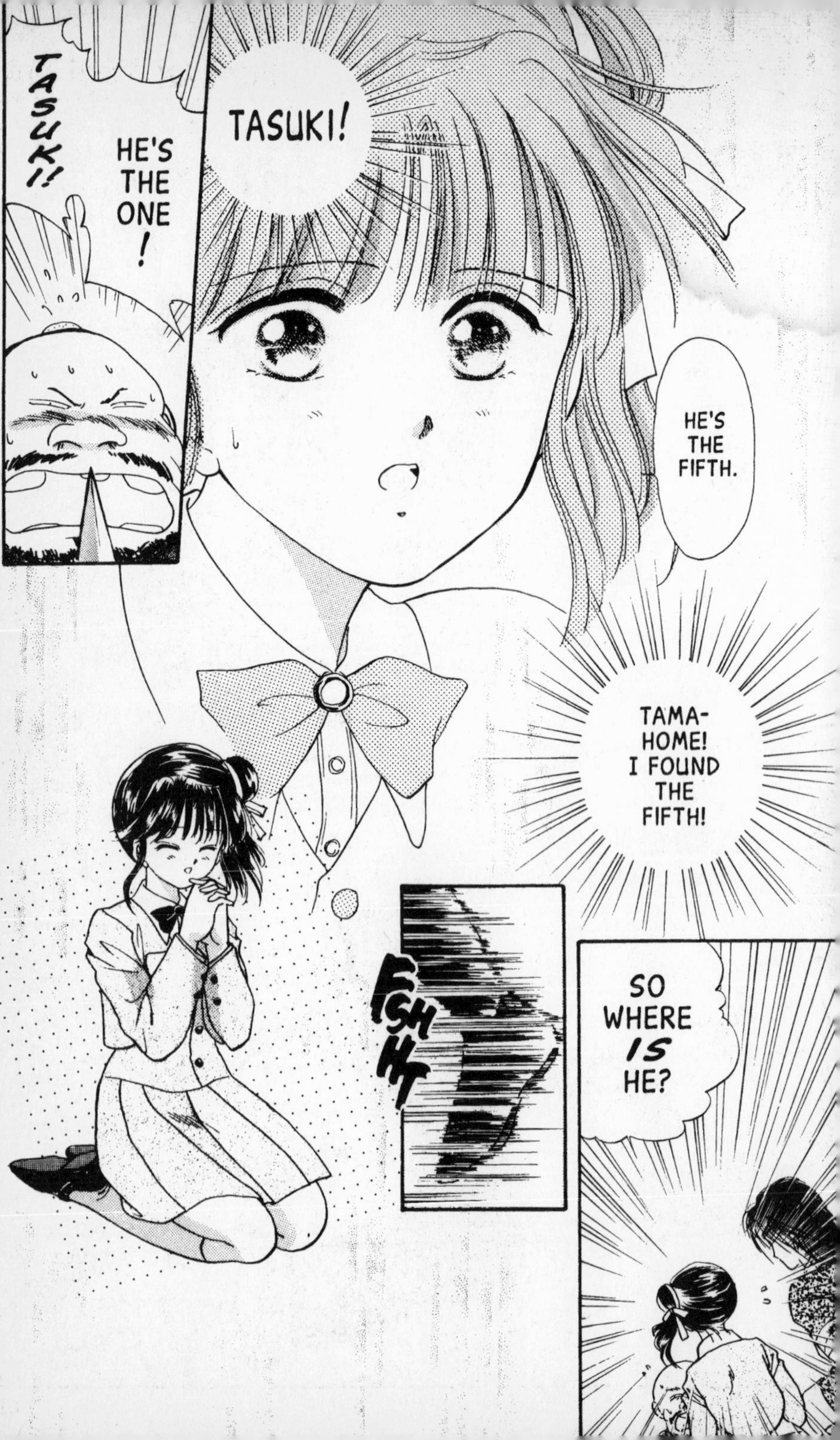
TASUKI!
HE'S THE FIFTH.
TASUKI!!
HE'S THE ONE!
TAMA-HOME! I FOUND THE FIFTH!
FSHHT
SO WHERE IS HE?

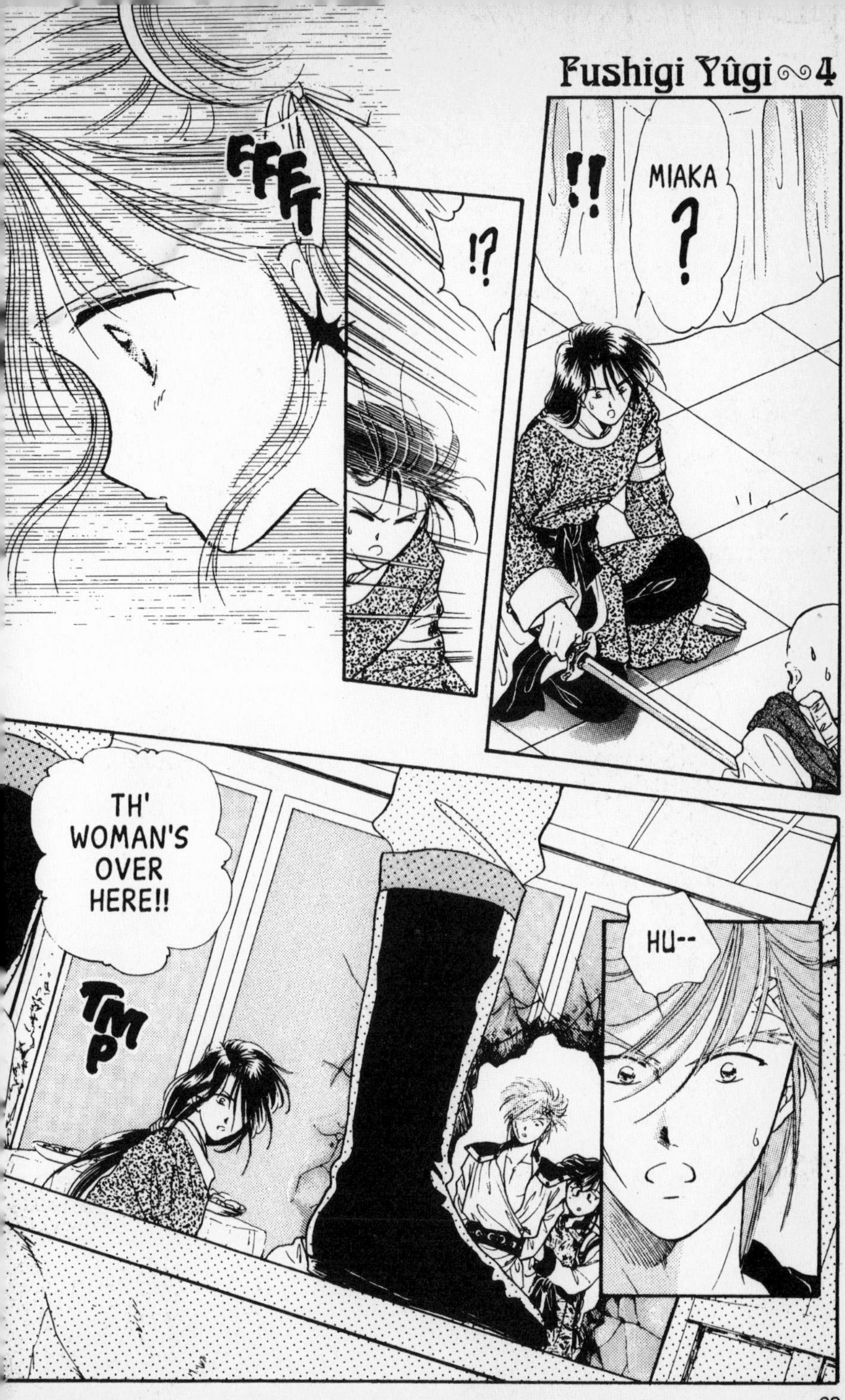
FFFT
!?
!!
MIAKA ?
TH' WOMAN'S OVER HERE!!
TMP
HU--

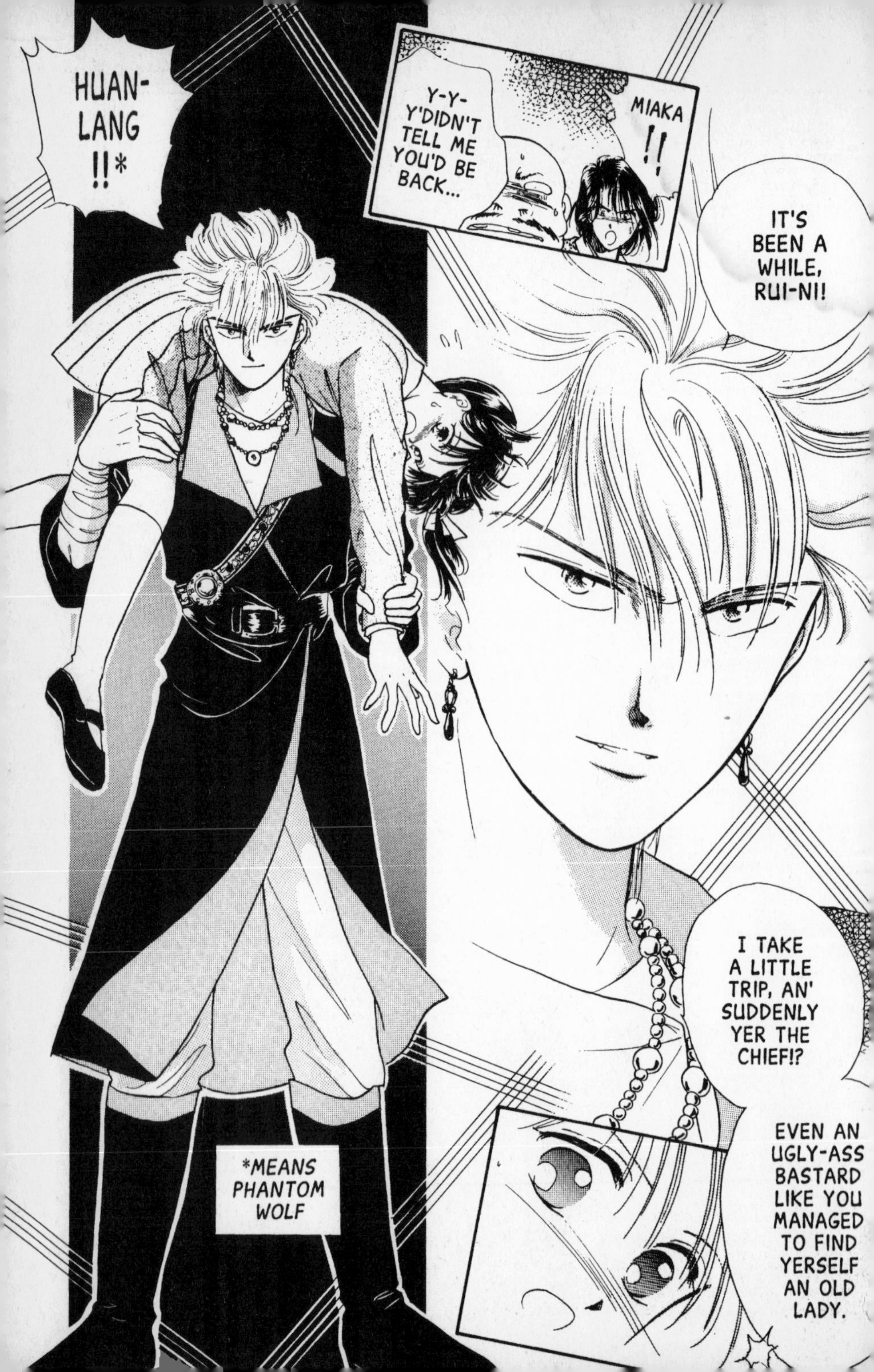
HUAN-LANG!!*
*MEANS PHANTOM WOLF
Y-Y-Y'DIDN'T TELL ME YOU'D BE BACK...
MIAKA !!
IT'S BEEN A WHILE, RUI-NI!
I TAKE A LITTLE TRIP, AN' SUDDENLY YER THE CHIEF!?
EVEN AN UGLY-ASS BASTARD LIKE YOU MANAGED TO FIND YERSELF AN OLD LADY.

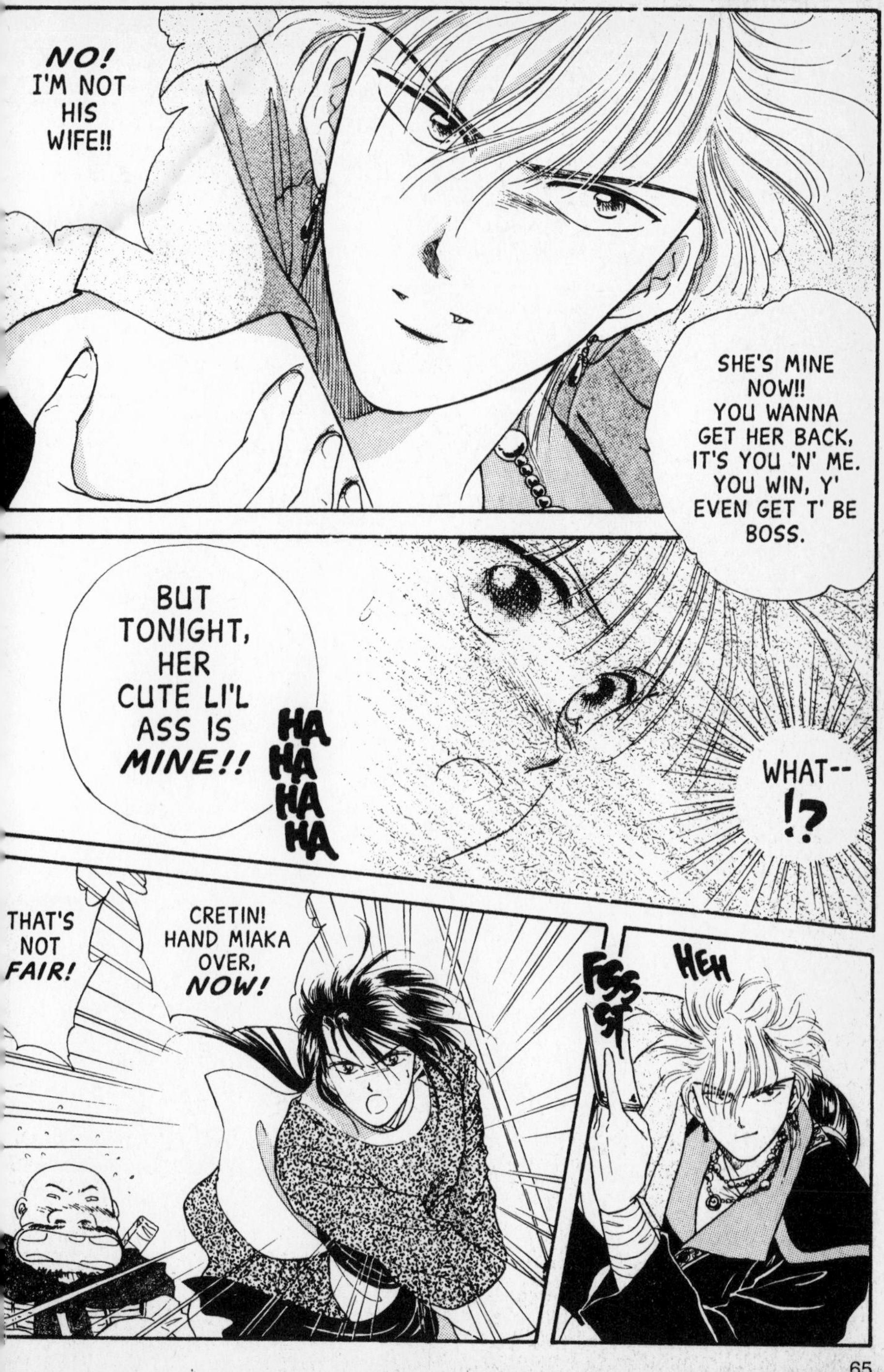
NO! I'M NOT HIS WIFE!!
SHE'S MINE NOW!! YOU WANNA GET HER BACK, IT'S YOU 'N' ME. YOU WIN, Y' EVEN GET T' BE BOSS.
BUT TONIGHT, HER CUTE LI'L ASS IS MINE!!
HA HA HA HA HA
WHAT-- !?
THAT'S NOT FAIR!
CRETIN! HAND MIAKA OVER, NOW!
FSSSST
HEH

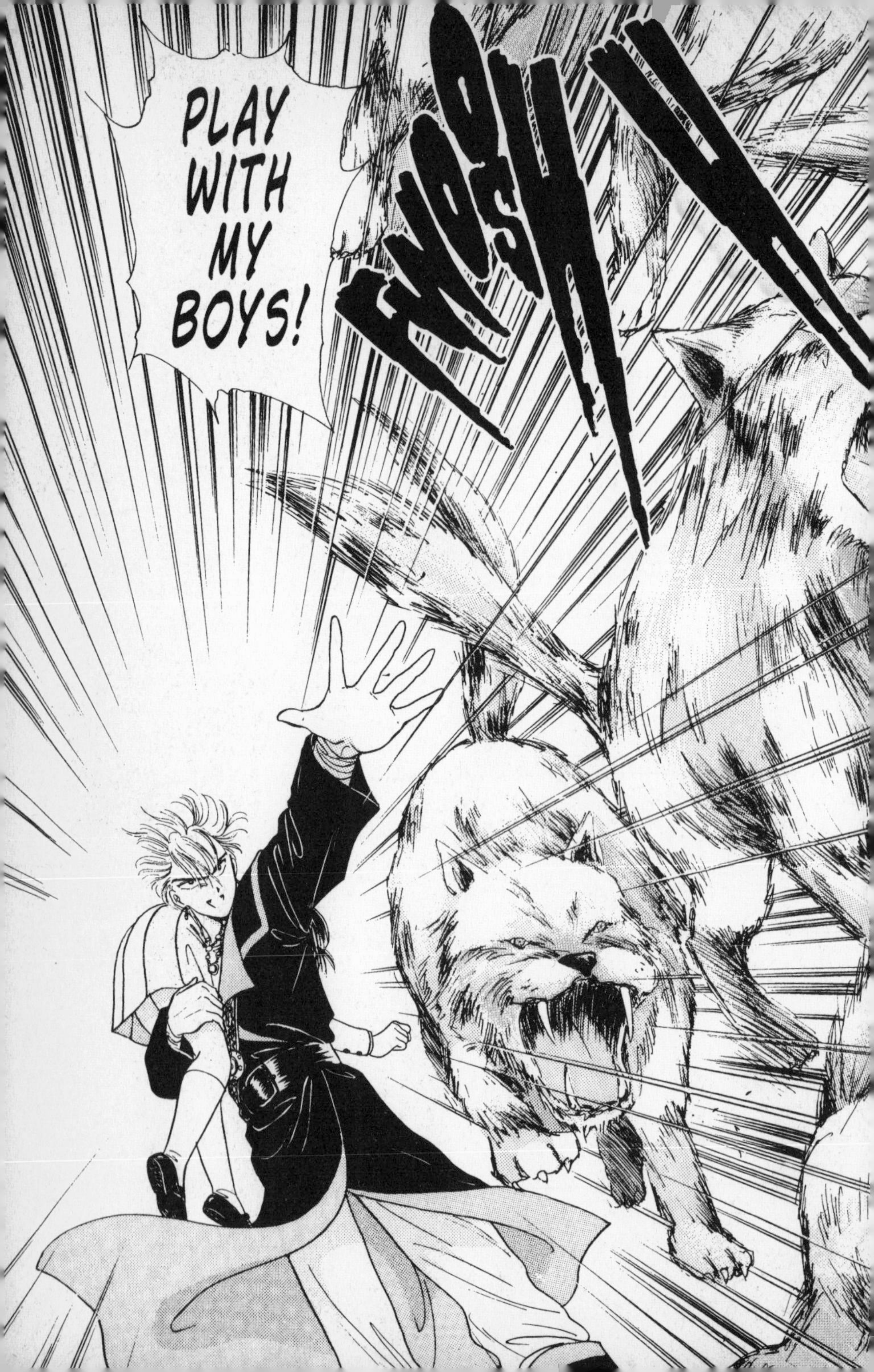
PLAY WITH MY BOYS!
FWOSH

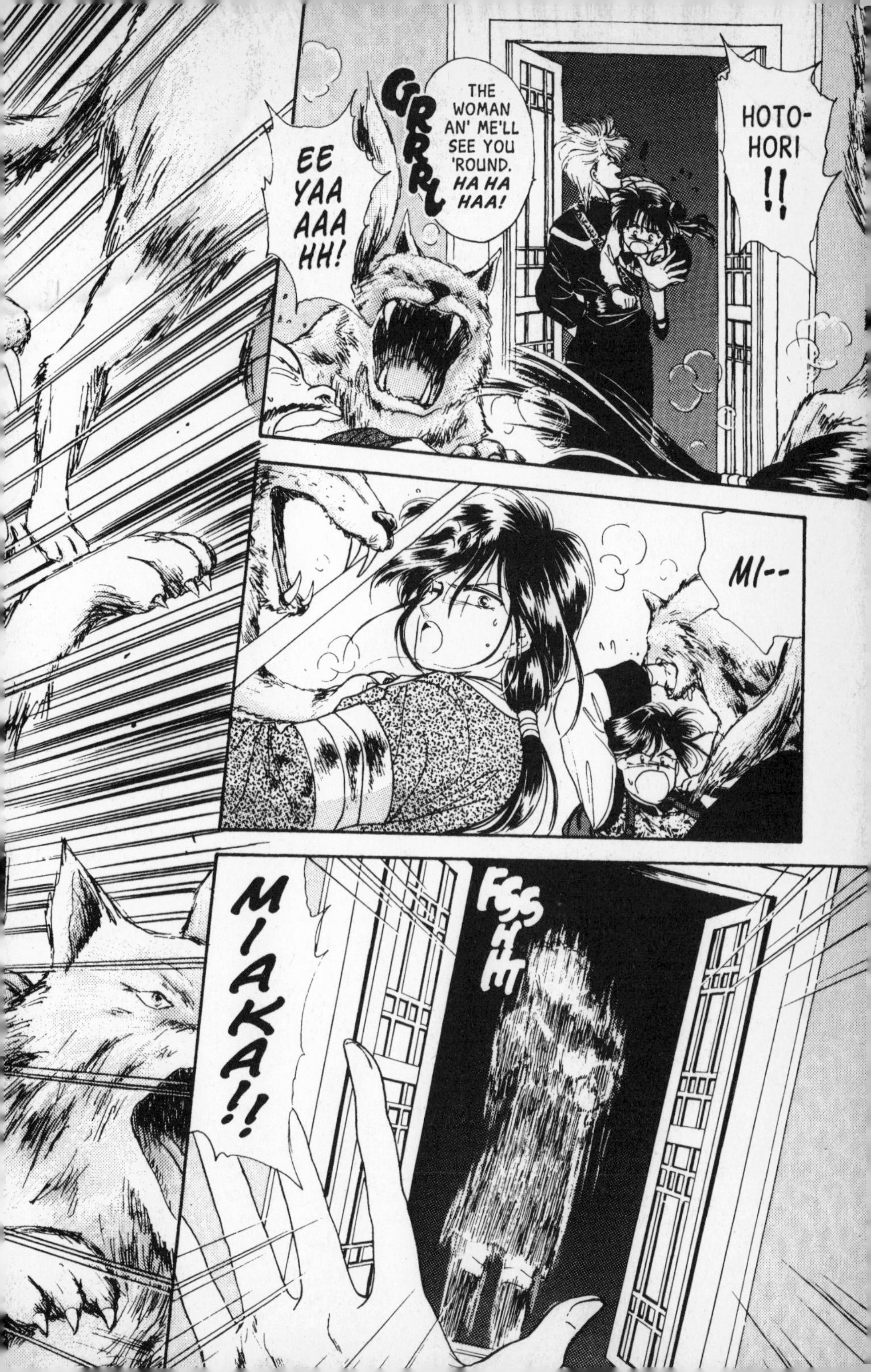
EE YAA AAA HH!
GRRRL
THE WOMAN AN' ME'LL SEE YOU 'ROUND. HA HA HAA!
HOTO-HORI!!
MI--
MIAKA!!
FSSHHT

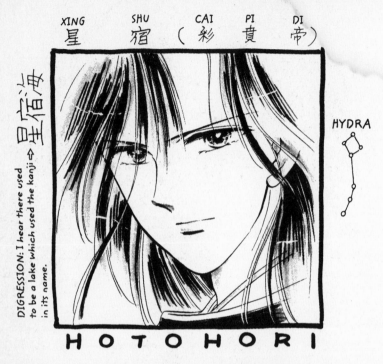

星宿海

DIGRESSION: I hear there used to be a lake which used the kanji ⇒ in its name.

HYDRA

H O T O H O R I

- Fourth Emperor of Hong-Nan. His palace is in the capital city of Rong-Yang where he reigns.

- Birthdate sometime between February and May. They don't make a big deal of it.

- He had two older brothers and one younger. 2 younger sisters (something like that). (There was probably quite a battle for succession.)

- 18 years old but he looks older.

- Height 6 feet, or there abouts. Blood type A? I don't know!!

- His specialty is fencing. But since he had the world's finest teachers since he was small, he can probably do anything.

- Personality: He seems like the type that hides his feelings, but he's actually a warm and peaceful man. As the ruler of his kingdom, he was raised surrounded by adults, so it's no wonder he looks old for his age. He looks cold and harsh when he's sitting on the throne because of his isolated and lonely upbringing.
  I figure he never had any love from his parents the previous emperor and empress, so he's very attracted to Miaka's warmth. When he's around her, he turns into a normal young man.
  The worst part (or best part) about him is that he's a TOTAL narcissist. Due to his sheltered background he doesn't know much about the world.

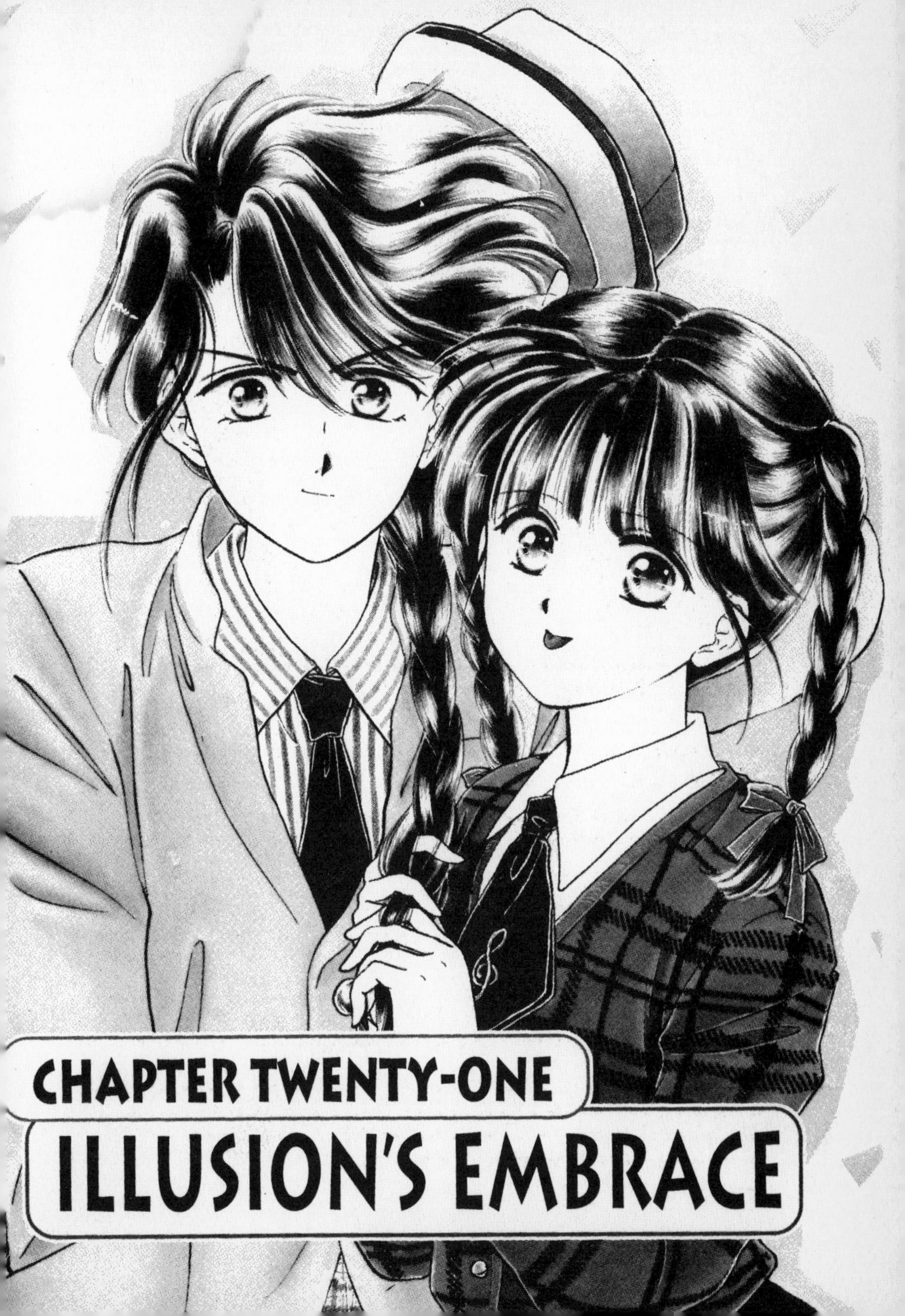
CHAPTER TWENTY-ONE
ILLUSION'S EMBRACE

NURIKO

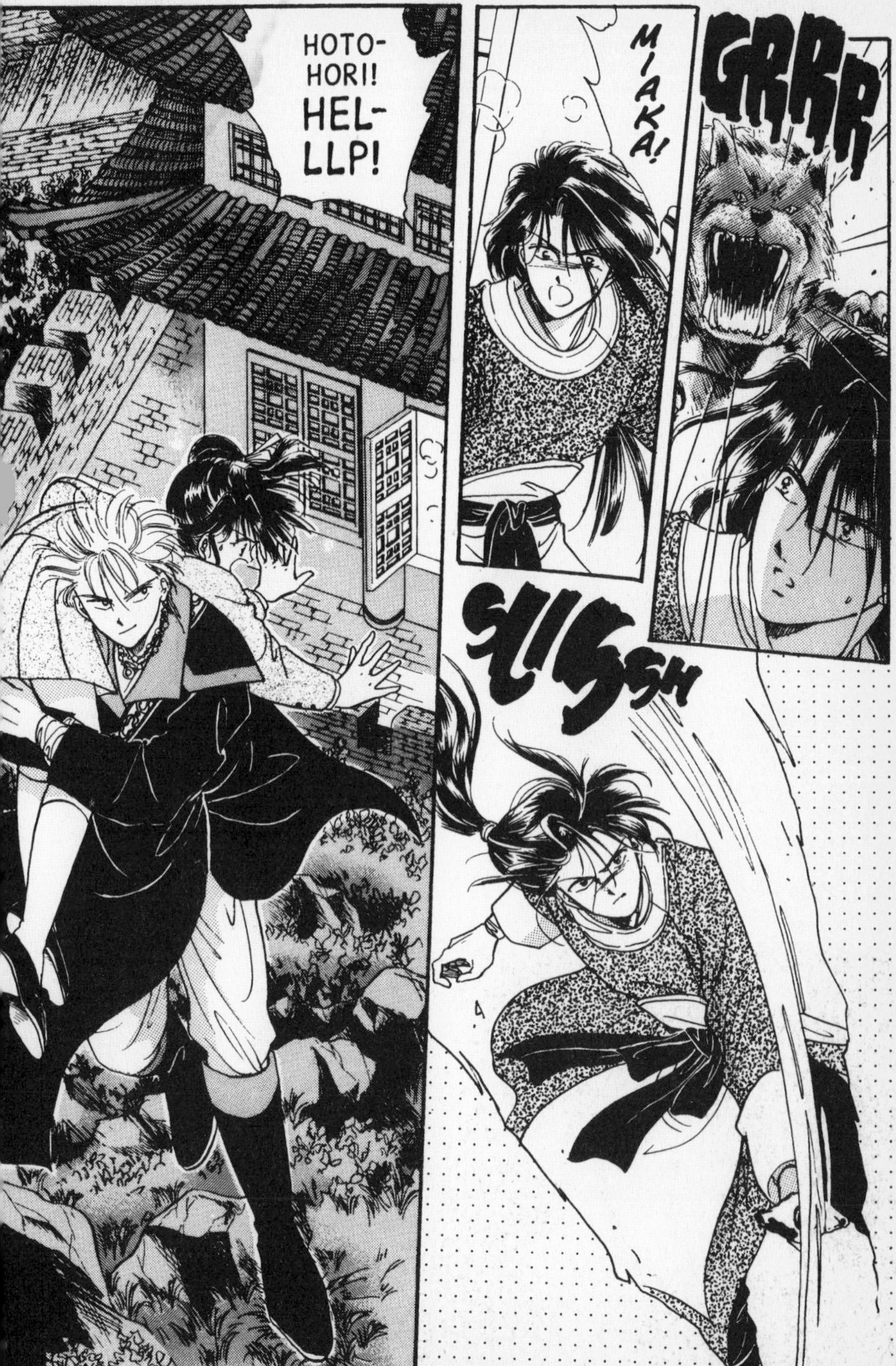
HOTO-
HORI!
HEL-
LLP!
MIAKA!
GRRR
SWISSH

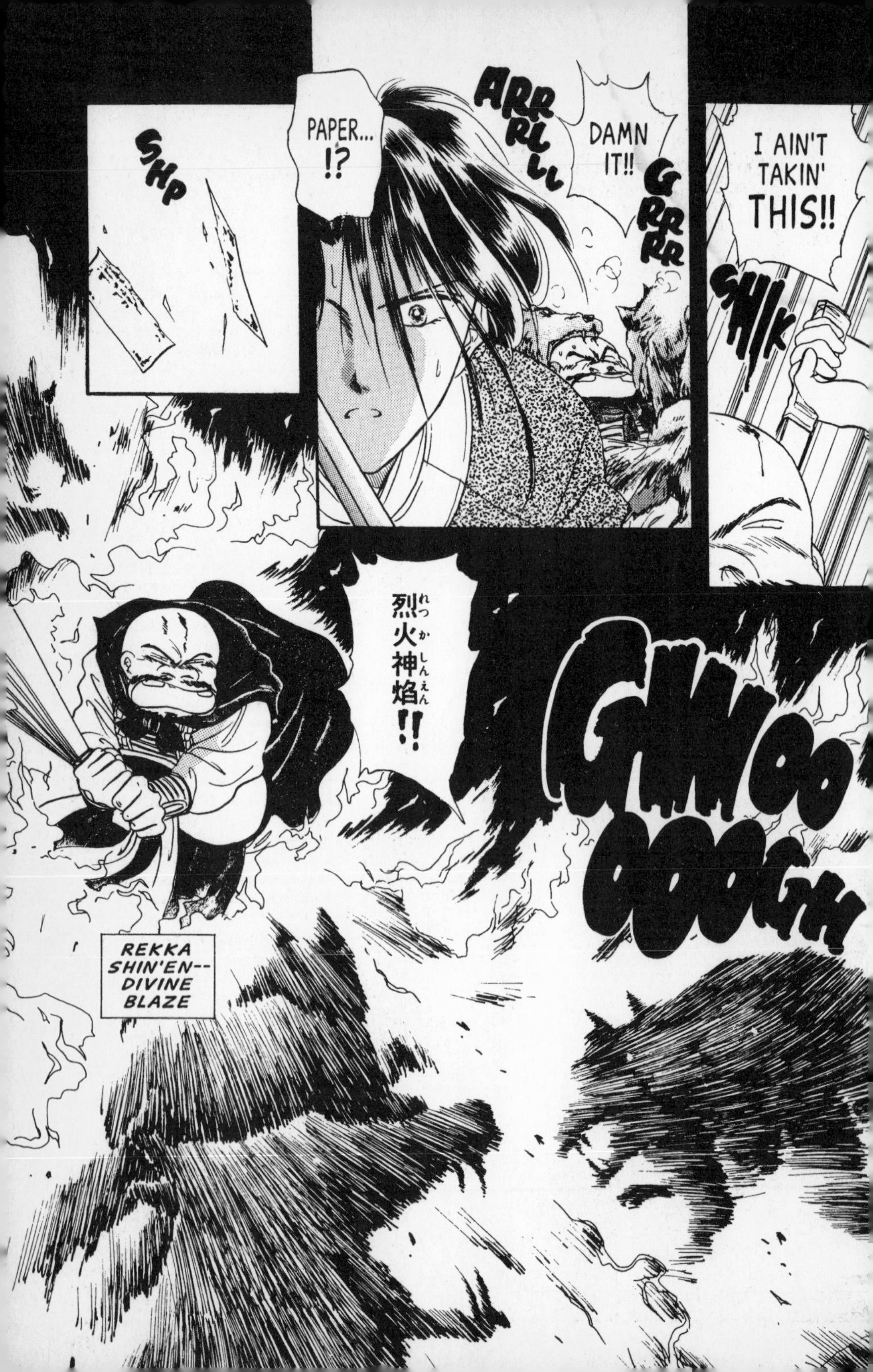
SHP
PAPER... !?
ARRRLLL
DAMN IT!!
GRRRR
I AIN'T TAKIN' THIS!!
SHIK
烈火神焔!!
GWOOOOOGH
REKKA SHIN'EN-- DIVINE BLAZE

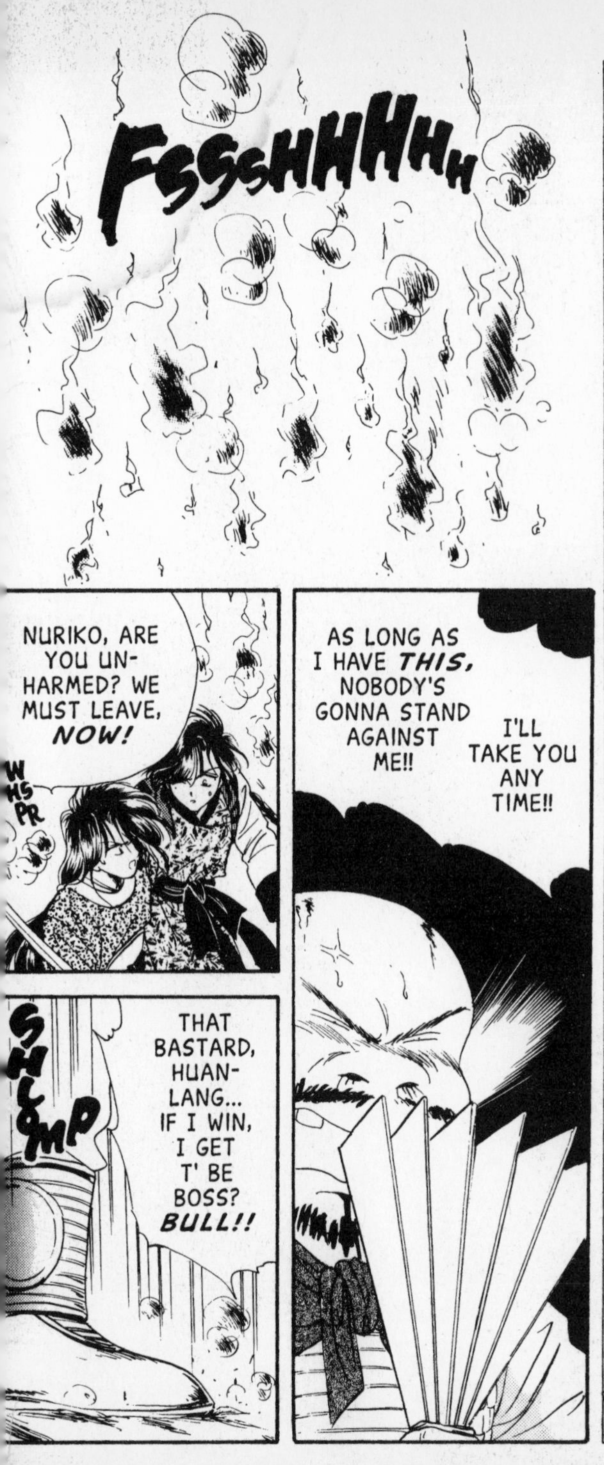
FSSSHHHHHH
NURIKO, ARE YOU UN-HARMED? WE MUST LEAVE, ***NOW!***
WHSPR
SHLOMP
THAT BASTARD, HUAN-LANG... IF I WIN, I GET T' BE BOSS? ***BULL!!***
AS LONG AS I HAVE ***THIS,*** NOBODY'S GONNA STAND AGAINST ME!!
I'LL TAKE YOU ANY TIME!!

Now I'm listening to the music for Street Fighter II. I just love the songs that sound Chinese. The commercial for the game has been playing since summer. It's sooo pretty! I love it!! That line, "I'll wander the Earth until I find someone stronger than I am," is so great.
That reminds me! A buddy of mine works at Capcom. Are you reading this? You're responsible for the computer backgrounds, right? I wonder if you're involved in the Street Fighter series. *I wanna play computer games, I wish I had free time.*
Come to think of it, I can't think of any ◊◊ of my friends who work normal office jobs (i.e. Office Ladies or OL). One of them, a friend from middle school, is in a puppet troupe (I get tapes from her that you can't find ANYWHERE). Another one's in a "human" theater troupe (or something like that). One who works at a bookstore, told a customer who was buying one of my books, "I'm pals with Yū Watase." I don't know WHAT she was thinking! (Sometimes she'll send me faxes with no warning.) Then there's one who's a newlywed housewife, and another who's a nurse. I guess Ms. A works at an office. Then there's one friend in a musical troupe (hurry and get a leading role. As a high school senior I drew Scarlett O'Hara for you, right?) *What does THAT have to do with anything?* The rest are manga artists. Birds of a feather, huh? Oh, yeah! There was one who became a banker. In any case they're all good people, which would have to mean that I'm good, too. (Hold on a sec...)
But with the distance between Tokyo and Osaka being 1/3 the entire length of Japan, I hardly ever see them. There's something soothing about friends who call you by your real name. I mean I've gotten used to being called "Ms. Watase."
Which reminds me, someone who wrote to me had the same first and last name as mine. I was amazed. (The characters were different, though.) That was more surprising than the time I received a letter from a boy with the same name as Manato Sudō in "Prepubescence" (I'm a little suspicious of this). How weird can this world be? Oh yes, a fan who's a housewife sent me a postcard saying that she named her son Manato. Isn't there a Tamahome out there somewhere?

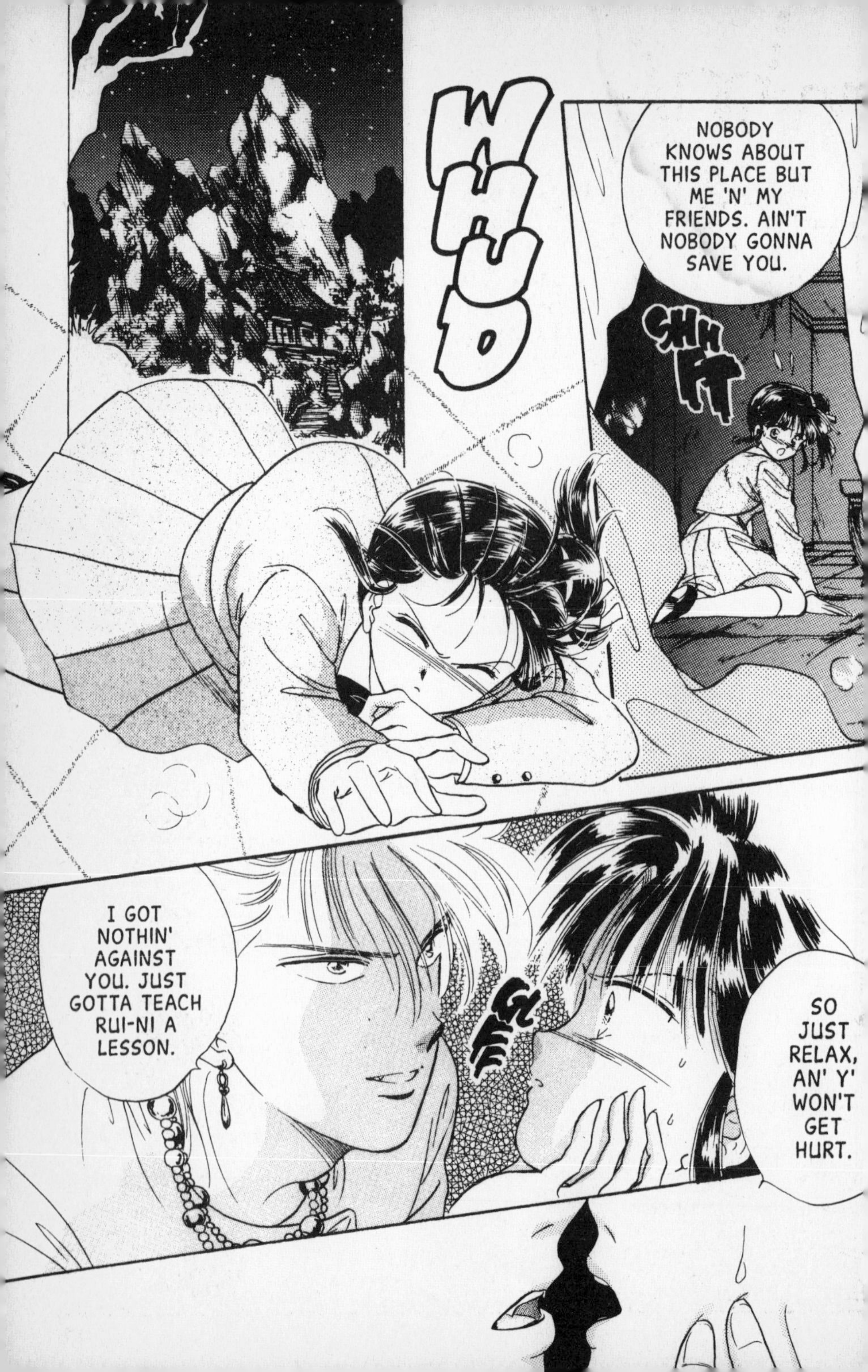
WHUD
NOBODY KNOWS ABOUT THIS PLACE BUT ME 'N' MY FRIENDS. AIN'T NOBODY GONNA SAVE YOU.
SHH FFT
I GOT NOTHIN' AGAINST YOU. JUST GOTTA TEACH RUI-NI A LESSON.
SO JUST RELAX, AN' Y' WON'T GET HURT.

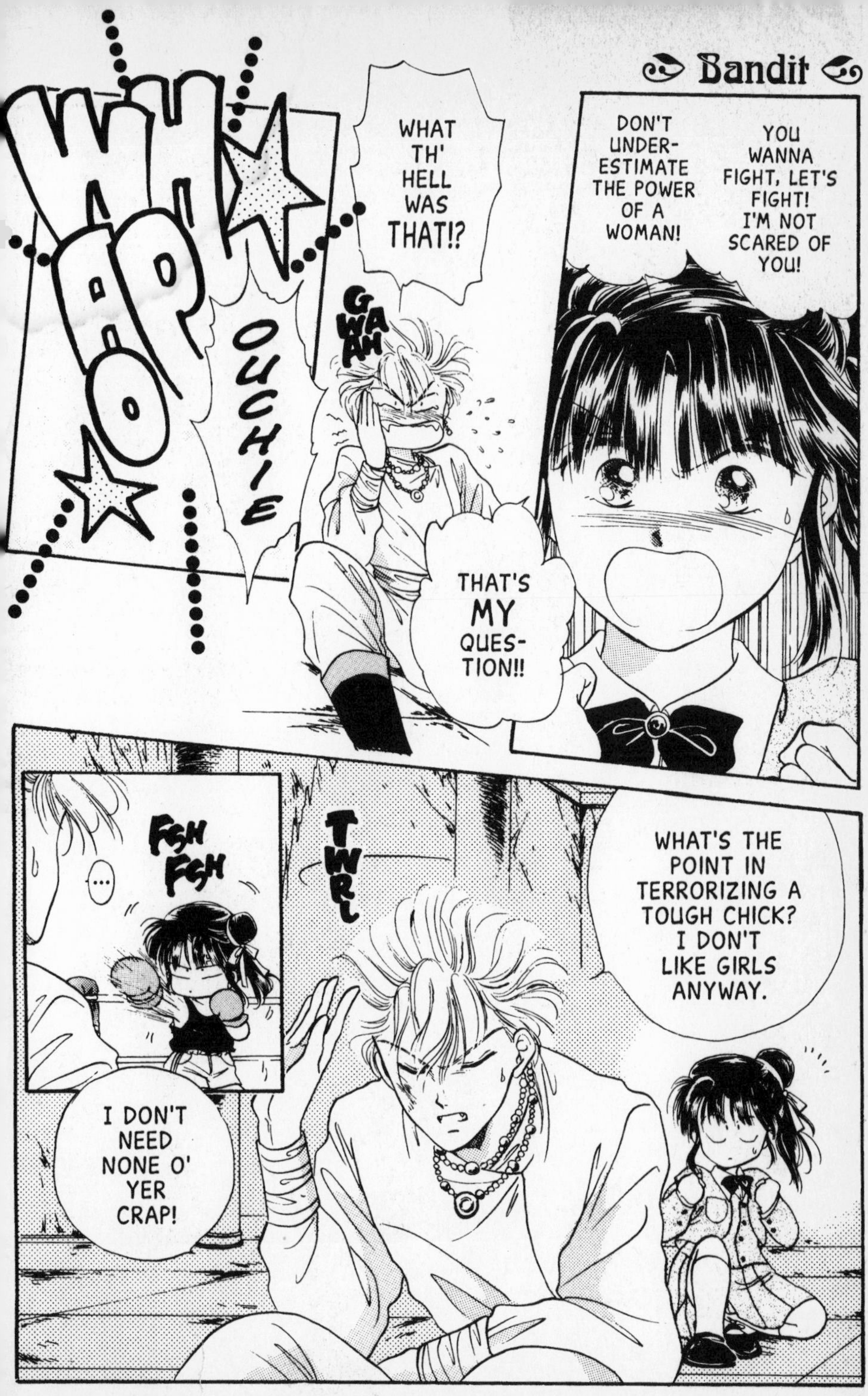
WHAP
OUCHIE
WHAT TH' HELL WAS THAT!?
GWAAH
DON'T UNDER-ESTIMATE THE POWER OF A WOMAN!
YOU WANNA FIGHT, LET'S FIGHT! I'M NOT SCARED OF YOU!
THAT'S MY QUES-TION!!
FSH FSH
...
I DON'T NEED NONE O' YER CRAP!
TWRL
WHAT'S THE POINT IN TERRORIZING A TOUGH CHICK? I DON'T LIKE GIRLS ANYWAY.

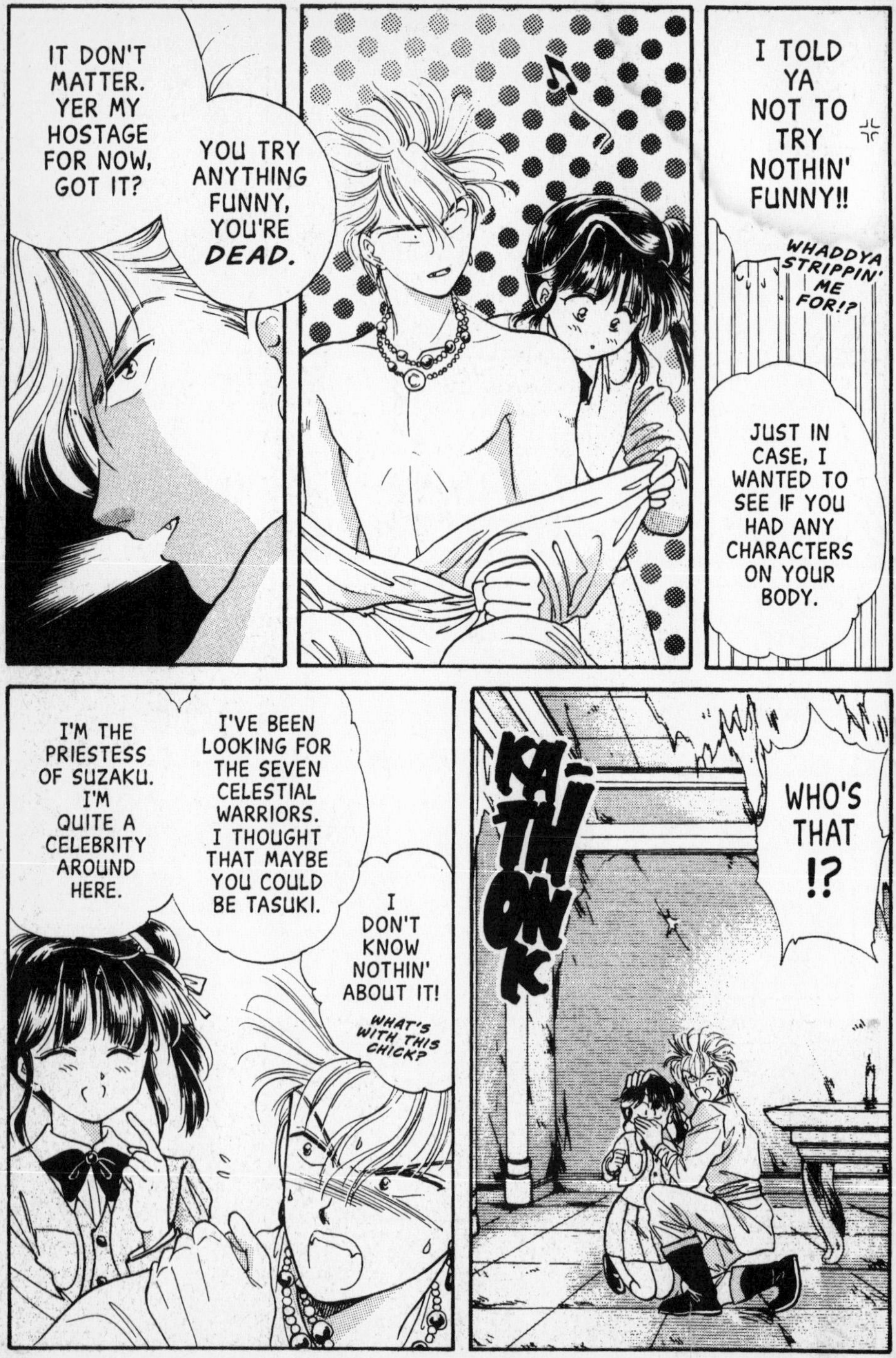
IT DON'T MATTER. YER MY HOSTAGE FOR NOW, GOT IT?
YOU TRY ANYTHING FUNNY, YOU'RE DEAD.
I TOLD YA NOT TO TRY NOTHIN' FUNNY!!
WHADDYA STRIPPIN' ME FOR!?
JUST IN CASE, I WANTED TO SEE IF YOU HAD ANY CHARACTERS ON YOUR BODY.
I'M THE PRIESTESS OF SUZAKU. I'M QUITE A CELEBRITY AROUND HERE.
I'VE BEEN LOOKING FOR THE SEVEN CELESTIAL WARRIORS. I THOUGHT THAT MAYBE YOU COULD BE TASUKI.
I DON'T KNOW NOTHIN' ABOUT IT!
WHAT'S WITH THIS CHICK?
KA-THONK
WHO'S THAT !?

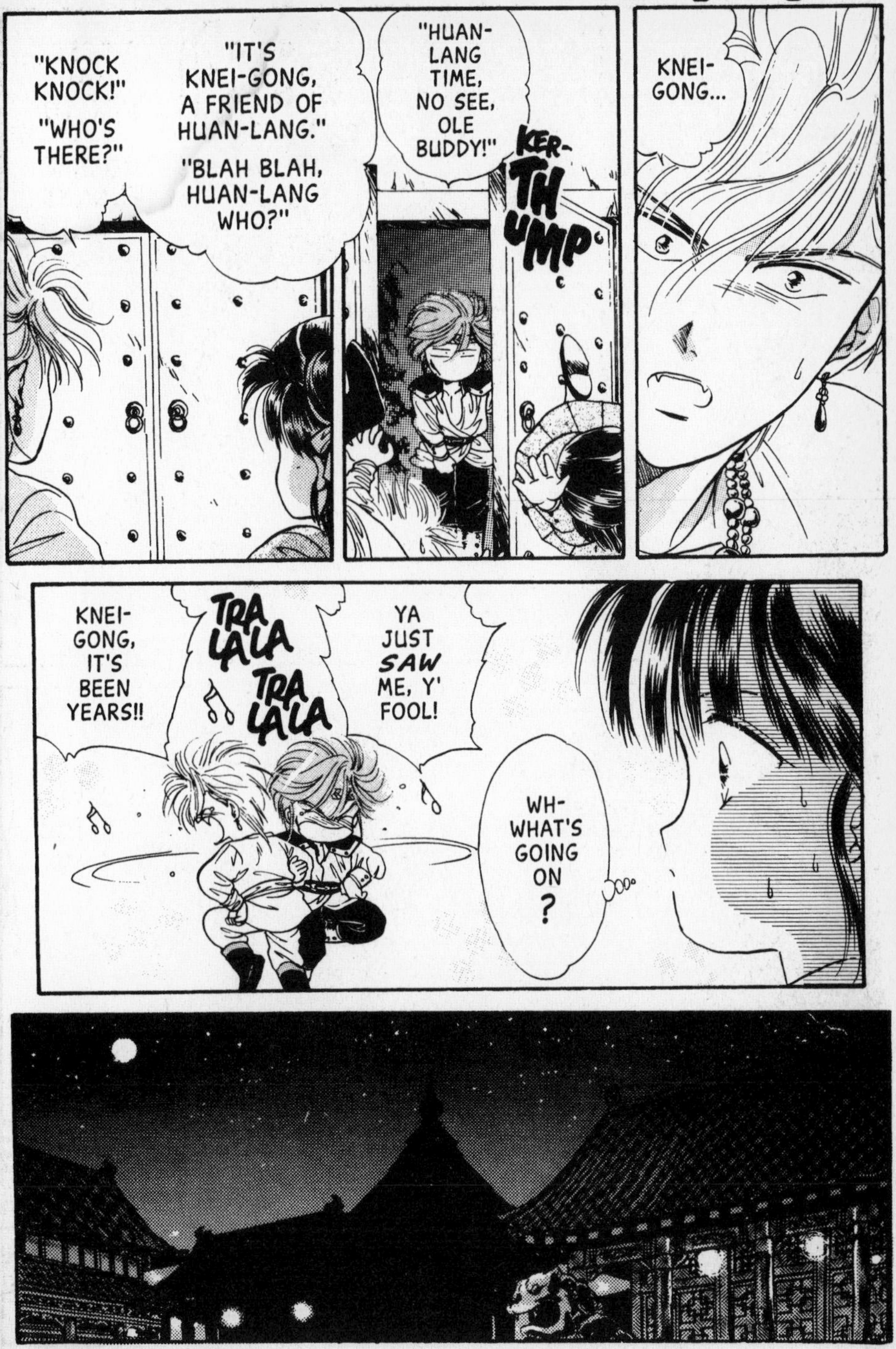
"KNOCK KNOCK!"
"WHO'S THERE?"
"IT'S KNEI-GONG, A FRIEND OF HUAN-LANG."
"BLAH BLAH, HUAN-LANG WHO?"
"HUAN-LANG TIME, NO SEE, OLE BUDDY!"
KER-THUMP
KNEI-GONG...
KNEI-GONG, IT'S BEEN YEARS!!
TRA LALA TRA LALA
YA JUST SAW ME, Y' FOOL!
WH-WHAT'S GOING ON ?

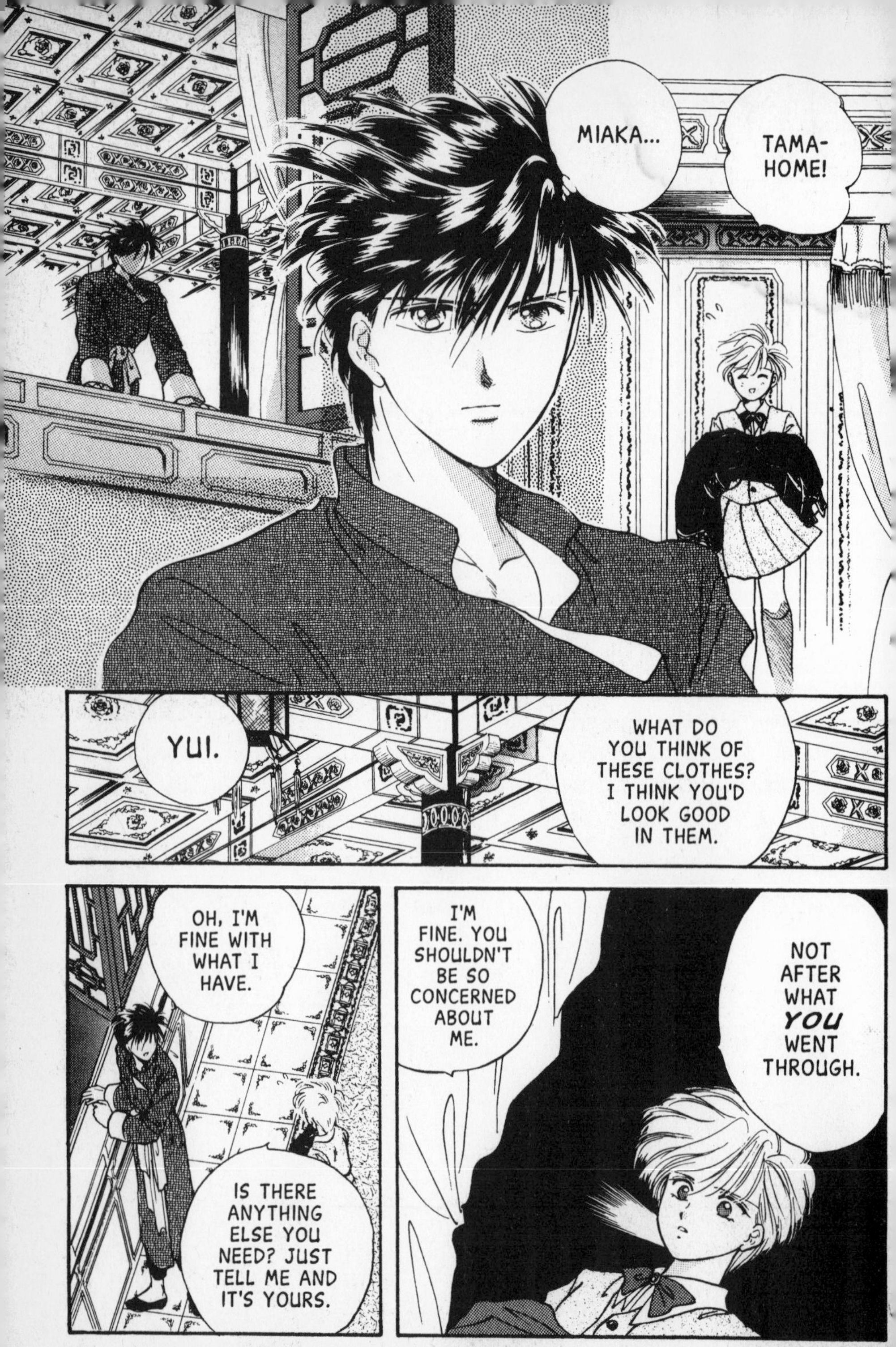
MIAKA...
TAMA-HOME!
YUI.
WHAT DO YOU THINK OF THESE CLOTHES? I THINK YOU'D LOOK GOOD IN THEM.
OH, I'M FINE WITH WHAT I HAVE.
IS THERE ANYTHING ELSE YOU NEED? JUST TELL ME AND IT'S YOURS.
I'M FINE. YOU SHOULDN'T BE SO CONCERNED ABOUT ME.
NOT AFTER WHAT *YOU* WENT THROUGH.

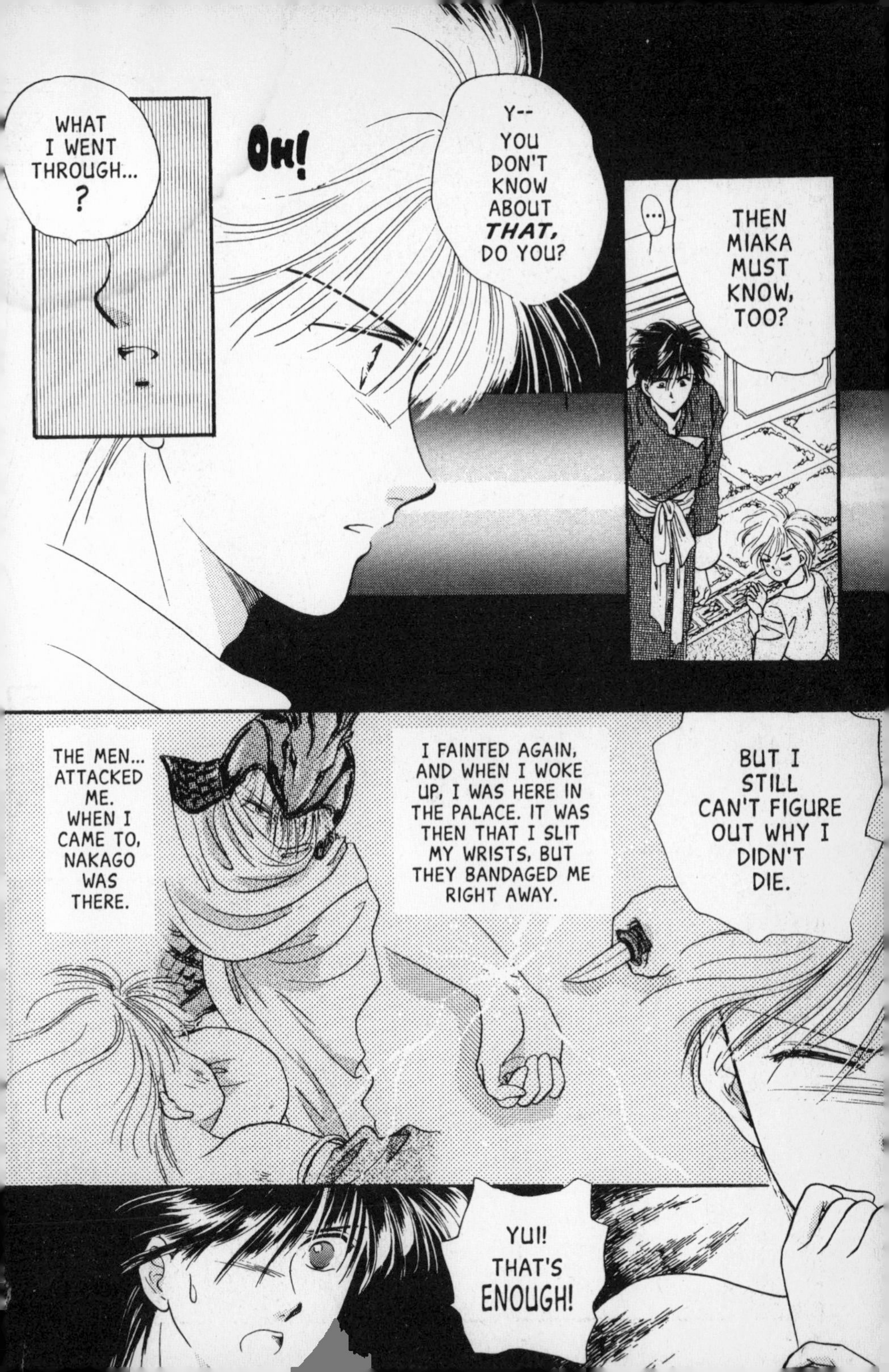
WHAT I WENT THROUGH... ?
OH!
Y-- YOU DON'T KNOW ABOUT THAT, DO YOU?
...
THEN MIAKA MUST KNOW, TOO?
THE MEN... ATTACKED ME. WHEN I CAME TO, NAKAGO WAS THERE.
I FAINTED AGAIN, AND WHEN I WOKE UP, I WAS HERE IN THE PALACE. IT WAS THEN THAT I SLIT MY WRISTS, BUT THEY BANDAGED ME RIGHT AWAY.
BUT I STILL CAN'T FIGURE OUT WHY I DIDN'T DIE.
YUI! THAT'S ENOUGH!

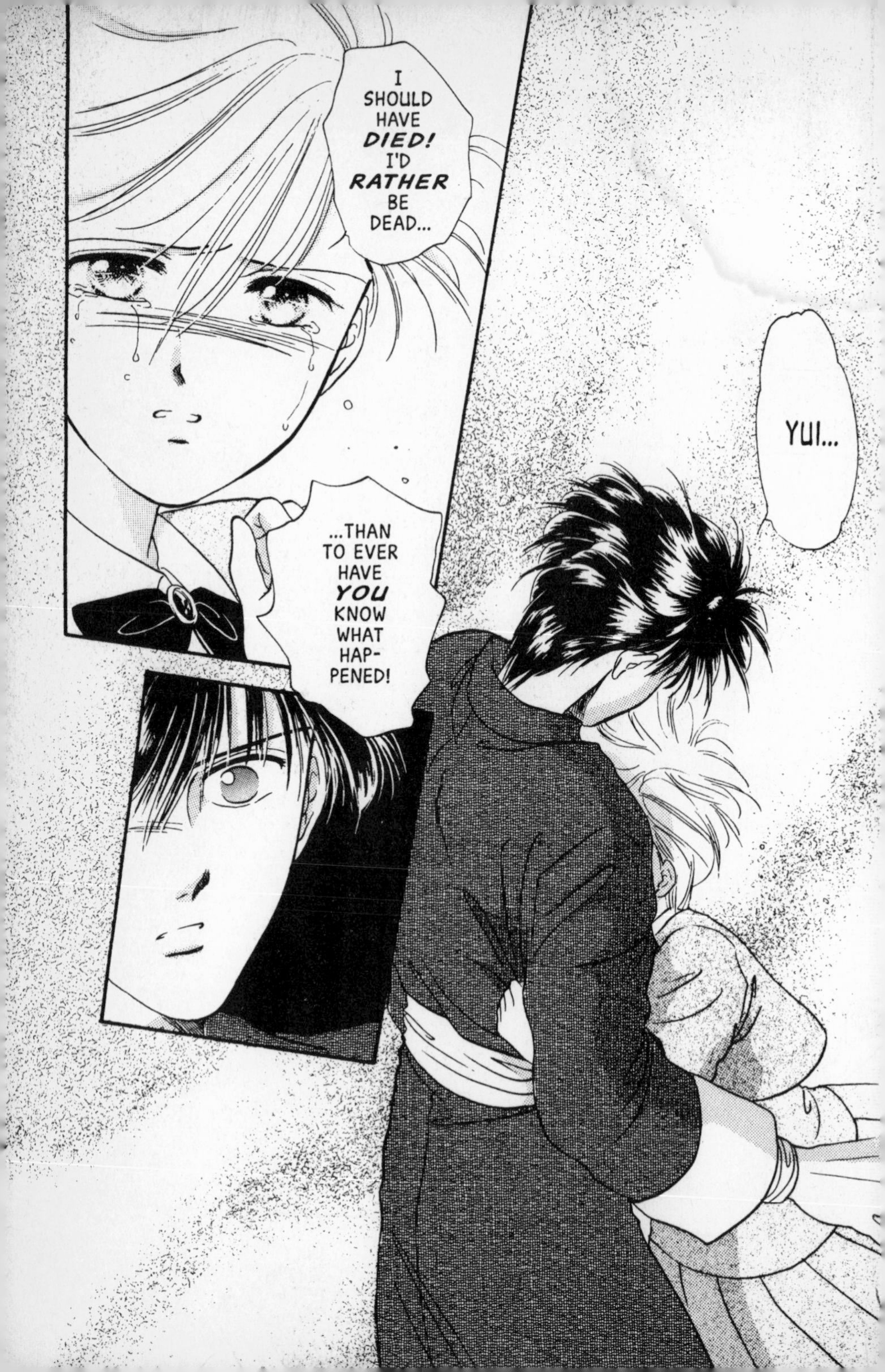
YUI...
I SHOULD HAVE DIED! I'D RATHER BE DEAD...
...THAN TO EVER HAVE YOU KNOW WHAT HAP-PENED!

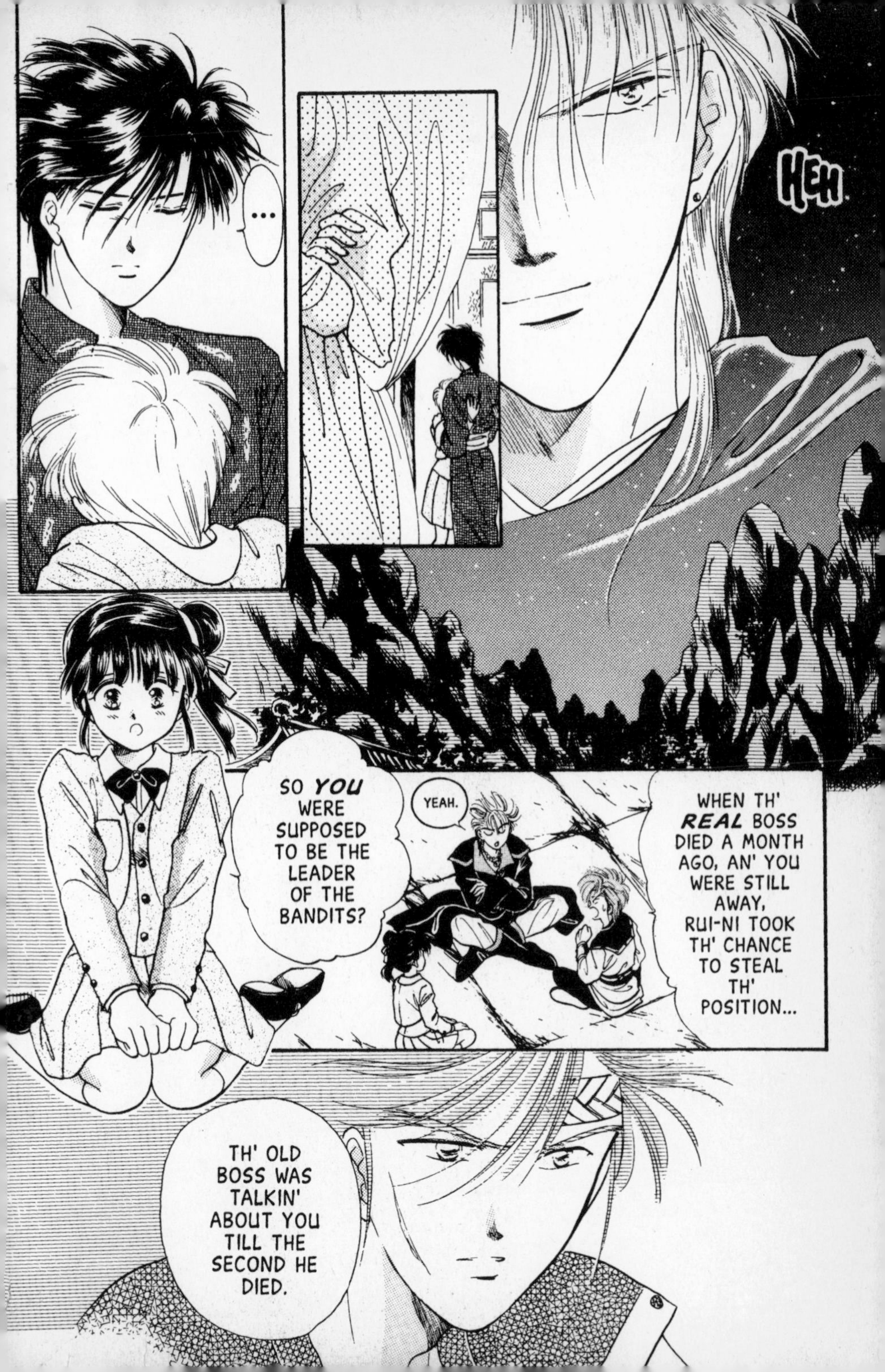
...
HEH
SO *YOU* WERE SUPPOSED TO BE THE LEADER OF THE BANDITS?
YEAH.
WHEN TH' ***REAL*** BOSS DIED A MONTH AGO, AN' YOU WERE STILL AWAY, RUI-NI TOOK TH' CHANCE TO STEAL TH' POSITION...
TH' OLD BOSS WAS TALKIN' ABOUT YOU TILL THE SECOND HE DIED.

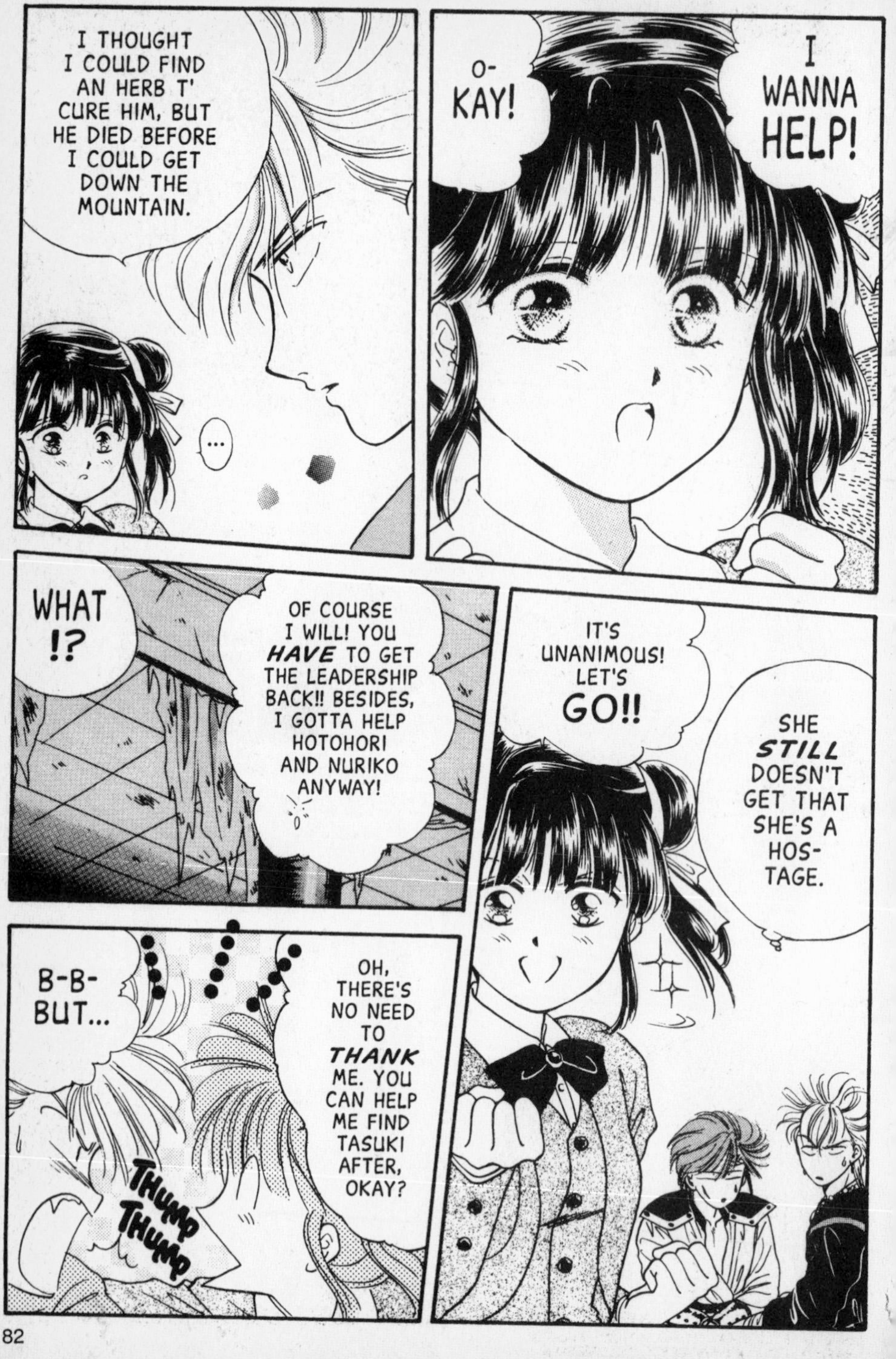

I THOUGHT I COULD FIND AN HERB T' CURE HIM, BUT HE DIED BEFORE I COULD GET DOWN THE MOUNTAIN.
...
O-KAY!
I WANNA HELP!
WHAT !?
OF COURSE I WILL! YOU *HAVE* TO GET THE LEADERSHIP BACK!! BESIDES, I GOTTA HELP HOTOHORI AND NURIKO ANYWAY!
IT'S UNANIMOUS! LET'S GO!!
SHE *STILL* DOESN'T GET THAT SHE'S A HOS-TAGE.
B-B-BUT...
OH, THERE'S NO NEED TO *THANK* ME. YOU CAN HELP ME FIND TASUKI AFTER, OKAY?
THUMP THUMP

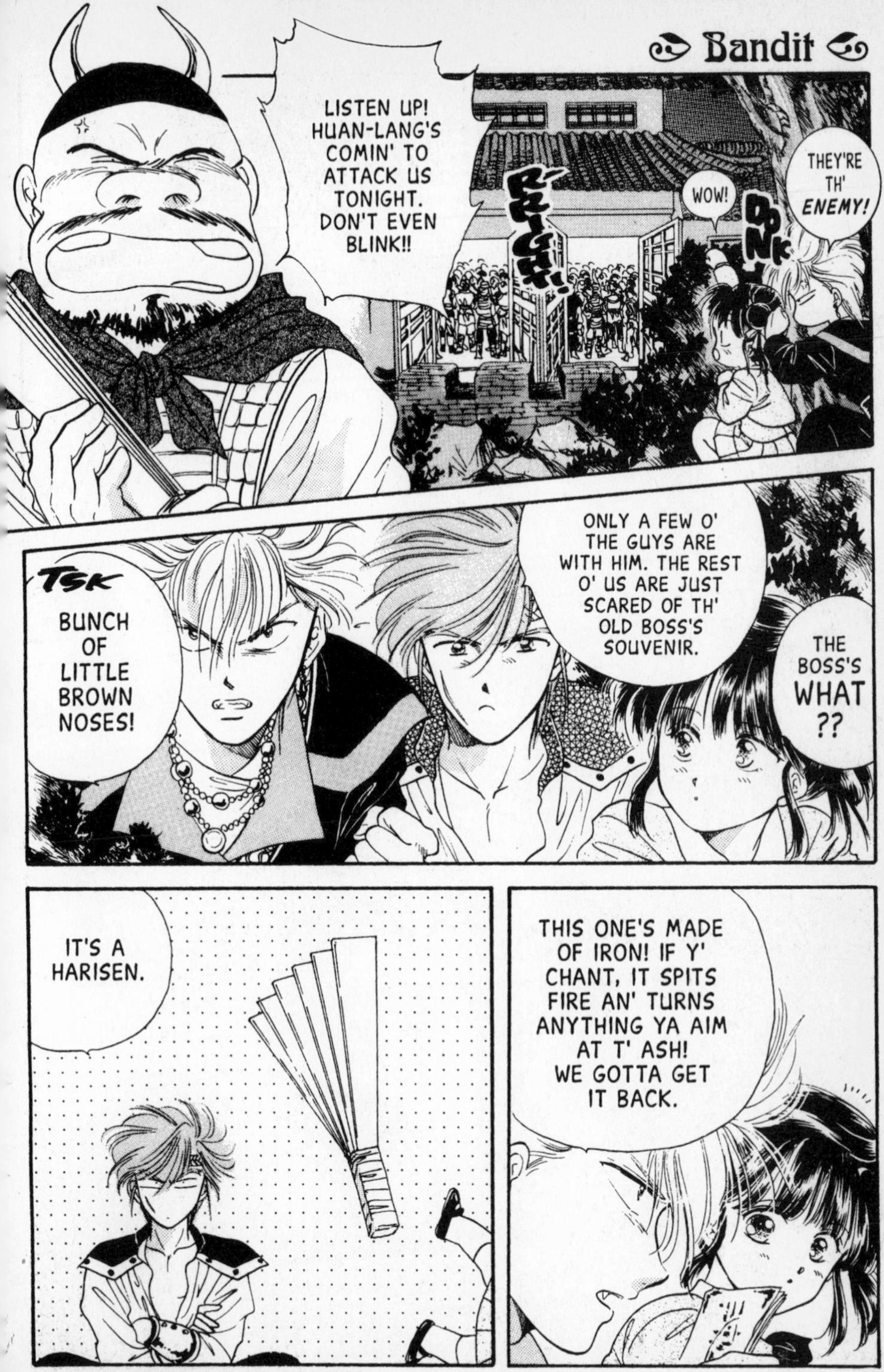
LISTEN UP! HUAN-LANG'S COMIN' TO ATTACK US TONIGHT. DON'T EVEN BLINK!!
RRIGHT!
WOW!
DONK
THEY'RE TH' ENEMY!
TSK
BUNCH OF LITTLE BROWN NOSES!
ONLY A FEW O' THE GUYS ARE WITH HIM. THE REST O' US ARE JUST SCARED OF TH' OLD BOSS'S SOUVENIR.
THE BOSS'S WHAT??
IT'S A HARISEN.
THIS ONE'S MADE OF IRON! IF Y' CHANT, IT SPITS FIRE AN' TURNS ANYTHING YA AIM AT T' ASH! WE GOTTA GET IT BACK.

A CLUB, USUALLY MADE OF PAPER, USED TO "MOTIVATE" STUDENTS.

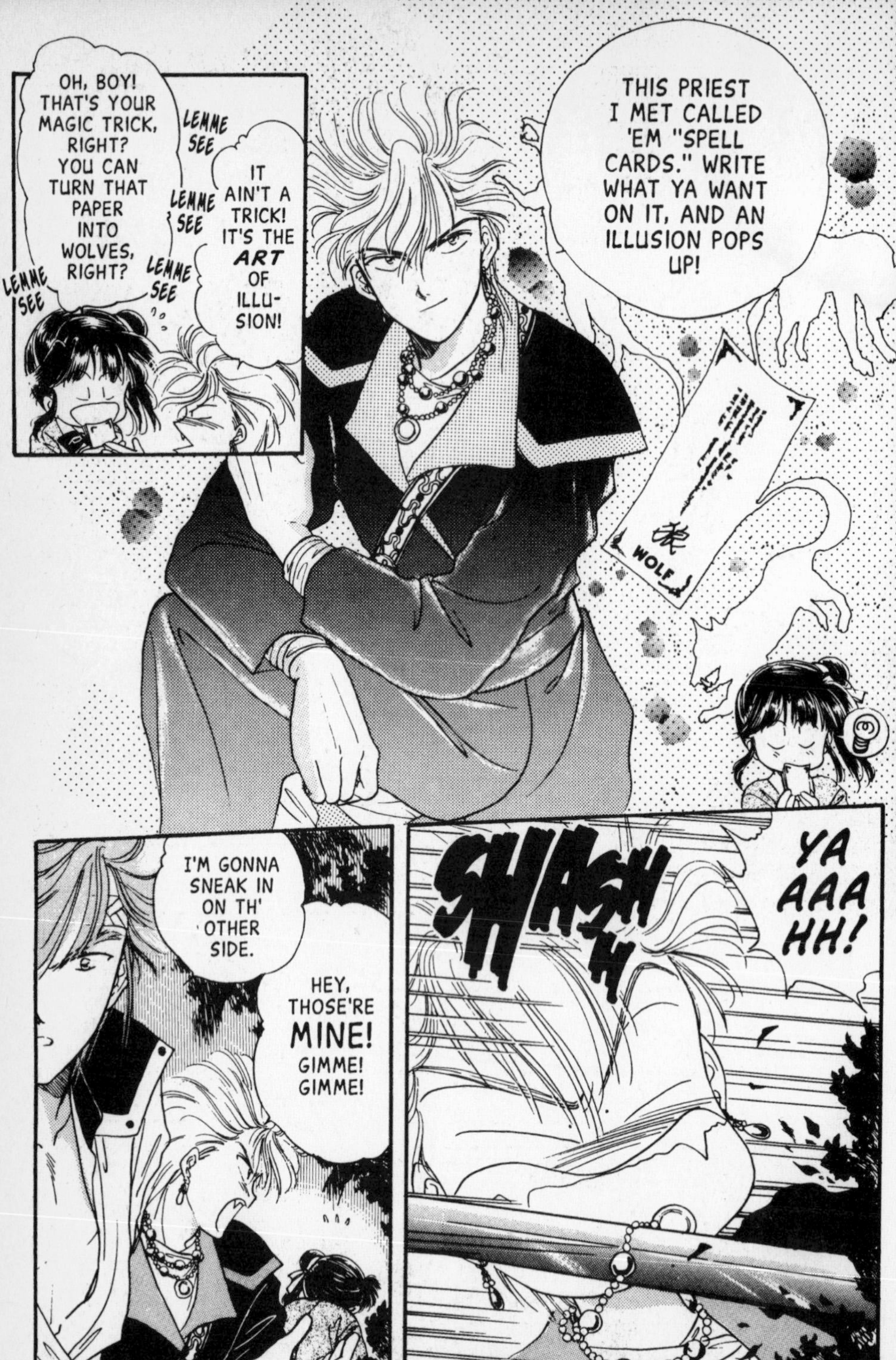
OH, BOY! THAT'S YOUR MAGIC TRICK, RIGHT? YOU CAN TURN THAT PAPER INTO WOLVES, RIGHT?
LEMME SEE
LEMME SEE
LEMME SEE
LEMME SEE
IT AIN'T A TRICK! IT'S THE ART OF ILLUSION!
THIS PRIEST I MET CALLED 'EM "SPELL CARDS." WRITE WHAT YA WANT ON IT, AND AN ILLUSION POPS UP!
WOLF
I'M GONNA SNEAK IN ON TH' OTHER SIDE.
HEY, THOSE'RE MINE! GIMME! GIMME!
SHASHH
YA AAA HH!

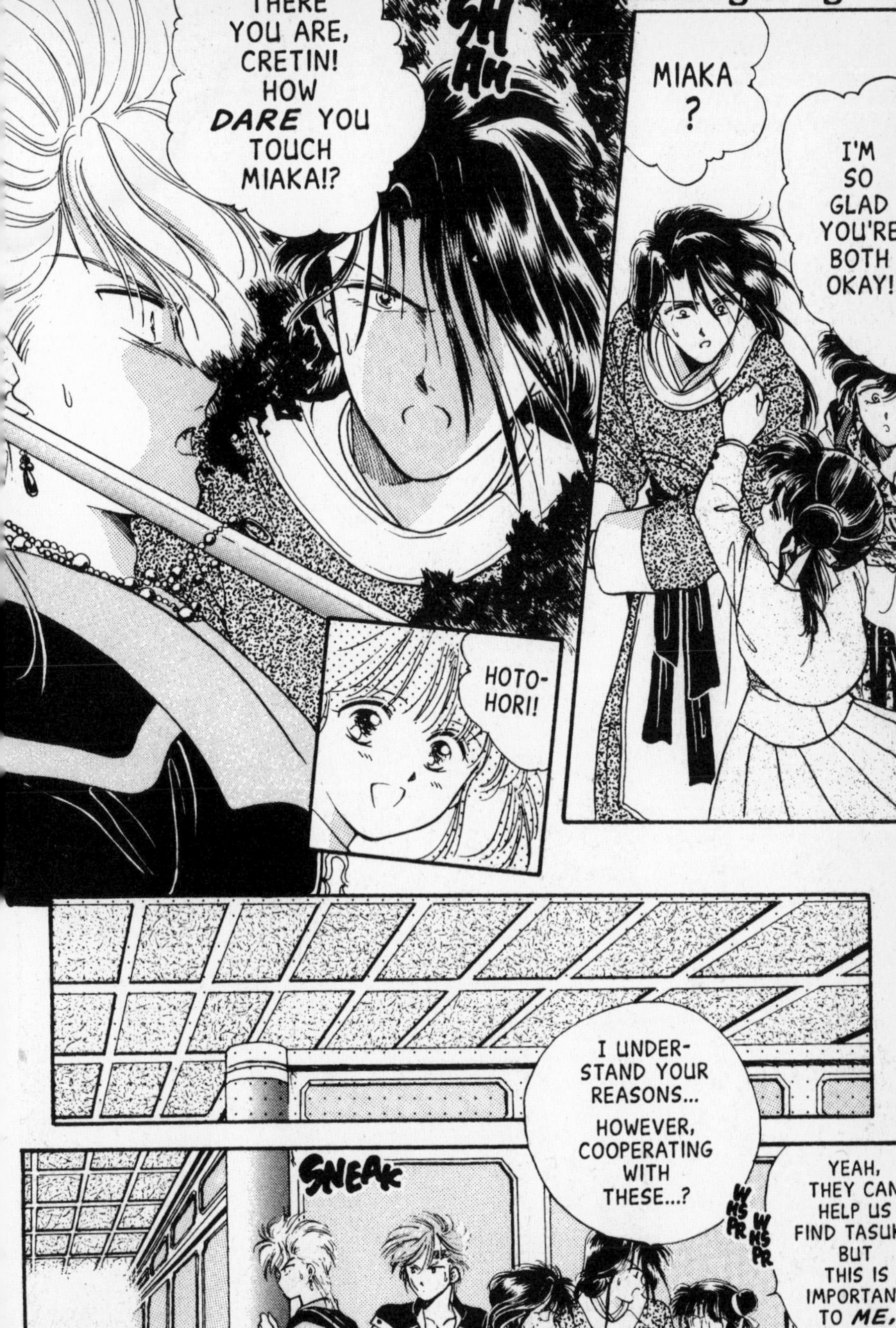
THERE YOU ARE, CRETIN! HOW *DARE* YOU TOUCH MIAKA!?
SHAH
HOTO-HORI!
MIAKA?
I'M SO GLAD YOU'RE BOTH OKAY!
I UNDER-STAND YOUR REASONS... HOWEVER, COOPERATING WITH THESE...?
SNEAK
WHSPR
WHSPR
YEAH, THEY CAN HELP US FIND TASUKI! BUT THIS IS IMPORTANT TO *ME,* TOO!

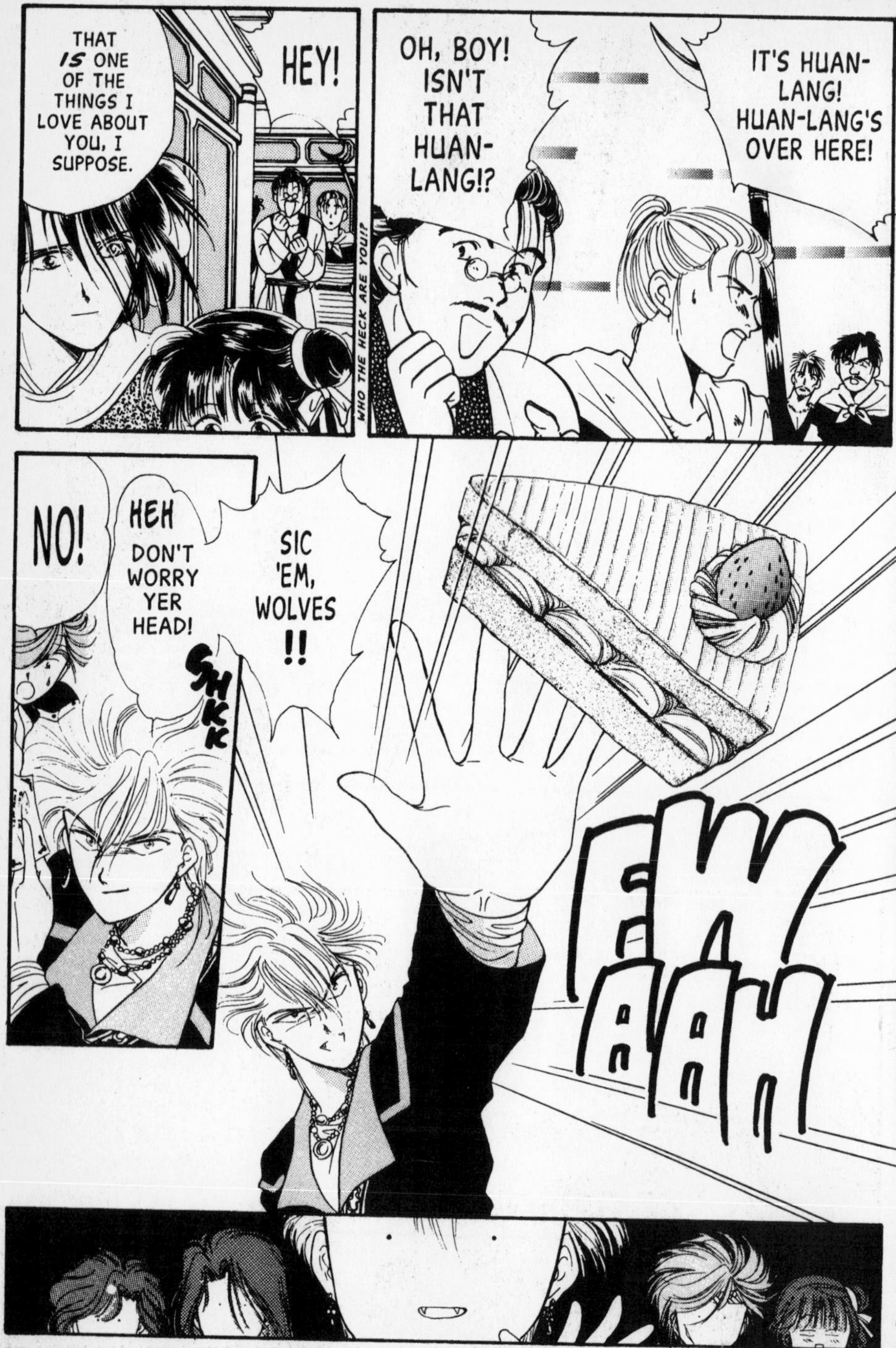
THAT IS ONE OF THE THINGS I LOVE ABOUT YOU, I SUPPOSE.
HEY!
WHO THE HECK ARE YOU!?
OH, BOY! ISN'T THAT HUAN-LANG!?
IT'S HUAN-LANG! HUAN-LANG'S OVER HERE!
NO!
HEH
DON'T WORRY YER HEAD!
SHKK
SIC 'EM, WOLVES!!
FWAAH

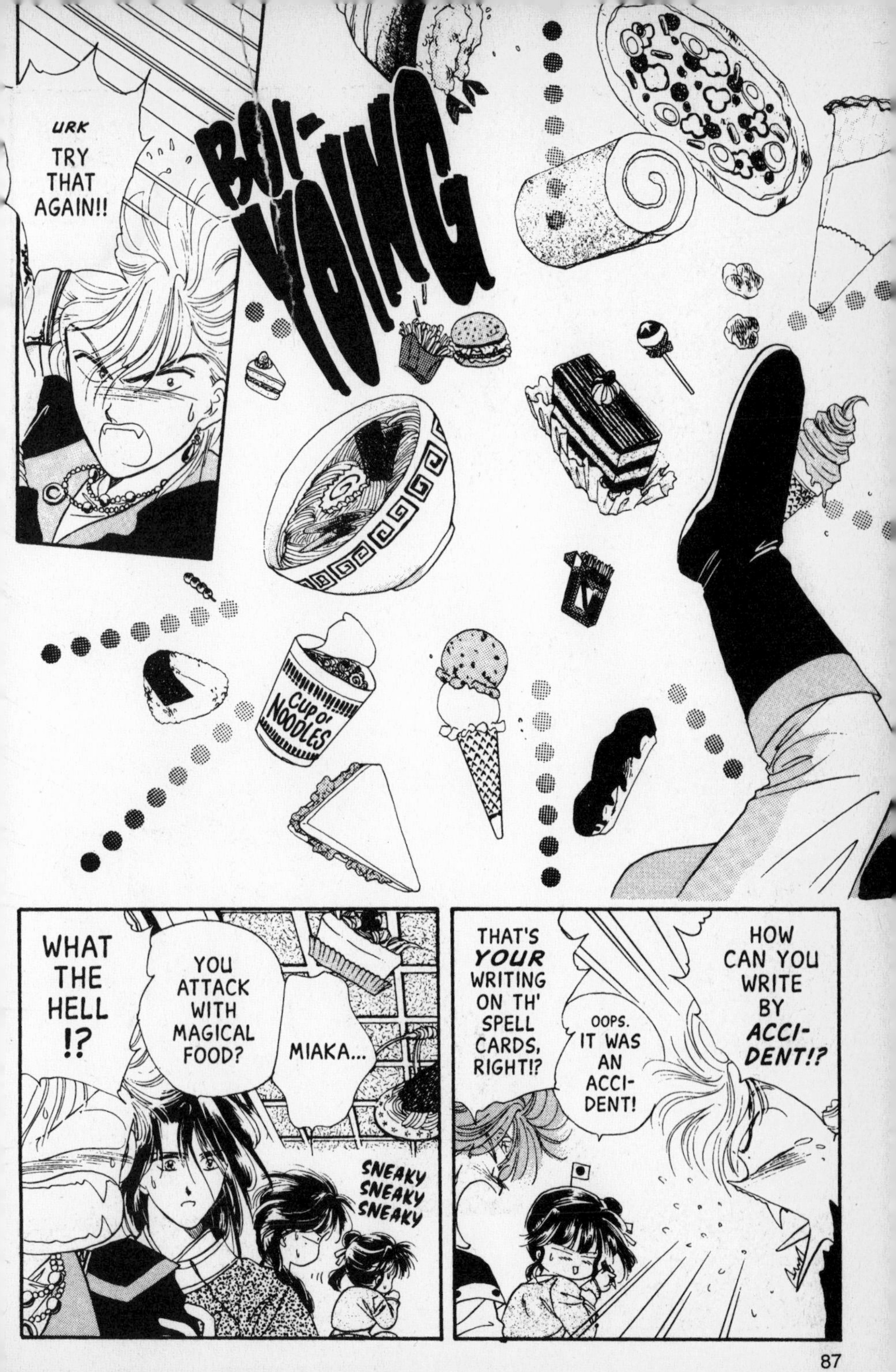
URK
TRY THAT AGAIN!!
BOI-YOING
CUP O' NOODLES
WHAT THE HELL!?
YOU ATTACK WITH MAGICAL FOOD?
MIAKA...
SNEAKY SNEAKY SNEAKY
THAT'S *YOUR* WRITING ON TH' SPELL CARDS, RIGHT!?
OOPS. IT WAS AN ACCIDENT!
HOW CAN YOU WRITE BY *ACCIDENT!?*

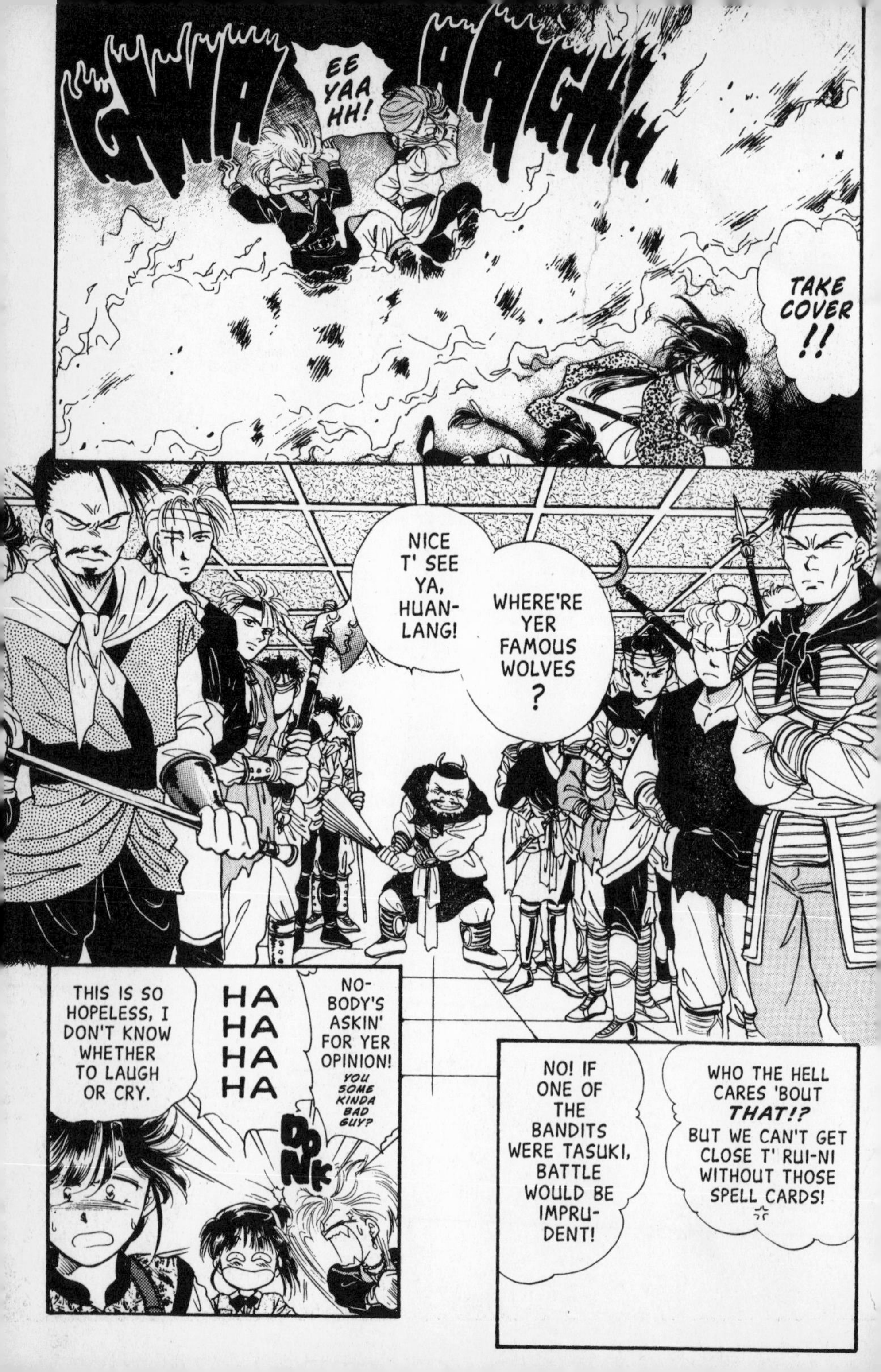
GWA AAGH
EE YAAHH!
TAKE COVER!!
NICE T' SEE YA, HUAN-LANG!
WHERE'RE YER FAMOUS WOLVES?
THIS IS SO HOPELESS, I DON'T KNOW WHETHER TO LAUGH OR CRY.
HA HA HA HA HA HA HA HA
NOBODY'S ASKIN' FOR YER OPINION!
YOU SOME KINDA BAD GUY?
DONK
NO! IF ONE OF THE BANDITS WERE TASUKI, BATTLE WOULD BE IMPRUDENT!
WHO THE HELL CARES 'BOUT *THAT!?* BUT WE CAN'T GET CLOSE T' RUI-NI WITHOUT THOSE SPELL CARDS!

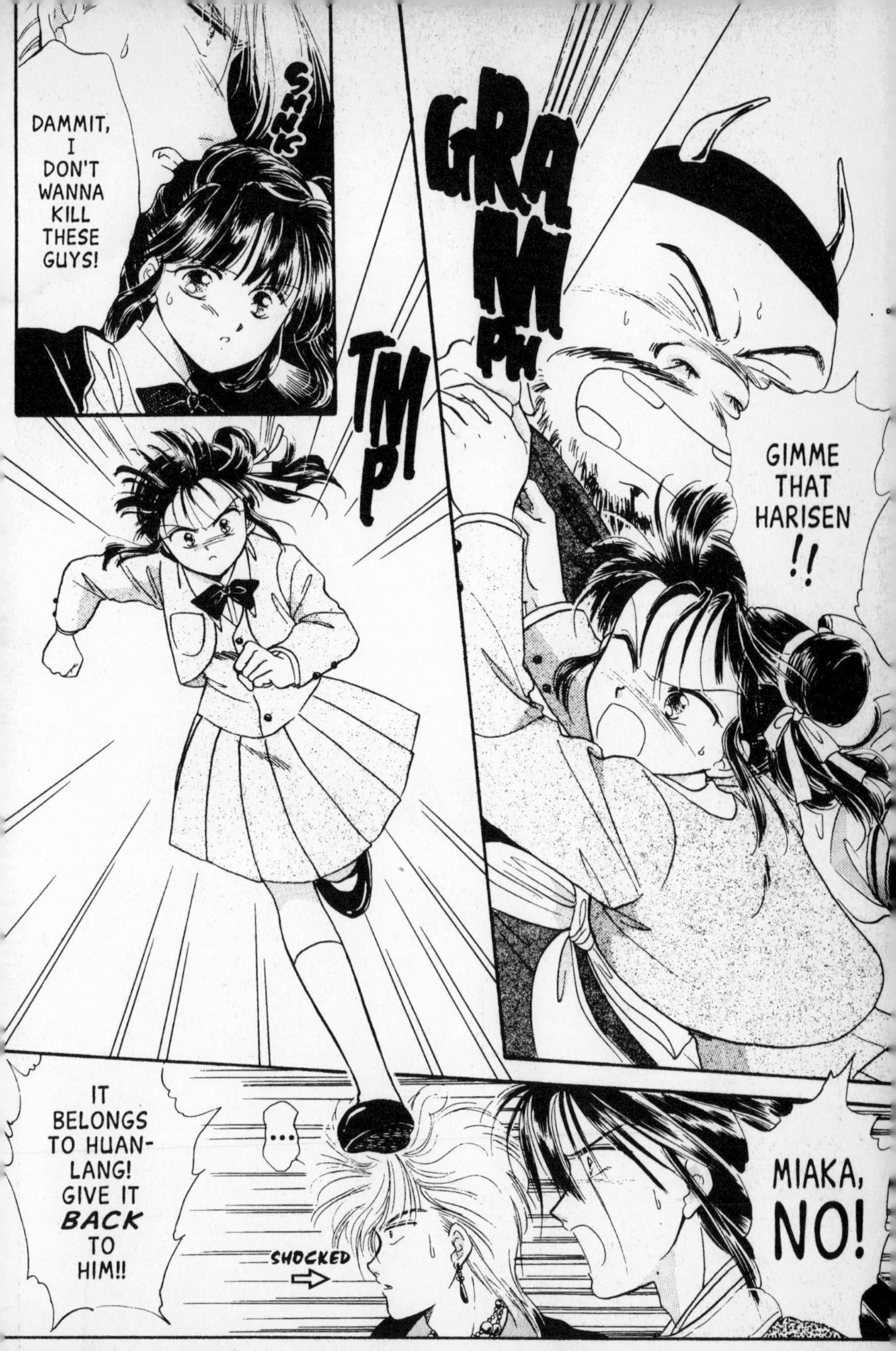
DAMMIT, I DON'T WANNA KILL THESE GUYS!
SHNK
TMP
GRAMPH
GIMME THAT HARISEN !!
IT BELONGS TO HUAN-LANG! GIVE IT BACK TO HIM!!
...
SHOCKED
MIAKA, NO!

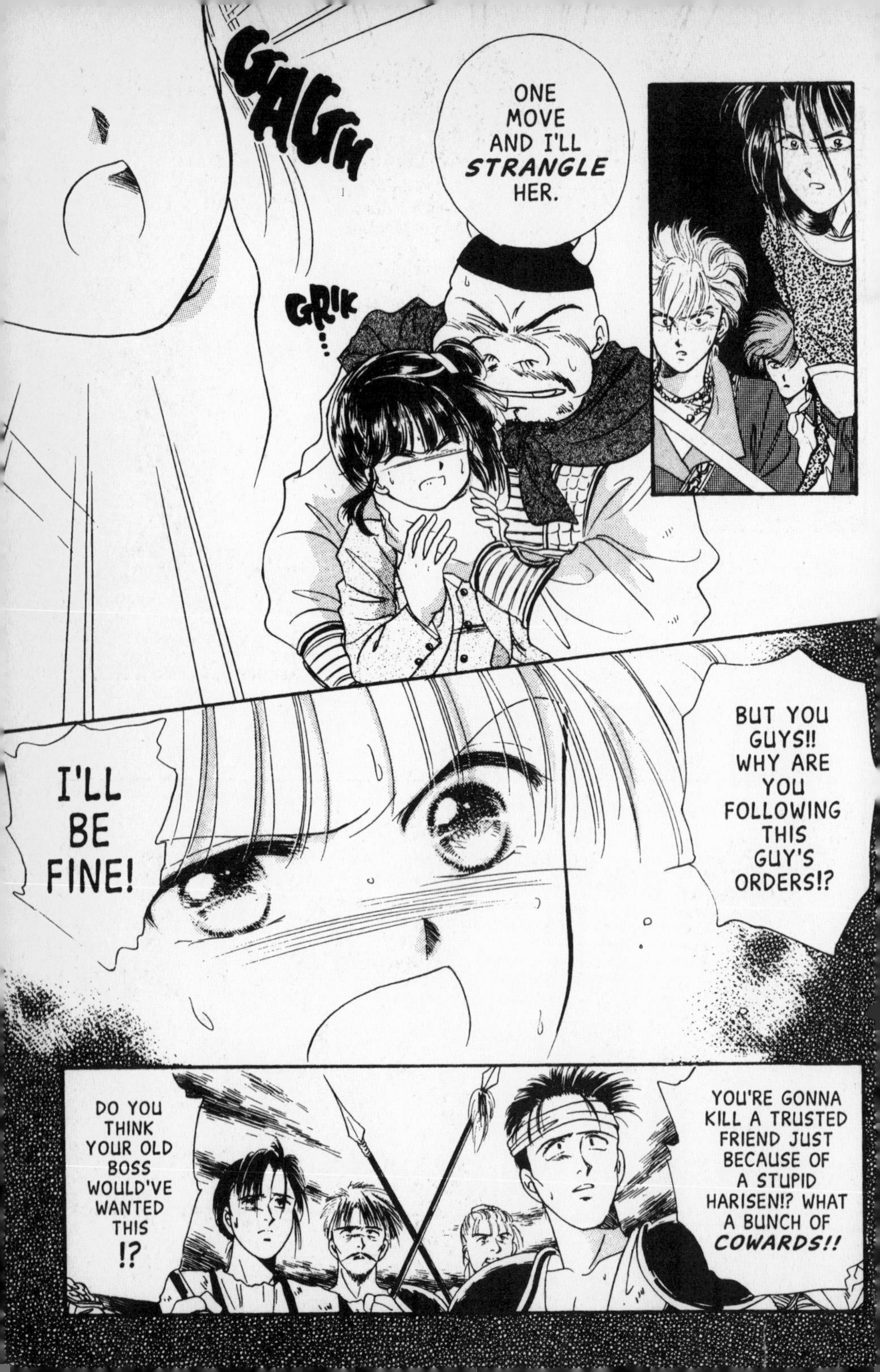
GAGH
ONE MOVE AND I'LL STRANGLE HER.
GRIK...
I'LL BE FINE!
BUT YOU GUYS!! WHY ARE YOU FOLLOWING THIS GUY'S ORDERS!?
DO YOU THINK YOUR OLD BOSS WOULD'VE WANTED THIS !?
YOU'RE GONNA KILL A TRUSTED FRIEND JUST BECAUSE OF A STUPID HARISEN!? WHAT A BUNCH OF COWARDS!!

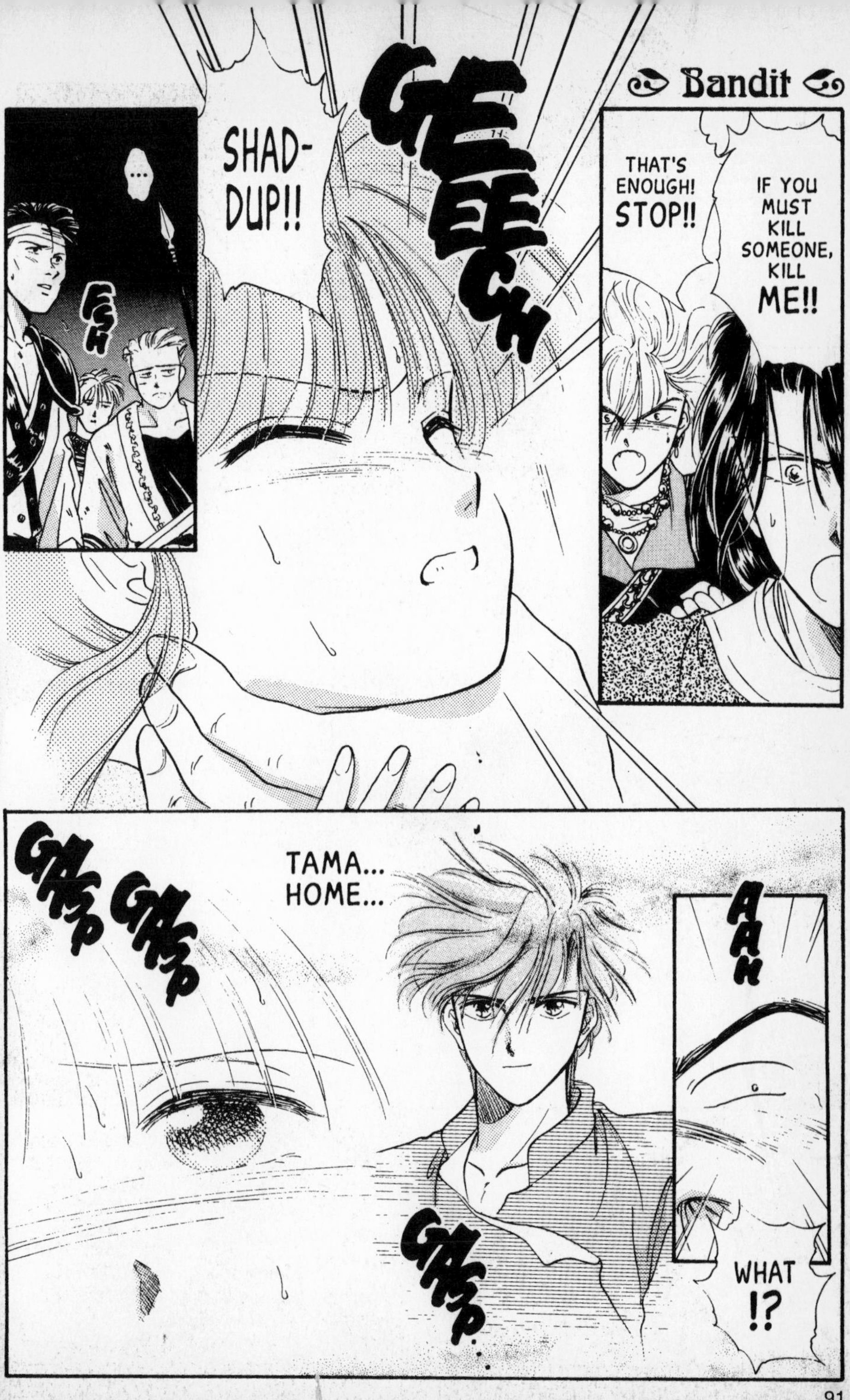
...
FSH
SHAD-DUP!!
GEEECH
THAT'S ENOUGH! STOP!!
IF YOU MUST KILL SOMEONE, KILL ME!!
GASP GASP
TAMA... HOME...
GASP...
AAH
WHAT!?

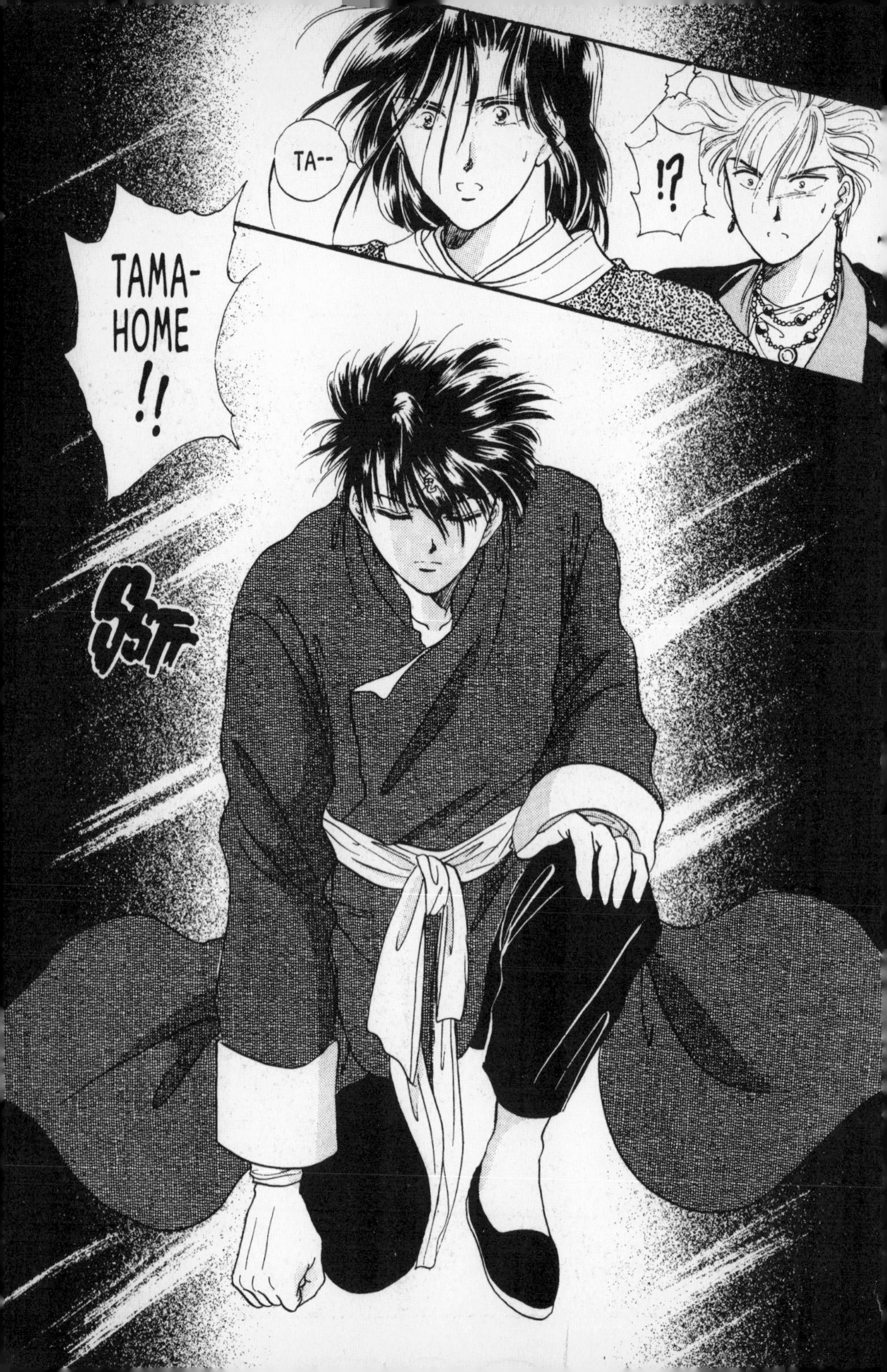
TA--
!?
TAMA-HOME !!
SSFF

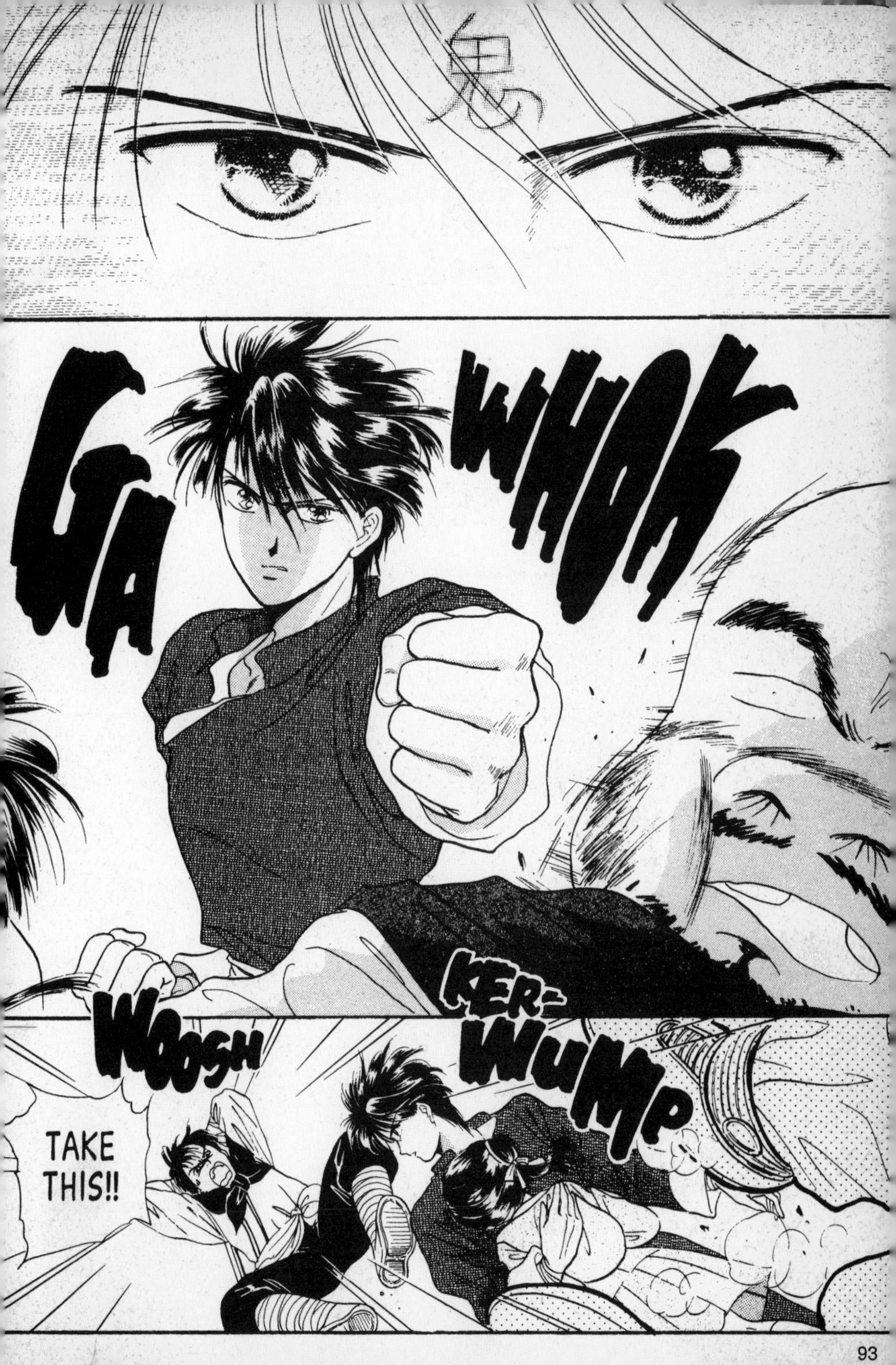
鬼
GA
WHOK
WOOSH
TAKE THIS!!
KER-WUMP

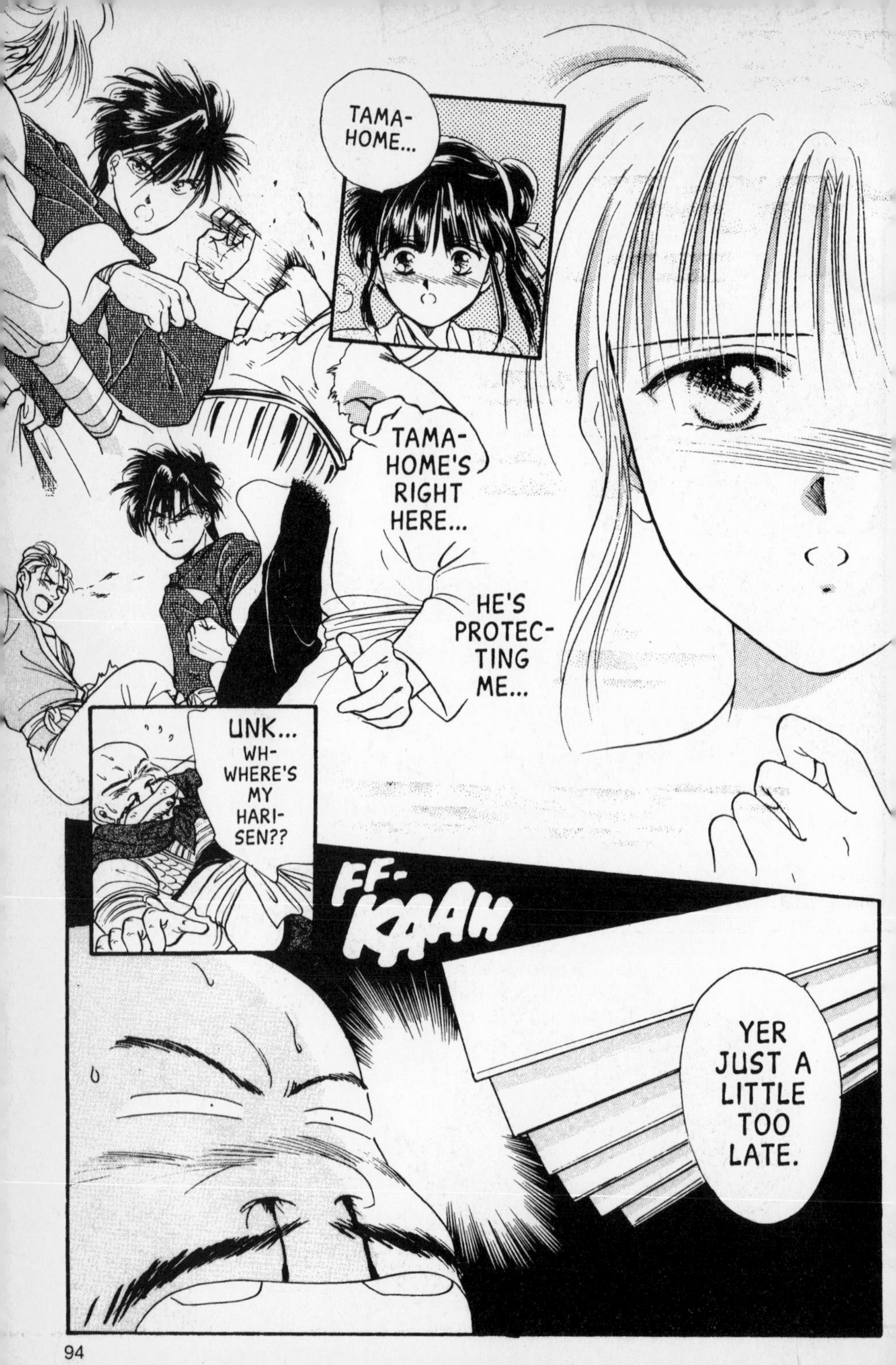
TAMA-HOME...
TAMA-HOME'S RIGHT HERE...
HE'S PROTEC-TING ME...
UNK... WH-WHERE'S MY HARI-SEN??
FF-KAAAH
YER JUST A LITTLE TOO LATE.

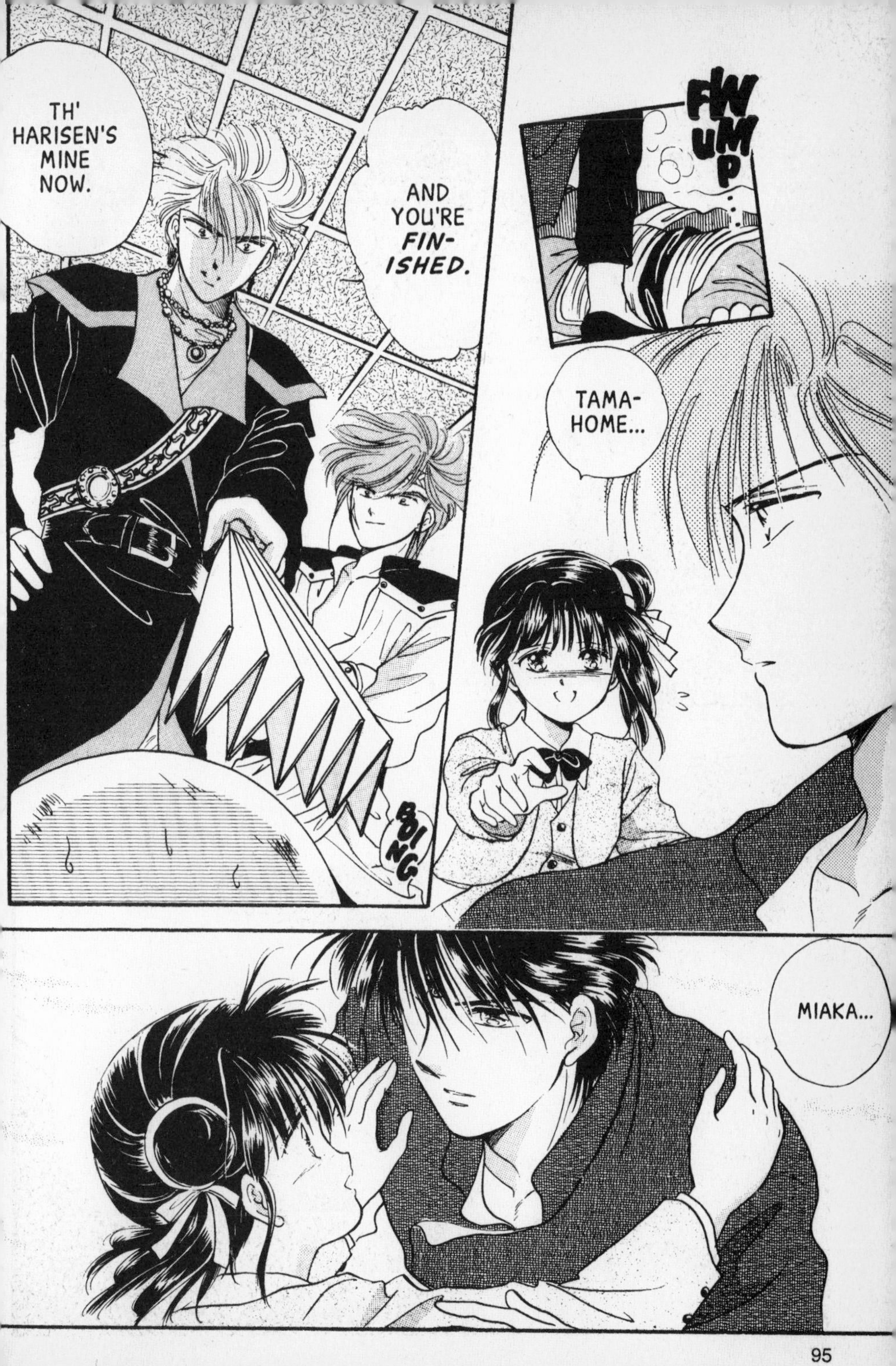
TH' HARISEN'S MINE NOW.
AND YOU'RE FIN-ISHED.
BOING
FWUMP
TAMA-HOME...
MIAKA...

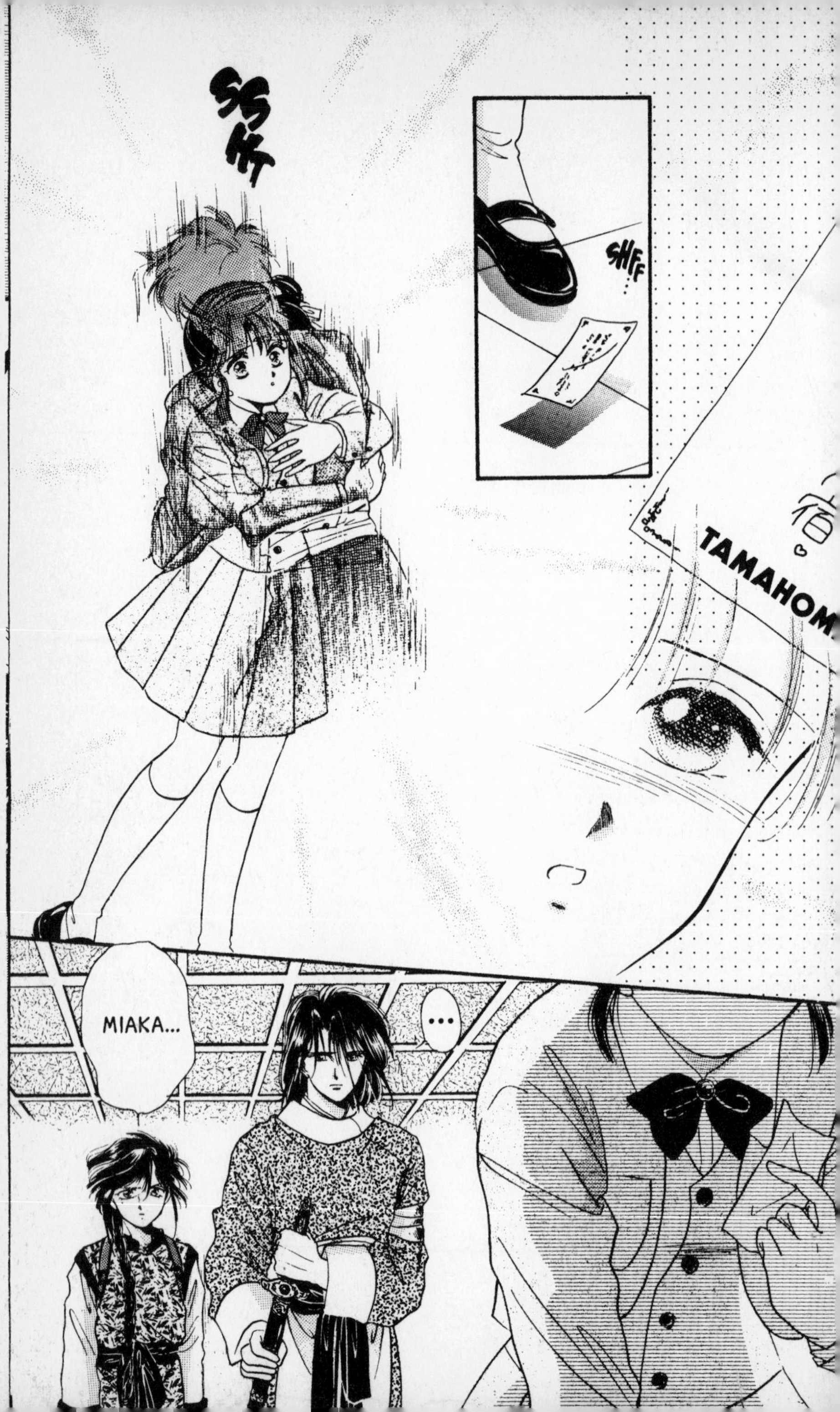
SSHT
SHFF...
TAMAHOM
MIAKA...
...

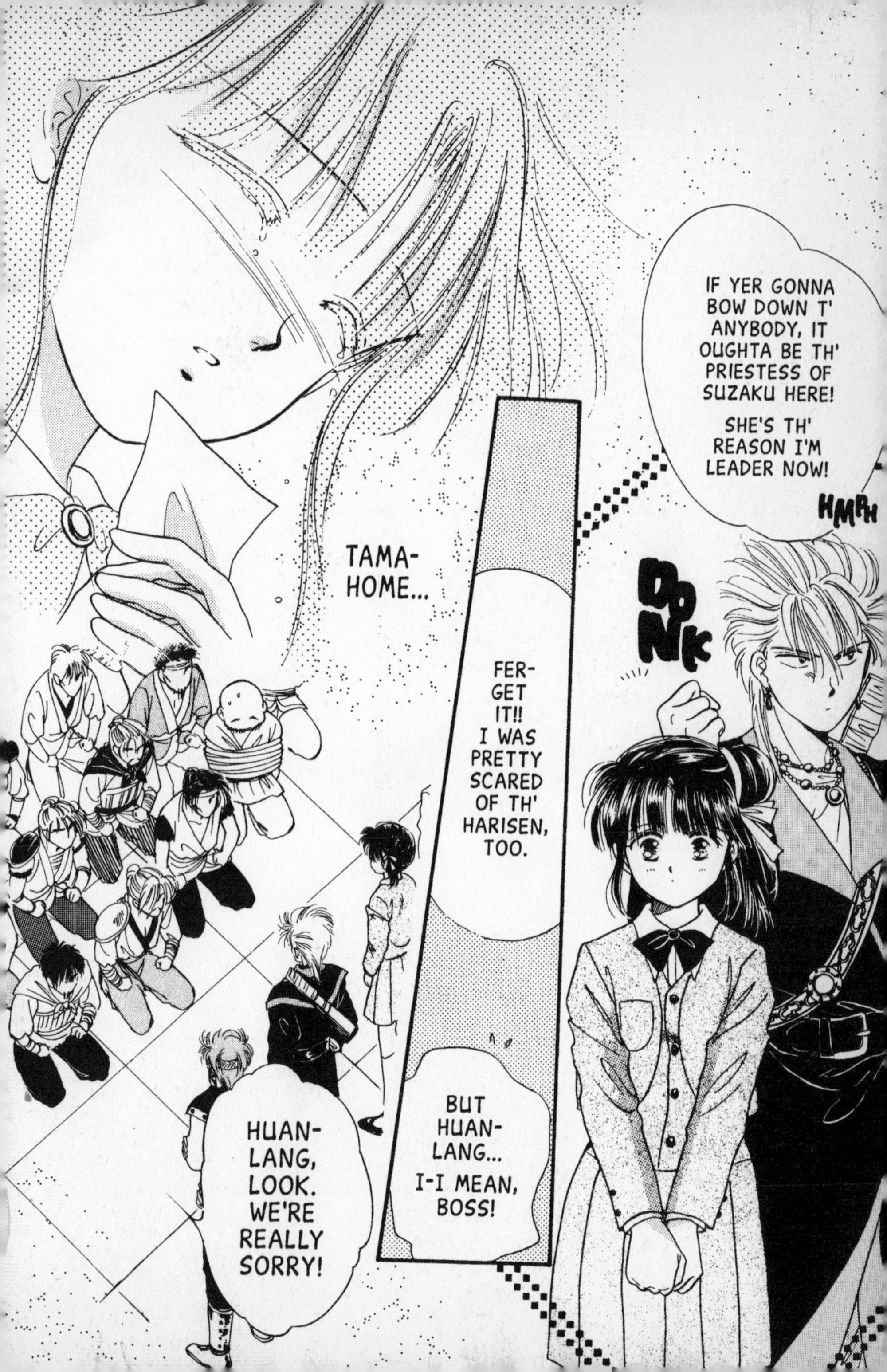
TAMA-HOME...
HUAN-LANG, LOOK. WE'RE REALLY SORRY!
FER-GET IT!! I WAS PRETTY SCARED OF TH' HARISEN, TOO.
BUT HUAN-LANG...
I-I MEAN, BOSS!
IF YER GONNA BOW DOWN T' ANYBODY, IT OUGHTA BE TH' PRIESTESS OF SUZAKU HERE!
SHE'S TH' REASON I'M LEADER NOW!
HMPH
DONK

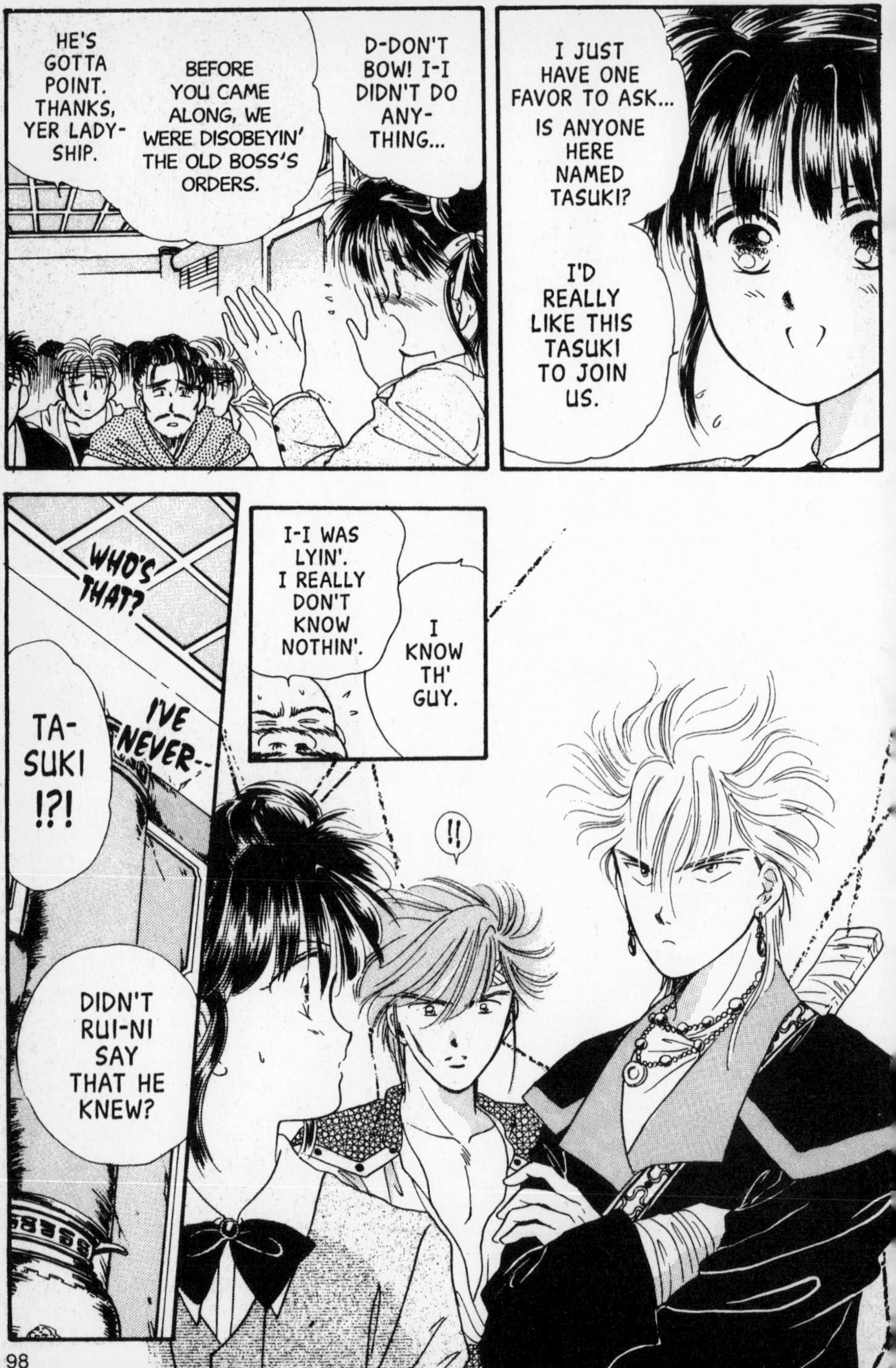
HE'S GOTTA POINT. THANKS, YER LADY-SHIP.
BEFORE YOU CAME ALONG, WE WERE DISOBEYIN' THE OLD BOSS'S ORDERS.
D-DON'T BOW! I-I DIDN'T DO ANY-THING...
I JUST HAVE ONE FAVOR TO ASK... IS ANYONE HERE NAMED TASUKI?
I'D REALLY LIKE THIS TASUKI TO JOIN US.
WHO'S THAT?
TA-SUKI !?!
I'VE NEVER--
DIDN'T RUI-NI SAY THAT HE KNEW?
I-I WAS LYIN'. I REALLY DON'T KNOW NOTHIN'.
I KNOW TH' GUY.
!!

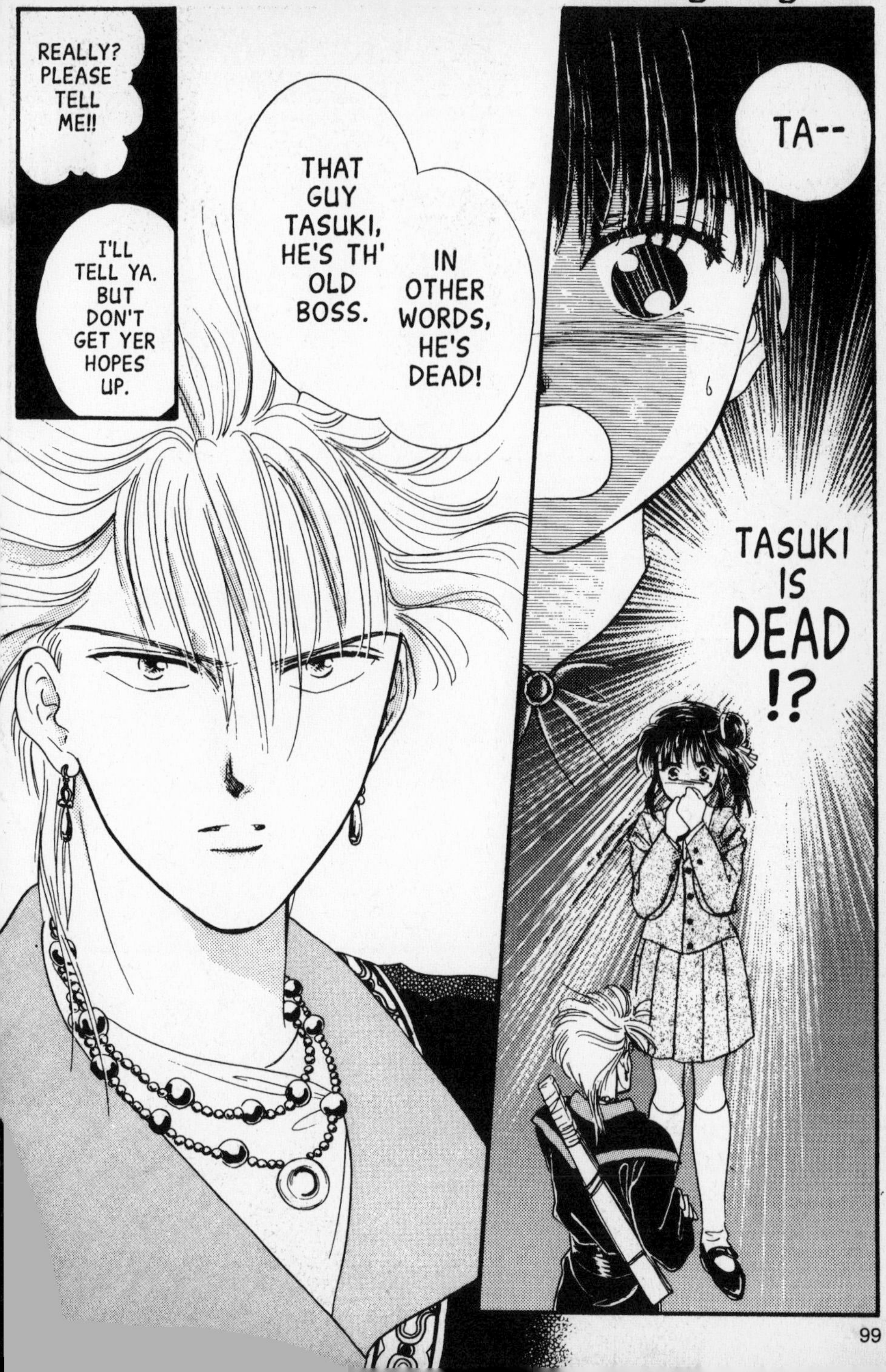
REALLY? PLEASE TELL ME!!
I'LL TELL YA. BUT DON'T GET YER HOPES UP.
THAT GUY TASUKI, HE'S TH' OLD BOSS.
IN OTHER WORDS, HE'S DEAD!
TA--
TASUKI IS DEAD!?

YOU TOO CAN DO IT!! CHICHIRI FASHION!!

EASILY!!

(MAYBE THIS IS JUST COSTUME PLAYING)

NO DA!

① First, prepare white T or V neck shirt, a large handkerchief, white boots, black string and belt.

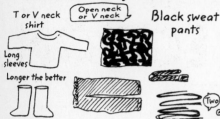

T or V neck shirt

Open neck or V neck

Black sweat pants

Long sleeves

Longer the better

Two

② Wear pants and then white shirt over pants. Fasten belt. Show leather side of the belt.

Bring up sleeves slightly to leave some → slack in them.

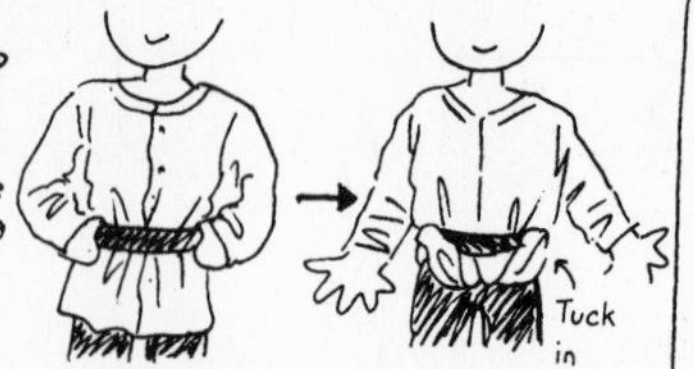

Tuck in shirt through belt.

Tuck only the tips of the shirt in.

③ Wear boots and wrap black string around them.

Shoes are critical. If you have Chinese shoes you're fine, but for those who don't I have a secret solution I'm revealing!!

MAGIC MARKER

Fake Shoes Using Black MAGIC MARKER. Make sure there are two open holes for air passage.

④ Now all you have to do is wear the furoshiki cloth like a surplice over your shoulder and your outfit's completed!

NO DA!

Make sure you speak with the same idiosyncracies as him. Also squint your eyes to make them thinner.

We have an advanced section below for those of you not quite satisfied.

—ADVANCED SECTION—

① I'm sure most of you have noticed that Chichiri's key possession is the rosary! You might not find such a big rosary.

You might have to go to a temple or occult group to find one.

② Not enough? Of course not. The second key props are... THE STAFF AND BAMBOO HAT!!

KRISH

Wait for that night when a traveling priest knocks on your door to ask for a night's lodging.

③ If you've gone this far, nothing can stop you! There is one last detail to be Chichiri and that's... THE MOHAWK!!

Note: Make sure you keep your hair here.

Bring a portrait of Chichiri to the beauty parlor and they'll be glad cut your hair accordingly, I'm sur

★ For those who have dared to go this far, with regard to being alienated from your neighbors or family, or ending up committing suicide, I assume no responsibility. It might be best at least for the sake of world peace if you train yourself to disappear into your straw hat and leave this world for good,

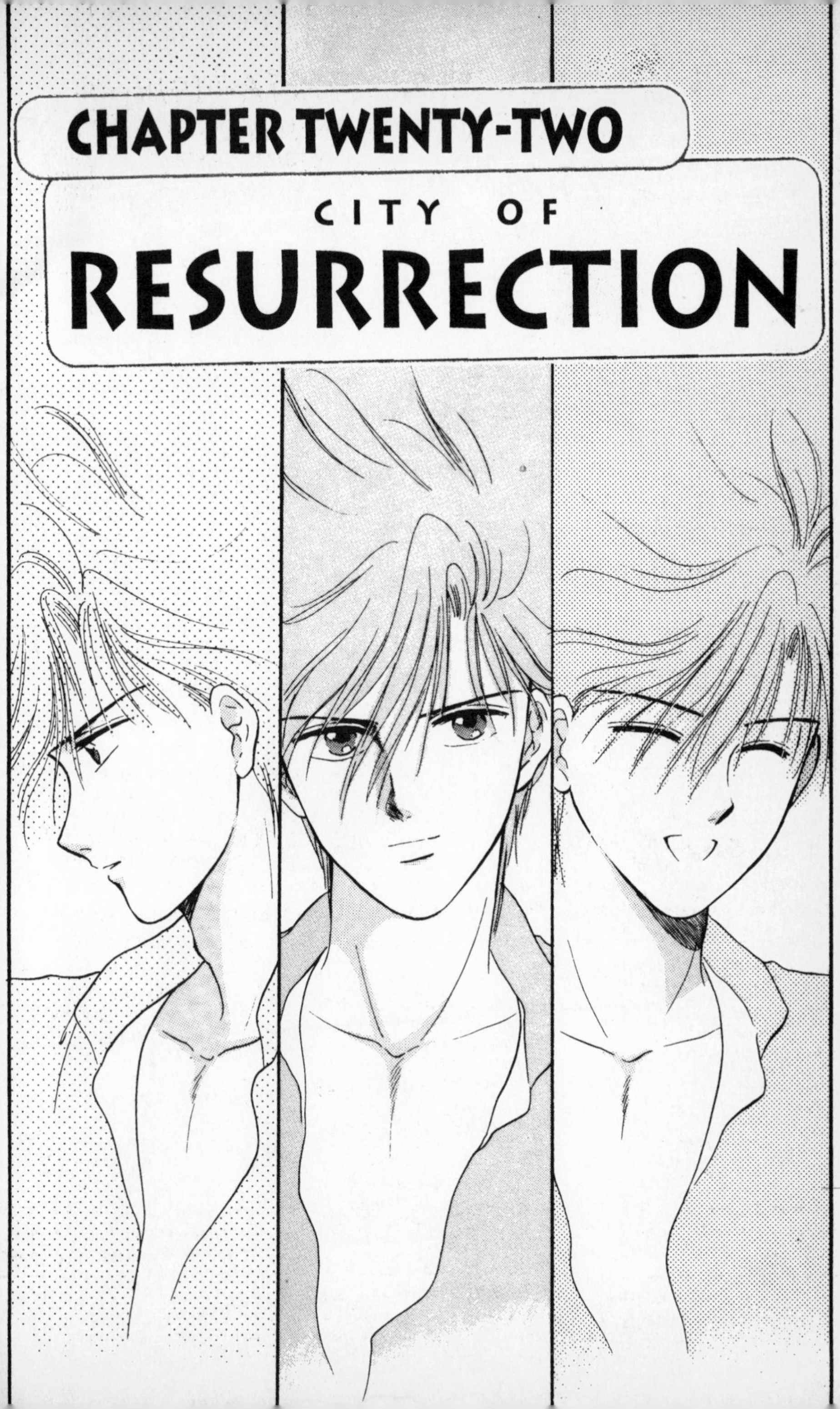
CHAPTER TWENTY-TWO
CITY OF
RESURRECTION

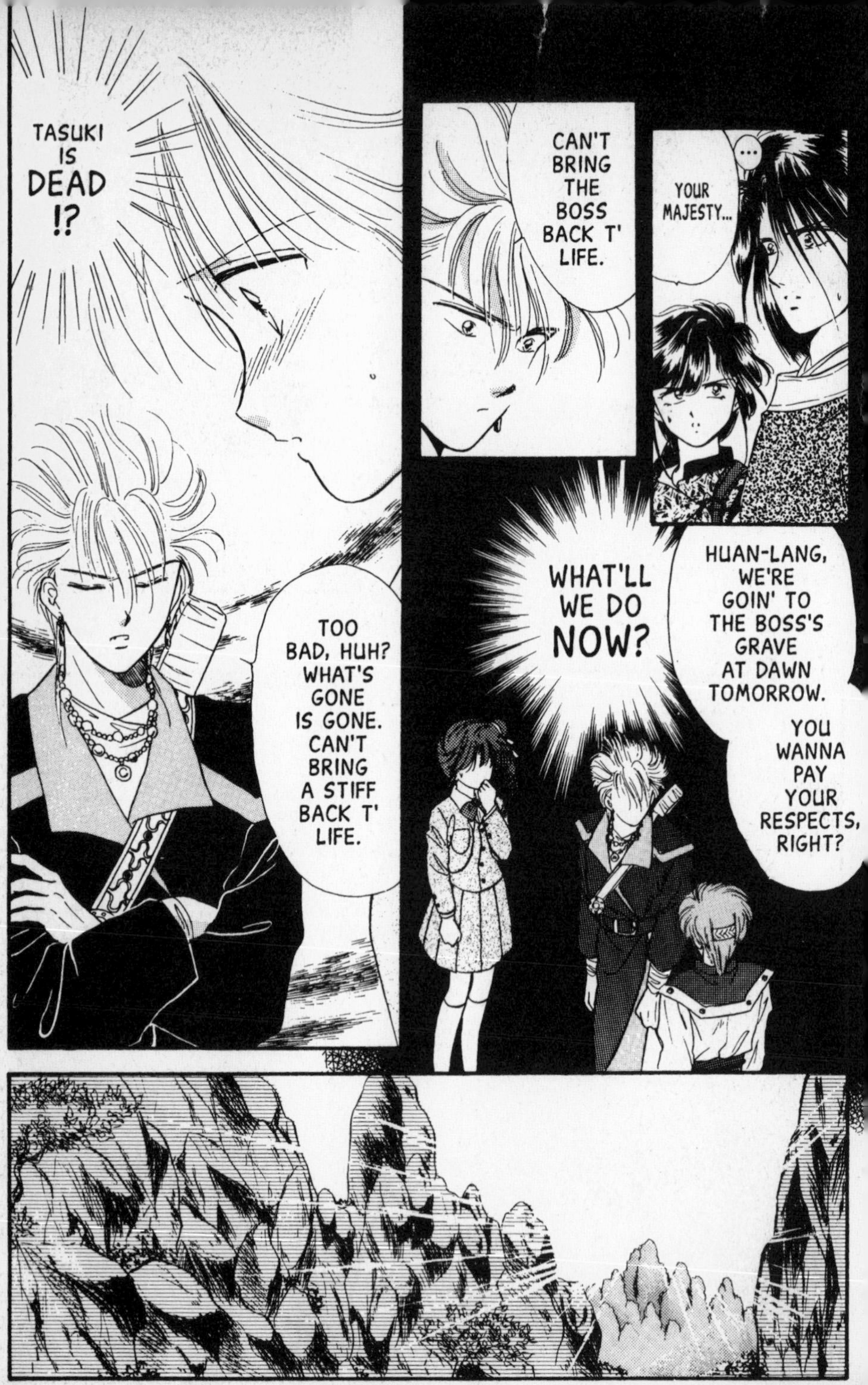
TASUKI IS DEAD !?
TOO BAD, HUH? WHAT'S GONE IS GONE. CAN'T BRING A STIFF BACK T' LIFE.
CAN'T BRING THE BOSS BACK T' LIFE.
...
YOUR MAJESTY...
WHAT'LL WE DO NOW?
HUAN-LANG, WE'RE GOIN' TO THE BOSS'S GRAVE AT DAWN TOMORROW.
YOU WANNA PAY YOUR RESPECTS, RIGHT?

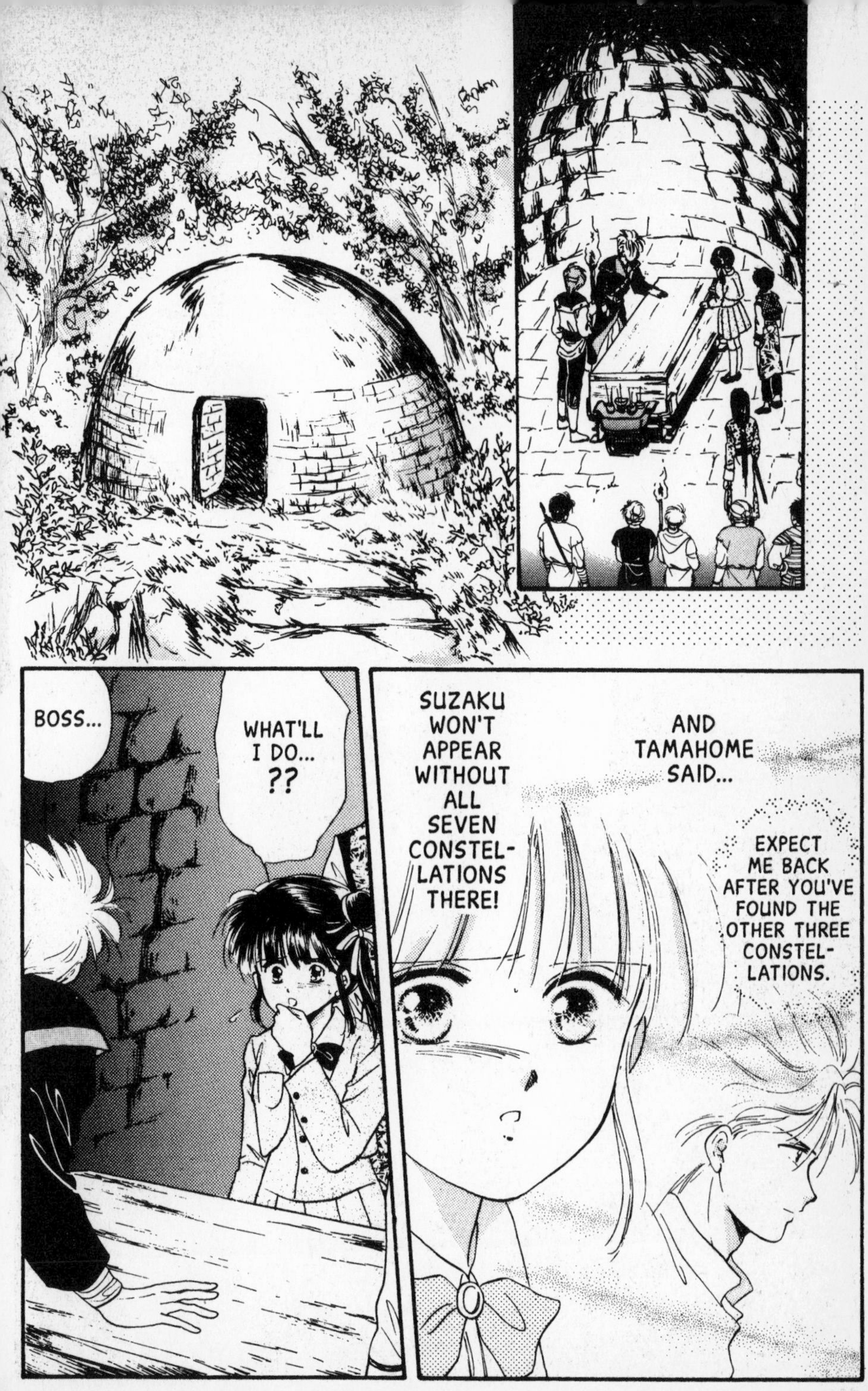
BOSS...
WHAT'LL I DO... ??
SUZAKU WON'T APPEAR WITHOUT ALL SEVEN CONSTEL-LATIONS THERE!
AND TAMAHOME SAID...
EXPECT ME BACK AFTER YOU'VE FOUND THE OTHER THREE CONSTEL-LATIONS.

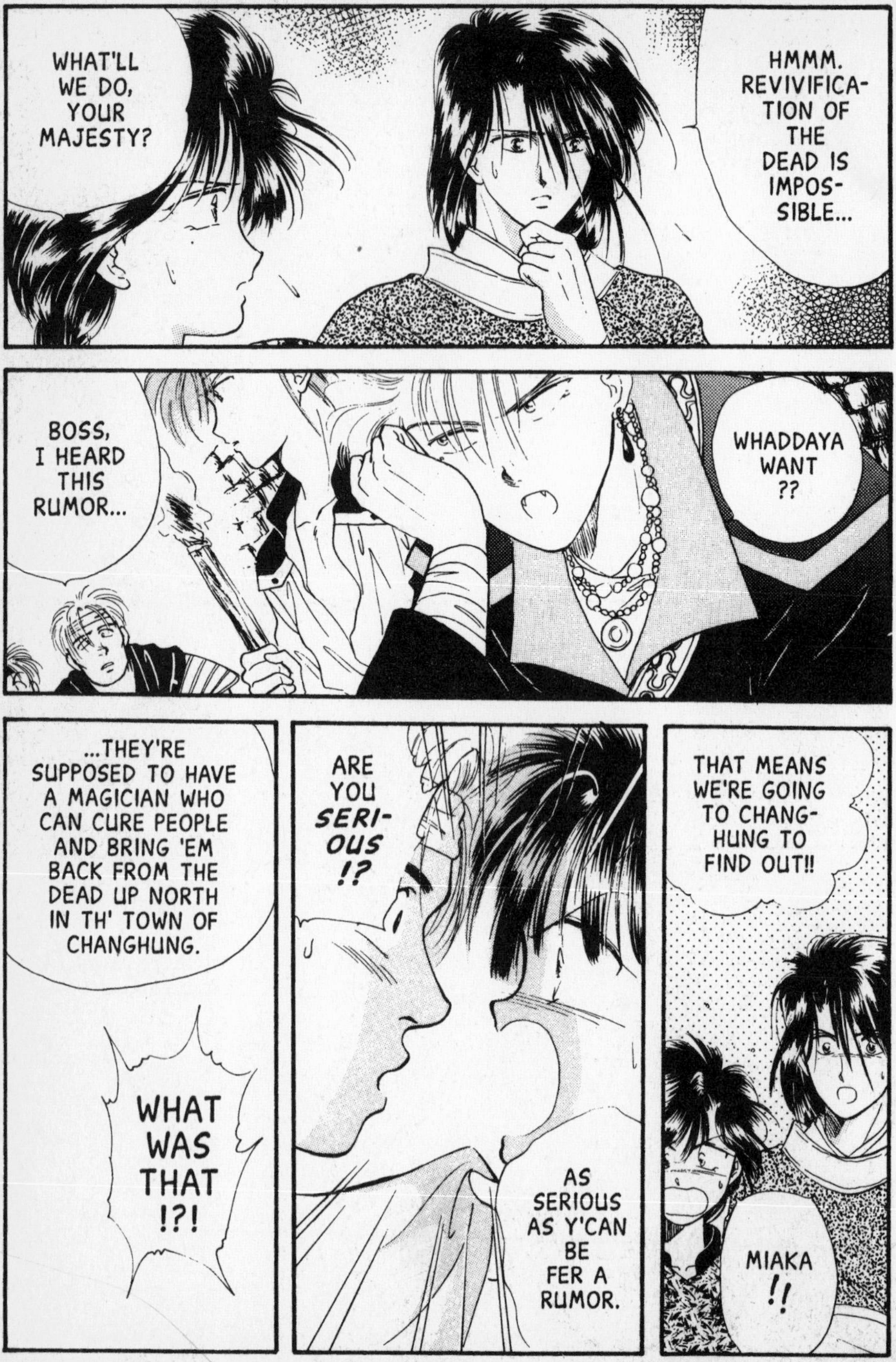
WHAT'LL WE DO, YOUR MAJESTY?
HMMM. REVIVIFICATION OF THE DEAD IS IMPOSSIBLE...
BOSS, I HEARD THIS RUMOR...
WHADDAYA WANT ??
...THEY'RE SUPPOSED TO HAVE A MAGICIAN WHO CAN CURE PEOPLE AND BRING 'EM BACK FROM THE DEAD UP NORTH IN TH' TOWN OF CHANGHUNG.
WHAT WAS THAT !?!
ARE YOU *SERIOUS* !?
AS SERIOUS AS Y'CAN BE FER A RUMOR.
THAT MEANS WE'RE GOING TO CHANGHUNG TO FIND OUT!!
MIAKA !!

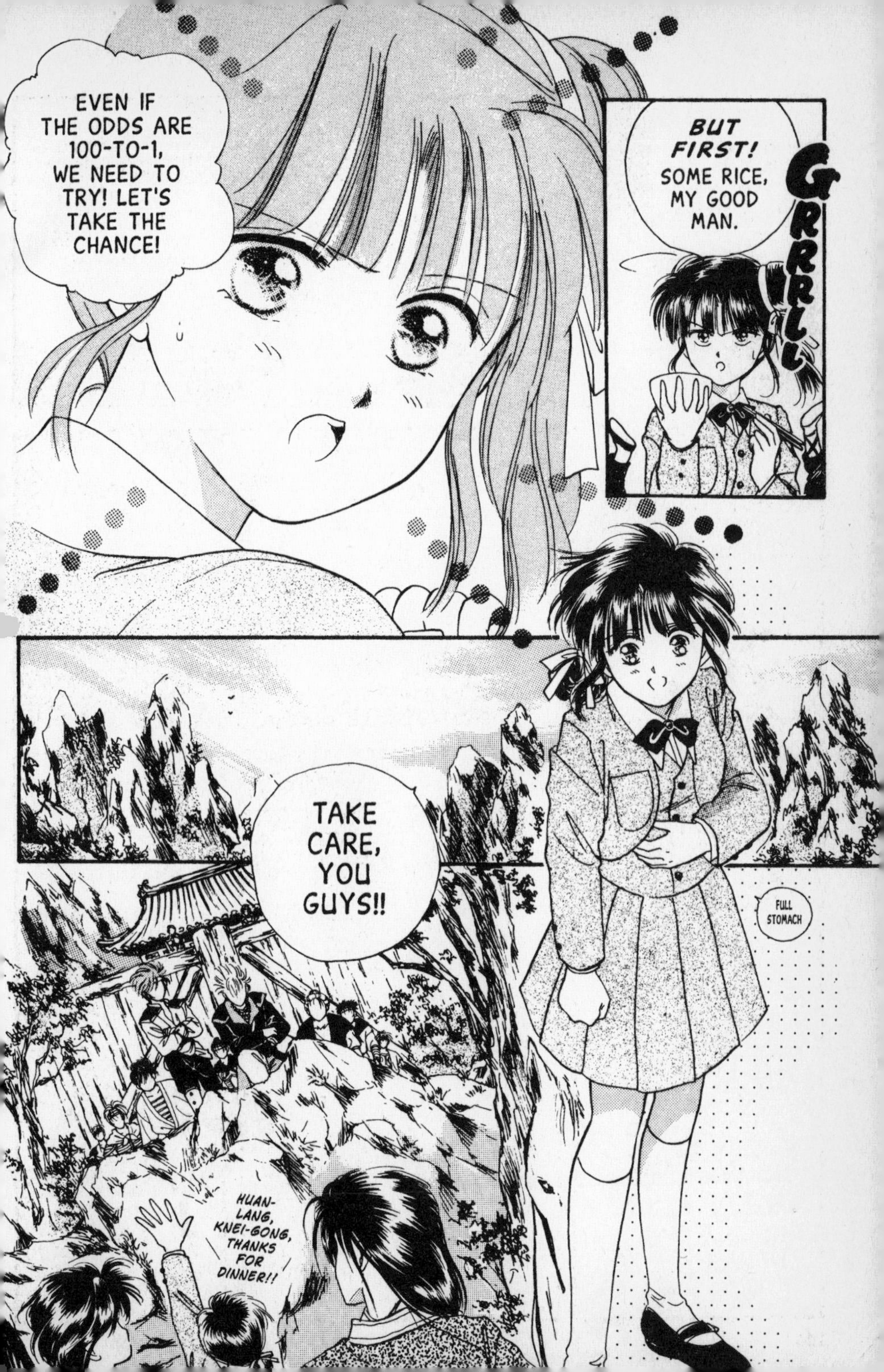
EVEN IF THE ODDS ARE 100-TO-1, WE NEED TO TRY! LET'S TAKE THE CHANCE!
BUT FIRST! SOME RICE, MY GOOD MAN.
GRRRLL
TAKE CARE, YOU GUYS!!
HUAN-LANG, KNEI-GONG, THANKS FOR DINNER!!
FULL STOMACH

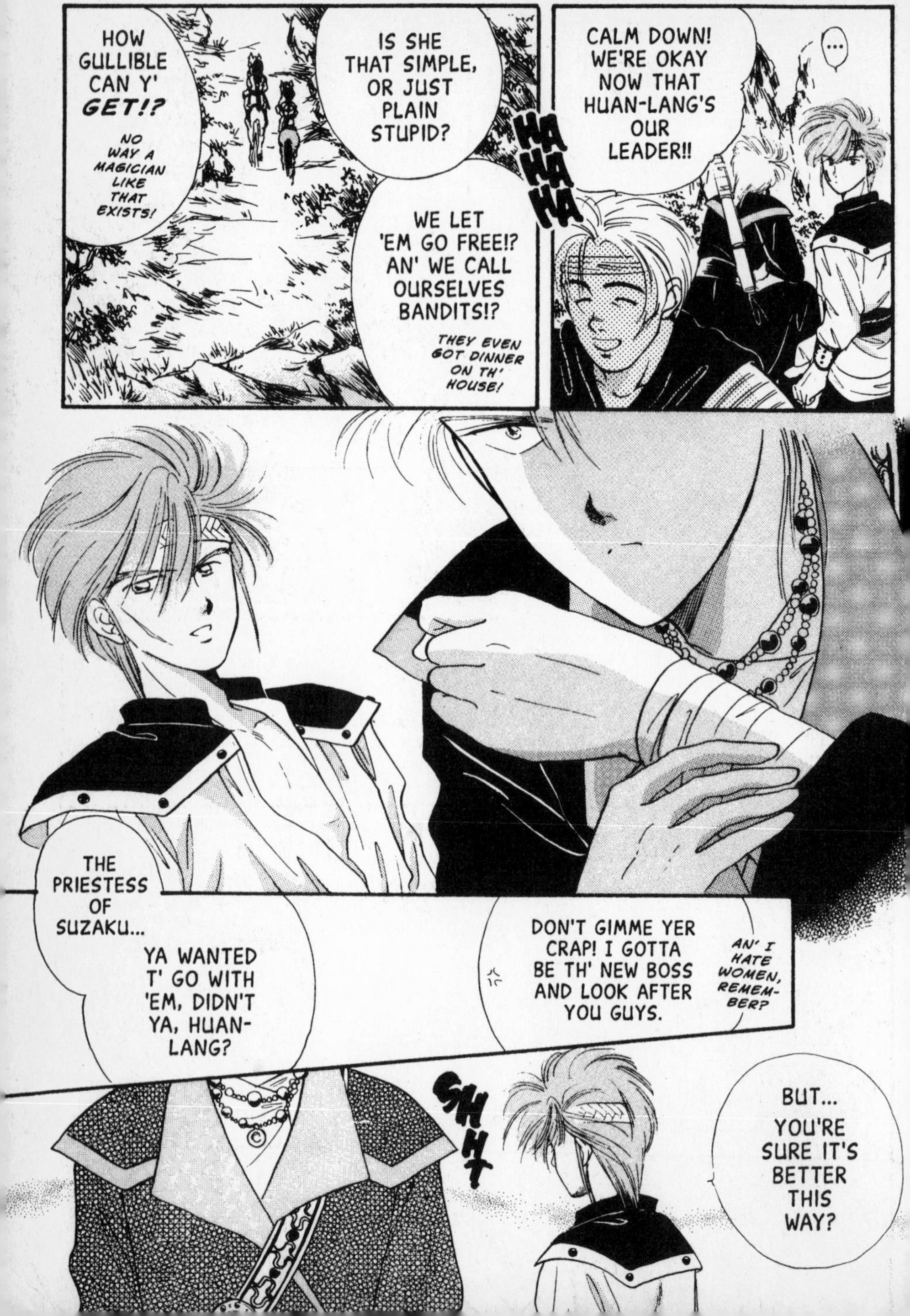
HOW GULLIBLE CAN Y' *GET!?*
NO WAY A MAGICIAN LIKE THAT EXISTS!
IS SHE THAT SIMPLE, OR JUST PLAIN STUPID?
WE LET 'EM GO FREE!? AN' WE CALL OURSELVES BANDITS!?
THEY EVEN GOT DINNER ON TH' HOUSE!
HAHAHAHA
CALM DOWN! WE'RE OKAY NOW THAT HUAN-LANG'S OUR LEADER!!
...
THE PRIESTESS OF SUZAKU...
YA WANTED T' GO WITH 'EM, DIDN'T YA, HUAN-LANG?
DON'T GIMME YER CRAP! I GOTTA BE TH' NEW BOSS AND LOOK AFTER YOU GUYS.
AN' I HATE WOMEN, REMEMBER?
SHHT
BUT... YOU'RE SURE IT'S BETTER THIS WAY?

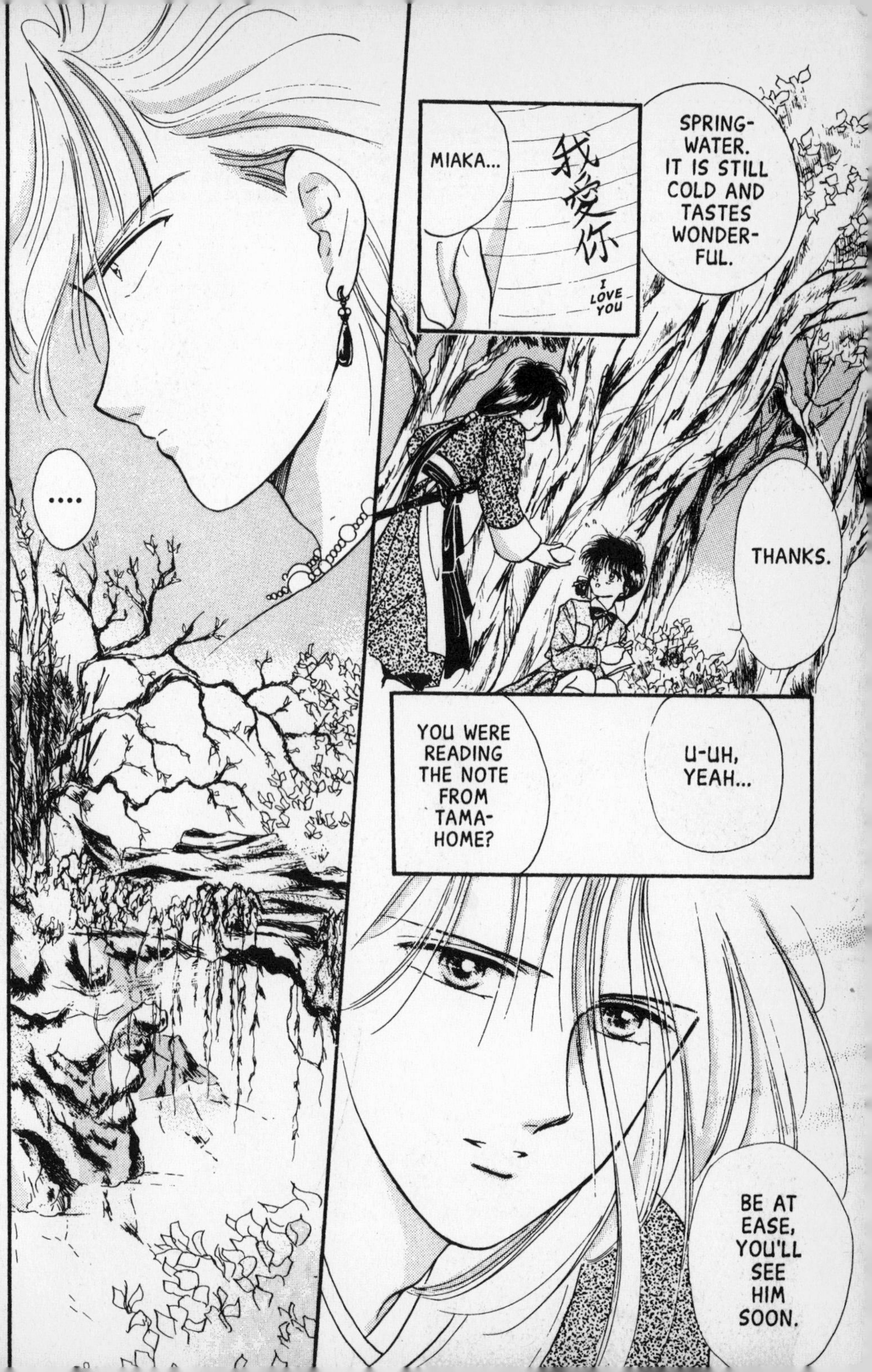
....
MIAKA...
我爱你
I LOVE YOU
SPRING-WATER. IT IS STILL COLD AND TASTES WONDERFUL.
THANKS.
YOU WERE READING THE NOTE FROM TAMAHOME?
U-UH, YEAH...
BE AT EASE, YOU'LL SEE HIM SOON.

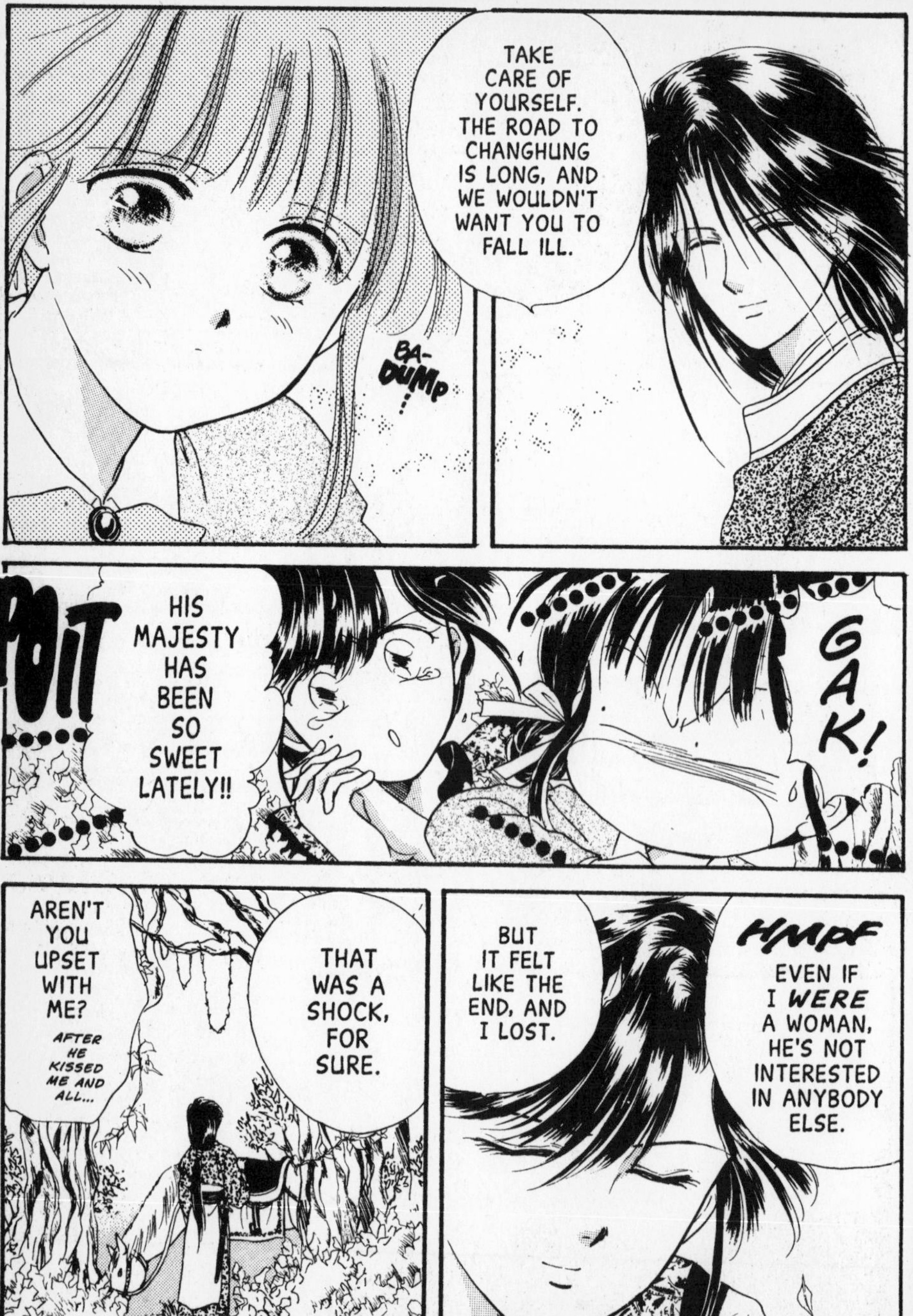
TAKE CARE OF YOURSELF. THE ROAD TO CHANGHUNG IS LONG, AND WE WOULDN'T WANT YOU TO FALL ILL.
BA-DUMP!
POIT
HIS MAJESTY HAS BEEN SO SWEET LATELY!!
GAK!
AREN'T YOU UPSET WITH ME?
AFTER HE KISSED ME AND ALL...
THAT WAS A SHOCK, FOR SURE.
BUT IT FELT LIKE THE END, AND I LOST.
HMPF
EVEN IF I WERE A WOMAN, HE'S NOT INTERESTED IN ANYBODY ELSE.

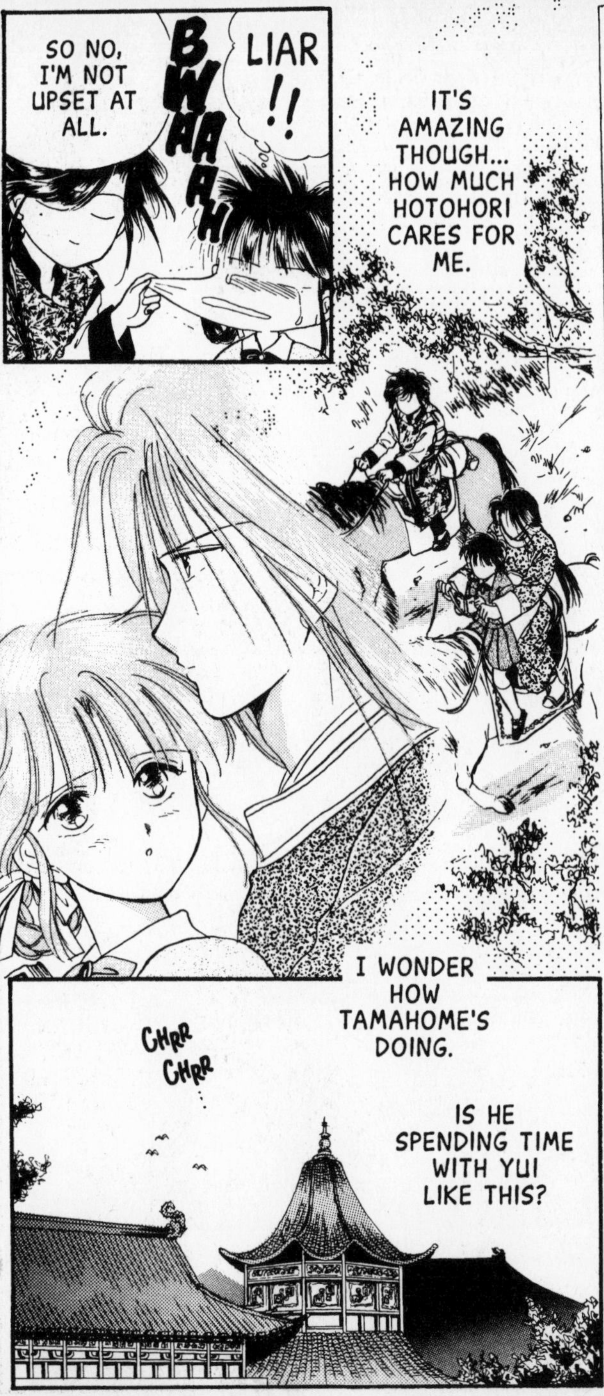
SO NO, I'M NOT UPSET AT ALL.
BWAAAAH
LIAR!!
IT'S AMAZING THOUGH... HOW MUCH HOTOHORI CARES FOR ME.
I WONDER HOW TAMAHOME'S DOING.
CHRR CHRR
IS HE SPENDING TIME WITH YUI LIKE THIS?

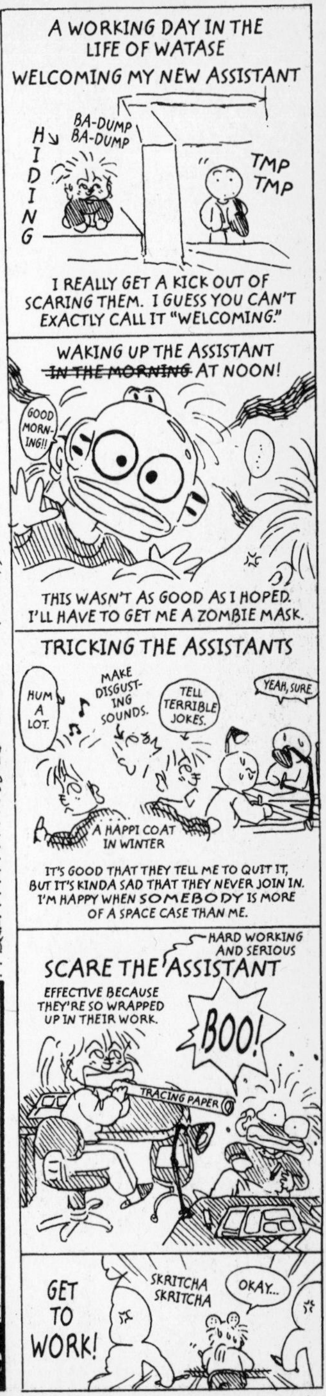
A WORKING DAY IN THE LIFE OF WATASE
WELCOMING MY NEW ASSISTANT
HIDING
BA-DUMP BA-DUMP
TMP TMP
I REALLY GET A KICK OUT OF SCARING THEM. I GUESS YOU CAN'T EXACTLY CALL IT "WELCOMING."
WAKING UP THE ASSISTANT ~~IN THE MORNING~~ AT NOON!
GOOD MORNING!!
THIS WASN'T AS GOOD AS I HOPED. I'LL HAVE TO GET ME A ZOMBIE MASK.
TRICKING THE ASSISTANTS
HUM A LOT.
MAKE DISGUSTING SOUNDS.
TELL TERRIBLE JOKES.
YEAH, SURE.
A HAPPI COAT IN WINTER
IT'S GOOD THAT THEY TELL ME TO QUIT IT, BUT IT'S KINDA SAD THAT THEY NEVER JOIN IN. I'M HAPPY WHEN SOMEBODY IS MORE OF A SPACE CASE THAN ME.
HARD WORKING AND SERIOUS
SCARE THE ASSISTANT
EFFECTIVE BECAUSE THEY'RE SO WRAPPED UP IN THEIR WORK.
BOO!
TRACING PAPER
GET TO WORK!
SKRITCHA SKRITCHA
OKAY...

Based on a true story (Well, it COULD be).

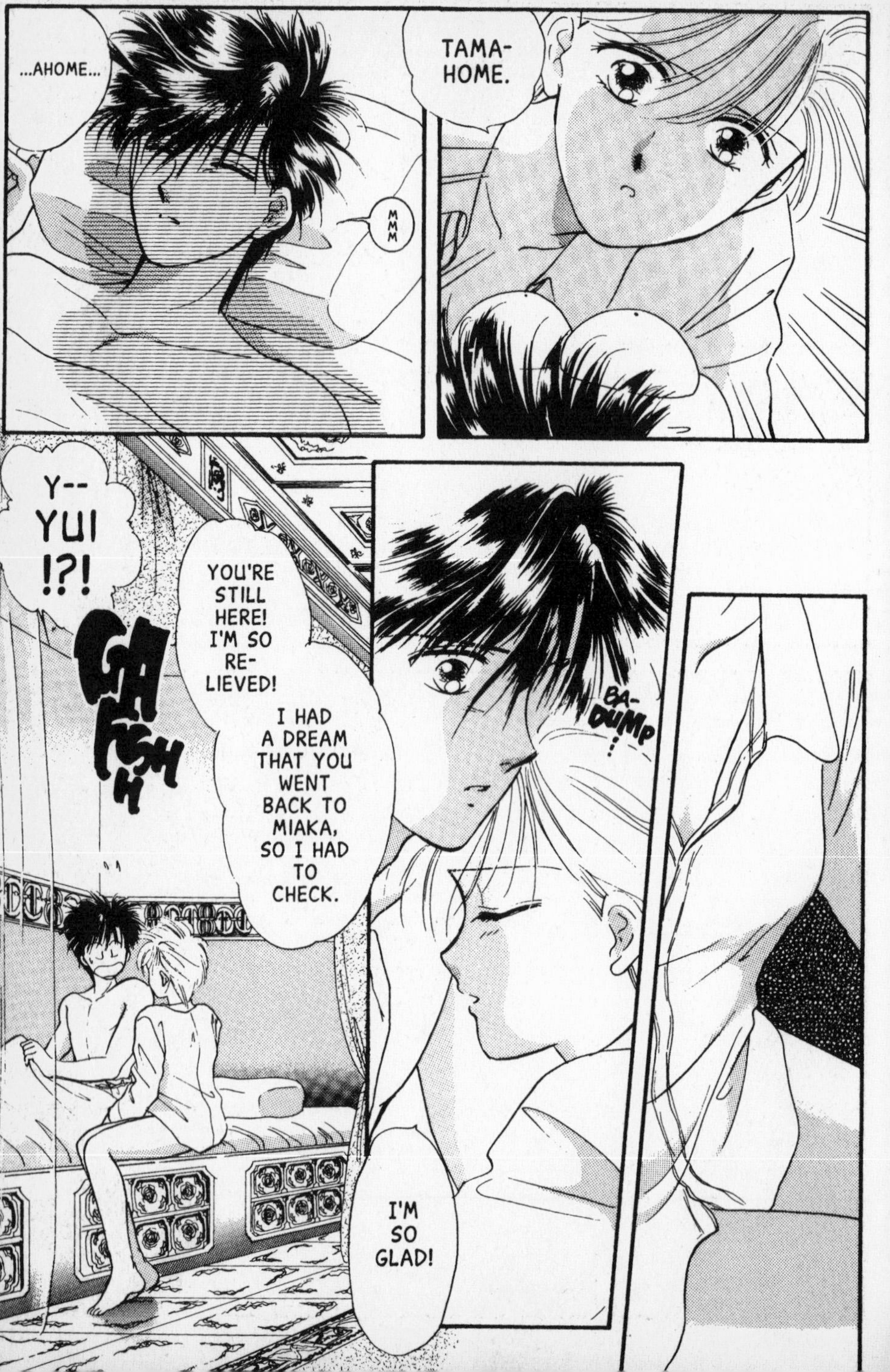
...AHOME...
MMM
TAMA-HOME.
Y-- YUI !?!
YOU'RE STILL HERE! I'M SO RE-LIEVED!
I HAD A DREAM THAT YOU WENT BACK TO MIAKA, SO I HAD TO CHECK.
BA-DUMP!
I'M SO GLAD!

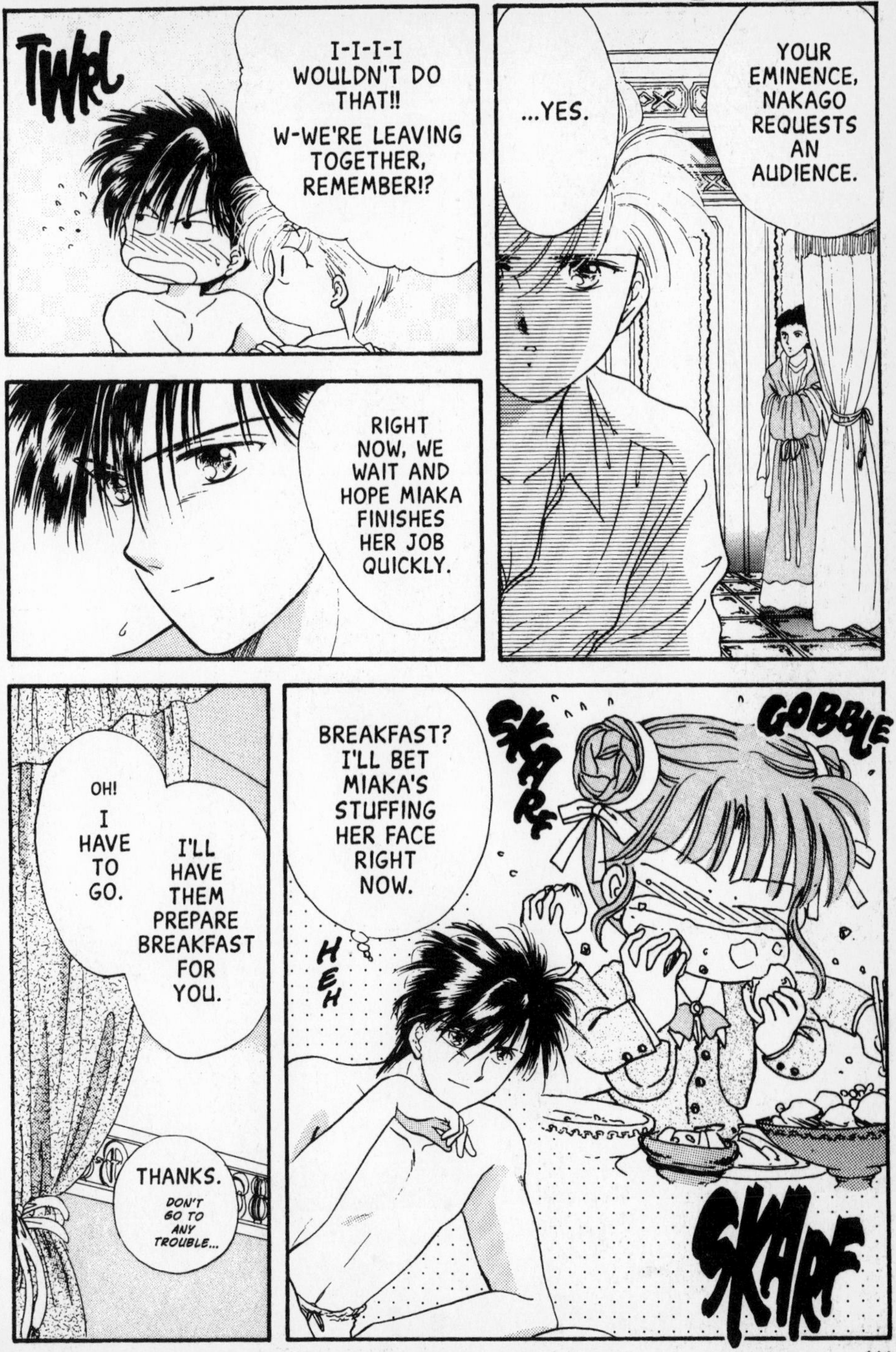
TWRL
I-I-I-I WOULDN'T DO THAT!!
W-WE'RE LEAVING TOGETHER, REMEMBER!?
RIGHT NOW, WE WAIT AND HOPE MIAKA FINISHES HER JOB QUICKLY.
...YES.
YOUR EMINENCE, NAKAGO REQUESTS AN AUDIENCE.
OH!
I HAVE TO GO.
I'LL HAVE THEM PREPARE BREAKFAST FOR YOU.
THANKS.
DON'T GO TO ANY TROUBLE...
BREAKFAST? I'LL BET MIAKA'S STUFFING HER FACE RIGHT NOW.
SKARF
GOBBLE
HEH
SKARF

WHEN WILL I GET TO SEE YOUR SMILING FACE AGAIN...

THE PRIESTESS OF SUZAKU IS NOW HEADED TO HONG-NAN'S NORTHERN CITY OF CHANGHUNG.

THEY SAY SOMEONE THERE CAN REVIVE THE DEAD.

SO, GATHERING HER CELESTIAL WARRIORS IS NO EASY TASK.

THEN... YOU'RE SAYING THE CELESTIAL WARRIOR TASUKI IS DEAD?

LET'S SEE HOW HARD SHE WORKS... ALL RIGHT, CONTINUE YOUR OBSERVATIONS.

YES, SIR!

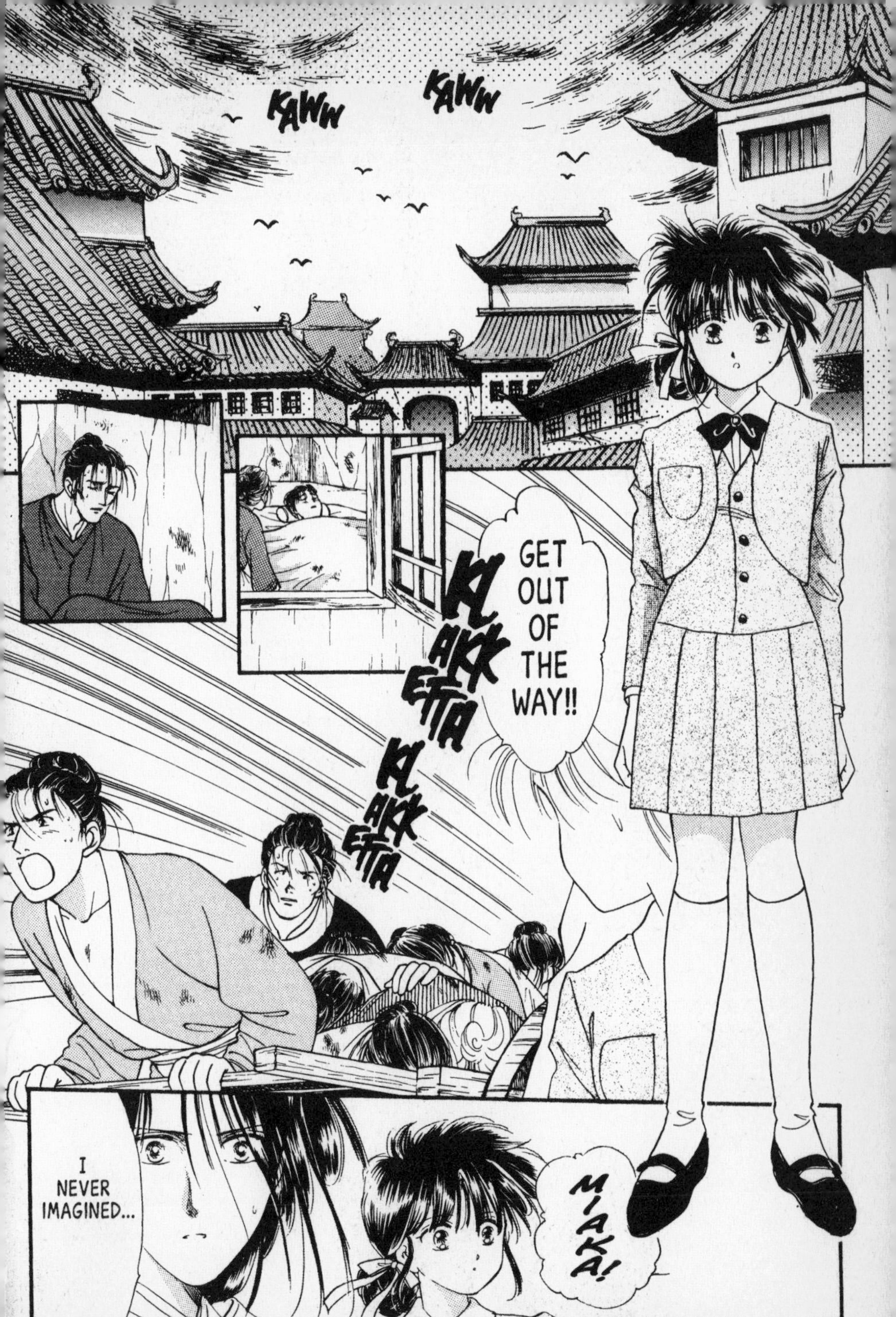
KAWW
KAWW
GET OUT OF THE WAY!!
KLAKKETTA
KLAKKETTA
I NEVER IMAGINED...
MIAKA!

LOOK AT THE CRYSTAL BALL!!

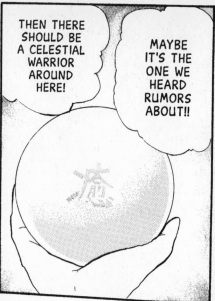

THEN THERE SHOULD BE A CELESTIAL WARRIOR AROUND HERE!

MAYBE IT'S THE ONE WE HEARD RUMORS ABOUT!!

YIPPEE!

WE'LL KILL TWO BIRDS WITH ONE STONE!

THONK

OWW!

WHUMP

OOPS! I'M SO SORRY!!

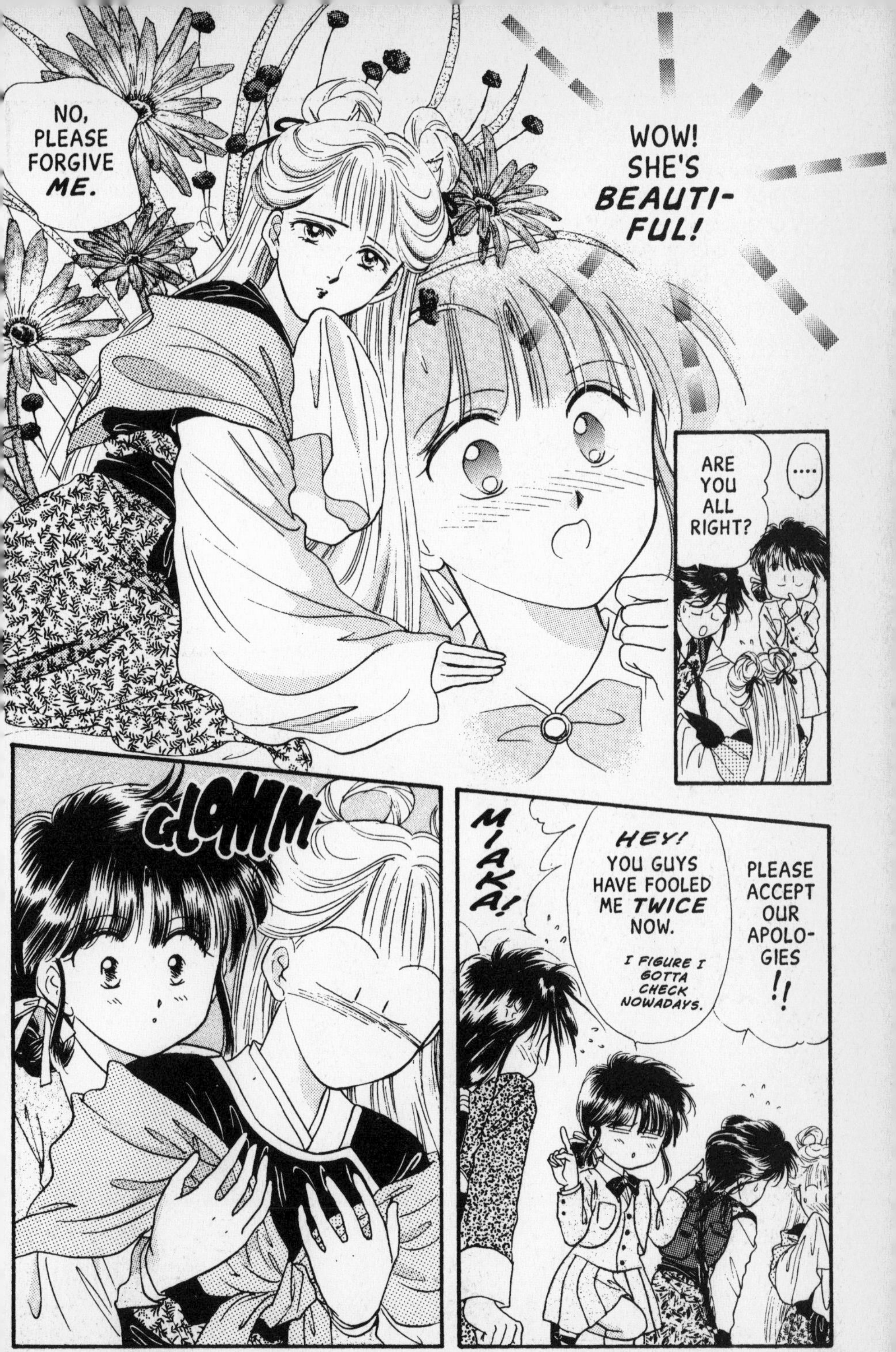
NO, PLEASE FORGIVE *ME.*
WOW! SHE'S *BEAUTI-FUL!*
ARE YOU ALL RIGHT?
....
GLOMM
MIAKA!
HEY! YOU GUYS HAVE FOOLED ME *TWICE* NOW.
I FIGURE I GOTTA CHECK NOWADAYS.
PLEASE ACCEPT OUR APOLO-GIES !!

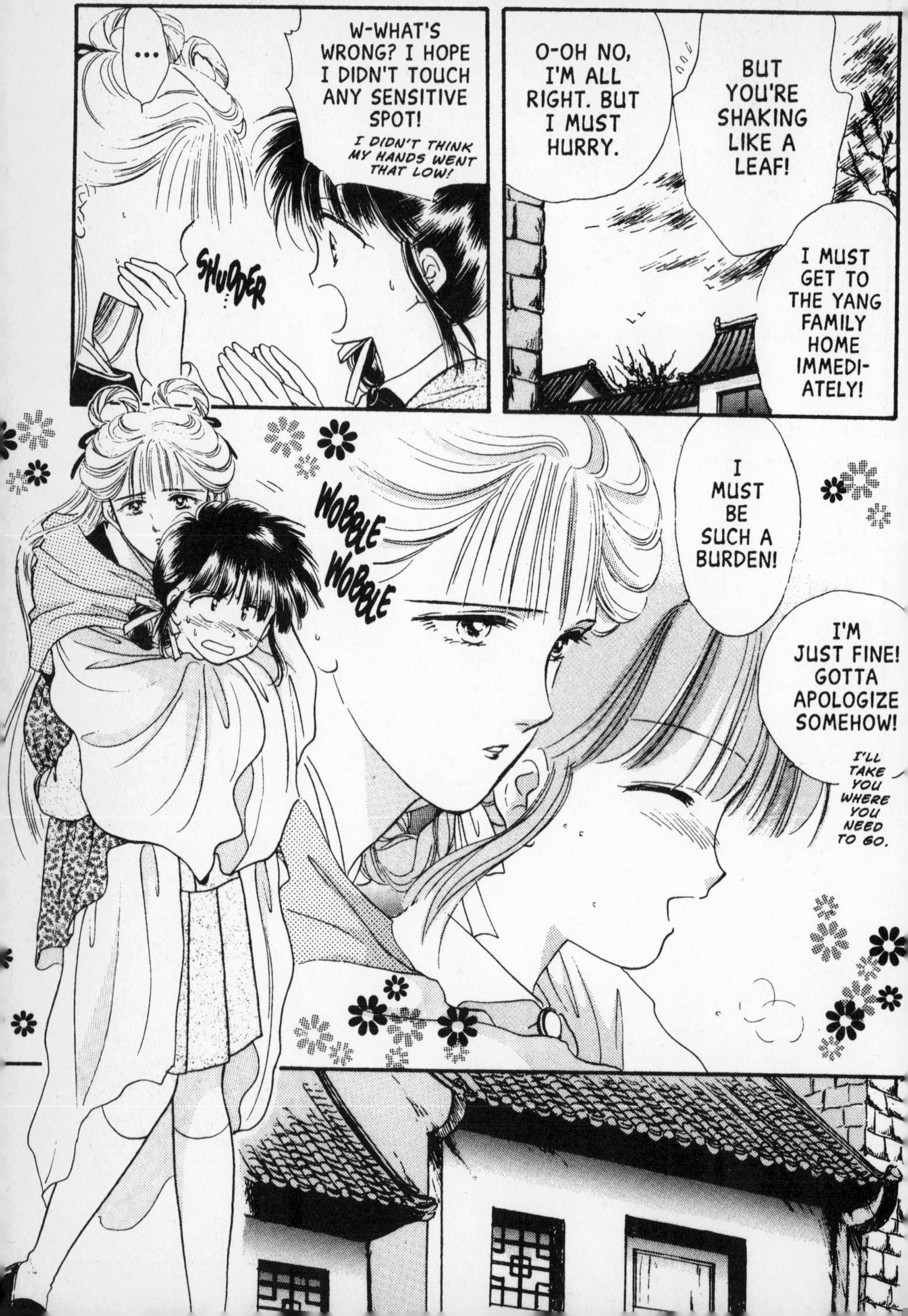
...
W-WHAT'S WRONG? I HOPE I DIDN'T TOUCH ANY SENSITIVE SPOT!
I DIDN'T THINK MY HANDS WENT THAT LOW!
SHUDDER
O-OH NO, I'M ALL RIGHT. BUT I MUST HURRY.
BUT YOU'RE SHAKING LIKE A LEAF!
I MUST GET TO THE YANG FAMILY HOME IMMEDI-ATELY!
WOBBLE WOBBLE
I MUST BE SUCH A BURDEN!
I'M JUST FINE! GOTTA APOLOGIZE SOMEHOW!
I'LL TAKE YOU WHERE YOU NEED TO GO.

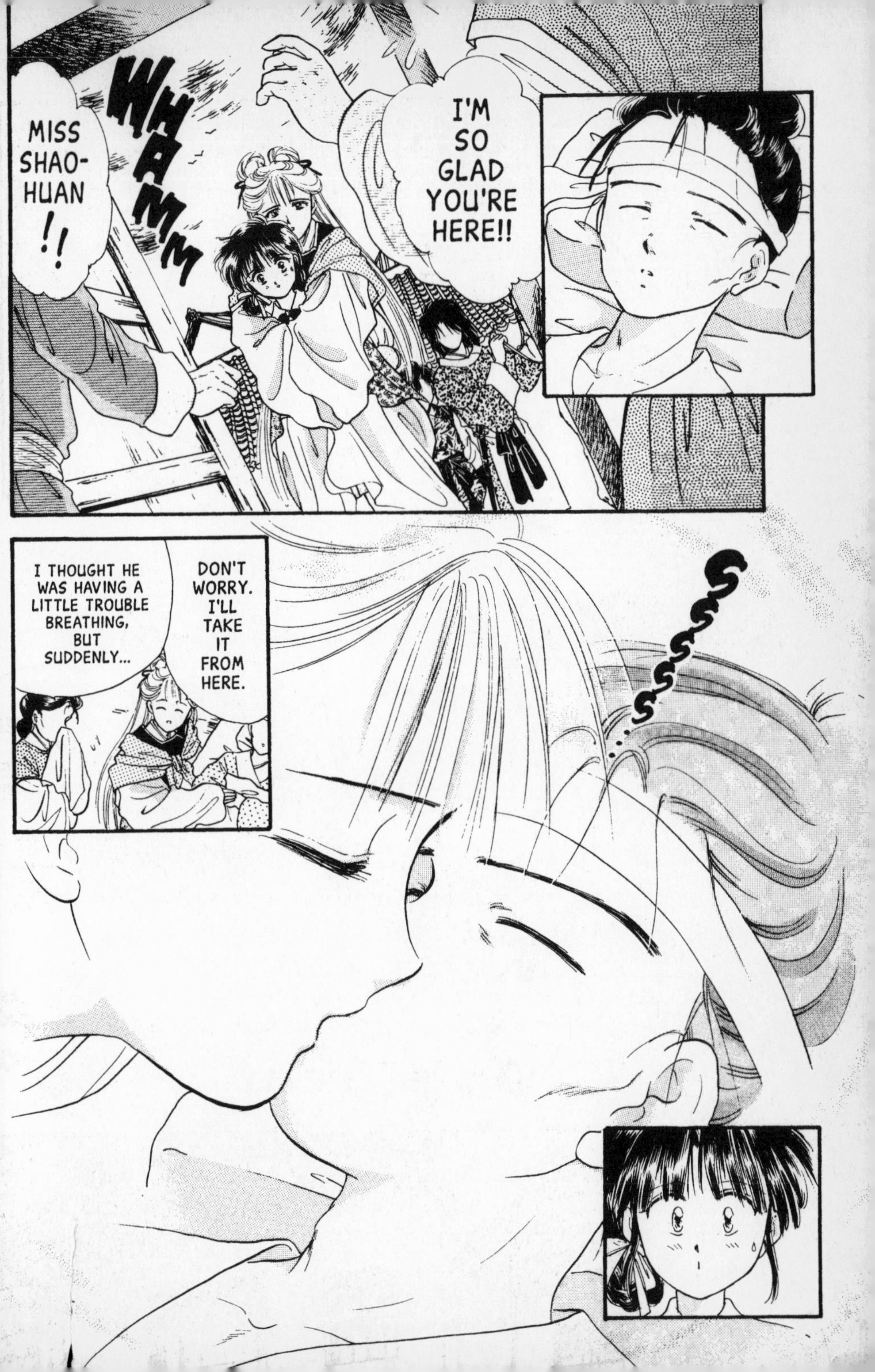
MISS SHAO-HUAN !!
WHAMMM
I'M SO GLAD YOU'RE HERE!!
I THOUGHT HE WAS HAVING A LITTLE TROUBLE BREATHING, BUT SUDDENLY...
DON'T WORRY. I'LL TAKE IT FROM HERE.
SSSSSS...

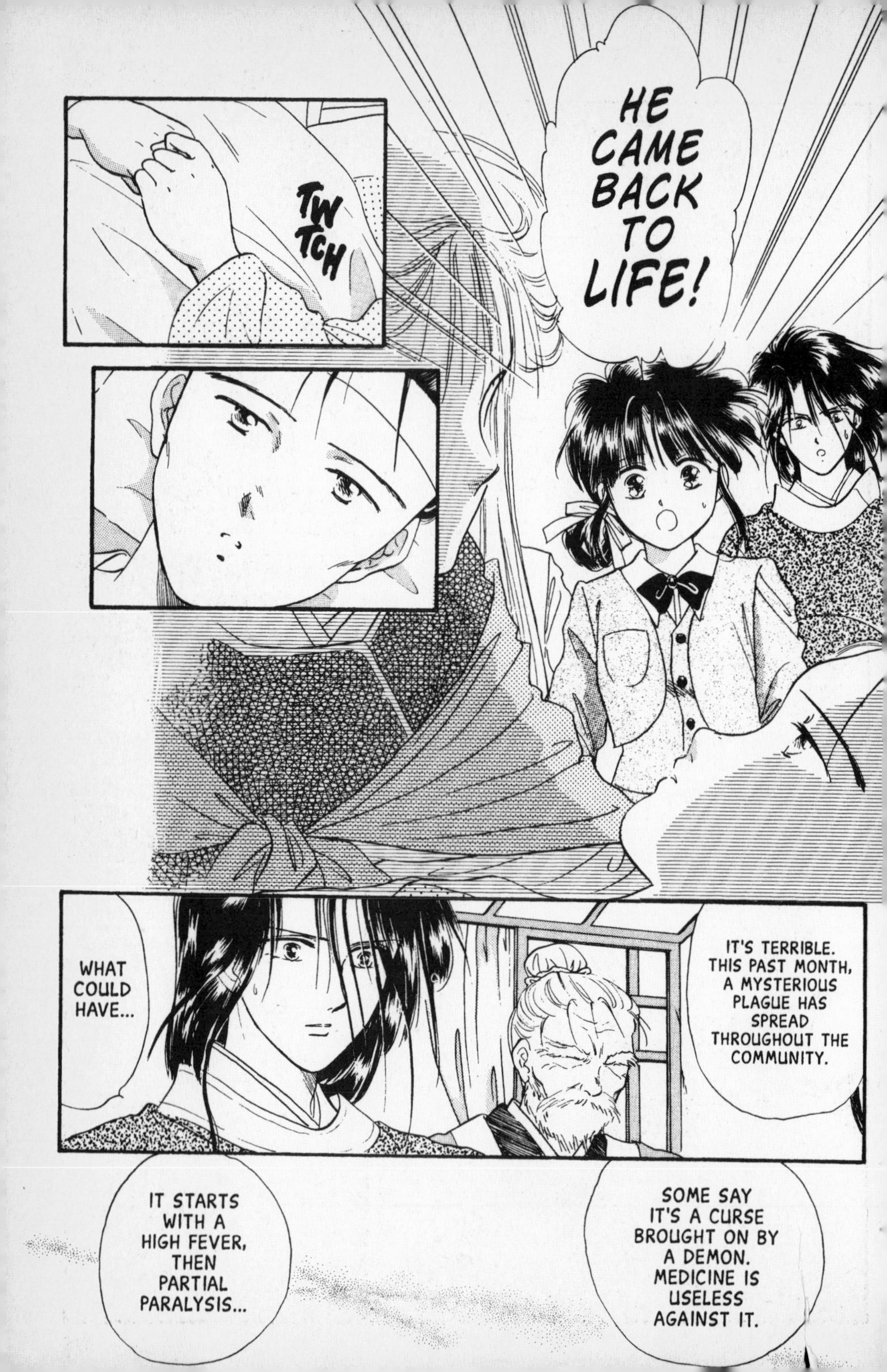
TWTCH
HE CAME BACK TO LIFE!
WHAT COULD HAVE...
IT'S TERRIBLE. THIS PAST MONTH, A MYSTERIOUS PLAGUE HAS SPREAD THROUGHOUT THE COMMUNITY.
IT STARTS WITH A HIGH FEVER, THEN PARTIAL PARALYSIS...
SOME SAY IT'S A CURSE BROUGHT ON BY A DEMON. MEDICINE IS USELESS AGAINST IT.

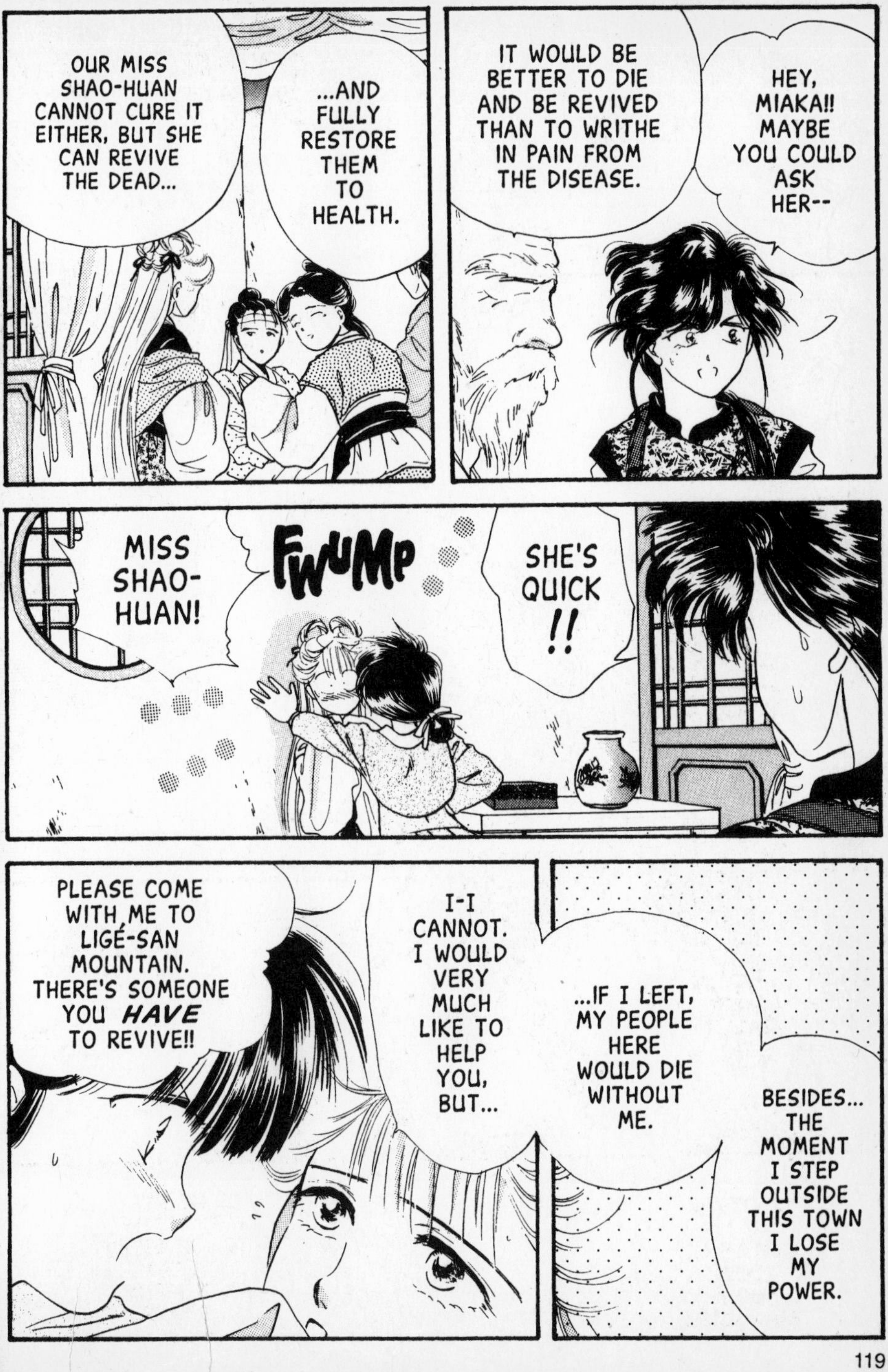
OUR MISS SHAO-HUAN CANNOT CURE IT EITHER, BUT SHE CAN REVIVE THE DEAD...
...AND FULLY RESTORE THEM TO HEALTH.
IT WOULD BE BETTER TO DIE AND BE REVIVED THAN TO WRITHE IN PAIN FROM THE DISEASE.
HEY, MIAKA!! MAYBE YOU COULD ASK HER--
MISS SHAO-HUAN!
FWUMP
SHE'S QUICK !!
PLEASE COME WITH ME TO LIGÉ-SAN MOUNTAIN. THERE'S SOMEONE YOU *HAVE* TO REVIVE!!
I-I CANNOT. I WOULD VERY MUCH LIKE TO HELP YOU, BUT...
...IF I LEFT, MY PEOPLE HERE WOULD DIE WITHOUT ME.
BESIDES... THE MOMENT I STEP OUTSIDE THIS TOWN I LOSE MY POWER.

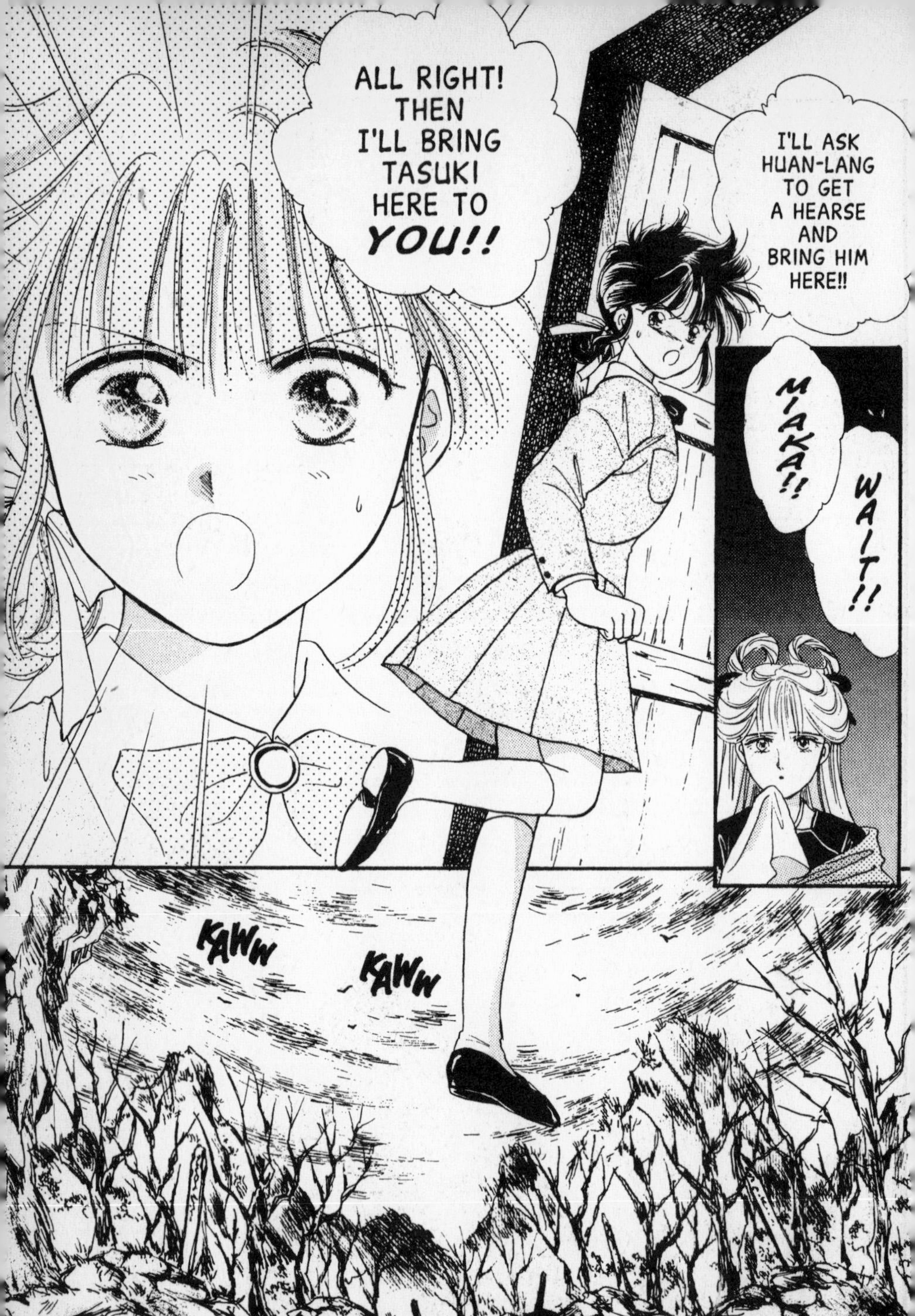
ALL RIGHT! THEN I'LL BRING TASUKI HERE TO YOU!!
I'LL ASK HUAN-LANG TO GET A HEARSE AND BRING HIM HERE!!
MIAKA!!
WAIT!!
KAWW
KAWW

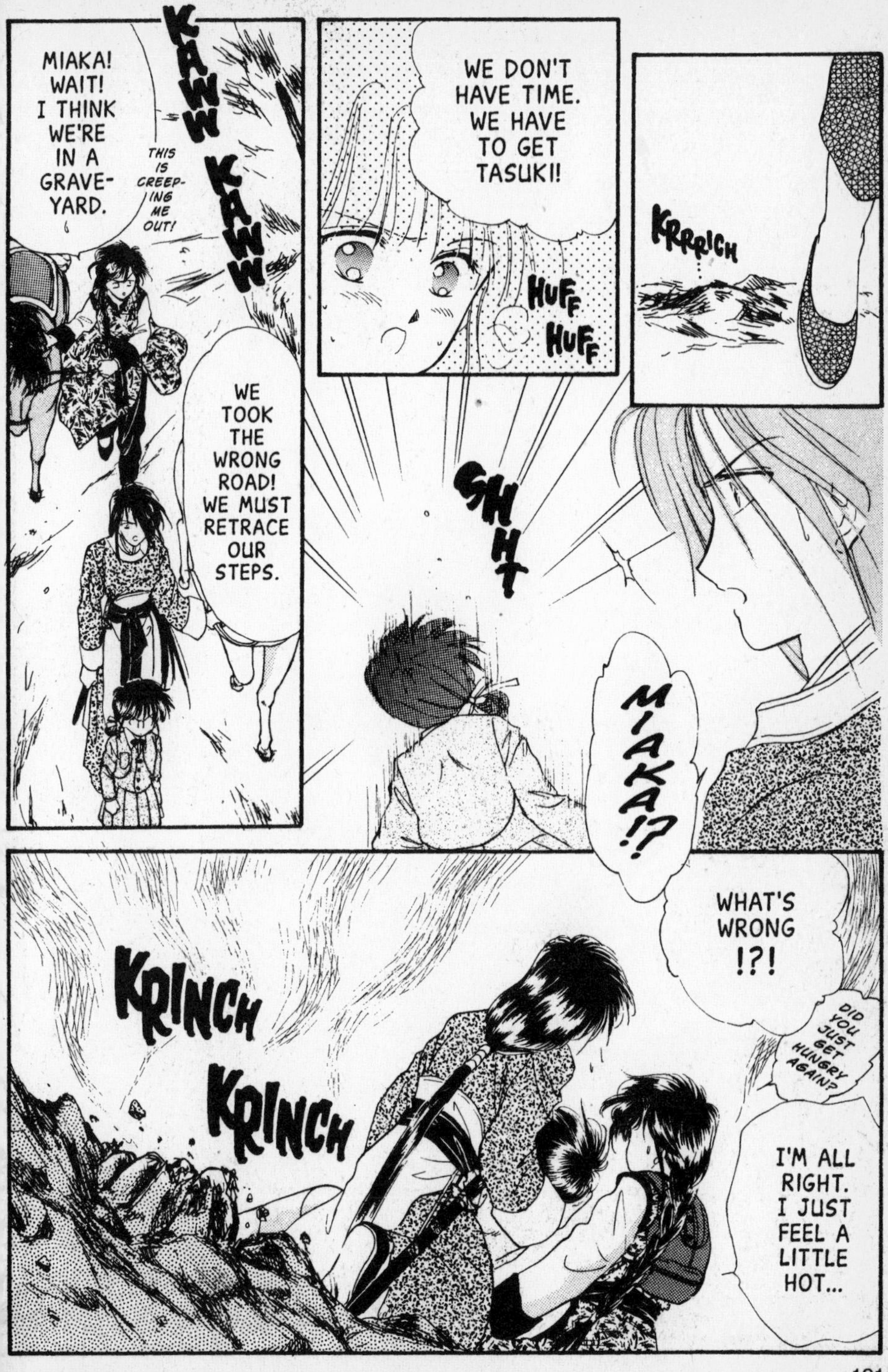
MIAKA! WAIT! I THINK WE'RE IN A GRAVEYARD.
THIS IS CREEPING ME OUT!
KAWW KAWW
WE TOOK THE WRONG ROAD! WE MUST RETRACE OUR STEPS.
WE DON'T HAVE TIME. WE HAVE TO GET TASUKI!
HUFF HUFF
KRRRICH
SHHT
MIAKA!?
WHAT'S WRONG !?!
KRINCH
KRINCH
DID YOU JUST GET HUNGRY AGAIN?
I'M ALL RIGHT. I JUST FEEL A LITTLE HOT...

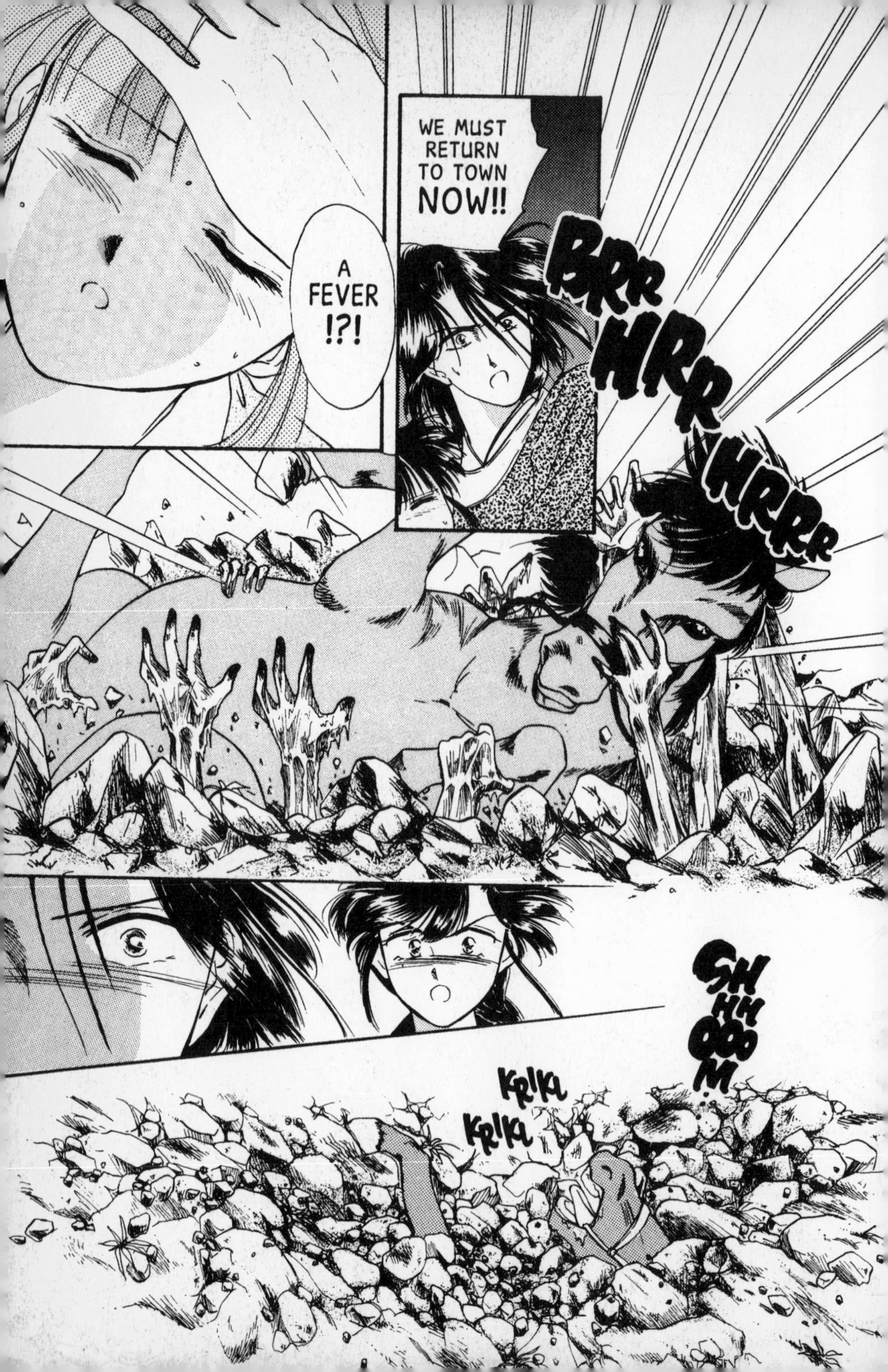
A FEVER !?!
WE MUST RETURN TO TOWN NOW!!
BRRR HRRR HRRRR
SHHHOOOM!
KRIKA KRIKA

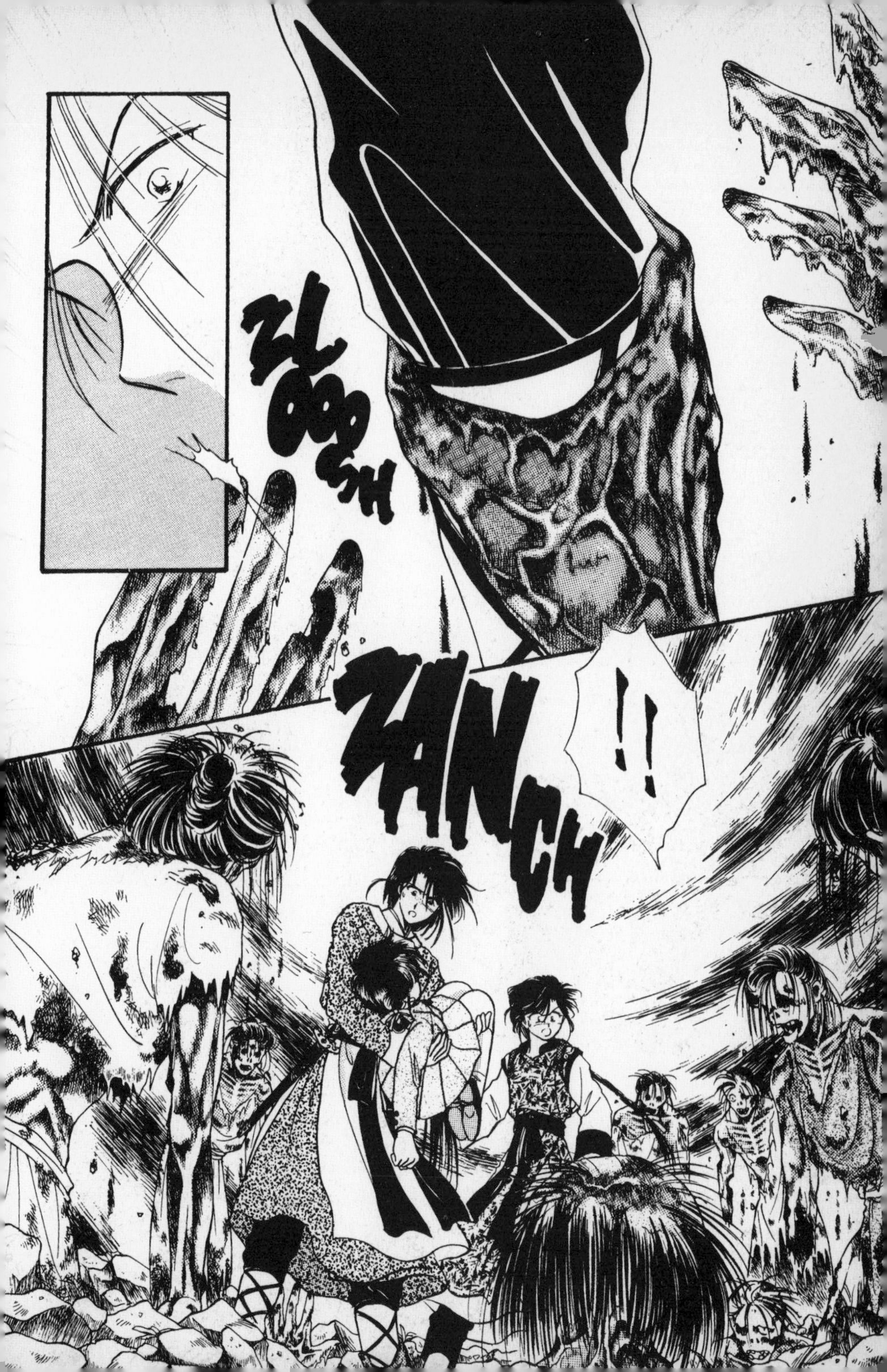
ZLOOOSH
ZANCH
!!

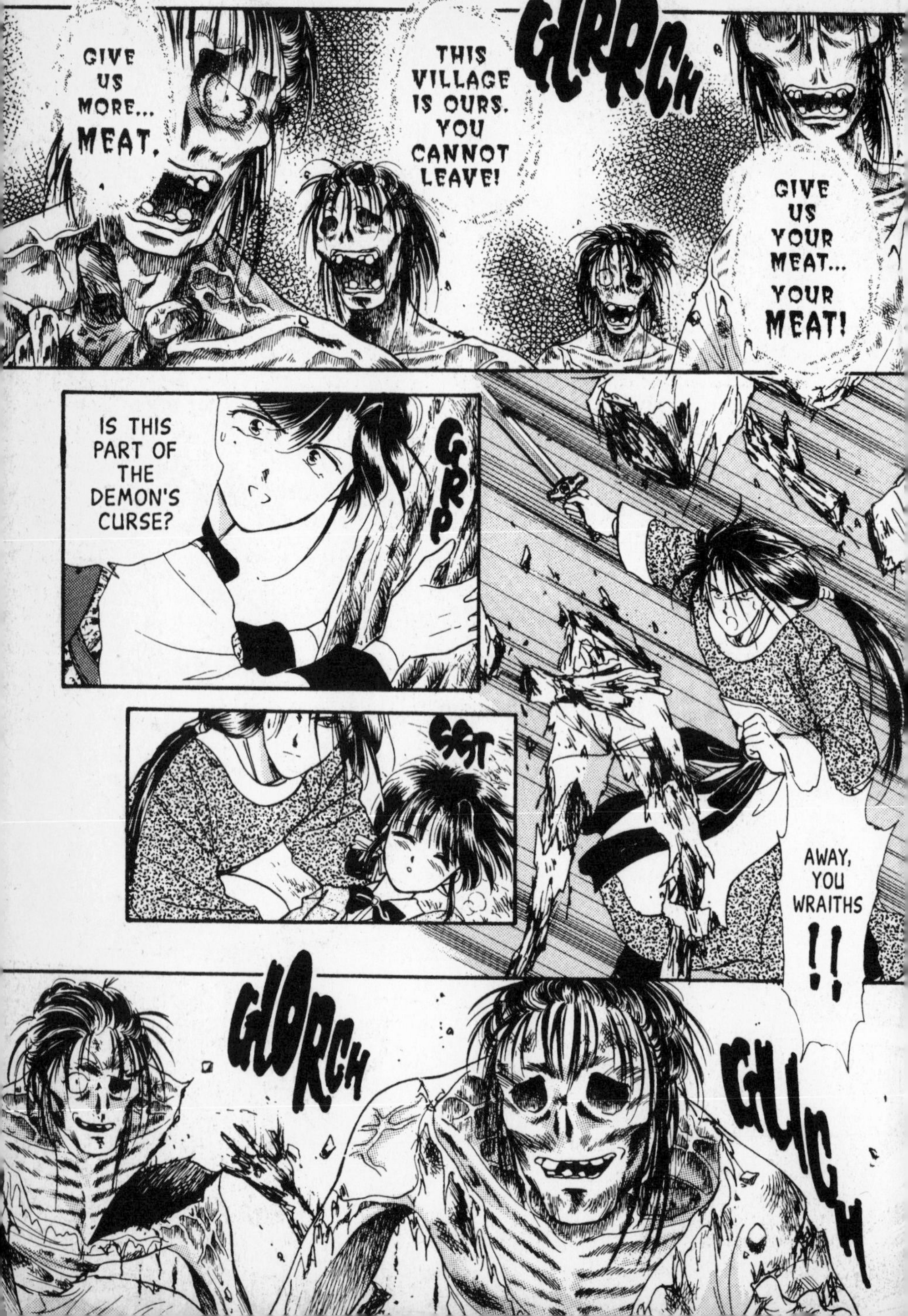

GIVE US MORE... MEAT.
THIS VILLAGE IS OURS. YOU CANNOT LEAVE!
GIRRRCH
GIVE US YOUR MEAT... YOUR MEAT!
IS THIS PART OF THE DEMON'S CURSE?
GRP
SST
AWAY, YOU WRAITHS!!
GLORCH
GUCHCH

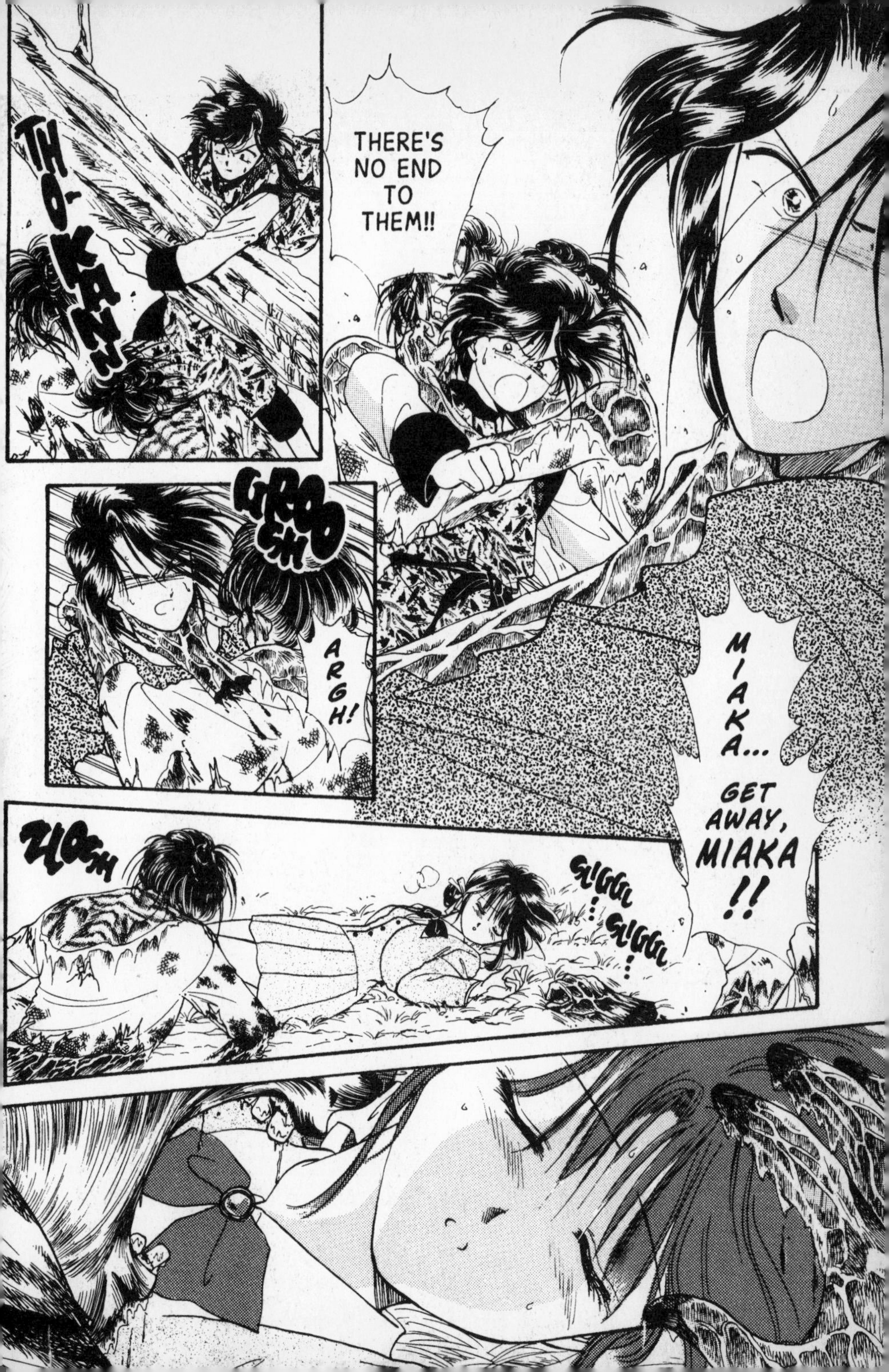
THO-KANN
GROOSH
ARGH!
THERE'S NO END TO THEM!!
MIAKA...
GET AWAY, MIAKA!!
ZUOSH
SLIGGL... SLIGGL...

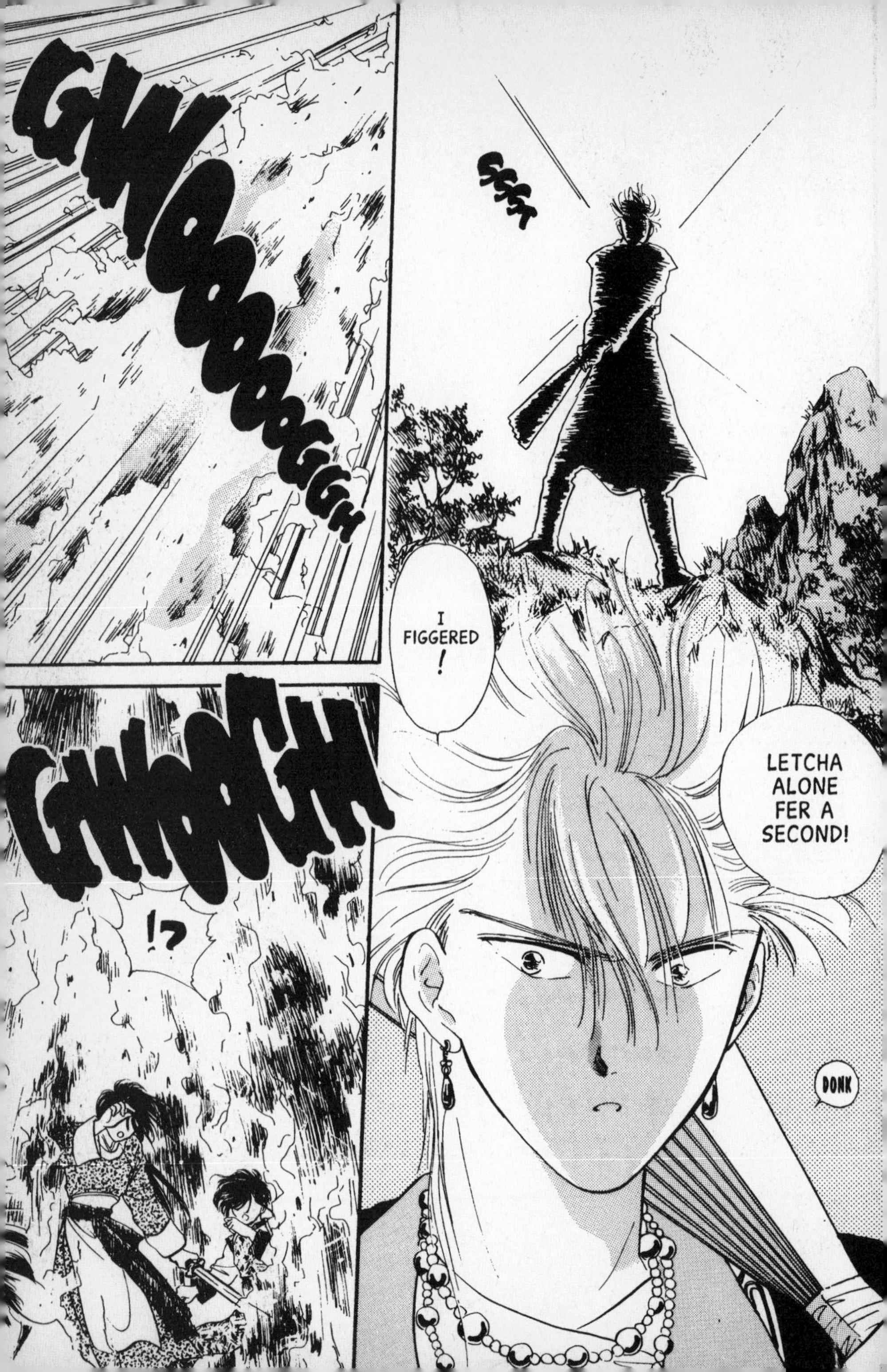
GWOOOOOOOGH
GWOOGH
!?
SSST
I FIGGERED!
LETCHA ALONE FER A SECOND!
DONK

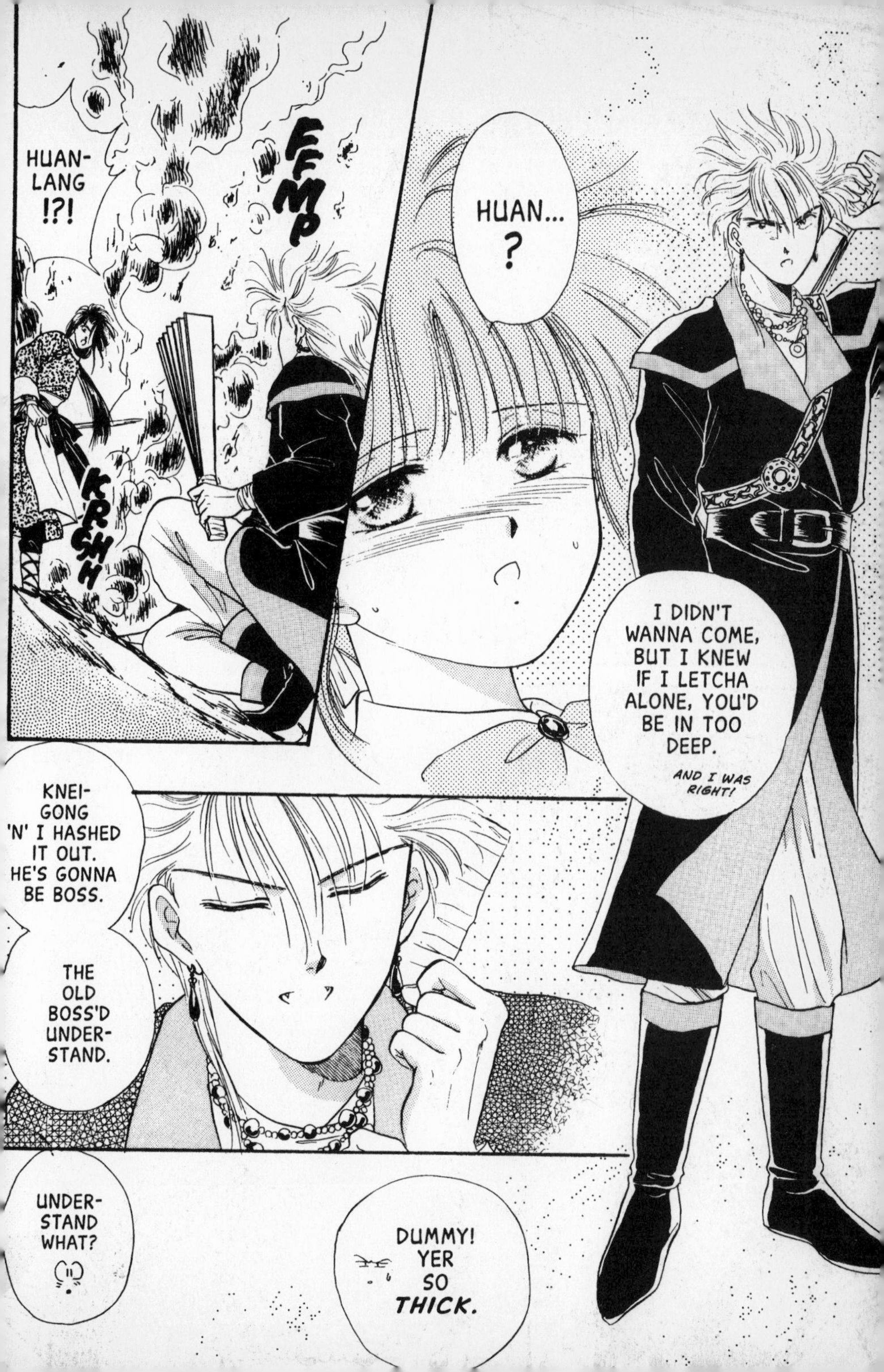
HUAN-LANG !?!
FFMP
KRSHH
HUAN... ?
KNEI-GONG 'N' I HASHED IT OUT. HE'S GONNA BE BOSS.
THE OLD BOSS'D UNDER-STAND.
UNDER-STAND WHAT?
DUMMY! YER SO THICK.
I DIDN'T WANNA COME, BUT I KNEW IF I LETCHA ALONE, YOU'D BE IN TOO DEEP.
AND I WAS RIGHT!

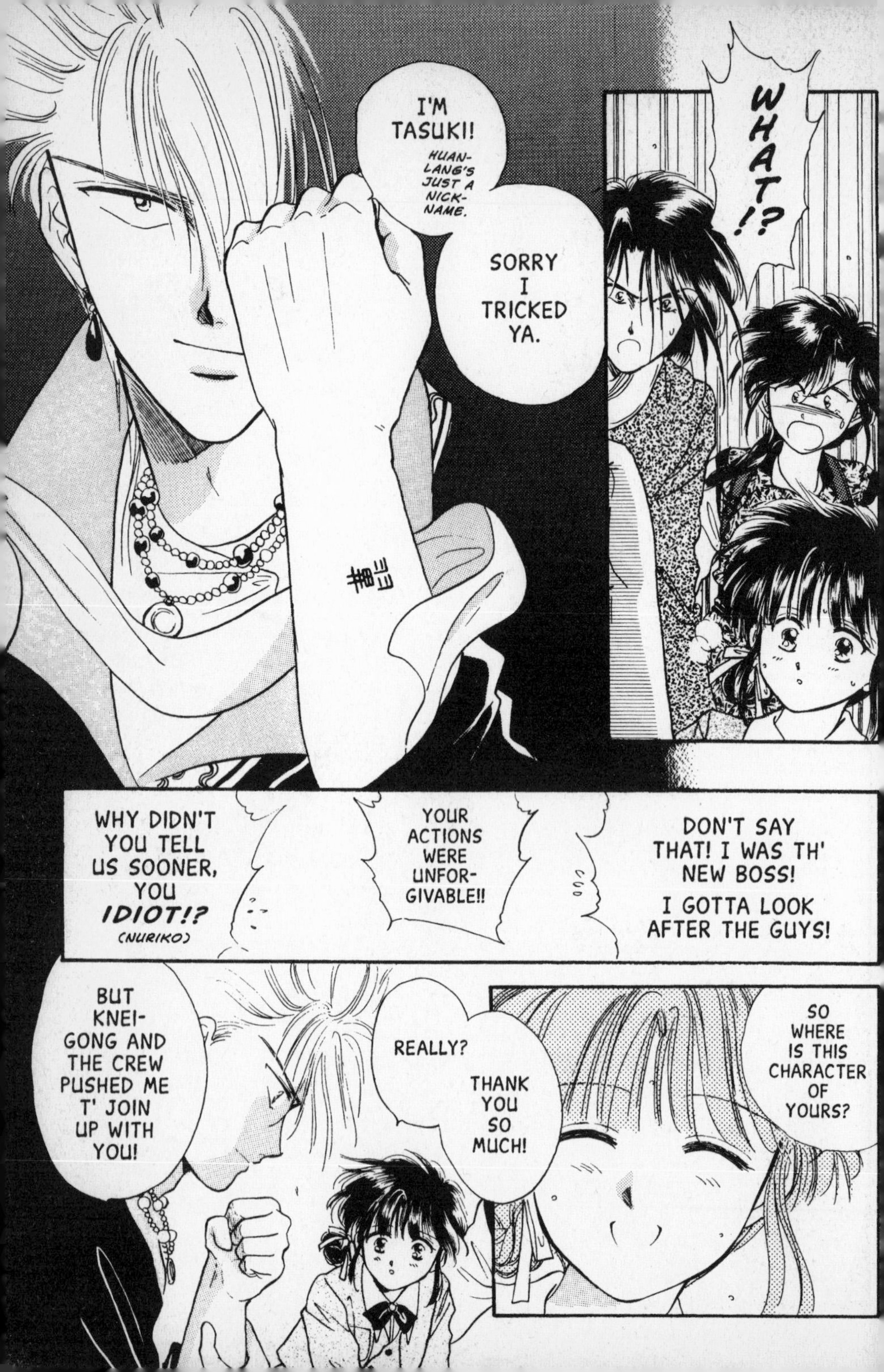
I'M TASUKI!
HUAN-LANG'S JUST A NICK-NAME.
SORRY I TRICKED YA.
WHAT!?
WHY DIDN'T YOU TELL US SOONER, YOU IDIOT!?
(NURIKO)
YOUR ACTIONS WERE UNFORGIVABLE!!
DON'T SAY THAT! I WAS TH' NEW BOSS!
I GOTTA LOOK AFTER THE GUYS!
BUT KNEI-GONG AND THE CREW PUSHED ME T' JOIN UP WITH YOU!
REALLY?
THANK YOU SO MUCH!
SO WHERE IS THIS CHARACTER OF YOURS?

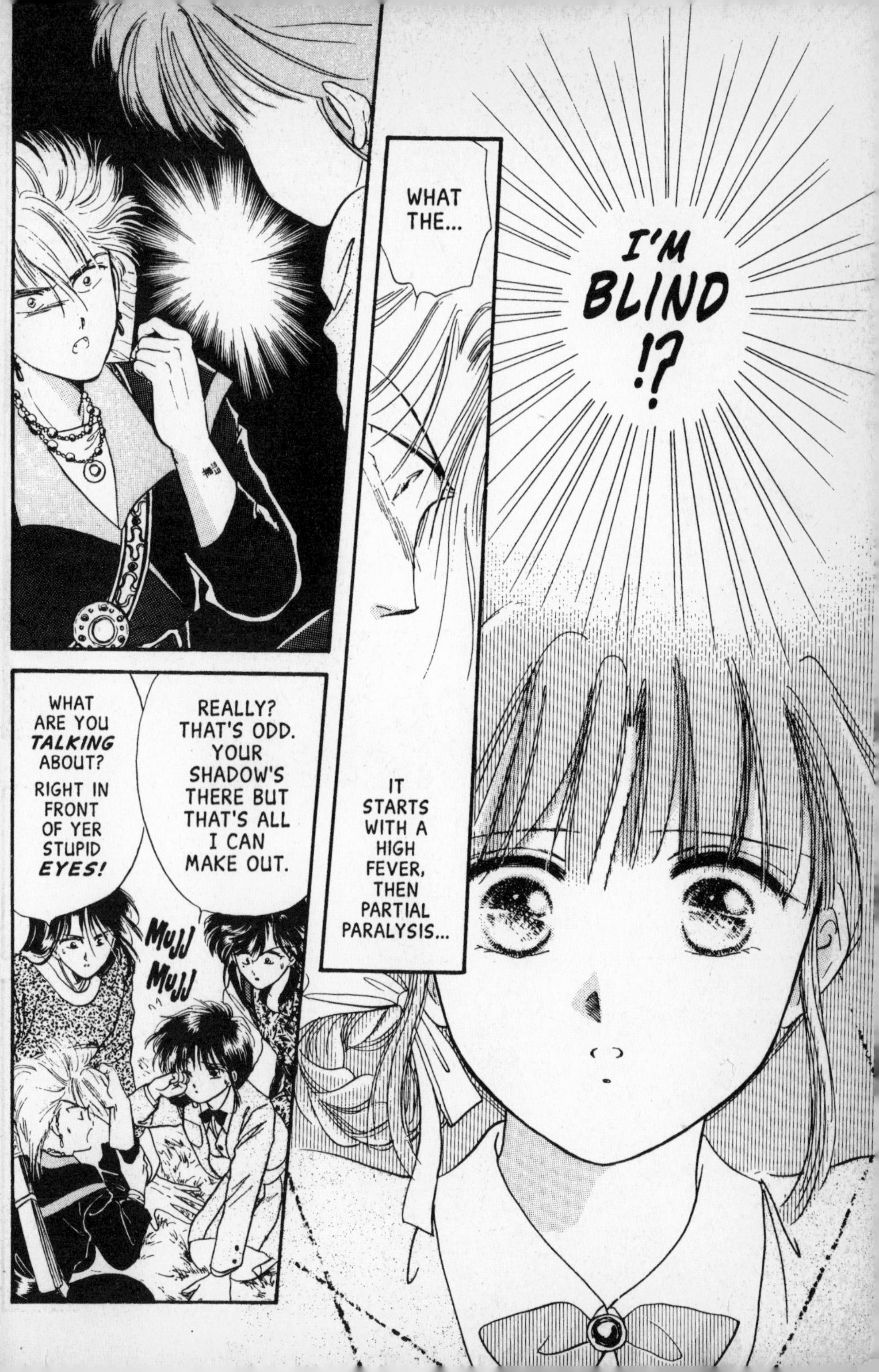
WHAT ARE YOU *TALKING* ABOUT? RIGHT IN FRONT OF YER STUPID *EYES!*
REALLY? THAT'S ODD. YOUR SHADOW'S THERE BUT THAT'S ALL I CAN MAKE OUT.
MUJJ MUJJ
WHAT THE...
I'M BLIND!?
IT STARTS WITH A HIGH FEVER, THEN PARTIAL PARALYSIS...

TASUKI

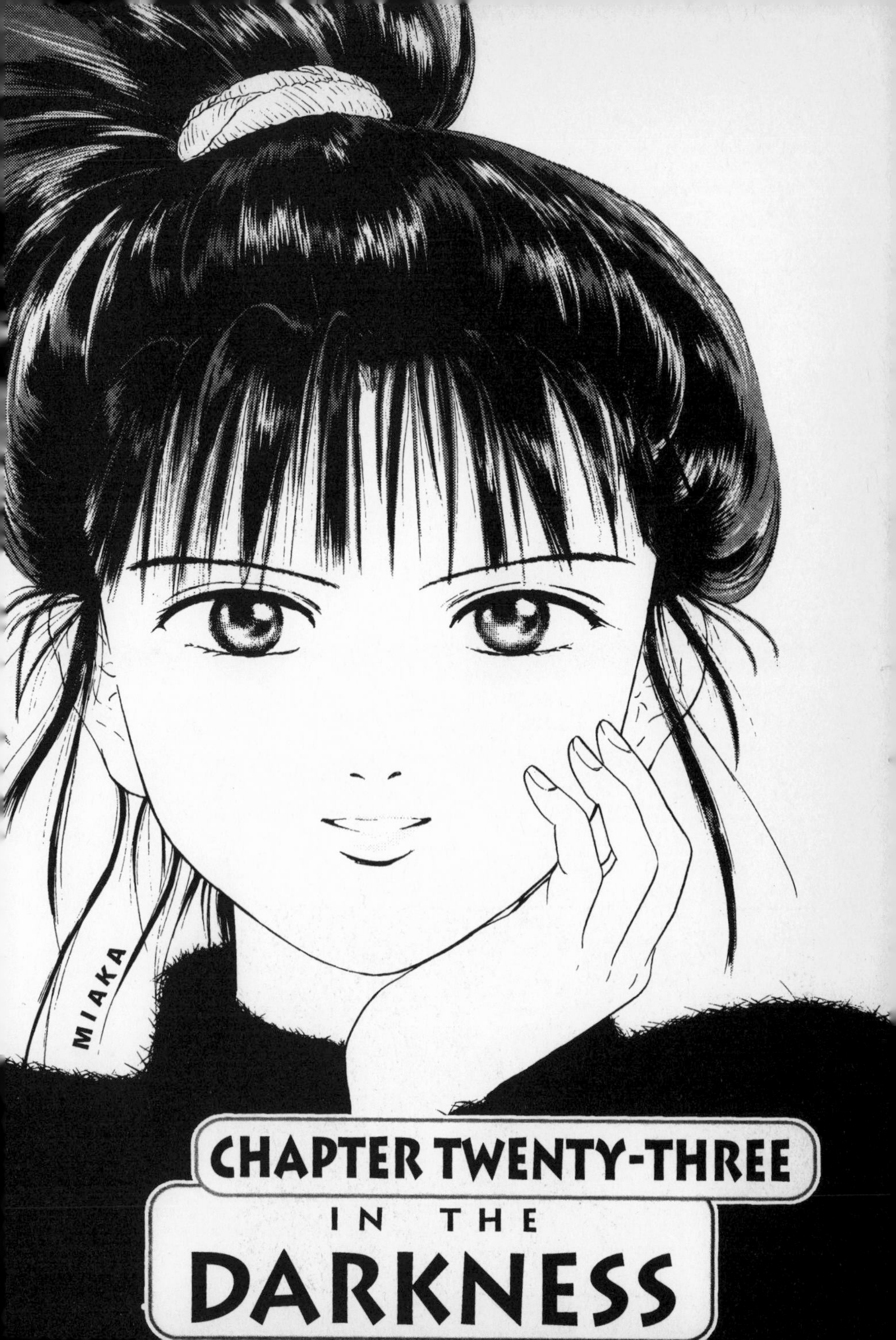
MIAKA
CHAPTER TWENTY-THREE
IN THE
DARKNESS

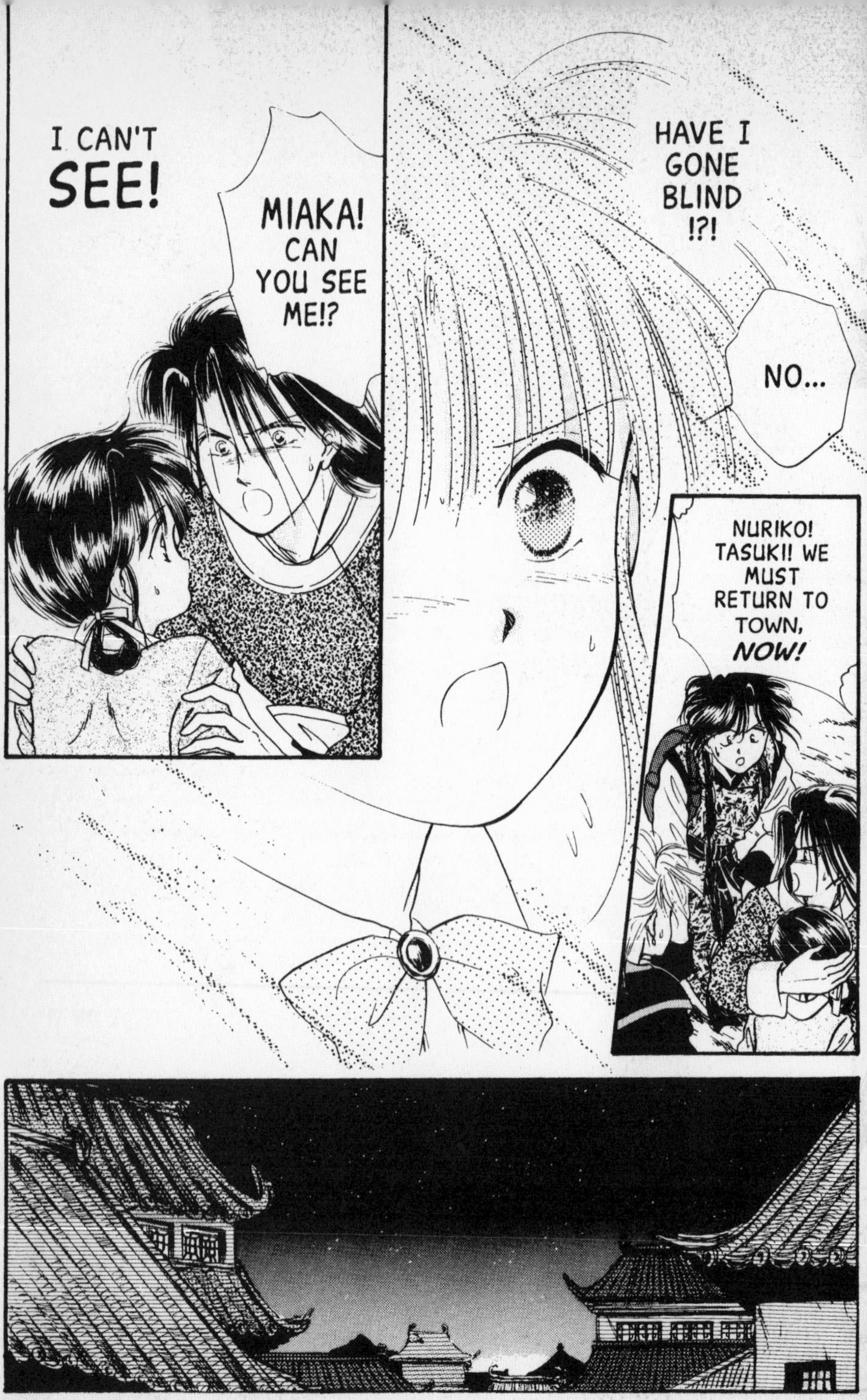
I CAN'T SEE!
MIAKA! CAN YOU SEE ME!?
HAVE I GONE BLIND !?!
NO...
NURIKO! TASUKI!! WE MUST RETURN TO TOWN, NOW!

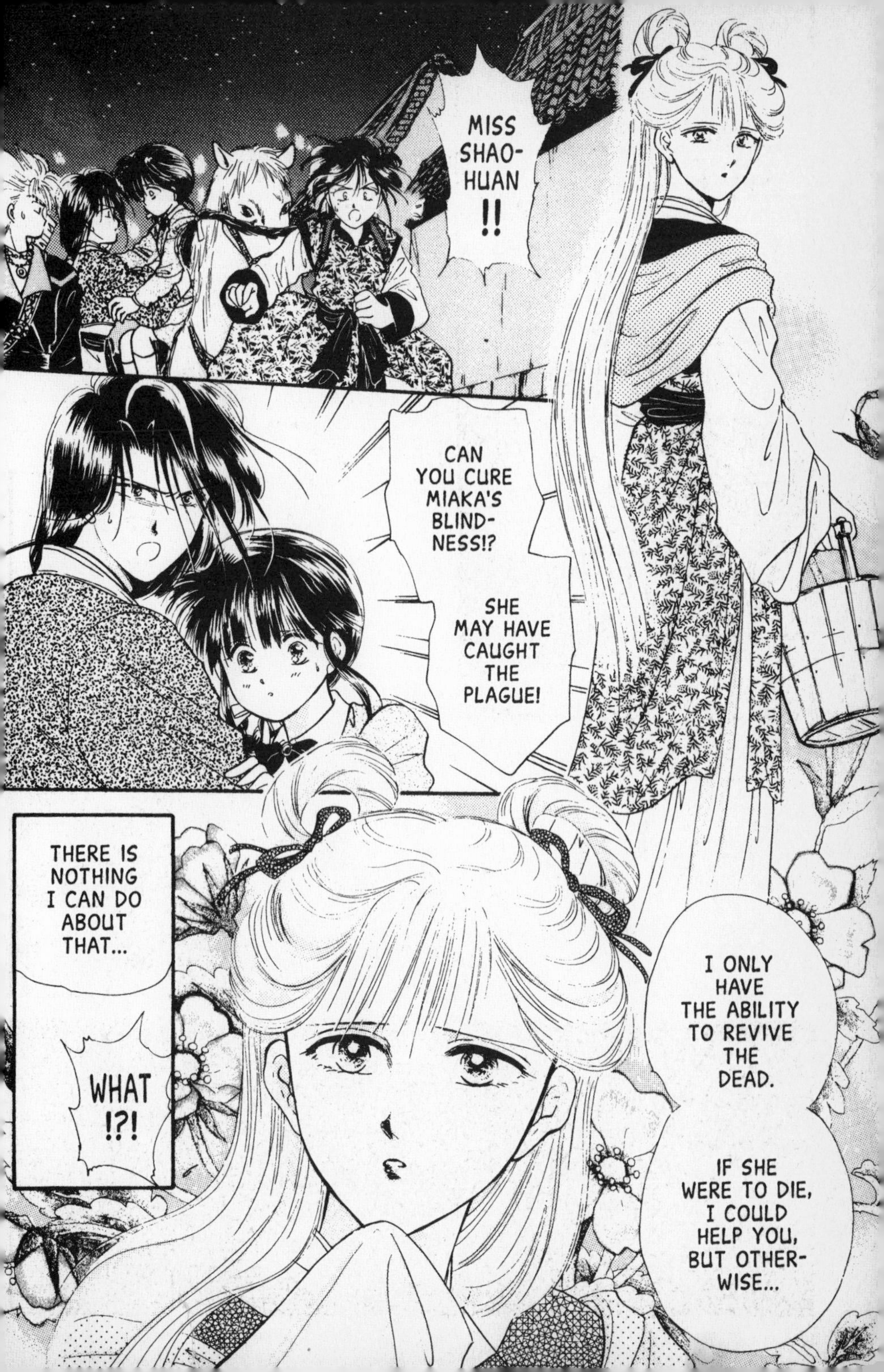
MISS SHAO-HUAN !!
CAN YOU CURE MIAKA'S BLIND-NESS!?
SHE MAY HAVE CAUGHT THE PLAGUE!
THERE IS NOTHING I CAN DO ABOUT THAT...
WHAT !?!
I ONLY HAVE THE ABILITY TO REVIVE THE DEAD.
IF SHE WERE TO DIE, I COULD HELP YOU, BUT OTHER-WISE...

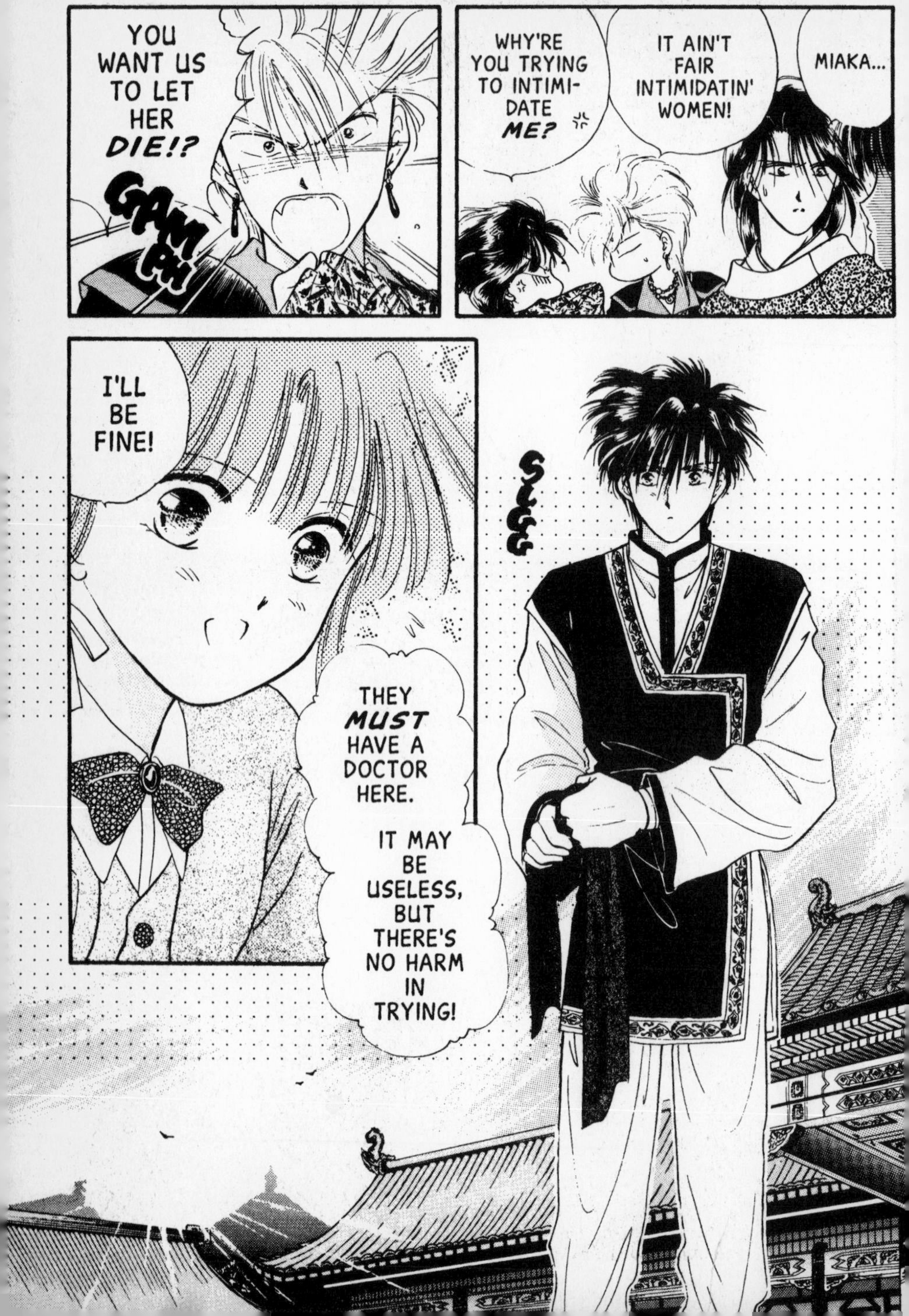
YOU WANT US TO LET HER *DIE!?*
GAMPH
WHY'RE YOU TRYING TO INTIMI-DATE *ME?*
IT AIN'T FAIR INTIMIDATIN' WOMEN!
MIAKA...
I'LL BE FINE!
THEY *MUST* HAVE A DOCTOR HERE.
IT MAY BE USELESS, BUT THERE'S NO HARM IN TRYING!
SIGG

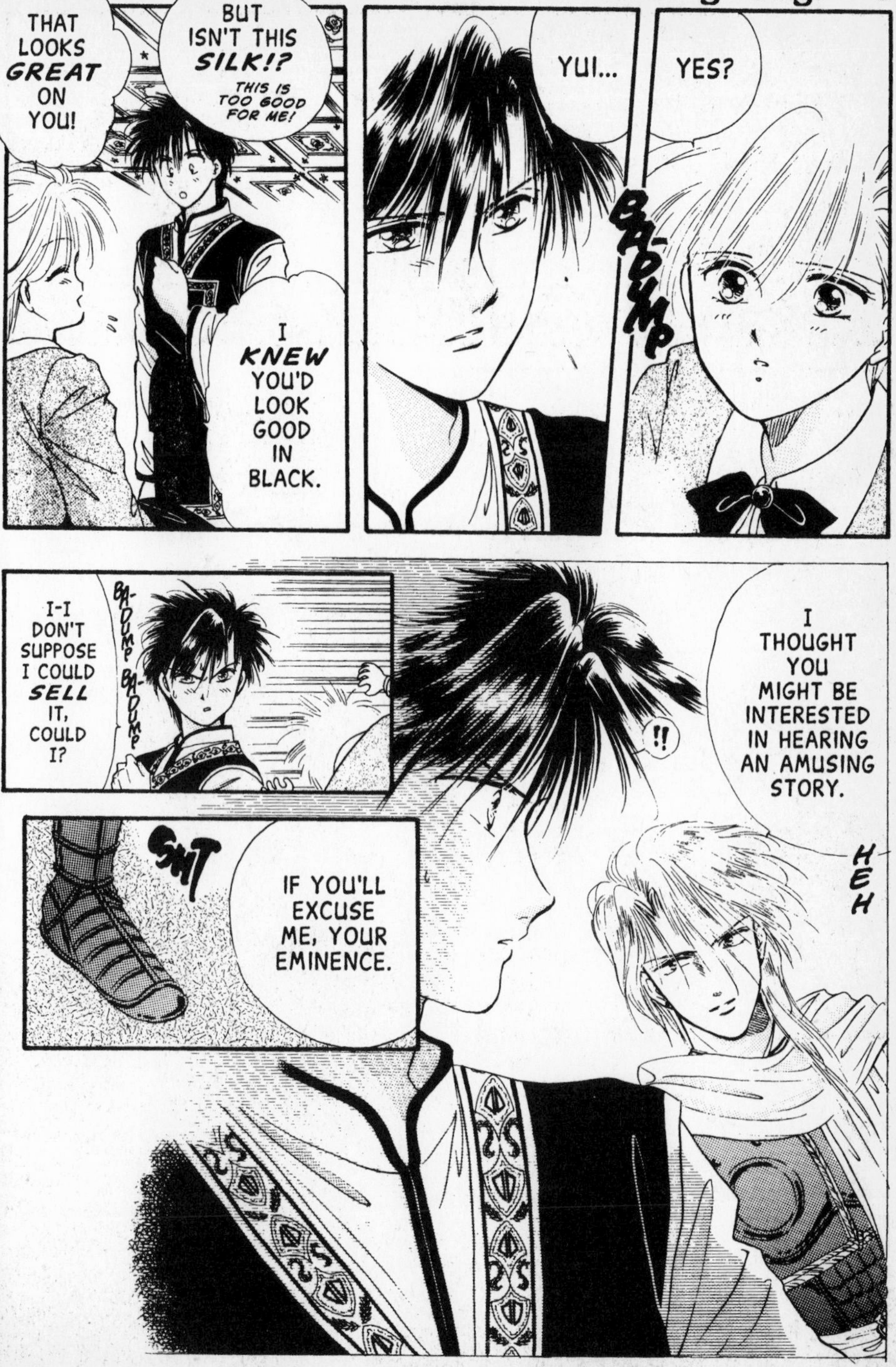
THAT LOOKS GREAT ON YOU!
BUT ISN'T THIS SILK!?
THIS IS TOO GOOD FOR ME!
I KNEW YOU'D LOOK GOOD IN BLACK.
YUI...
YES?
BA-DUMP
I-I DON'T SUPPOSE I COULD SELL IT, COULD I?
BA-DUMP BA-DUMP
SHT
IF YOU'LL EXCUSE ME, YOUR EMINENCE.
I THOUGHT YOU MIGHT BE INTERESTED IN HEARING AN AMUSING STORY.
!!
HEH

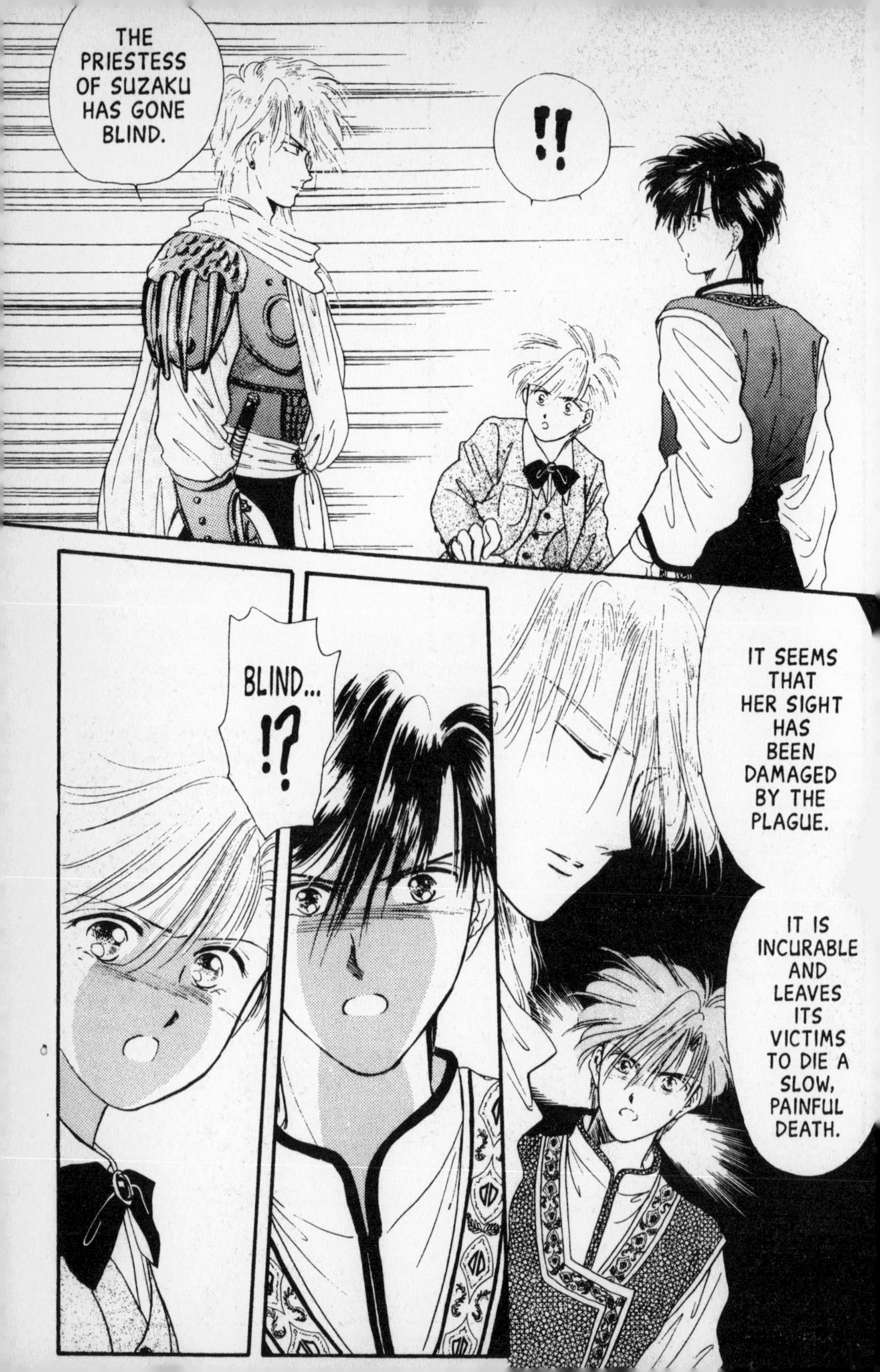
THE PRIESTESS OF SUZAKU HAS GONE BLIND.
!!
BLIND... !?
IT SEEMS THAT HER SIGHT HAS BEEN DAMAGED BY THE PLAGUE.
IT IS INCURABLE AND LEAVES ITS VICTIMS TO DIE A SLOW, PAINFUL DEATH.

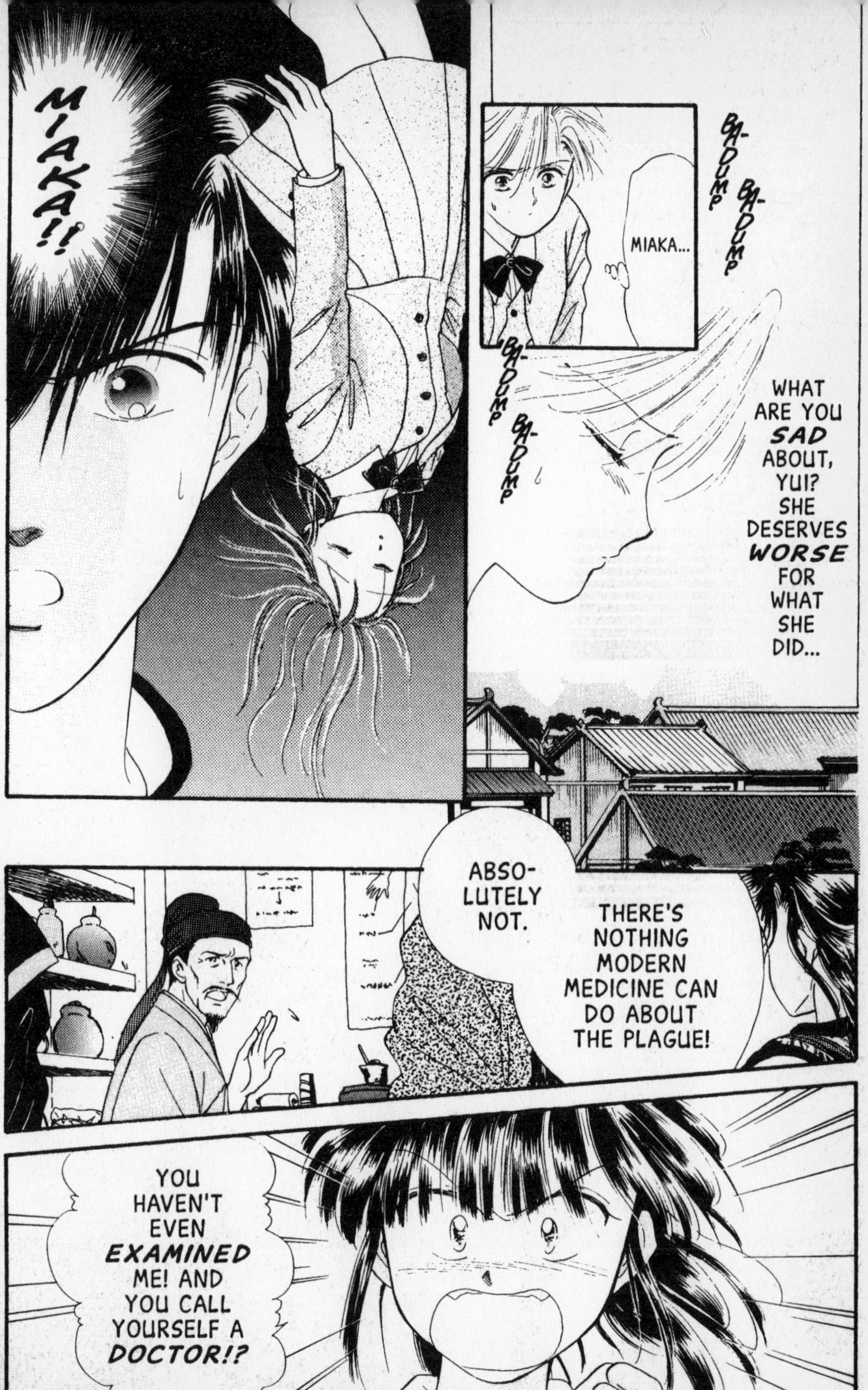
MIAKA!!
BA-DUMP BA-DUMP
MIAKA...
BA-DUMP BA-DUMP
WHAT ARE YOU *SAD* ABOUT, YUI? SHE DESERVES *WORSE* FOR WHAT SHE DID...
ABSO-LUTELY NOT.
THERE'S NOTHING MODERN MEDICINE CAN DO ABOUT THE PLAGUE!
YOU HAVEN'T EVEN *EXAMINED* ME! AND YOU CALL YOURSELF A *DOCTOR!?*

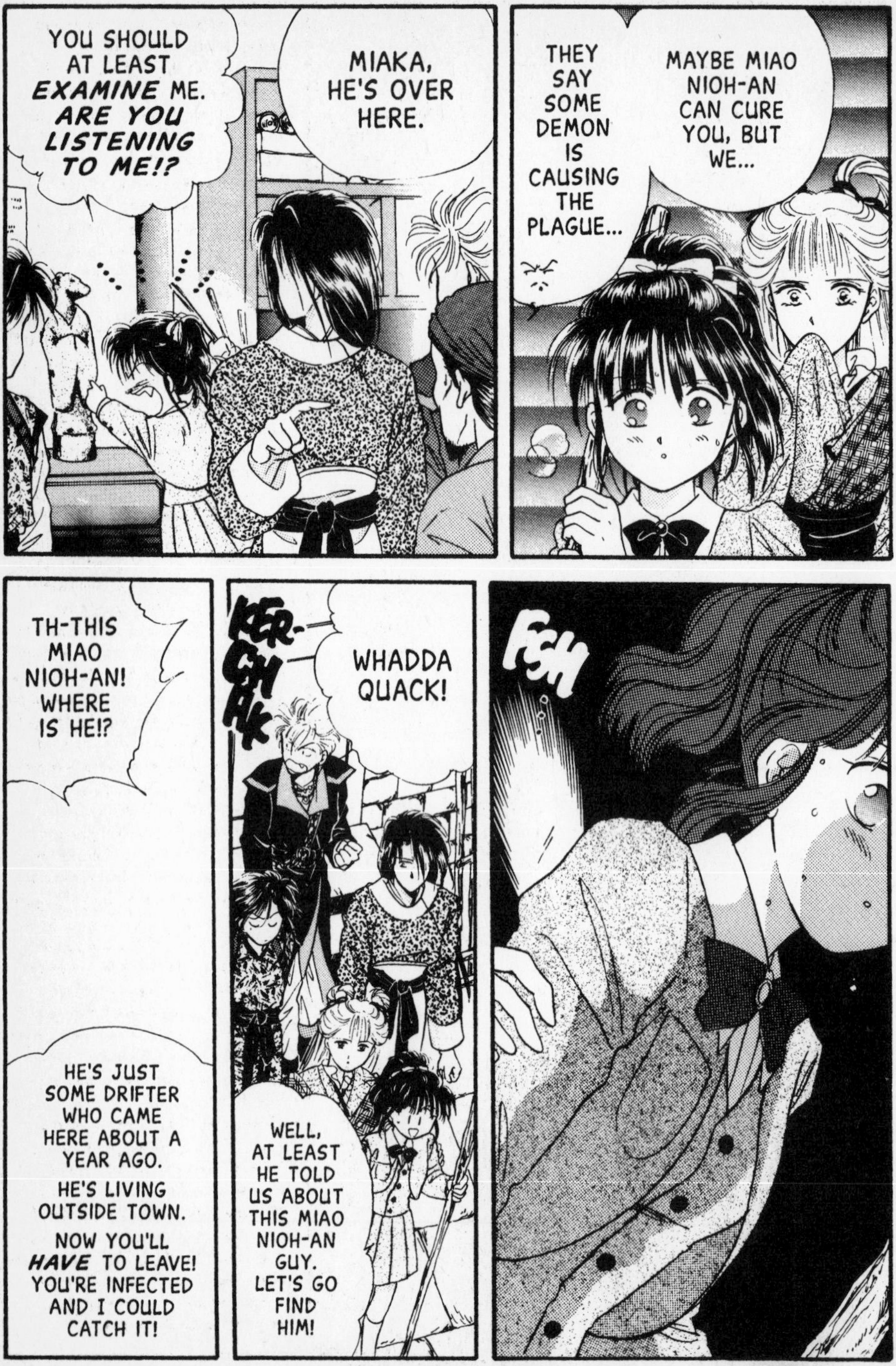
YOU SHOULD AT LEAST *EXAMINE* ME. ***ARE YOU LISTENING TO ME!?***
MIAKA, HE'S OVER HERE.
THEY SAY SOME DEMON IS CAUSING THE PLAGUE...
MAYBE MIAO NIOH-AN CAN CURE YOU, BUT WE...
TH-THIS MIAO NIOH-AN! WHERE IS HE!?
HE'S JUST SOME DRIFTER WHO CAME HERE ABOUT A YEAR AGO.
HE'S LIVING OUTSIDE TOWN.
NOW YOU'LL ***HAVE*** TO LEAVE! YOU'RE INFECTED AND I COULD CATCH IT!
KER-CHAK
WHADDA QUACK!
WELL, AT LEAST HE TOLD US ABOUT THIS MIAO NIOH-AN GUY. LET'S GO FIND HIM!
FSH

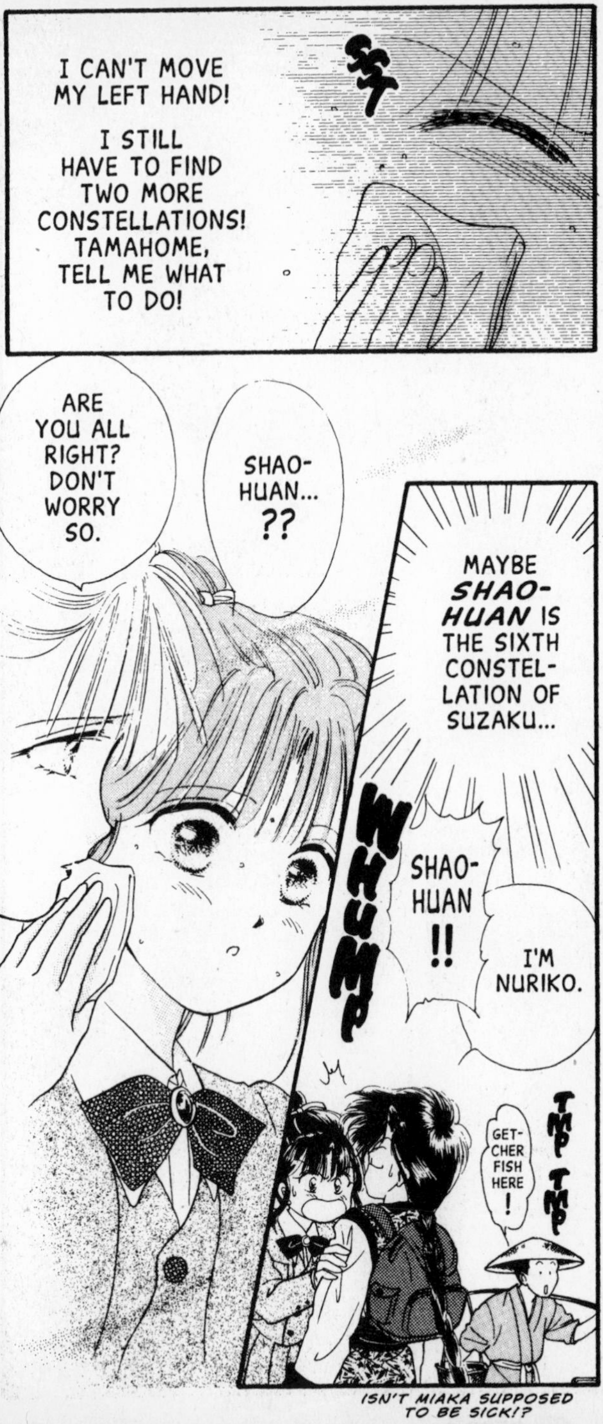
I CAN'T MOVE MY LEFT HAND!
I STILL HAVE TO FIND TWO MORE CONSTELLATIONS! TAMAHOME, TELL ME WHAT TO DO!
ARE YOU ALL RIGHT? DON'T WORRY SO.
SHAO-HUAN... ??
MAYBE *SHAO-HUAN* IS THE SIXTH CONSTELLATION OF SUZAKU...
WHUMP
SHAO-HUAN !!
I'M NURIKO.
GET-CHER FISH HERE !
TMP TMP

ISN'T MIAKA SUPPOSED TO BE SICK!?

Bandit

So... Twin Peaks is about to begin! Today is Saturday. Shogakukan's editorial offices should be closed. So why do I get a call from my editor!? Comic editors work on the weekend. Let's applaud all their hard work. Now then, lately I haven't found any interesting TV shows so I've been watching Sekai Fushigi Hakken ("Strange Discoveries!") and The Wonder Zone, as well as Terebi Tokusōbu ("Special Investigation TV"). Beat Takeshi is the best! Bokutachi no Drama Series ("Our Drama Series") and Hōkago ("After School") are just remakes of the masterpiece Tenkōsei ("Transfer Student") so I haven't been watching them, but I have been watching Sono Toki, Heart wa Nusumareta ("That Was When My Heart Was Stolen.") I guess none of this will matter by the time this is printed, but a character in that series really reminds me of Yui. My assistant agrees! She wears a brown school uniform; she has her hair cut short; and she even slashed her wrists. But Yui is purer. There aren't that many brat girls who are that jaded at the age of 15 or 16. *Well, maybe there are.* It's supposed to be a high-school romantic comedy, but there's also this stuff about who slept with whom--it's a bit much. *The youth of today!* Don't they have anything more interesting to think about? Huh? Not very convincing coming from me? Well, I guess I depict my share of kiss scenes, corny men's dialogue and racy scenes... HOLD ON!! I just realized I've dug myself into a hole. I tell you though, art work can be really hard. Now then, how else do I spend my day? I read the Asahi News. *I'm so sophisticated!* Actually, I mostly read the funnies, but I really do read the articles. The mother in Tonari no Yamada-kun ("My Neighbors the Yamadas") reminds me a lot of my mom. They both speak in a Kansai dialect, although my mom's thinner. Their conversations are just like the ones I have with my mom. My mom plays passive, while I'm always the aggressor. Why is it always that way? That's just how folks in the Kansai area are, I guess. Daily conversations are a comedy routine. *That's why I like Tasuki so much!*

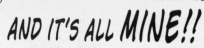

AND IT'S ALL **MINE**!!

TH **WAP**

I KNOW THAT SMELL! **FISH!**

EH?

GA— **FUMP**

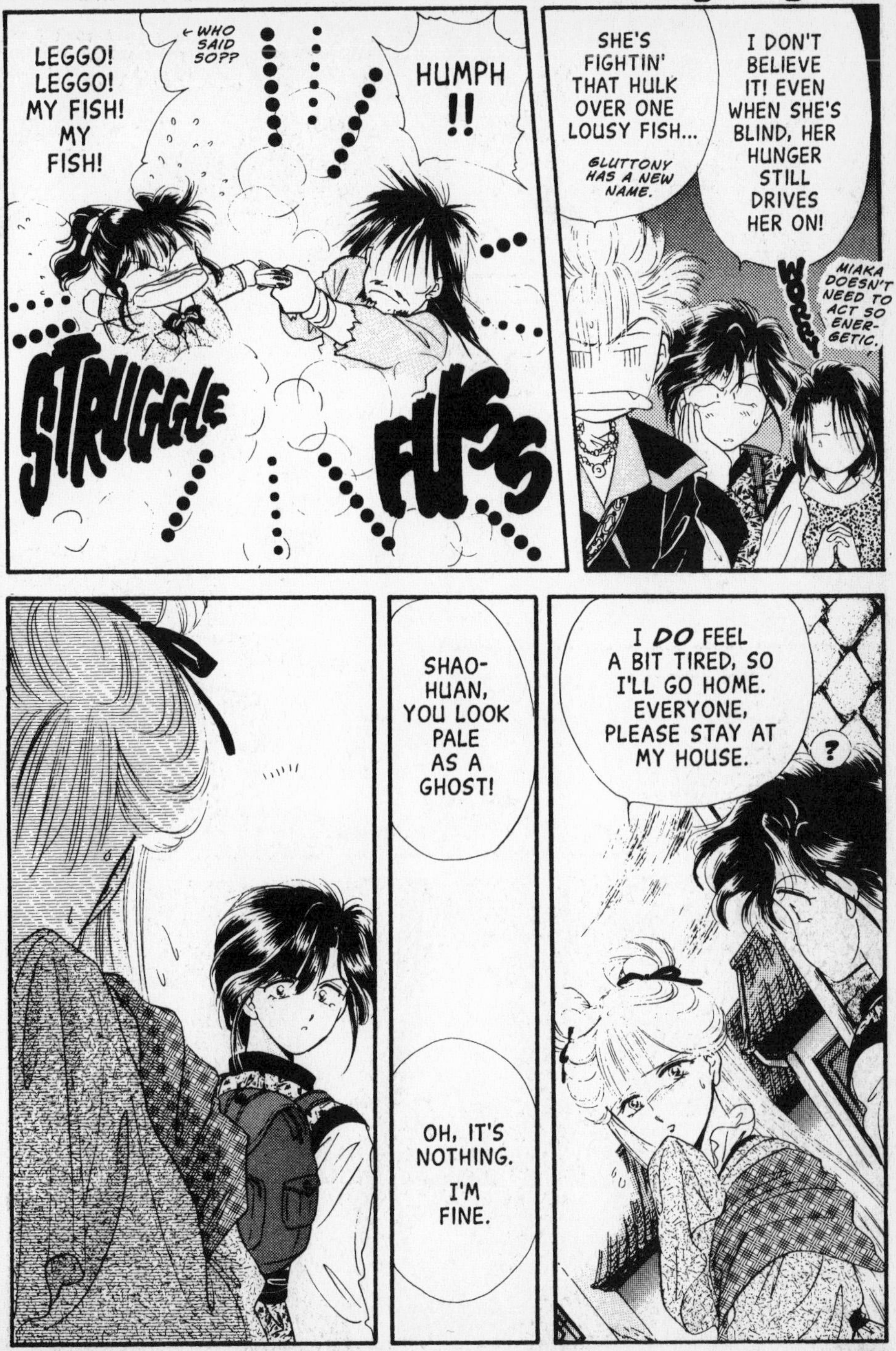
LEGGO! LEGGO! MY FISH! MY FISH!
WHO SAID SO??
HUMPH!!
STRUGGLE
FUSS
SHE'S FIGHTIN' THAT HULK OVER ONE LOUSY FISH...
GLUTTONY HAS A NEW NAME.
I DON'T BELIEVE IT! EVEN WHEN SHE'S BLIND, HER HUNGER STILL DRIVES HER ON!
WORRY
MIAKA DOESN'T NEED TO ACT SO ENERGETIC.
SHAO-HUAN, YOU LOOK PALE AS A GHOST!
OH, IT'S NOTHING.
I'M FINE.
I DO FEEL A BIT TIRED, SO I'LL GO HOME. EVERYONE, PLEASE STAY AT MY HOUSE.
?

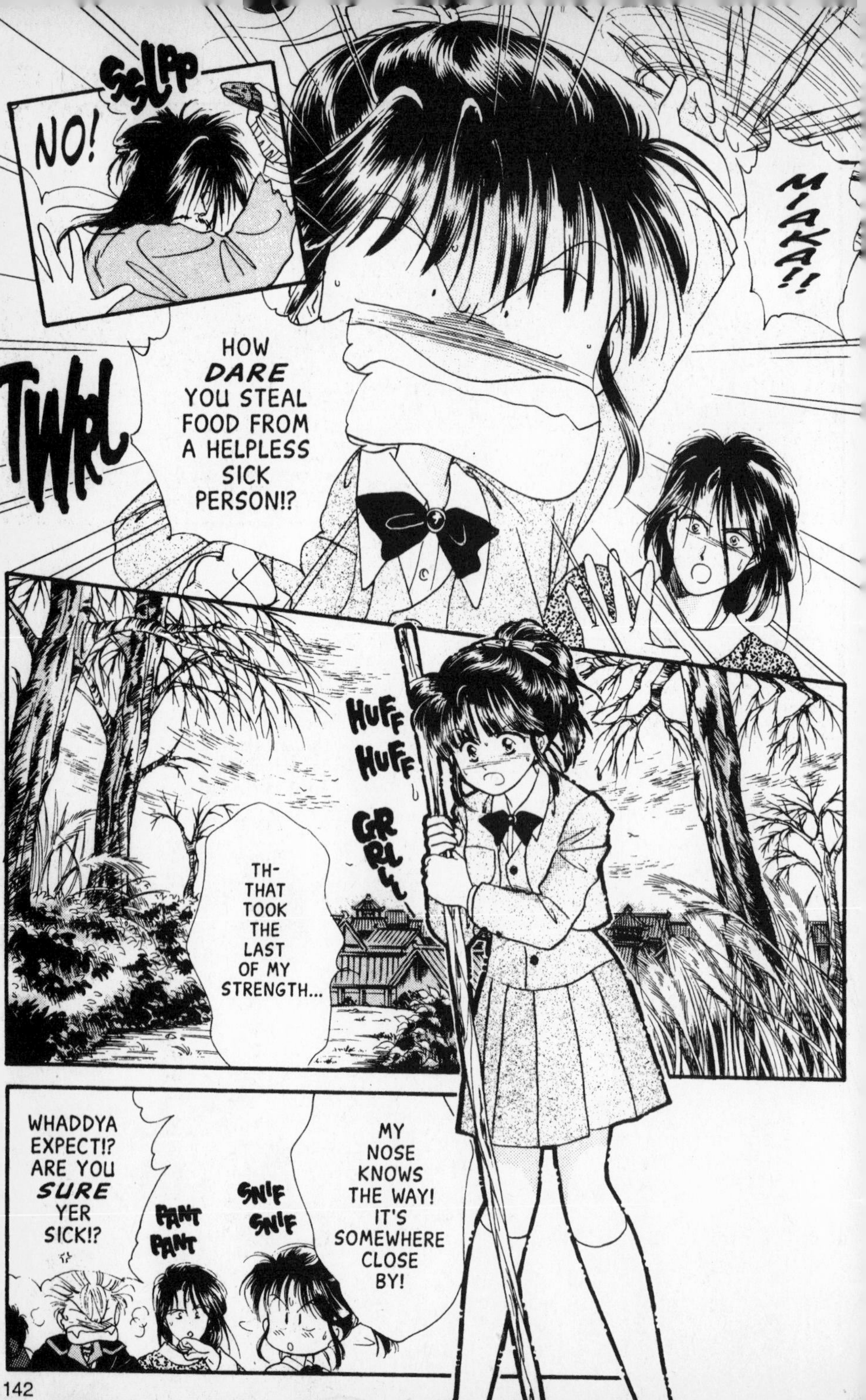
SSSLPP
NO!
MIAKA!!
TWIRL
HOW DARE YOU STEAL FOOD FROM A HELPLESS SICK PERSON!?
HUFF HUFF
GRRLLL
TH-THAT TOOK THE LAST OF MY STRENGTH...
WHADDYA EXPECT!? ARE YOU SURE YER SICK!?
PANT PANT
SNIF SNIF
MY NOSE KNOWS THE WAY! IT'S SOMEWHERE CLOSE BY!

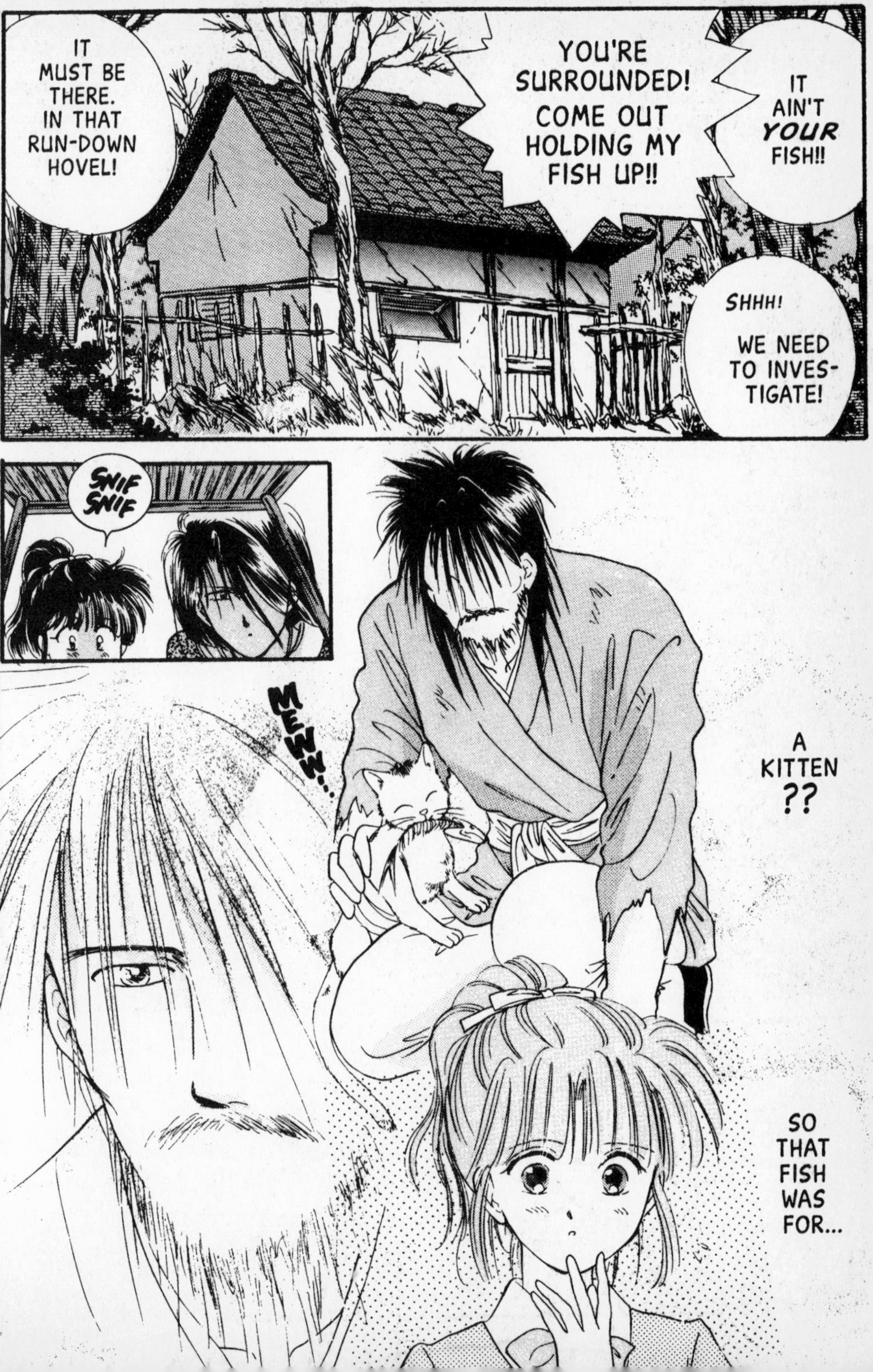
IT MUST BE THERE. IN THAT RUN-DOWN HOVEL!
YOU'RE SURROUNDED! COME OUT HOLDING MY FISH UP!!
IT AIN'T *YOUR* FISH!!
SHHH!
WE NEED TO INVES-TIGATE!
SNIF SNIF
MEWW...
A KITTEN ??
SO THAT FISH WAS FOR...

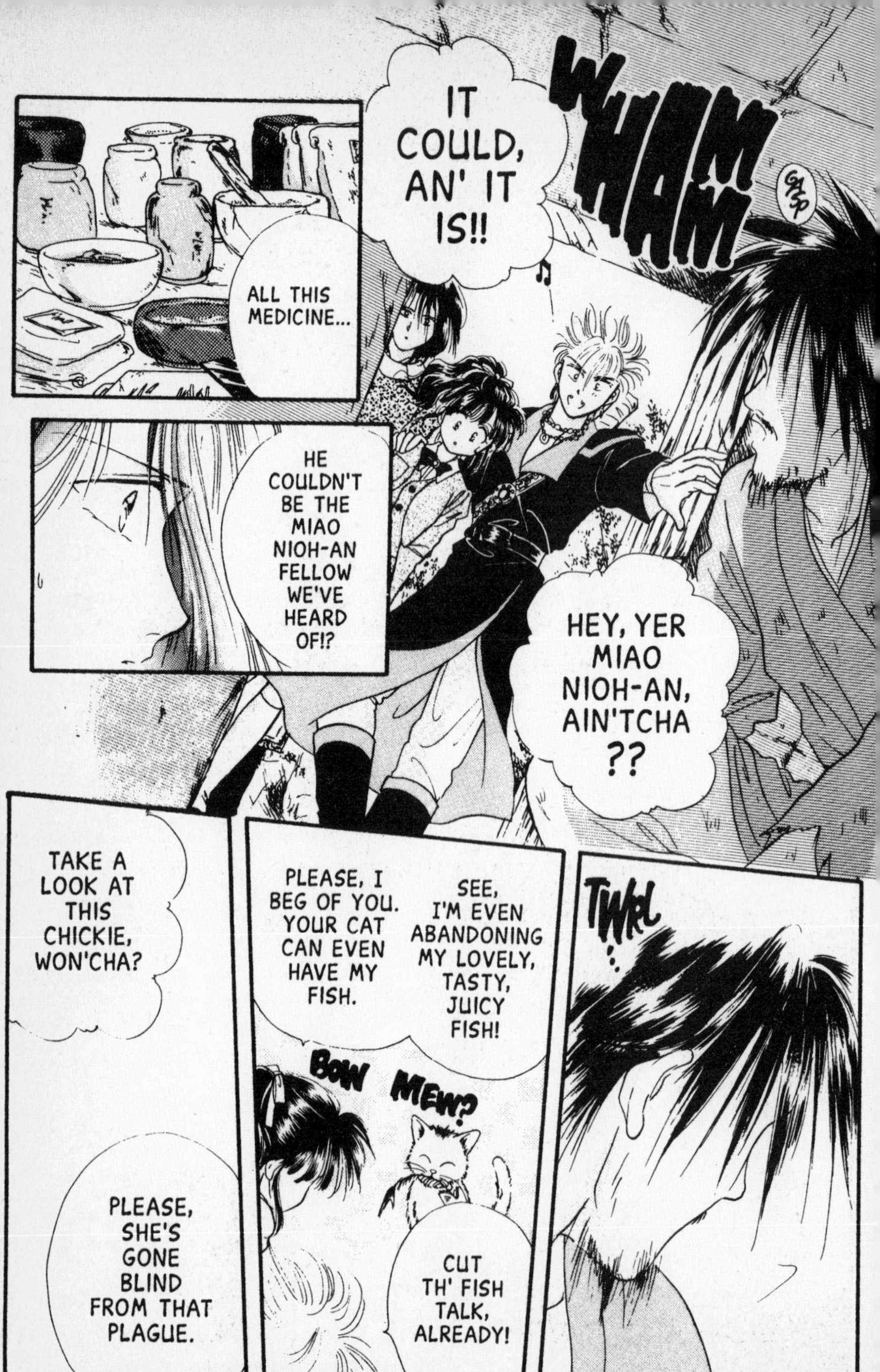
ALL THIS MEDICINE...
HE COULDN'T BE THE MIAO NIOH-AN FELLOW WE'VE HEARD OF!?
IT COULD, AN' IT IS!!
WHAM WHAM
GASP
HEY, YER MIAO NIOH-AN, AIN'TCHA ??
TAKE A LOOK AT THIS CHICKIE, WON'CHA?
PLEASE, SHE'S GONE BLIND FROM THAT PLAGUE.
PLEASE, I BEG OF YOU. YOUR CAT CAN EVEN HAVE MY FISH.
SEE, I'M EVEN ABANDONING MY LOVELY, TASTY, JUICY FISH!
BOW
MEW?
CUT TH' FISH TALK, ALREADY!
TWRL

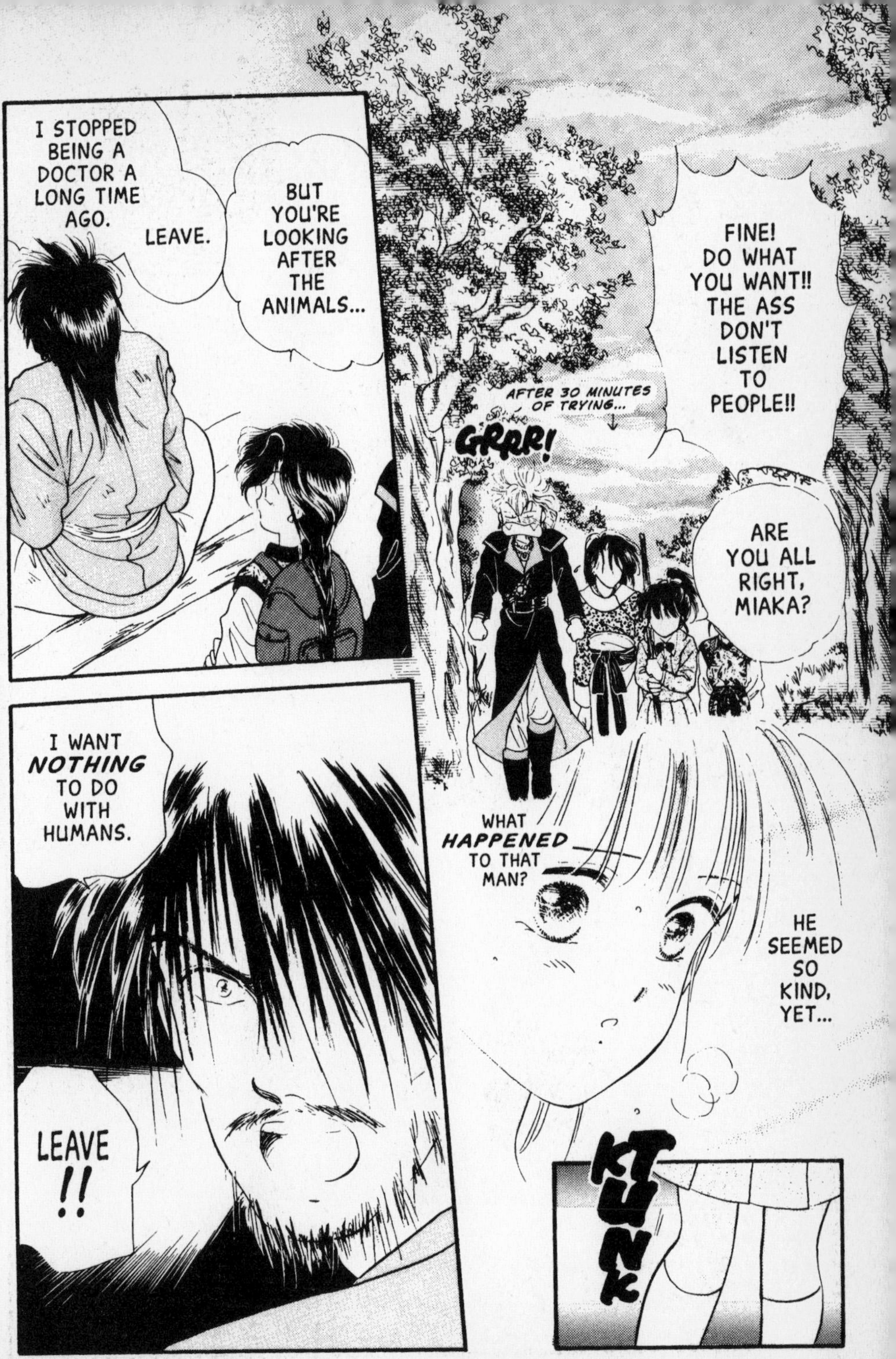
I STOPPED BEING A DOCTOR A LONG TIME AGO.
LEAVE.
BUT YOU'RE LOOKING AFTER THE ANIMALS...
I WANT NOTHING TO DO WITH HUMANS.
LEAVE!!
FINE! DO WHAT YOU WANT!! THE ASS DON'T LISTEN TO PEOPLE!!
AFTER 30 MINUTES OF TRYING...
GRRR!
ARE YOU ALL RIGHT, MIAKA?
WHAT HAPPENED TO THAT MAN?
HE SEEMED SO KIND, YET...
KTUNK

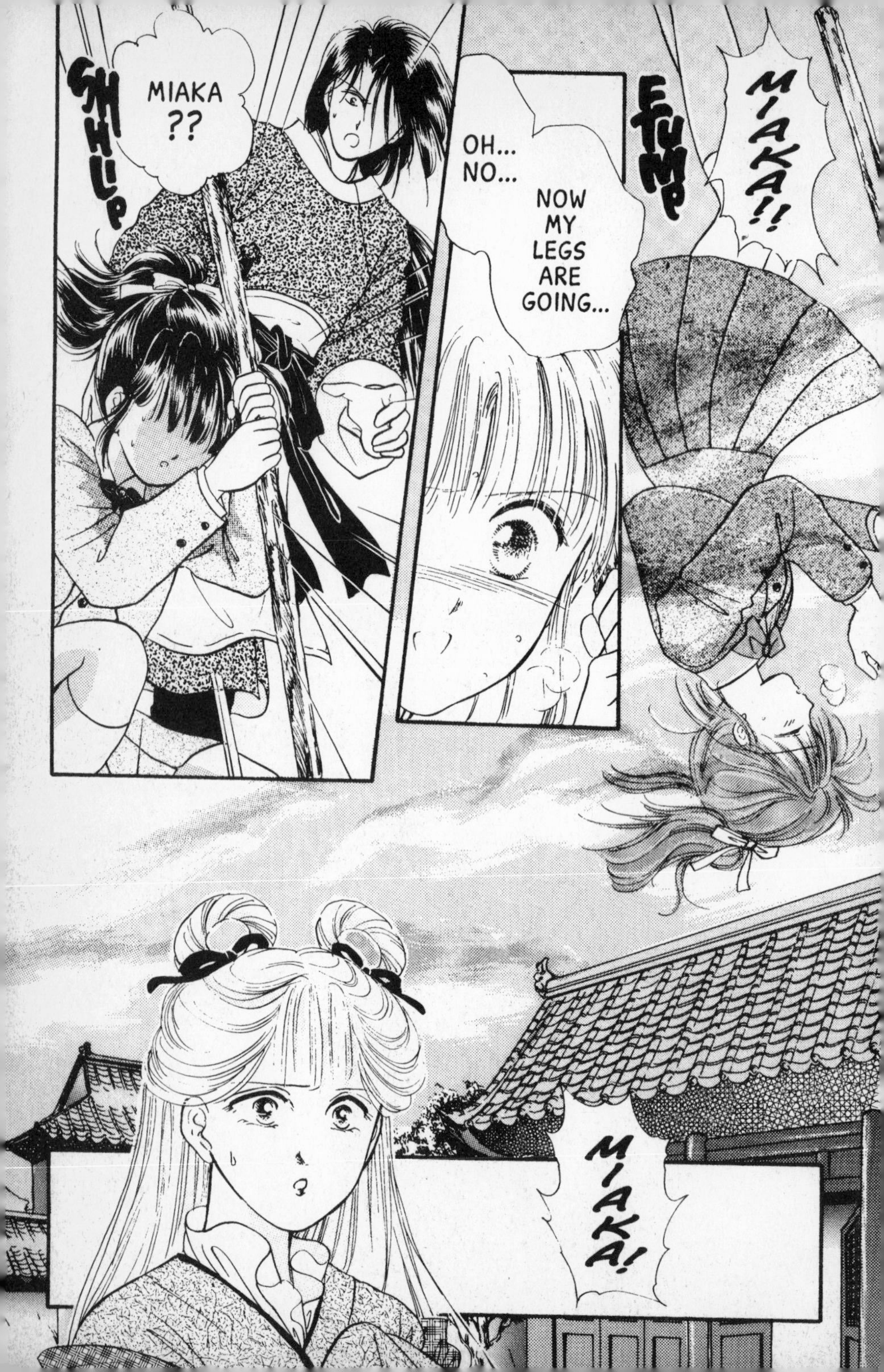
SHHLIP
MIAKA ??
OH... NO...
NOW MY LEGS ARE GOING...
FUMP
MIAKA!!
MIAKA!

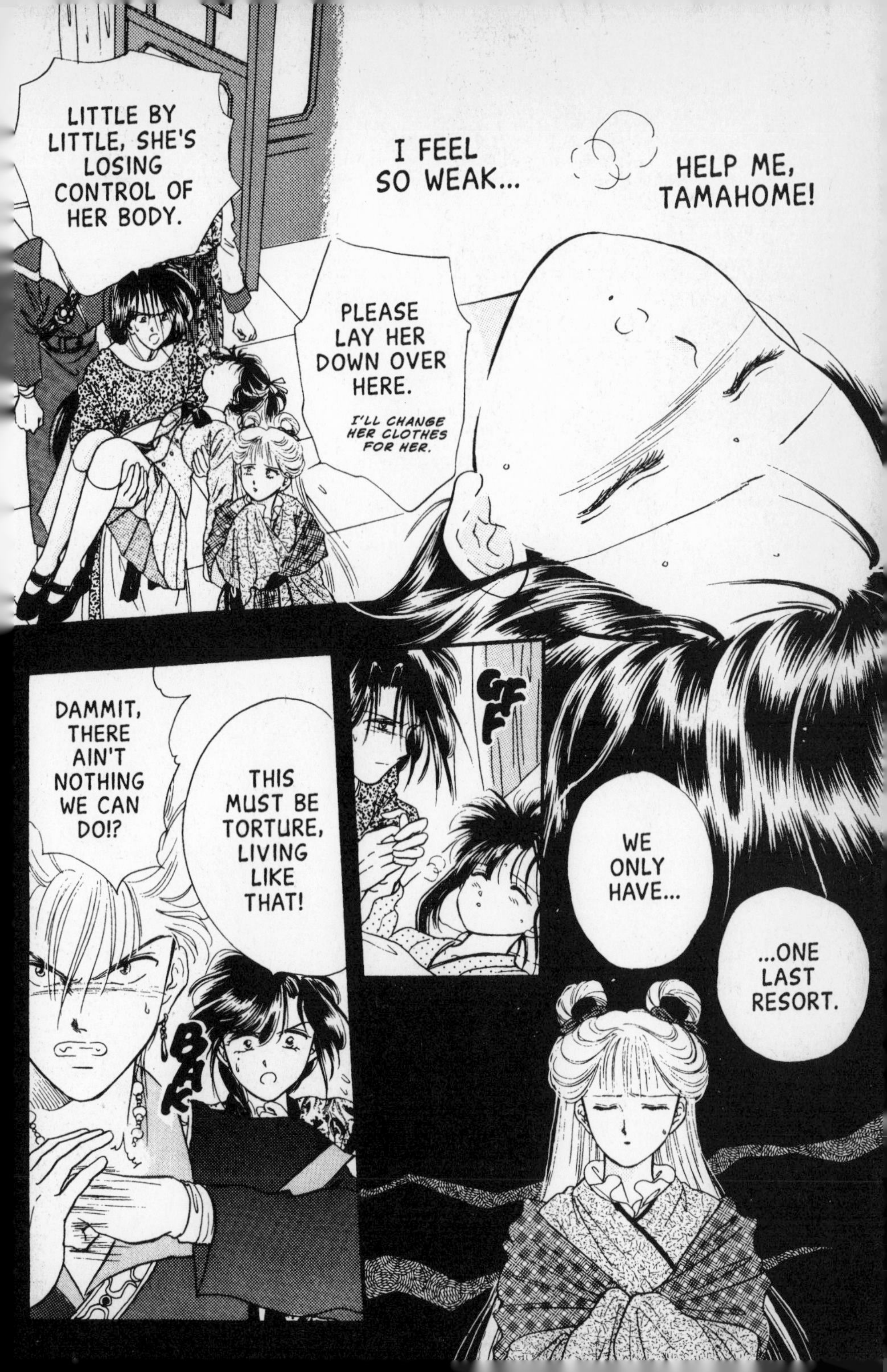
LITTLE BY LITTLE, SHE'S LOSING CONTROL OF HER BODY.
I FEEL SO WEAK...
HELP ME, TAMAHOME!
PLEASE LAY HER DOWN OVER HERE.
I'LL CHANGE HER CLOTHES FOR HER.
DAMMIT, THERE AIN'T NOTHING WE CAN DO!?
THIS MUST BE TORTURE, LIVING LIKE THAT!
BAK
GFF
WE ONLY HAVE...
...ONE LAST RESORT.

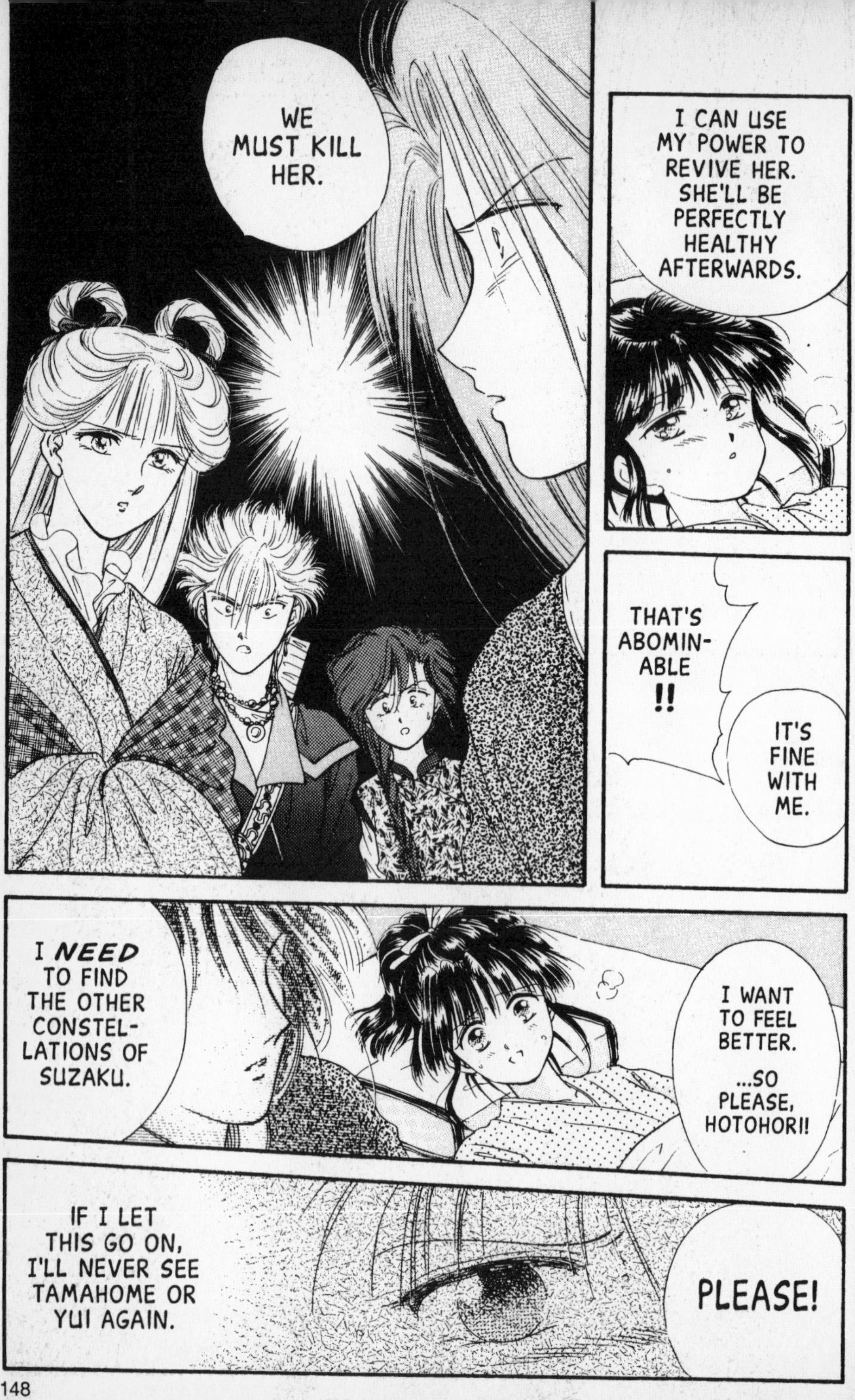
WE MUST KILL HER.
I CAN USE MY POWER TO REVIVE HER. SHE'LL BE PERFECTLY HEALTHY AFTERWARDS.
THAT'S ABOMIN-ABLE!!
IT'S FINE WITH ME.
I *NEED* TO FIND THE OTHER CONSTEL-LATIONS OF SUZAKU.
I WANT TO FEEL BETTER.
...SO PLEASE, HOTOHORI!!
IF I LET THIS GO ON, I'LL NEVER SEE TAMAHOME OR YUI AGAIN.
PLEASE!

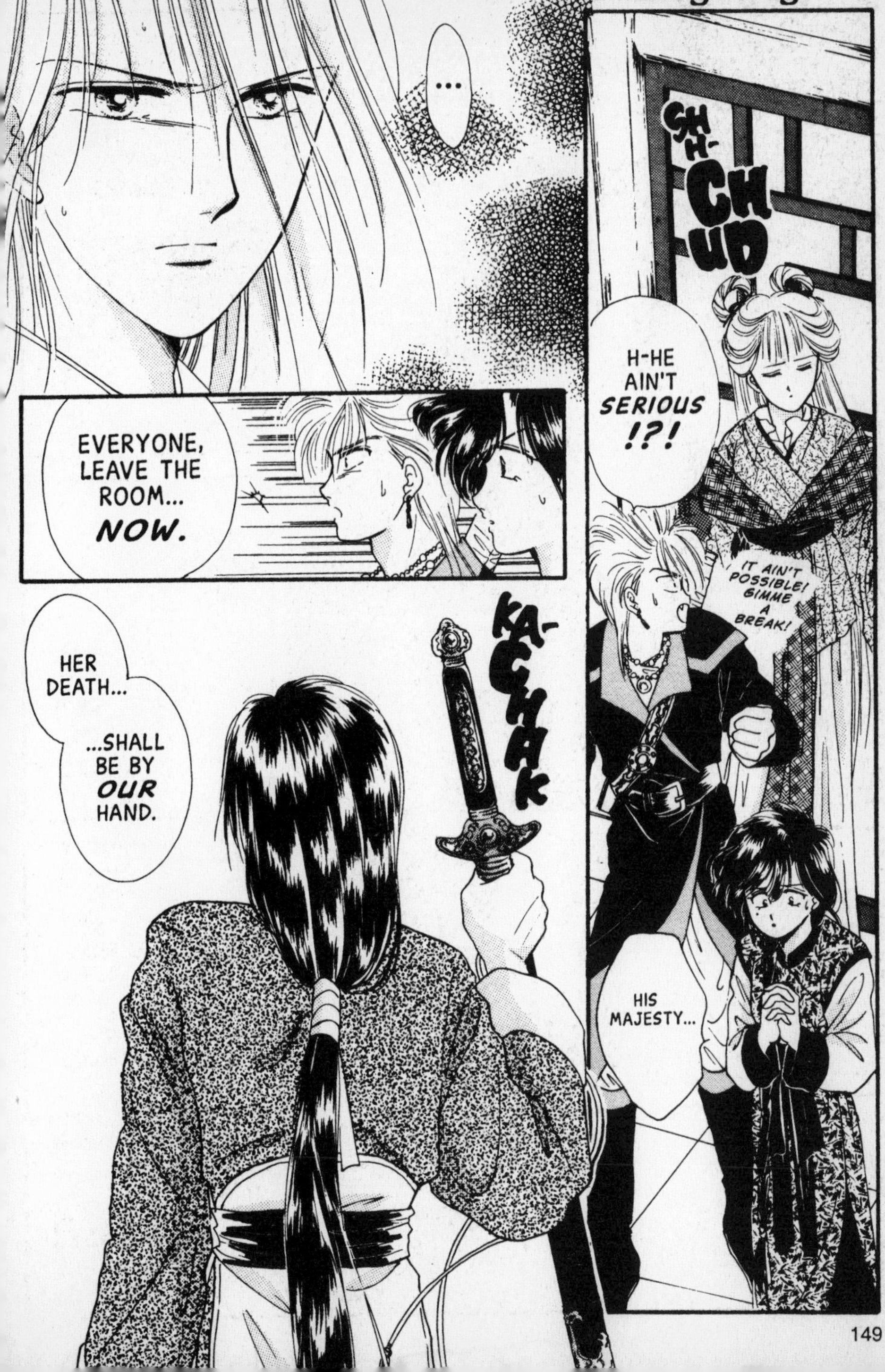
...
EVERYONE, LEAVE THE ROOM... NOW.
HER DEATH...
...SHALL BE BY OUR HAND.
KA-CHAK
SHH-CHUD
H-HE AIN'T SERIOUS !?!
IT AIN'T POSSIBLE! GIMME A BREAK!
HIS MAJESTY...

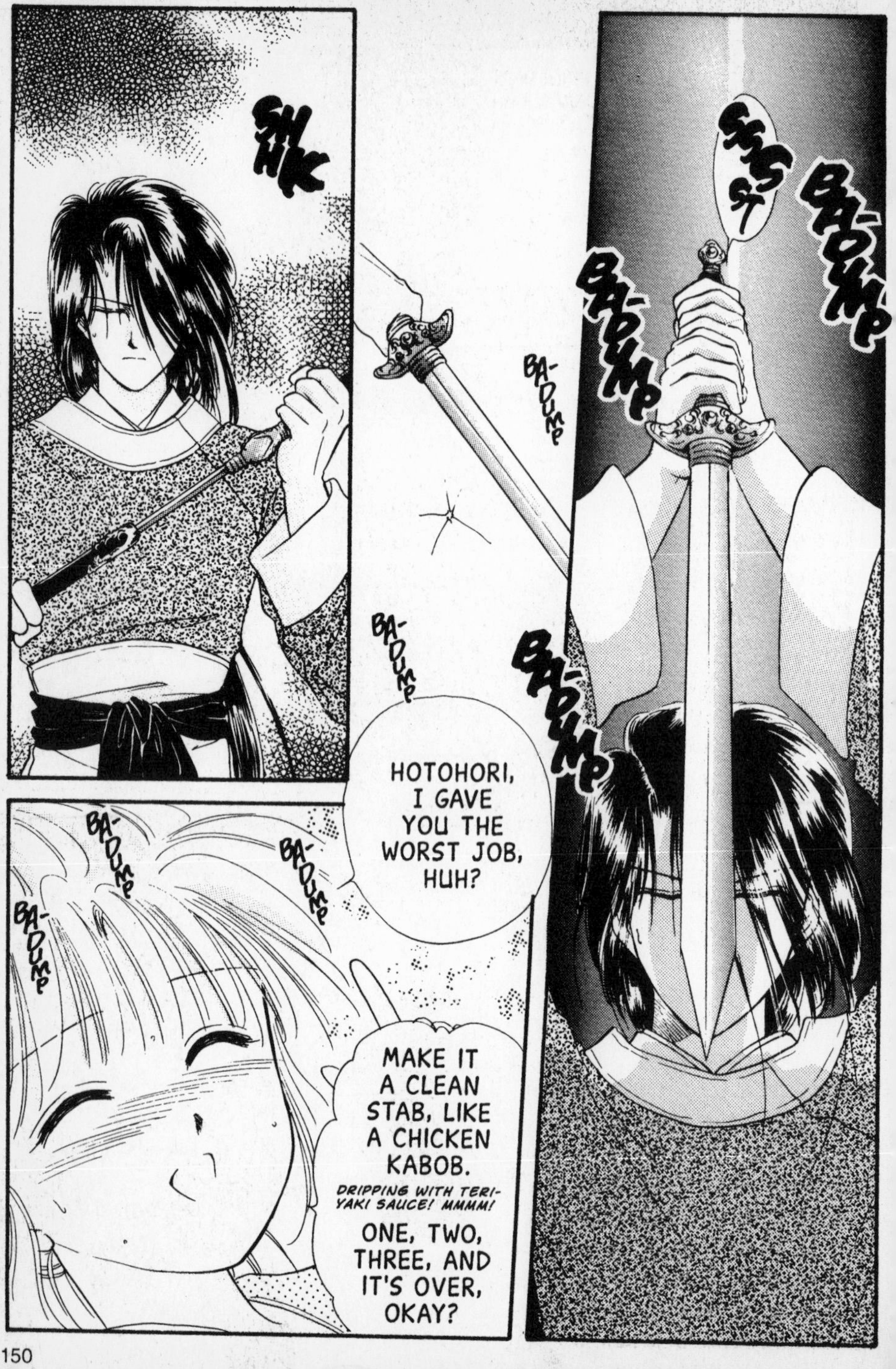
SHHK
BA-DUMP
BA-DUMP
HOTOHORI, I GAVE YOU THE WORST JOB, HUH?
BA-DUMP
BA-DUMP
BA-DUMP
MAKE IT A CLEAN STAB, LIKE A CHICKEN KABOB.
DRIPPING WITH TERI-YAKI SAUCE! MMMM!
ONE, TWO, THREE, AND IT'S OVER, OKAY?
BA-DUMP
BA-DUMP
BA-DUMP

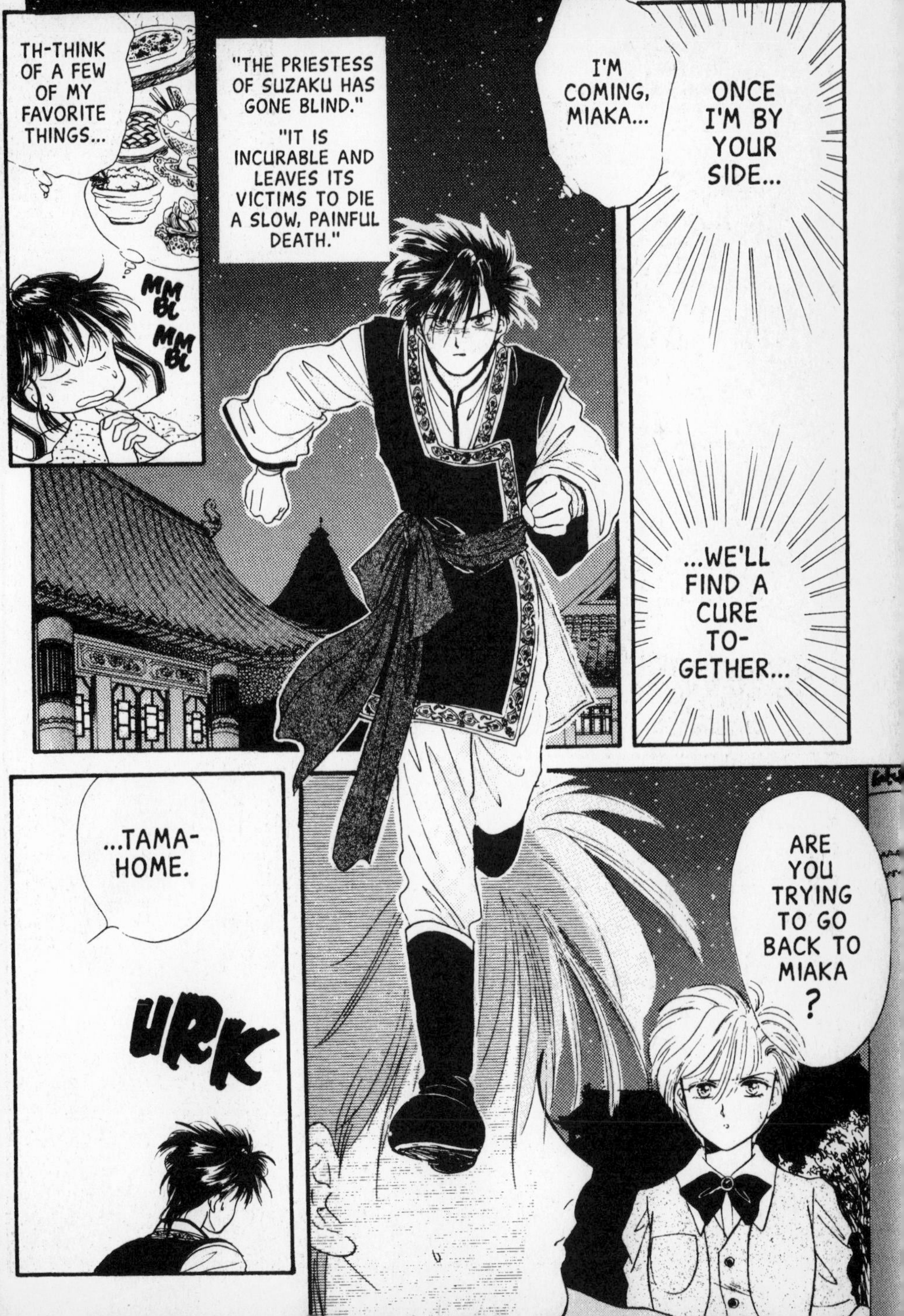
TH-THINK OF A FEW OF MY FAVORITE THINGS...
MMBL MMBL
"THE PRIESTESS OF SUZAKU HAS GONE BLIND."
"IT IS INCURABLE AND LEAVES ITS VICTIMS TO DIE A SLOW, PAINFUL DEATH."
I'M COMING, MIAKA...
ONCE I'M BY YOUR SIDE...
...WE'LL FIND A CURE TO-GETHER...
...TAMA-HOME.
URK
ARE YOU TRYING TO GO BACK TO MIAKA?

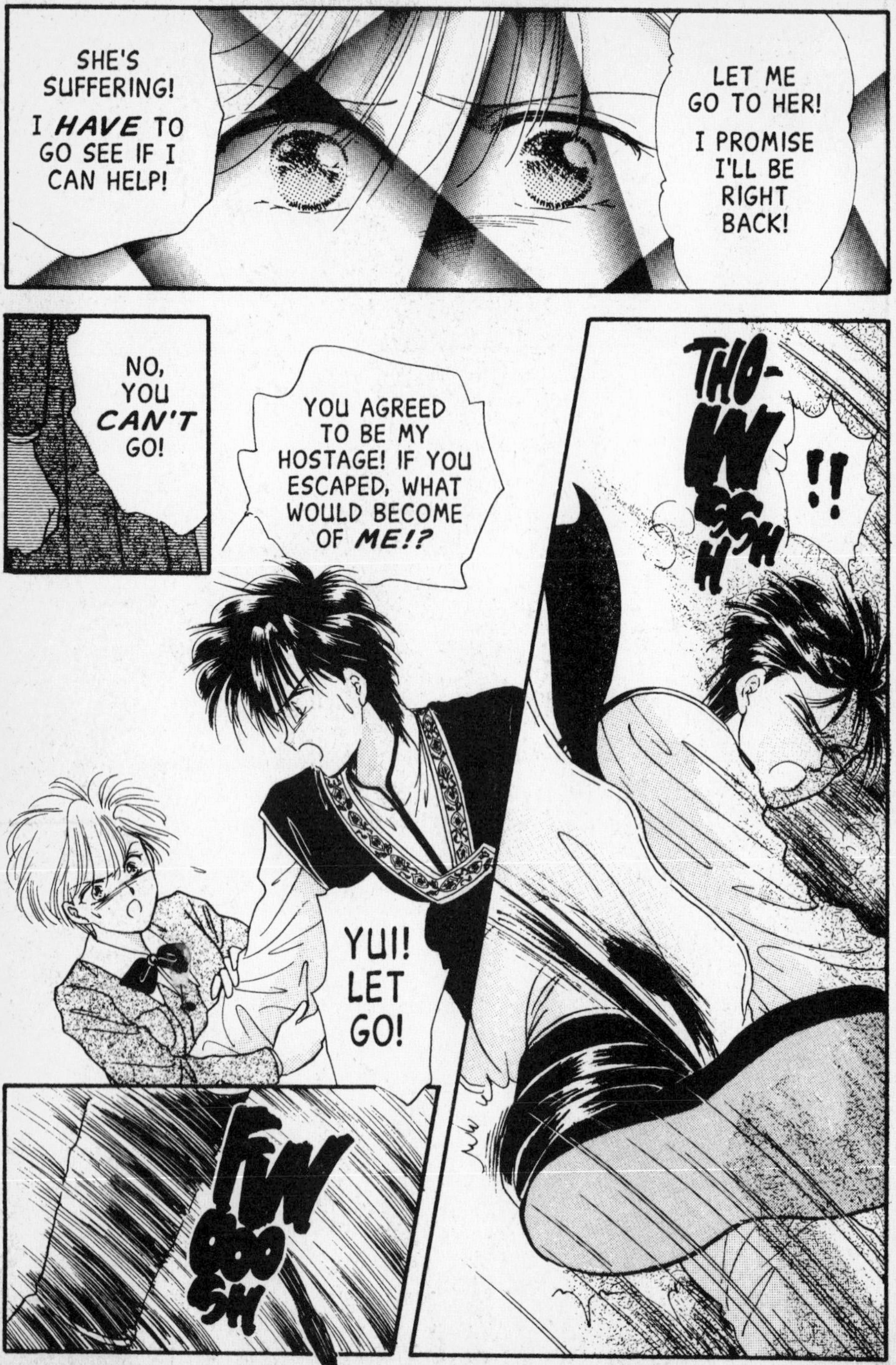

SHE'S SUFFERING! I *HAVE* TO GO SEE IF I CAN HELP!
LET ME GO TO HER! I PROMISE I'LL BE RIGHT BACK!
NO, YOU *CAN'T* GO!
YOU AGREED TO BE MY HOSTAGE! IF YOU ESCAPED, WHAT WOULD BECOME OF *ME!?*
YUI! LET GO!
THO-WWOSSH
!!
FWOOOSH

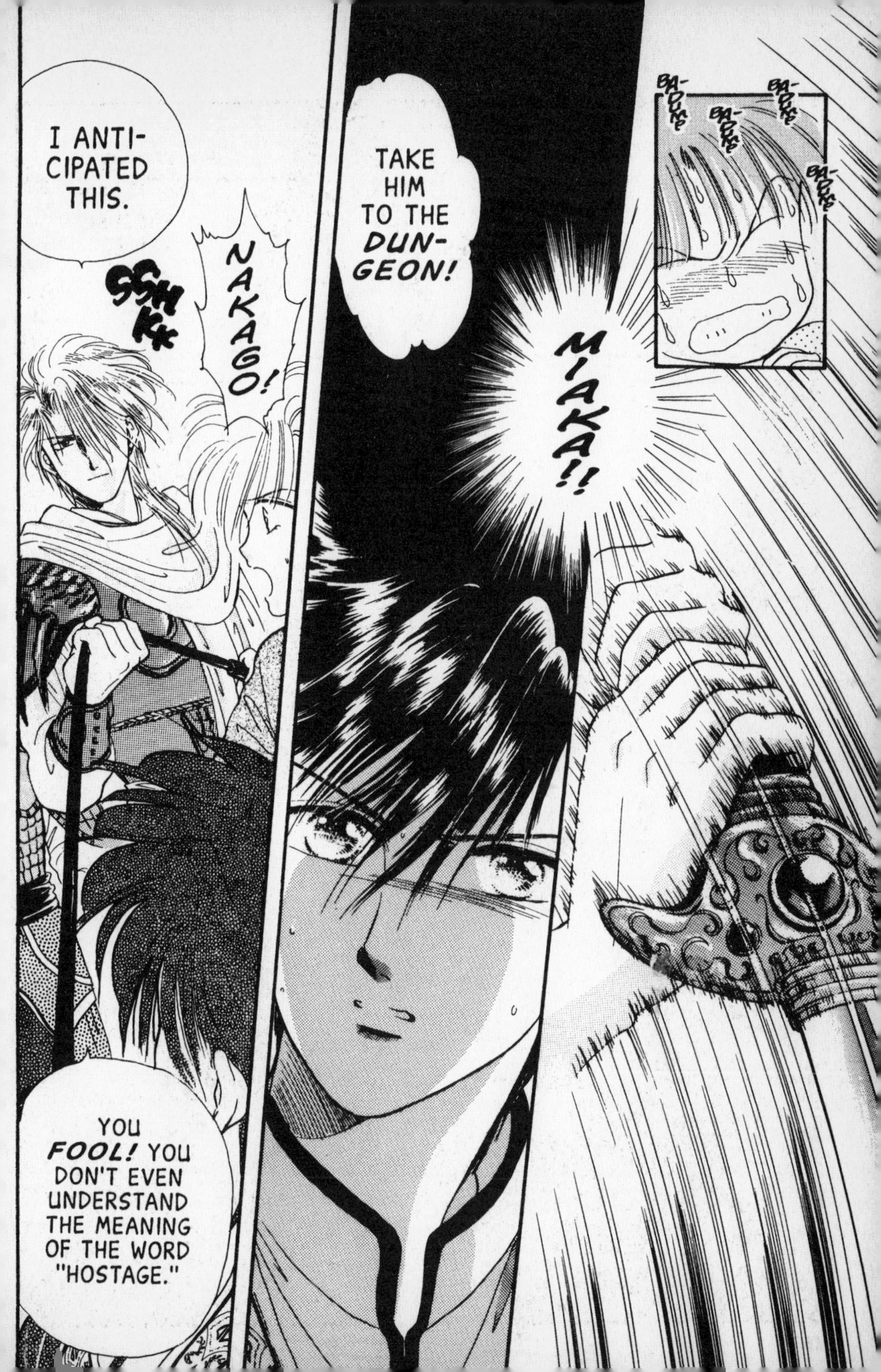
I ANTI-CIPATED THIS.
SSHKK
NAKAGO!
YOU FOOL! YOU DON'T EVEN UNDERSTAND THE MEANING OF THE WORD "HOSTAGE."
TAKE HIM TO THE DUNGEON!
MIAKA!!
BA-DUMP
BA-DUMP
BA-DUMP
BA-DUMP

…?

HOTO-
HORI…
?

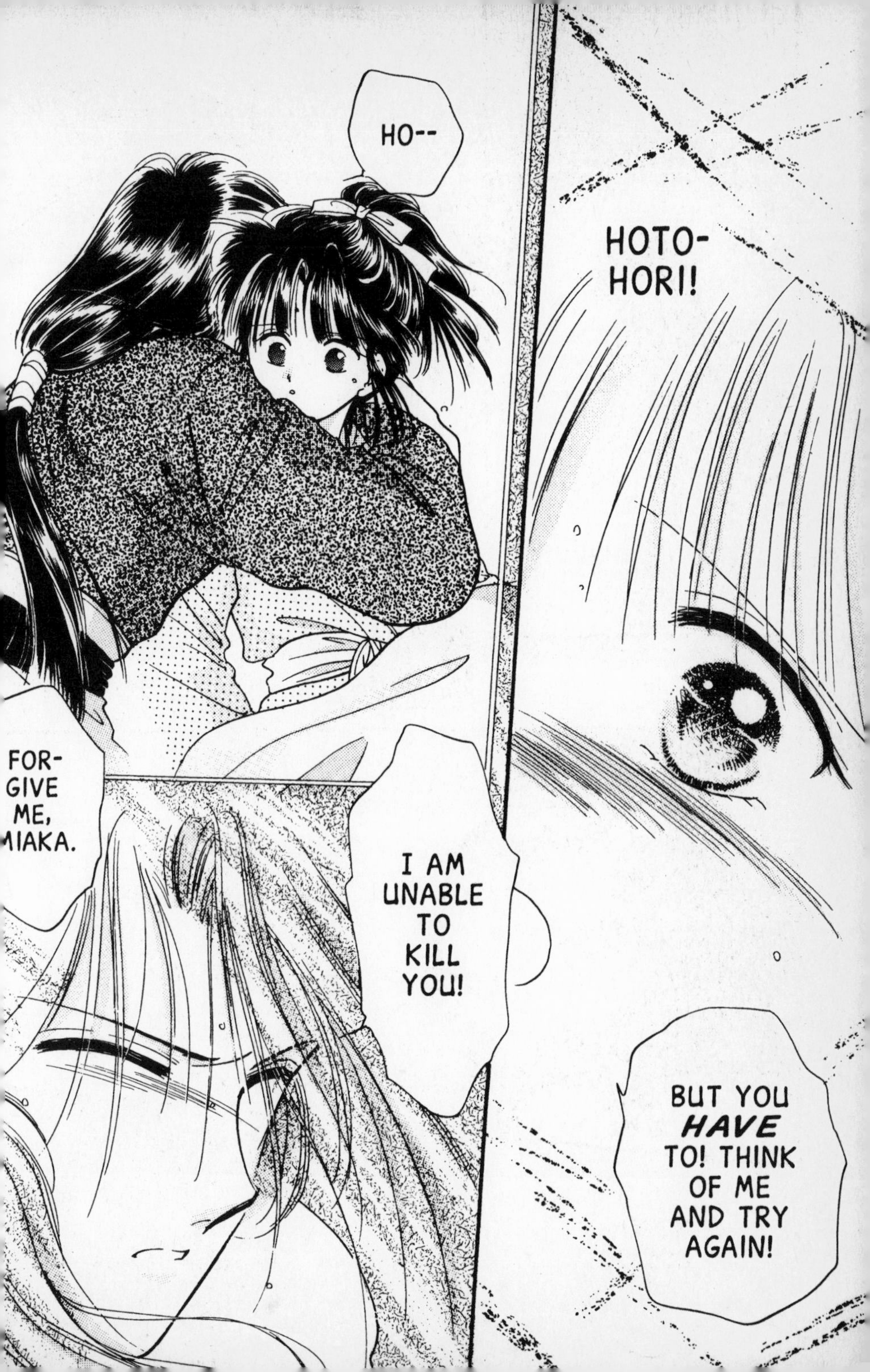
HO--
FOR-GIVE ME, MIAKA.
I AM UNABLE TO KILL YOU!
HOTO-HORI!
BUT YOU *HAVE* TO! THINK OF ME AND TRY AGAIN!

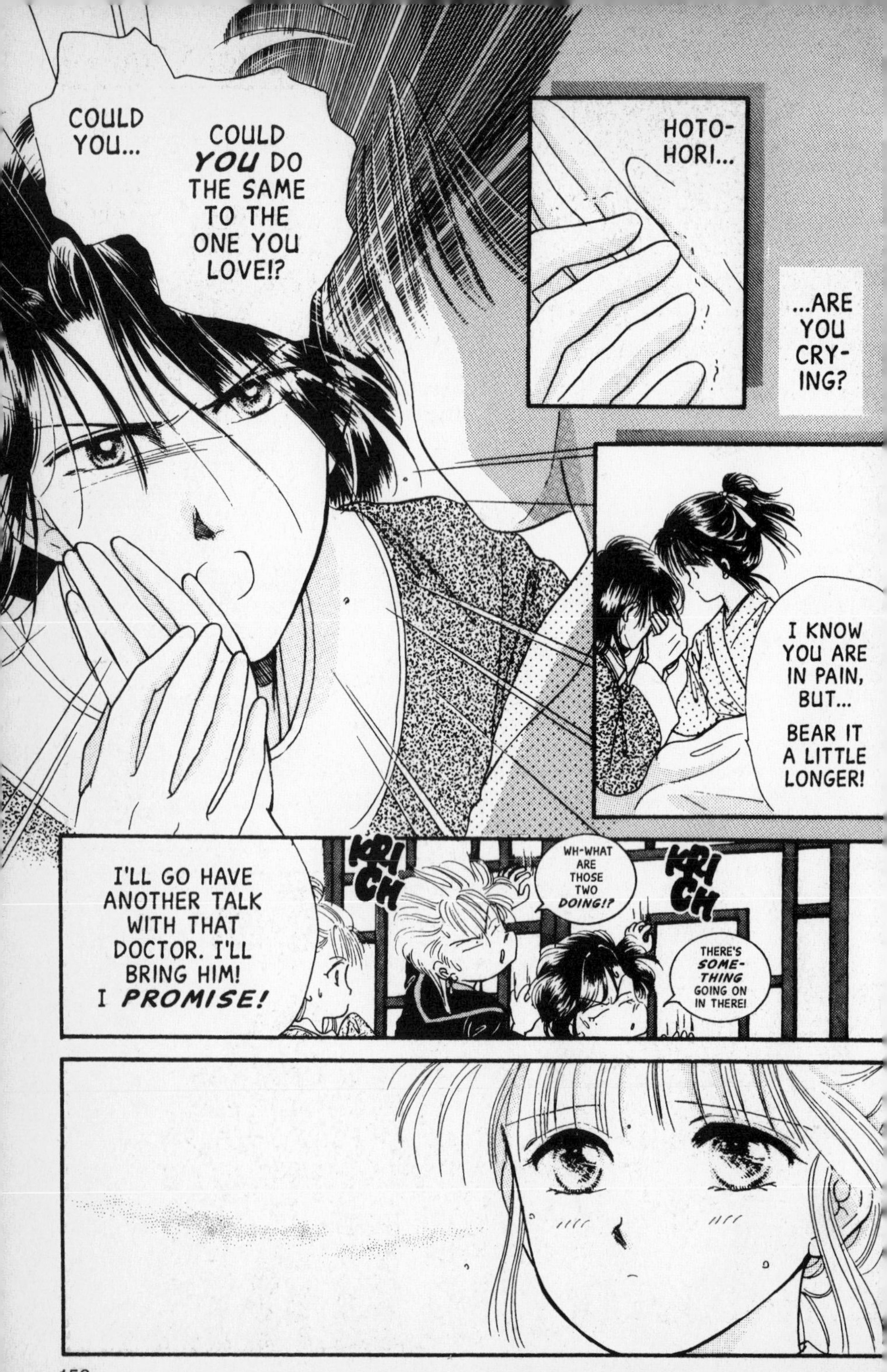
COULD YOU...
COULD *YOU* DO THE SAME TO THE ONE YOU LOVE!?
HOTO-HORI...
...ARE YOU CRY-ING?
I KNOW YOU ARE IN PAIN, BUT...
BEAR IT A LITTLE LONGER!
I'LL GO HAVE ANOTHER TALK WITH THAT DOCTOR. I'LL BRING HIM! I *PROMISE!*
KRI CH
WH-WHAT ARE THOSE TWO *DOING!?*
KRI CH
THERE'S *SOME-THING* GOING ON IN THERE!

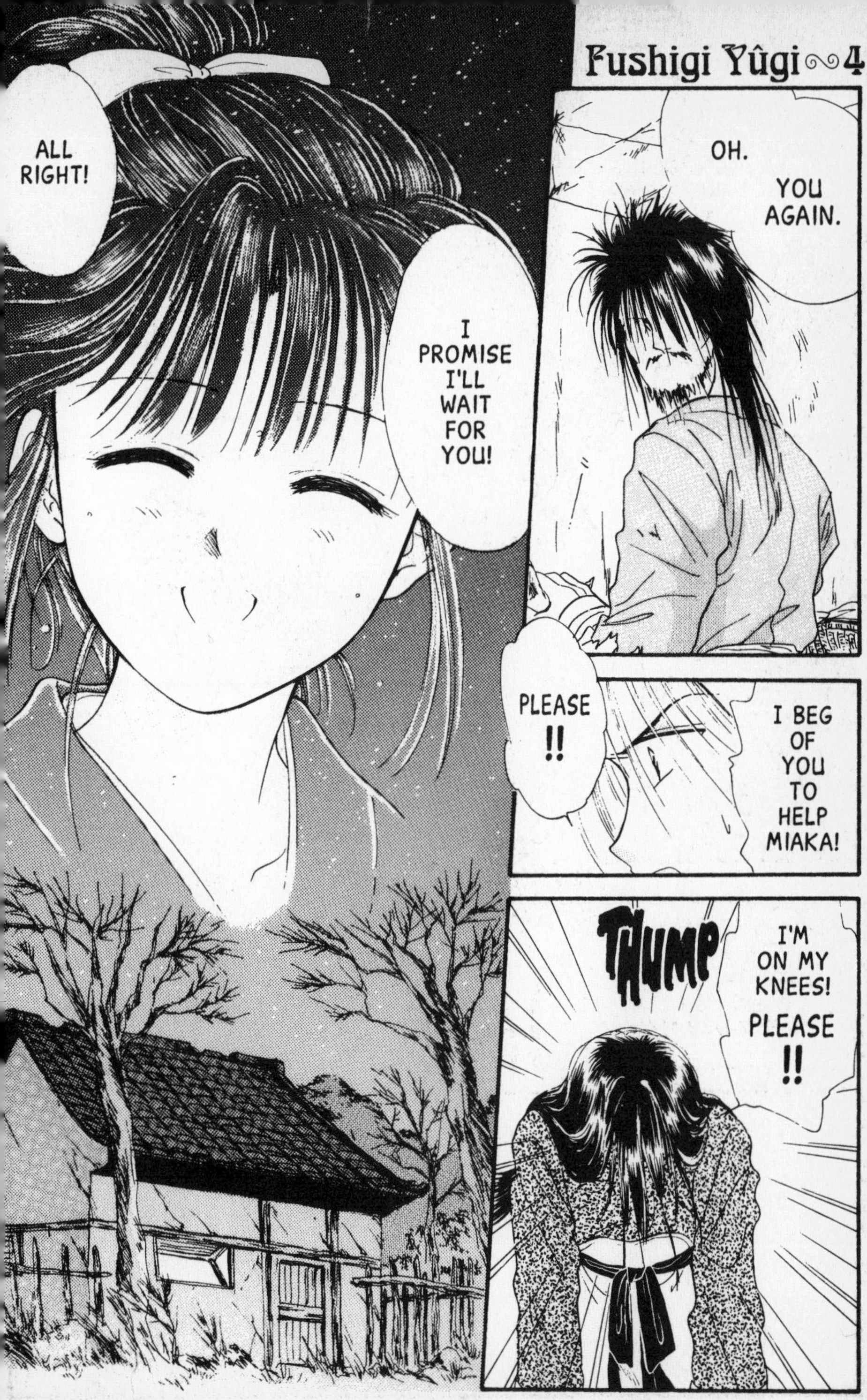
ALL RIGHT!
I PROMISE I'LL WAIT FOR YOU!
OH.
YOU AGAIN.
PLEASE !!
I BEG OF YOU TO HELP MIAKA!
THUMP
I'M ON MY KNEES!
PLEASE !!

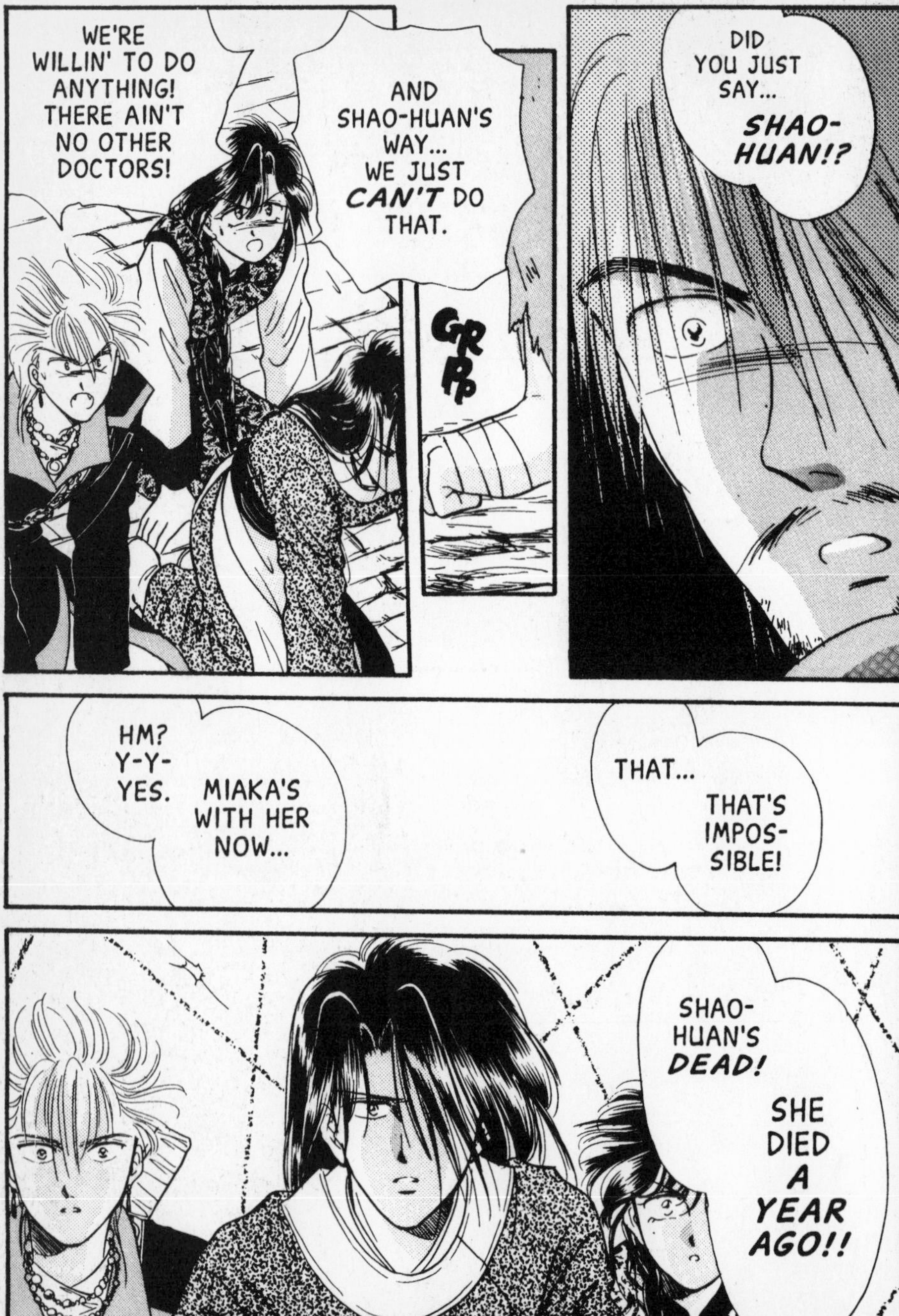
WE'RE WILLIN' TO DO ANYTHING! THERE AIN'T NO OTHER DOCTORS!
AND SHAO-HUAN'S WAY... WE JUST *CAN'T* DO THAT.
GRRPP
DID YOU JUST SAY... ***SHAO-HUAN!?***
HM? Y-Y-YES.
MIAKA'S WITH HER NOW...
THAT...
THAT'S IMPOSSIBLE!
SHAO-HUAN'S ***DEAD!***
SHE DIED ***A YEAR AGO!!***

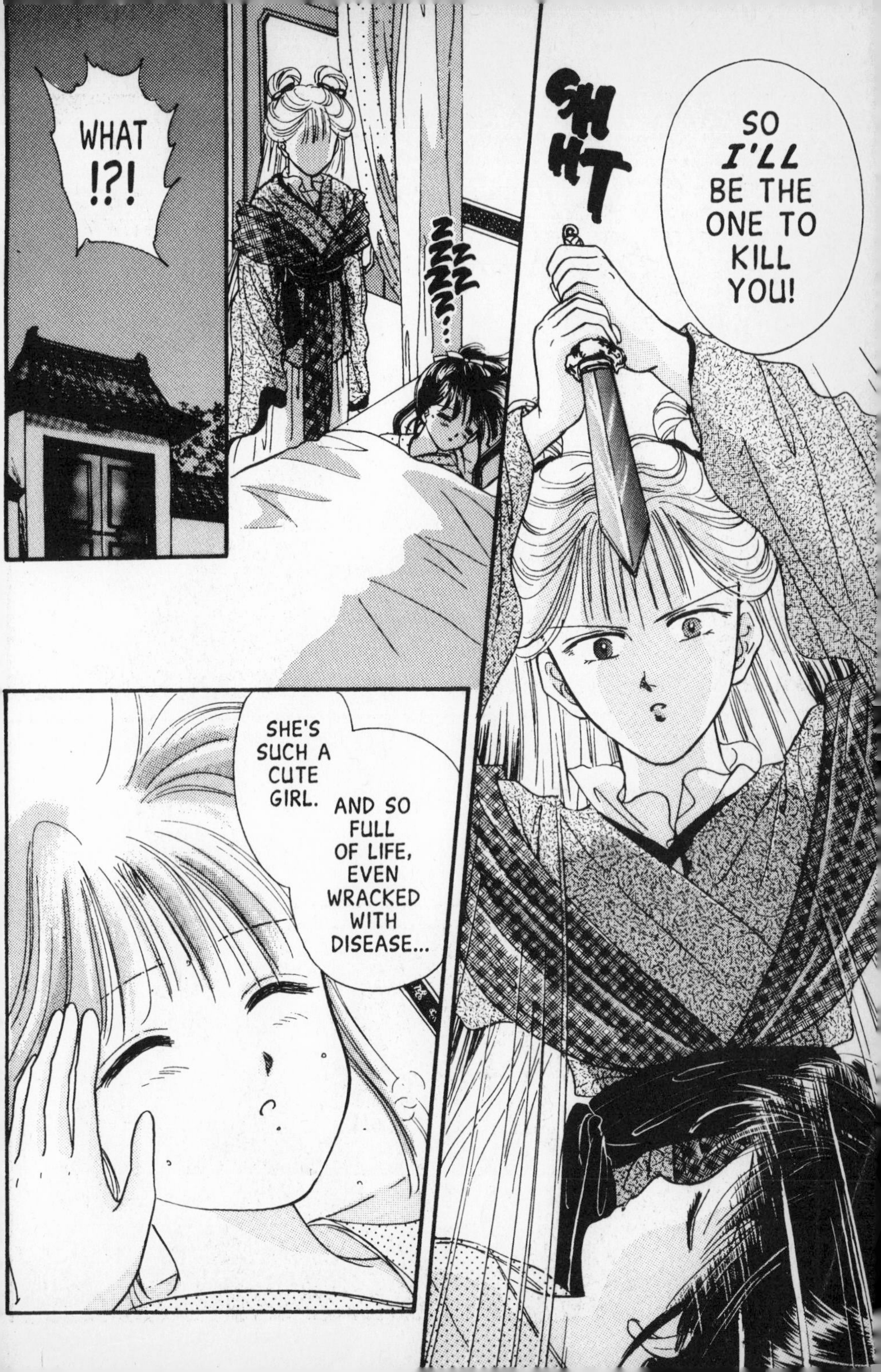
WHAT !?!
ZZZZZ...
SHE'S SUCH A CUTE GIRL.
AND SO FULL OF LIFE, EVEN WRACKED WITH DISEASE...
SHHT
SO I'LL BE THE ONE TO KILL YOU!

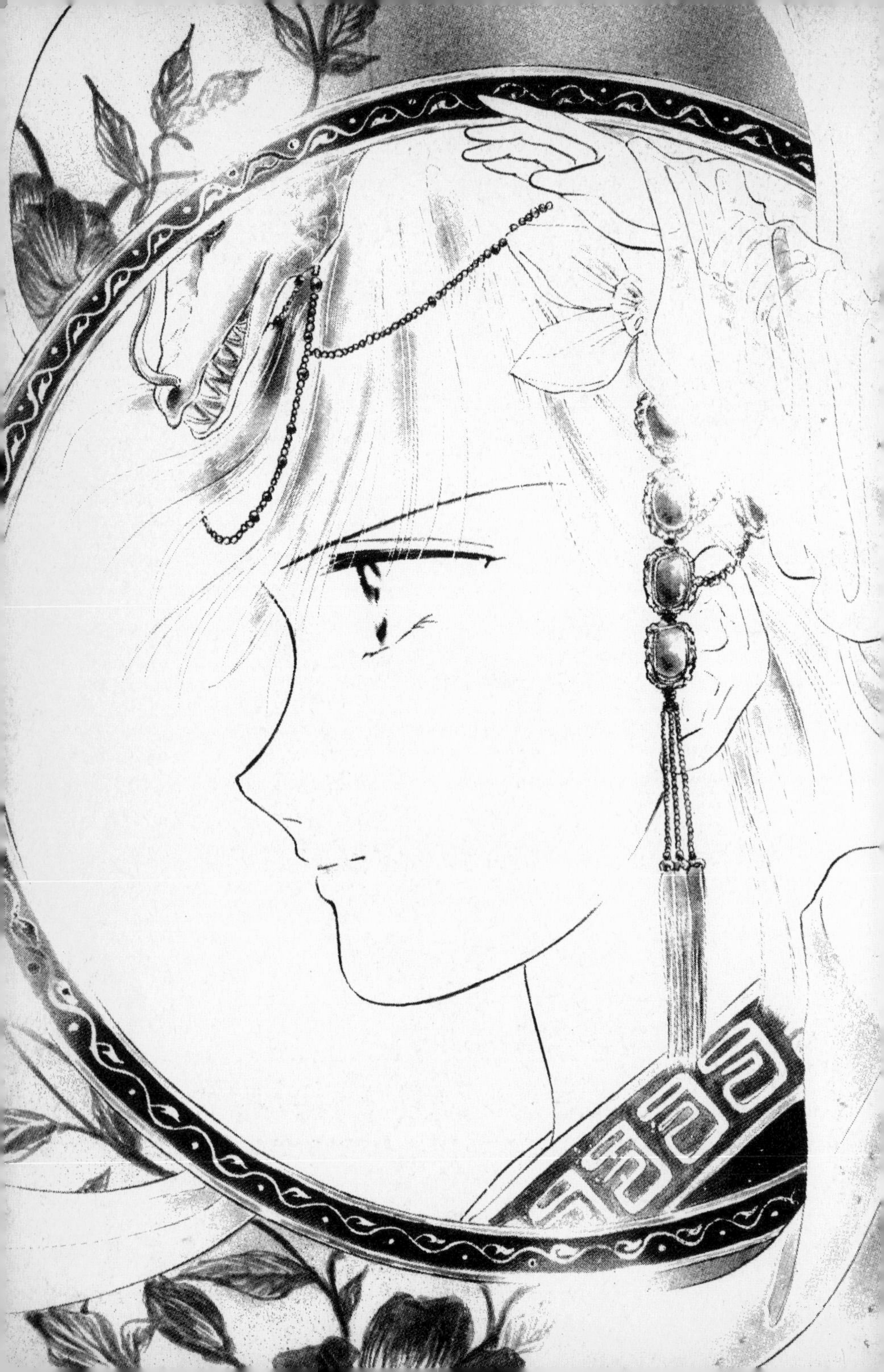

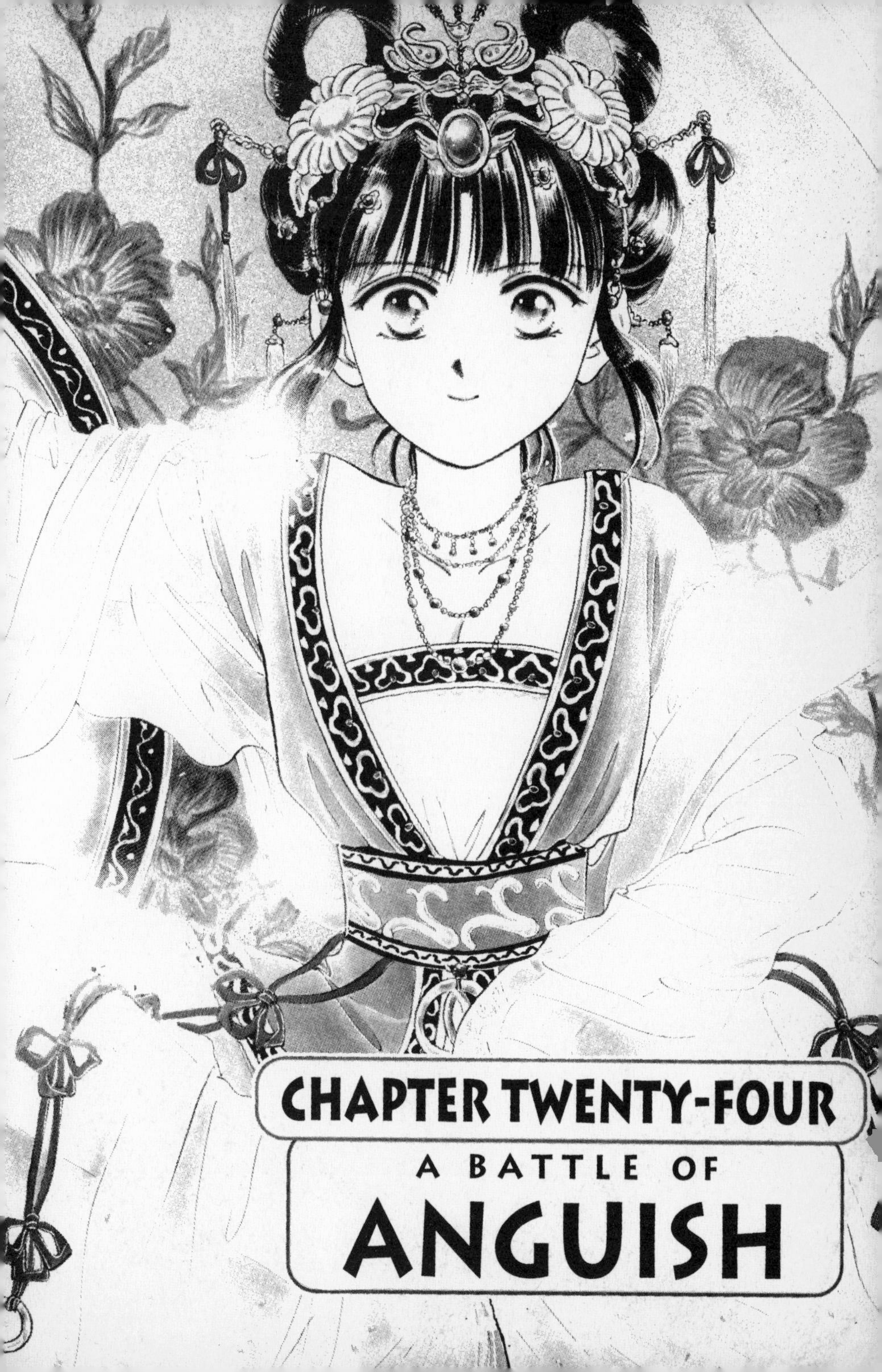
CHAPTER TWENTY-FOUR
A BATTLE OF
ANGUISH

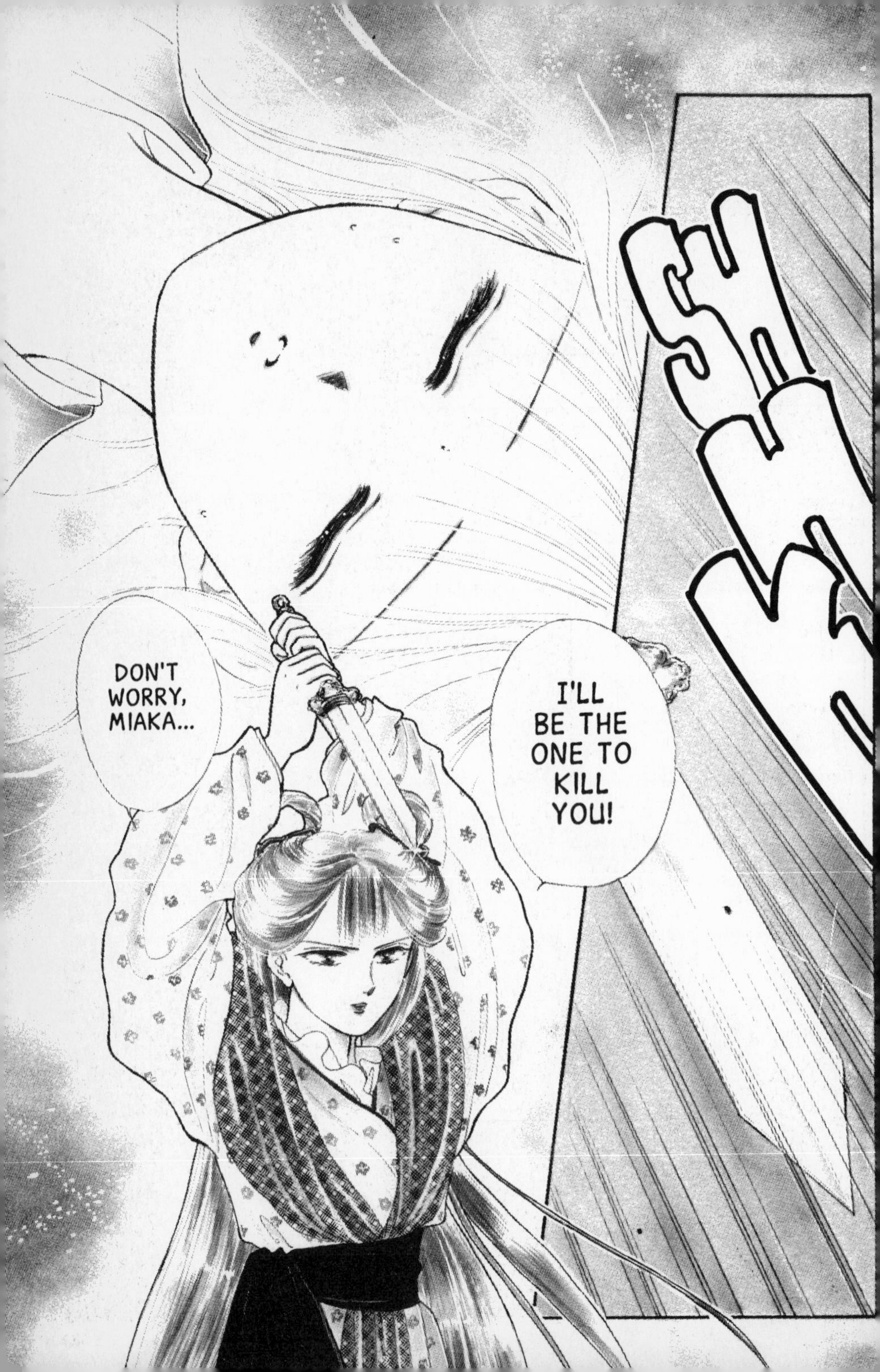
DON'T WORRY, MIAKA...
I'LL BE THE ONE TO KILL YOU!

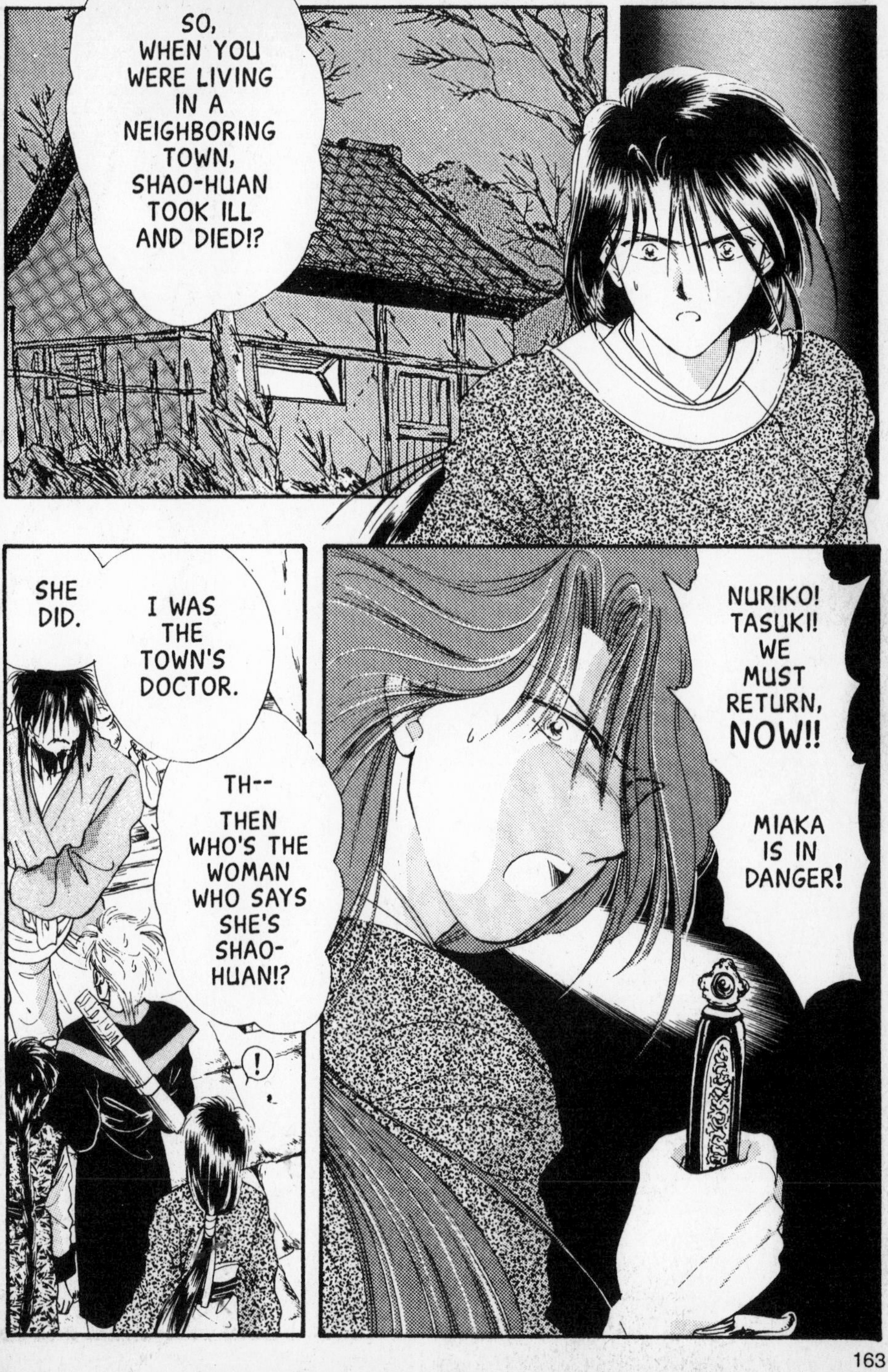
SO, WHEN YOU WERE LIVING IN A NEIGHBORING TOWN, SHAO-HUAN TOOK ILL AND DIED!?
SHE DID.
I WAS THE TOWN'S DOCTOR.
TH--
THEN WHO'S THE WOMAN WHO SAYS SHE'S SHAO-HUAN!?
!
NURIKO! TASUKI!! WE MUST RETURN, NOW!!
MIAKA IS IN DANGER!

THUDDA THUDDA MEEW

SHAO-HUAN...

...COULDN'T BE...

SLLSH

GROLLL

.....

HM.... HMM...

AN ICE CREAM DRUM-STICK!

CHOMP

AIEEE

NO, IT'S NOT!

FLUMPH

MMMM. POTATO CHIPS.

BA-DUMP BA-DUMP BA-DUMP

SLISH

ZZ

SLISH

ZZZZ

ZZZZ

SLISH

FWOO

PANT PANT

I-IS SHE REALLY ASLEEP??

SHAO-HUAN...

GASP

I APPRECIATE WHAT YOU'RE TRYING TO DO, BUT I CAN'T LET YOU KILL ME.

I PROMISED HOTOHORI I'D WAIT FOR HIM.

Y-Y-YOU WERE AWAKE??

IT WOULD HAVE BEEN EASIER TO DIE AND HAVE YOU REVIVE ME, BUT...

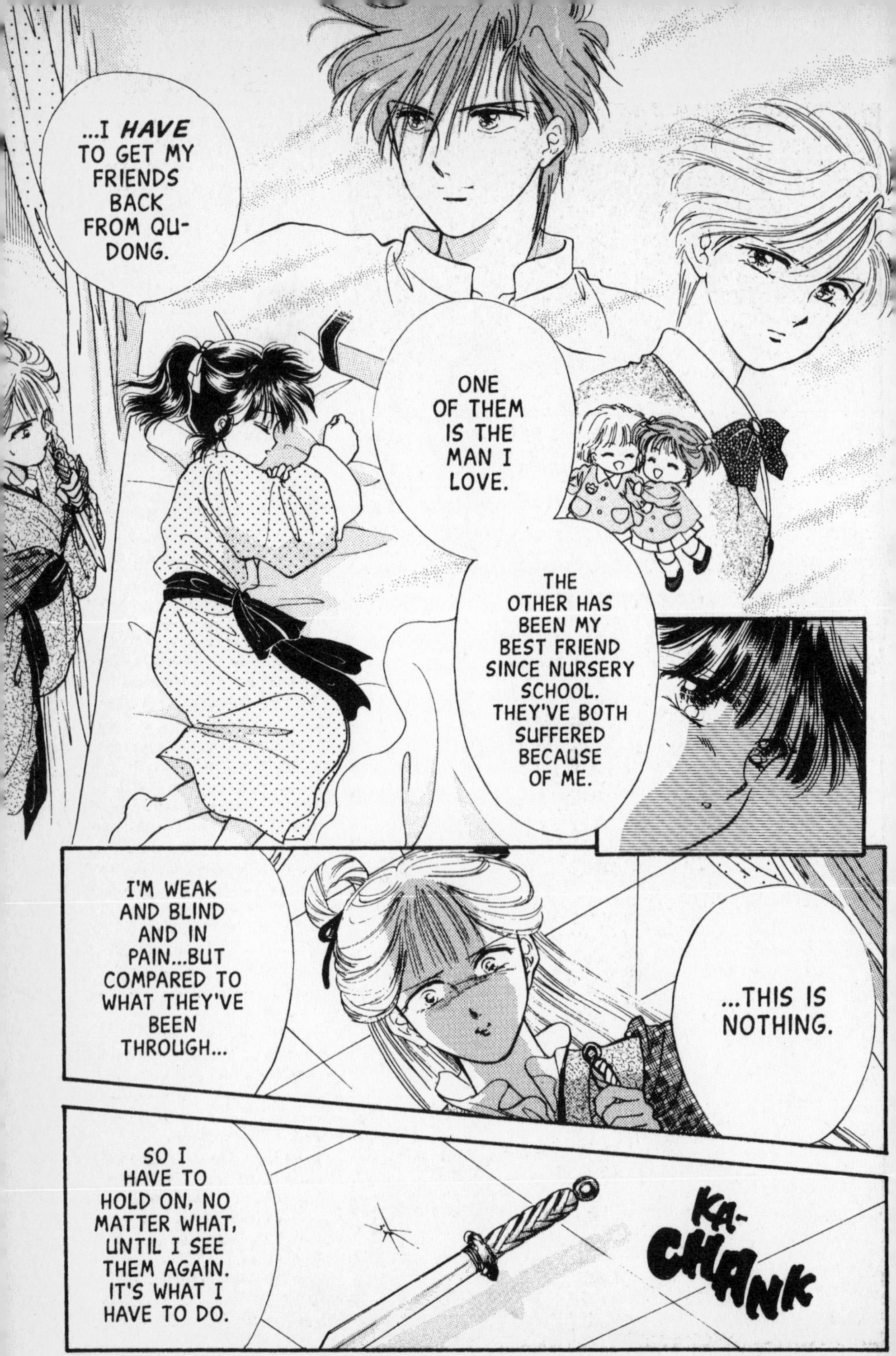
...I *HAVE* TO GET MY FRIENDS BACK FROM QU-DONG.
ONE OF THEM IS THE MAN I LOVE.
THE OTHER HAS BEEN MY BEST FRIEND SINCE NURSERY SCHOOL. THEY'VE BOTH SUFFERED BECAUSE OF ME.
I'M WEAK AND BLIND AND IN PAIN...BUT COMPARED TO WHAT THEY'VE BEEN THROUGH...
...THIS IS NOTHING.
SO I HAVE TO HOLD ON, NO MATTER WHAT, UNTIL I SEE THEM AGAIN. IT'S WHAT I HAVE TO DO.
KA-CHANK

Bandit

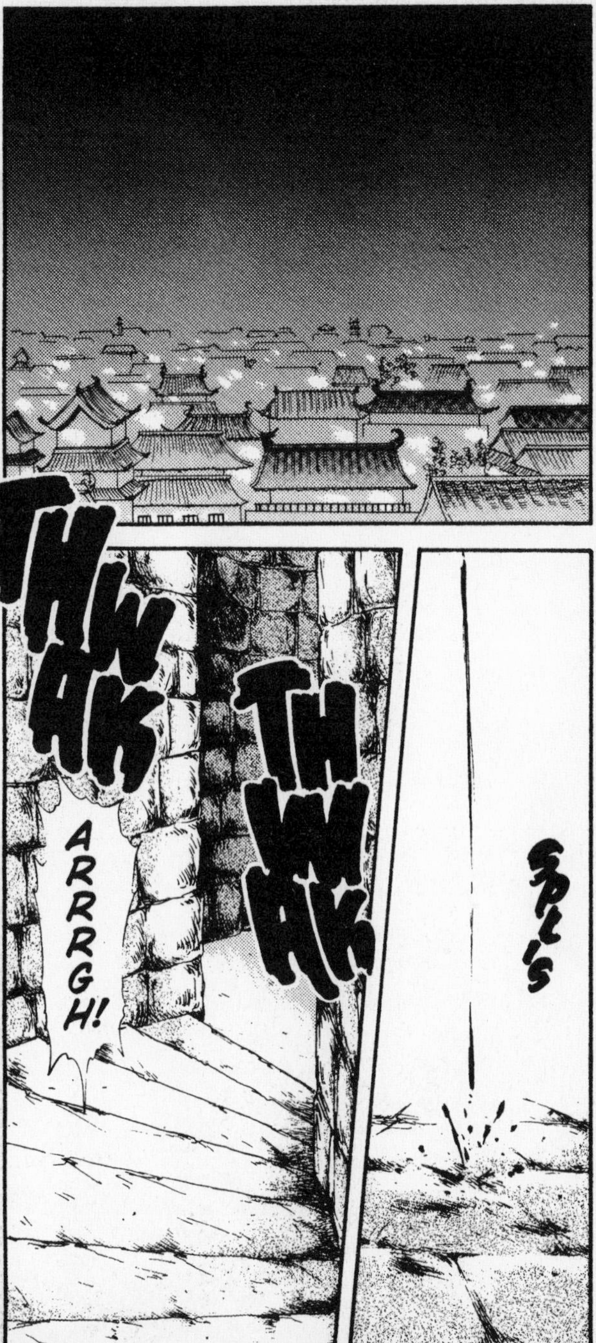
THWAK
ARRRGH!
THWAK
SPLIS

One thing I find interesting in the Asahi News are the letters to the editor. There are so many interesting opinions. There was a really interesting piece on corporal punishment recently. If you push a teacher too far... hey, he's only human. A teacher can't get carried away, but you need to maintain SOME discipline in the class room. When I was young, my parents put me in my place all the time. But everybody says I've got a great relationship with my mother. She'd scold me, or she'd praise me whenever the occasion called for it. But slapping your child, like Miaka's mom did, might not be appropriate. In any case, don't just use the paper for the TV listings! You don't learn anything about the world. So let's read a few articles now and again! You hear me, people?
Oh, no! It's 2 a.m. already. I'm half asleep. ⊖⊖ I'm huuungry! They say that manga reveals the artist's personality. I wonder whether Miaka's appetite says something about me... (The editorial department thinks that my first editor, Ms. Y., is the model.) I washed my face and applied some skin lotion. *This is the way I spend my free time.* And the lotion's yogurt smell just gets me going!! It's addictive! When I met with my editor at the cafe, I ordered some cocoa, and it looked so delicious, I couldn't contain my smile. I don't hold back at mealtime... Hey! It's healthy! No matter how determined I am to lose weight, when I try to control myself, I wind up eating. We're human, aren't we? We gotta eat!
My pen's running out of ink!
The stuffed cabbage I had for dinner was so good! But right now, I have a craving for crab. The next time I visit home, I have a reservation for Chanko Nabe.
I don't know what to do! I have to wrap this up! (And I've written to the point where I have to find a good conclusion to this chat section!) It's no conclusion, but I've filled up enough space.
DUM DA DA DUM DUM--
DUM DUM (curtain) *What the heck was this chat section about?*

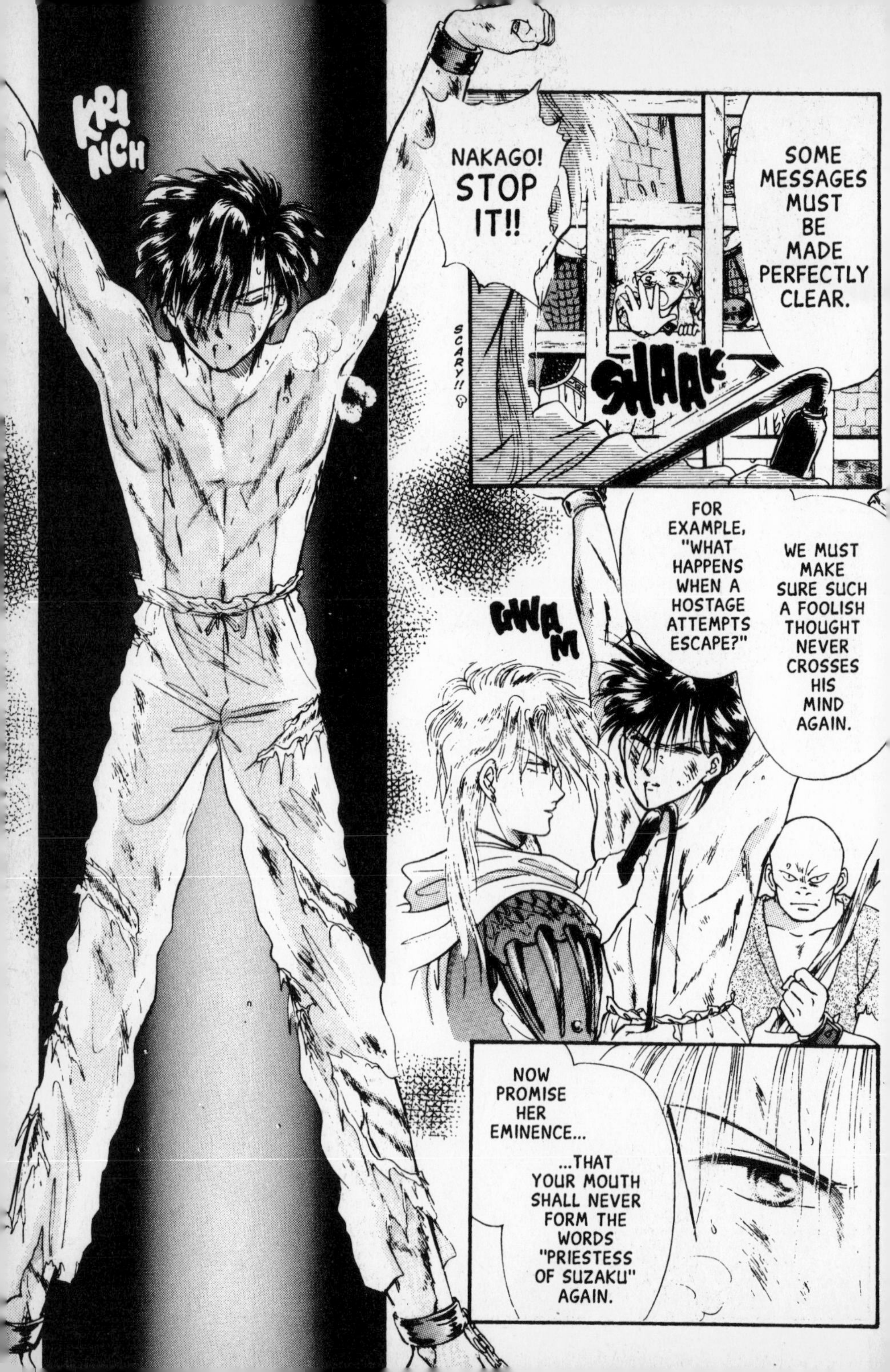
KRINCH
NAKAGO! STOP IT!!
SOME MESSAGES MUST BE MADE PERFECTLY CLEAR.
SCARY!!
SHAAK
FOR EXAMPLE, "WHAT HAPPENS WHEN A HOSTAGE ATTEMPTS ESCAPE?"
WE MUST MAKE SURE SUCH A FOOLISH THOUGHT NEVER CROSSES HIS MIND AGAIN.
GWAM
NOW PROMISE HER EMINENCE...
...THAT YOUR MOUTH SHALL NEVER FORM THE WORDS "PRIESTESS OF SUZAKU" AGAIN.

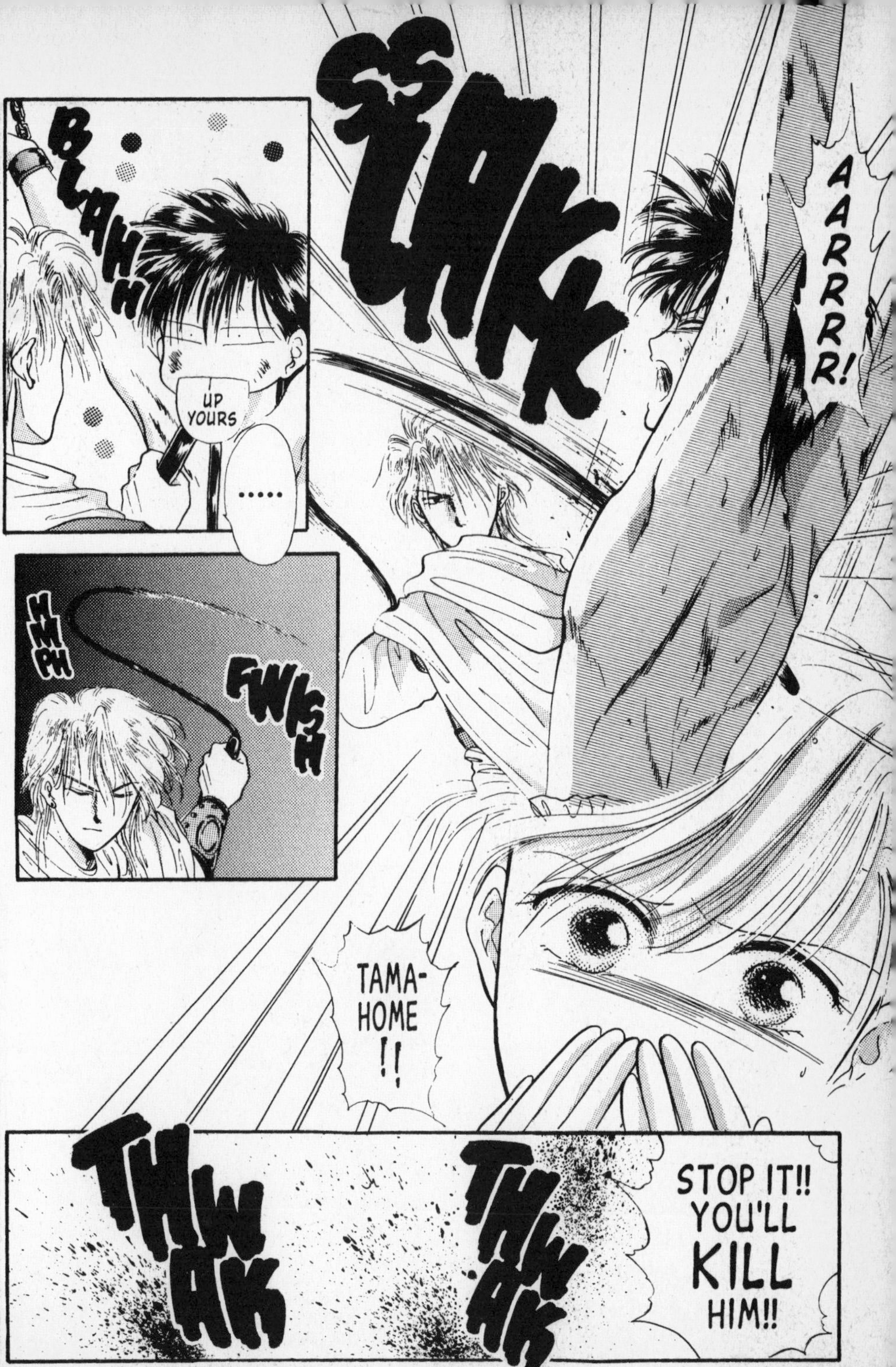
BLAHHH
UP YOURS
.....
HMPH
FWISH
SSLAKK
AARRRR!
TAMA-HOME!!
THWAK
THWAK
STOP IT!! YOU'LL KILL HIM!!

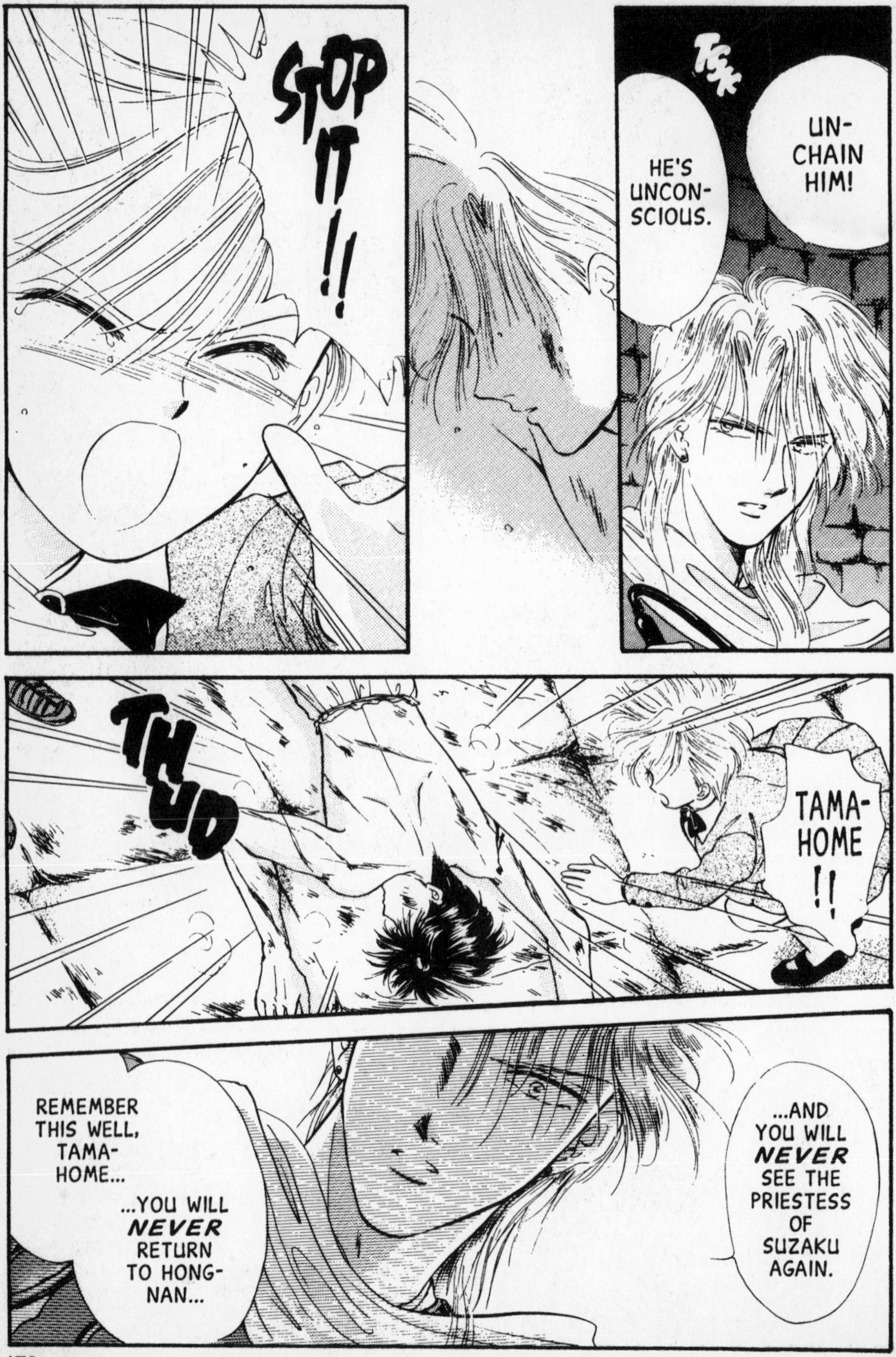
STOP IT!!
TSK
HE'S UNCON-SCIOUS.
UN-CHAIN HIM!
THUD
TAMA-HOME!!
REMEMBER THIS WELL, TAMA-HOME...
...YOU WILL *NEVER* RETURN TO HONG-NAN...
...AND YOU WILL *NEVER* SEE THE PRIESTESS OF SUZAKU AGAIN.

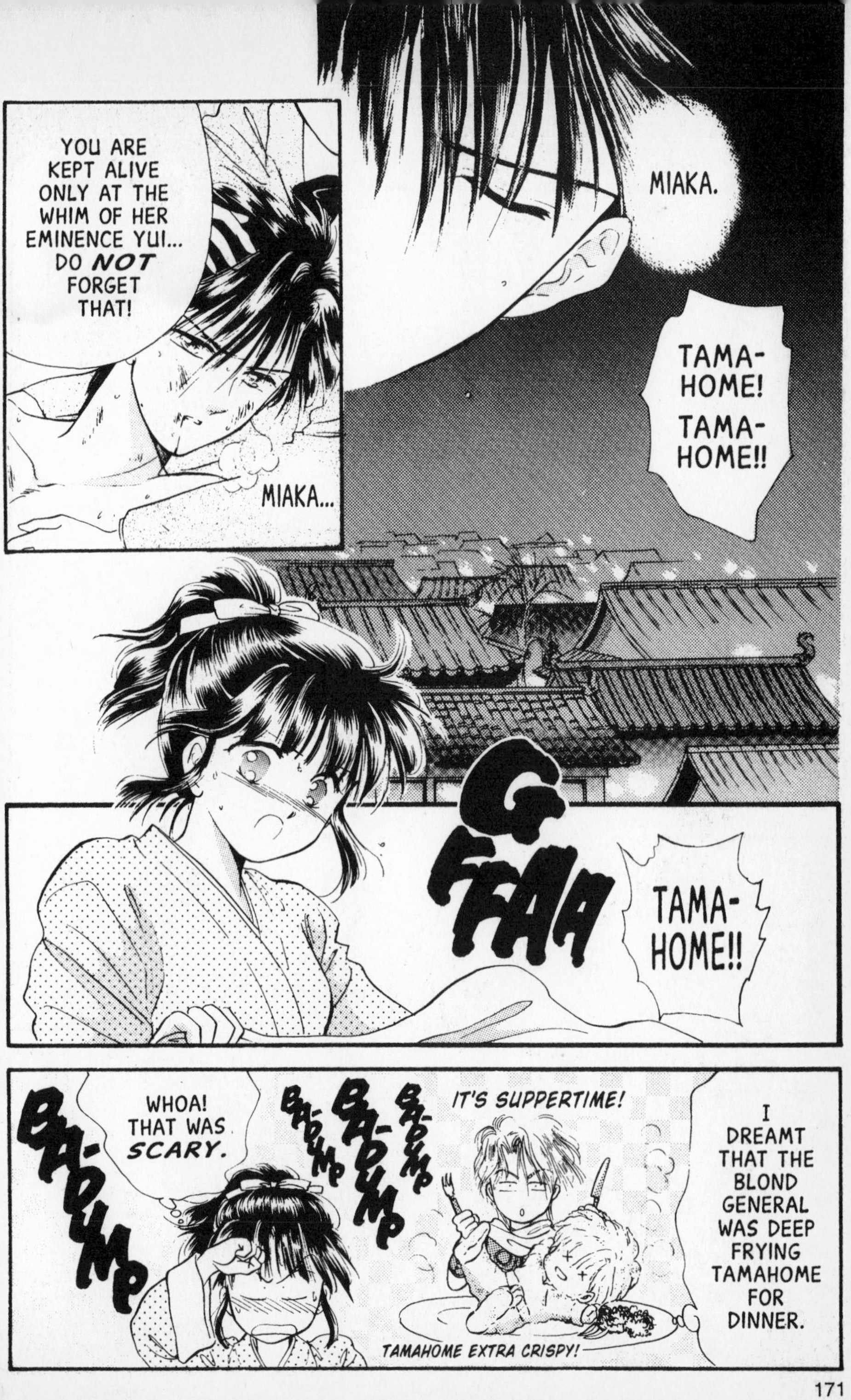
YOU ARE KEPT ALIVE ONLY AT THE WHIM OF HER EMINENCE YUI... DO NOT FORGET THAT!
MIAKA...
MIAKA.
TAMA-HOME! TAMA-HOME!!
GFAA
TAMA-HOME!!
BA-DUMP
WHOA! THAT WAS SCARY.
BA-DUMP BA-DUMP BA-DUMP
IT'S SUPPERTIME!
I DREAMT THAT THE BLOND GENERAL WAS DEEP FRYING TAMAHOME FOR DINNER.
TAMAHOME EXTRA CRISPY!

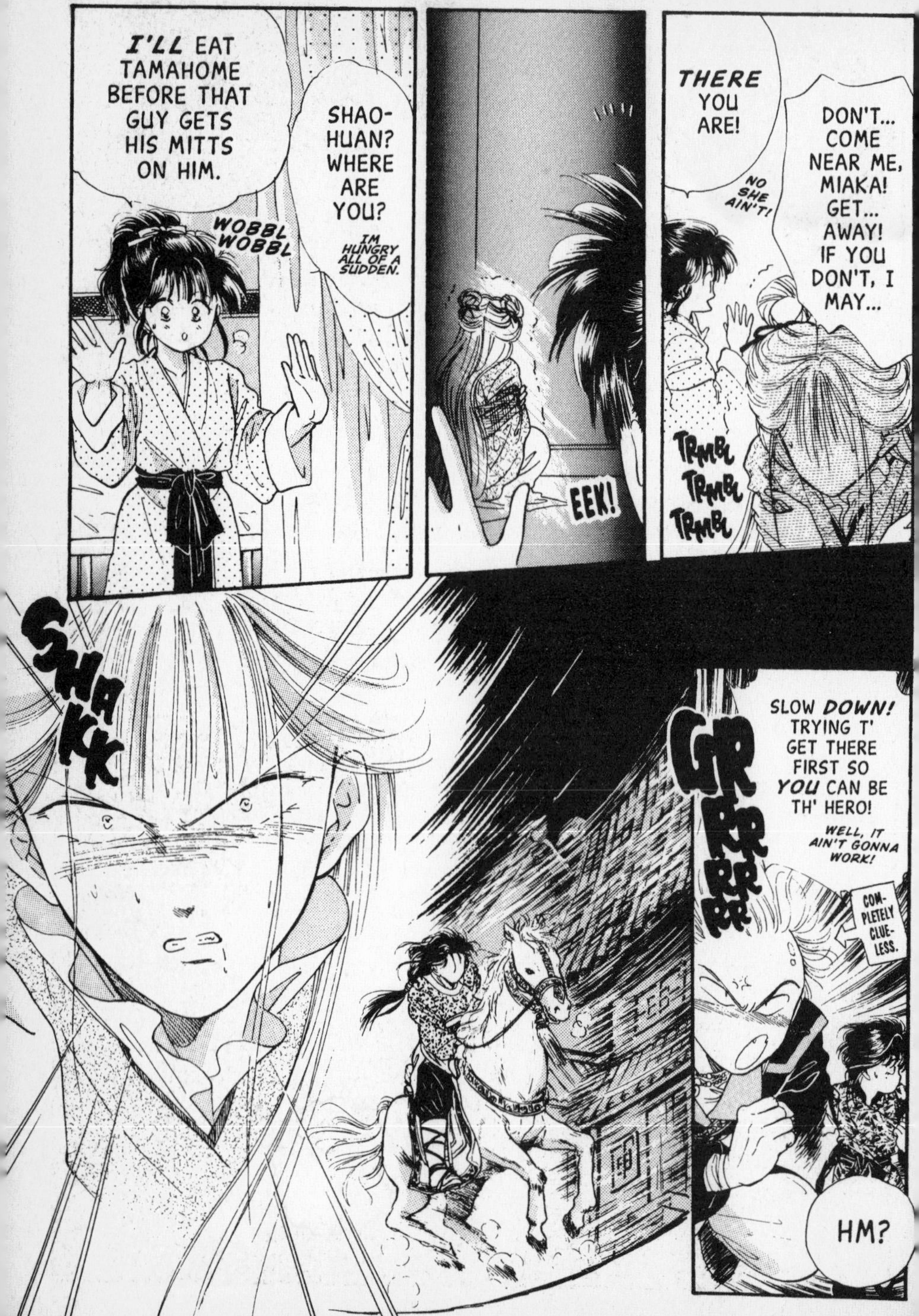
I'LL EAT TAMAHOME BEFORE THAT GUY GETS HIS MITTS ON HIM.
WOBBL WOBBL
SHAO-HUAN? WHERE ARE YOU?
IM HUNGRY ALL OF A SUDDEN.
EEK!
THERE YOU ARE!
NO SHE AIN'T!
DON'T... COME NEAR ME, MIAKA! GET... AWAY! IF YOU DON'T, I MAY...
TRMBL TRMBL TRMBL
SHAKK
GRRRRRRR
SLOW DOWN! TRYING T' GET THERE FIRST SO YOU CAN BE TH' HERO!
WELL, IT AIN'T GONNA WORK!
COMPLETELY CLUELESS.
HM?

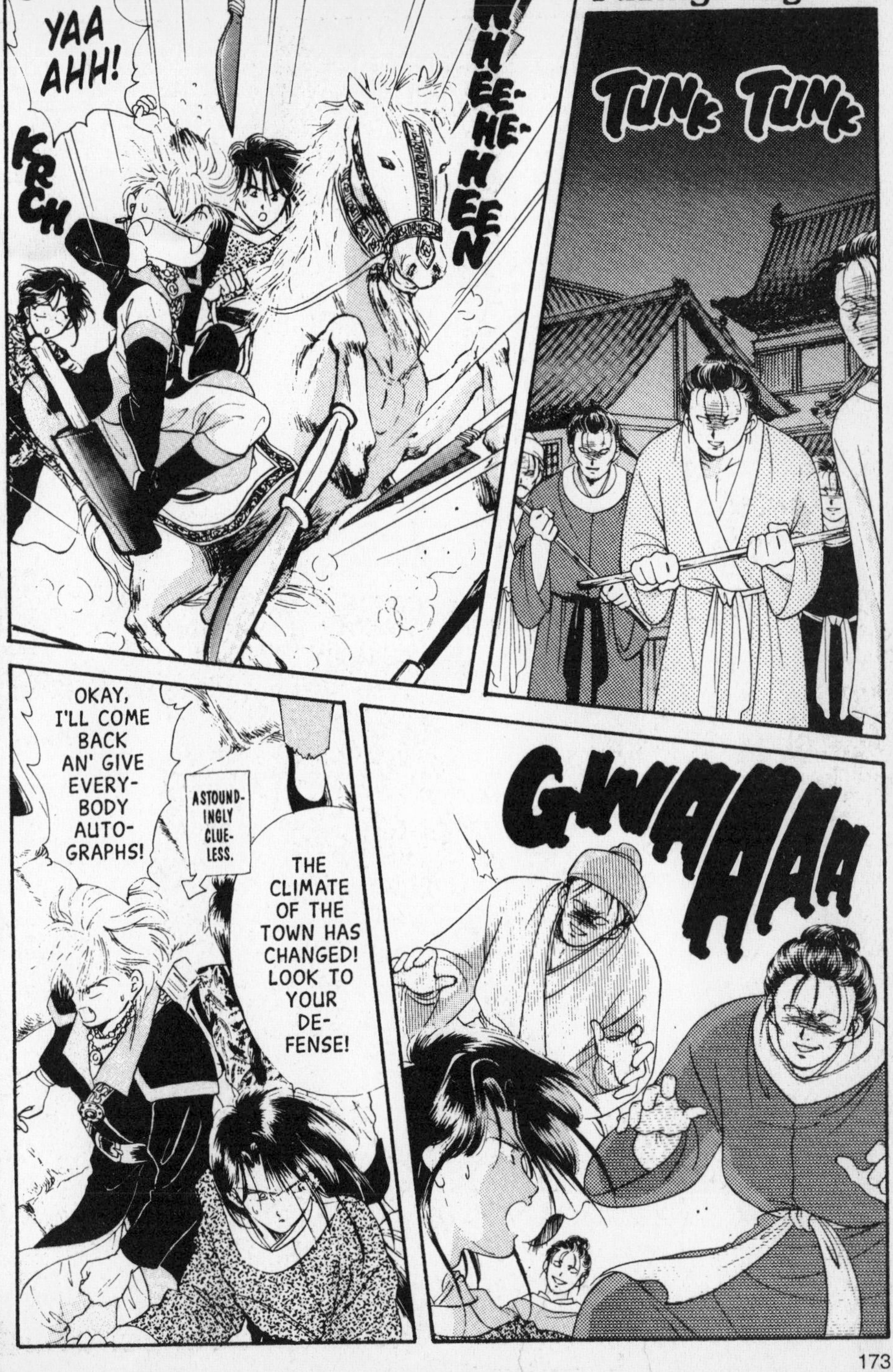
YAA AHH!
KRCH
WHEE-HE-HEEN
TUNK TUNK
OKAY, I'LL COME BACK AN' GIVE EVERY-BODY AUTO-GRAPHS!
ASTOUND-INGLY CLUE-LESS.
THE CLIMATE OF THE TOWN HAS CHANGED! LOOK TO YOUR DE-FENSE!
GWAAAAA

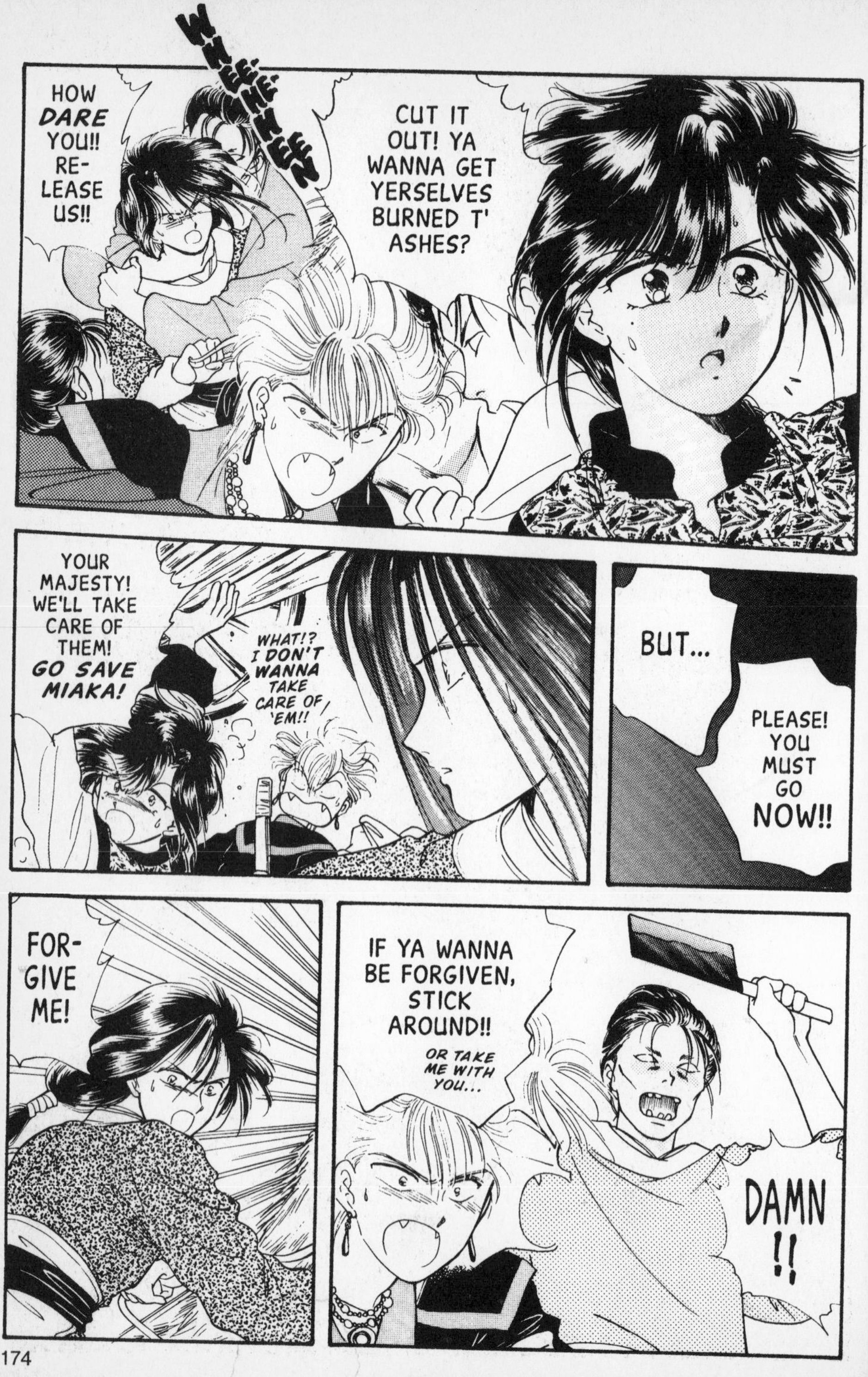
HOW DARE YOU!! RE-LEASE US!!
WHEEHEHEEN
CUT IT OUT! YA WANNA GET YERSELVES BURNED T' ASHES?
YOUR MAJESTY! WE'LL TAKE CARE OF THEM! GO SAVE MIAKA!
WHAT!? I DON'T WANNA TAKE CARE OF 'EM!!
BUT...
PLEASE! YOU MUST GO NOW!!
FOR-GIVE ME!
IF YA WANNA BE FORGIVEN, STICK AROUND!!
OR TAKE ME WITH YOU...
DAMN !!

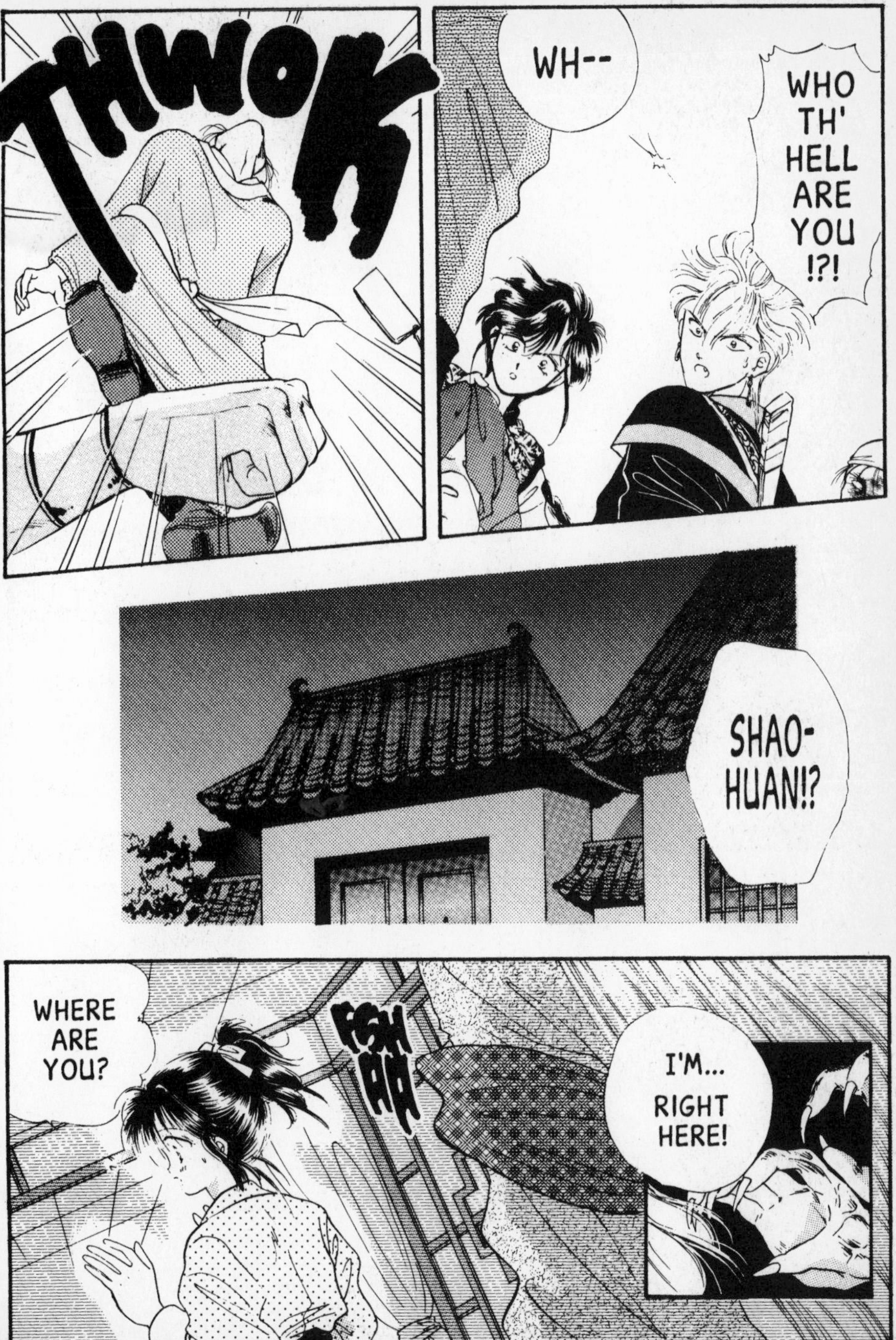
THWOK
WH--
WHO TH' HELL ARE YOU !?!
SHAO-HUAN!?
WHERE ARE YOU?
FSH AAA
I'M... RIGHT HERE!

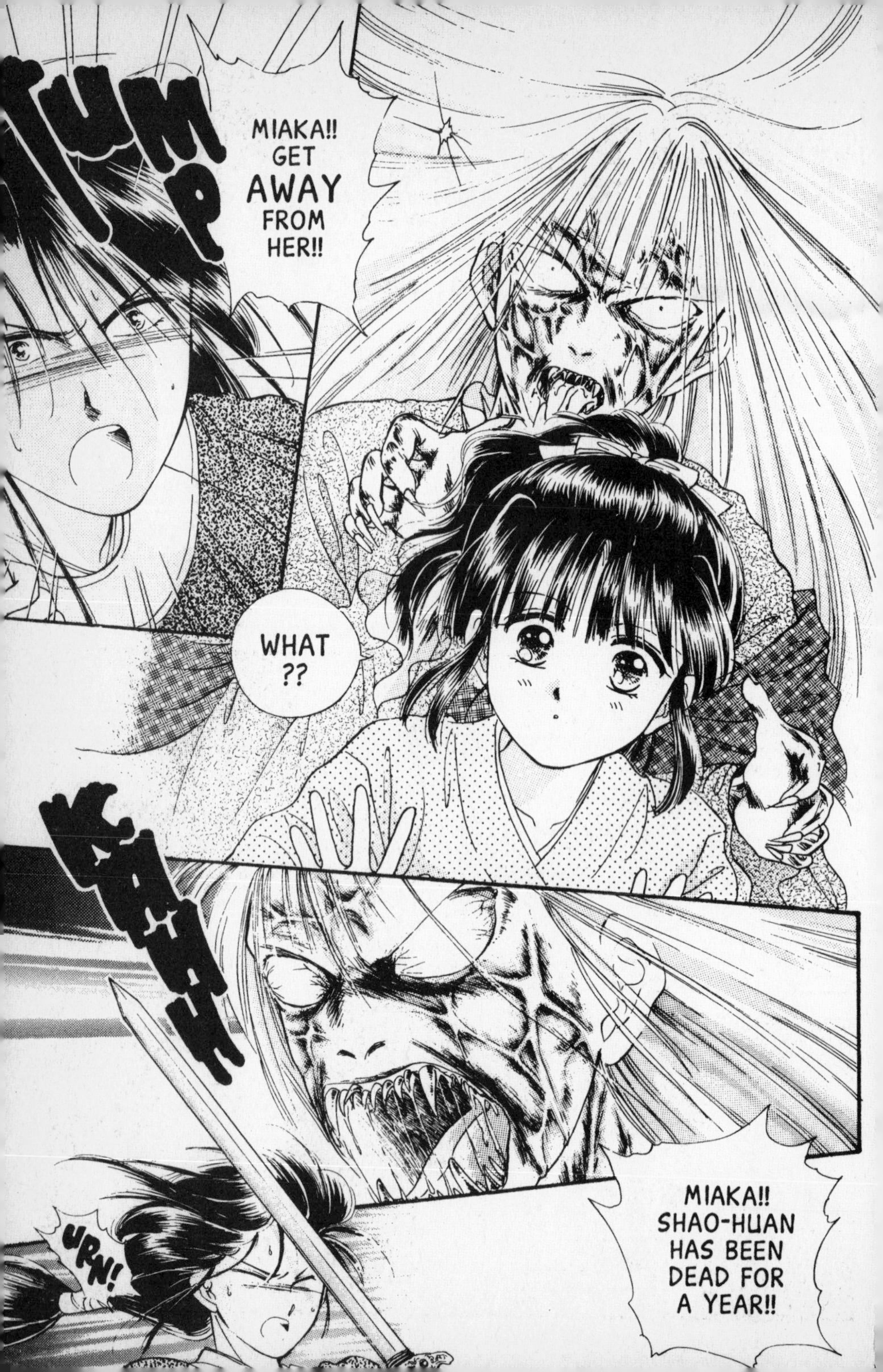
THUMP
MIAKA!! GET AWAY FROM HER!!
WHAT ??
URN!
MIAKA!! SHAO-HUAN HAS BEEN DEAD FOR A YEAR!!

WHAT??

GATCH

KRCH KRCH KRCH KRCH KRCH

OUCH-IE OUCH-IE OUCH-IE OUCH-IE

YOU'RE TOO LATE. THIS GIRL IS *MINE!* HER BONES WILL TASTE DELICIOUS!

SSHHT

I-I'M SO WEAK...

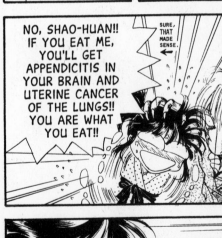

NO, SHAO-HUAN!! IF YOU EAT ME, YOU'LL GET APPENDICITIS IN YOUR BRAIN AND UTERINE CANCER OF THE LUNGS!! YOU ARE WHAT YOU EAT!!

SURE, THAT MADE SENSE. ←

!!

STOP !!

TMP

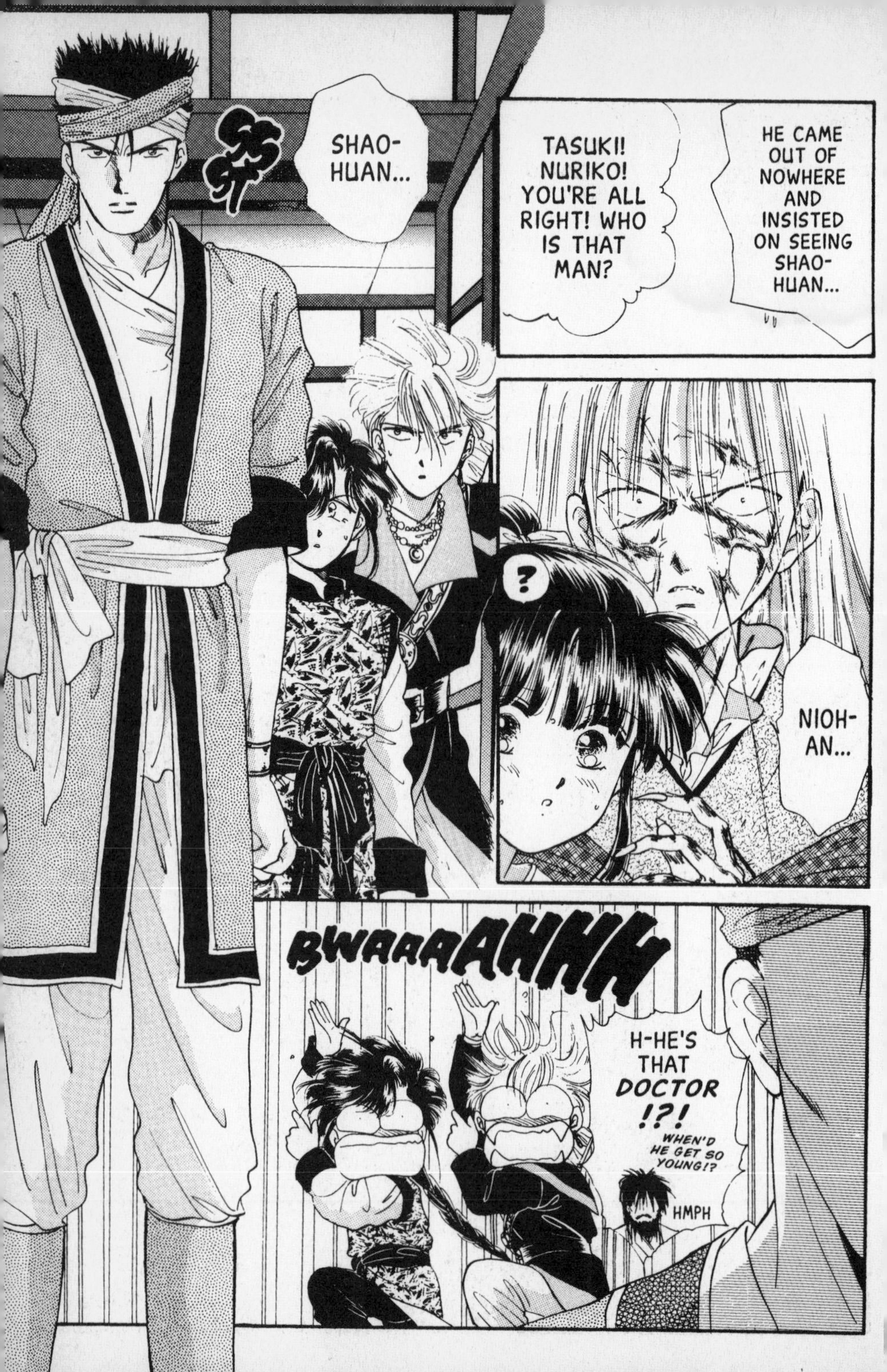
SHAO-HUAN...
TASUKI!! NURIKO! YOU'RE ALL RIGHT! WHO IS THAT MAN?
HE CAME OUT OF NOWHERE AND INSISTED ON SEEING SHAO-HUAN...
?
NIOH-AN...
BWAAAAHHHH
H-HE'S THAT DOCTOR !?!
WHEN'D HE GET SO YOUNG!?
HMPH

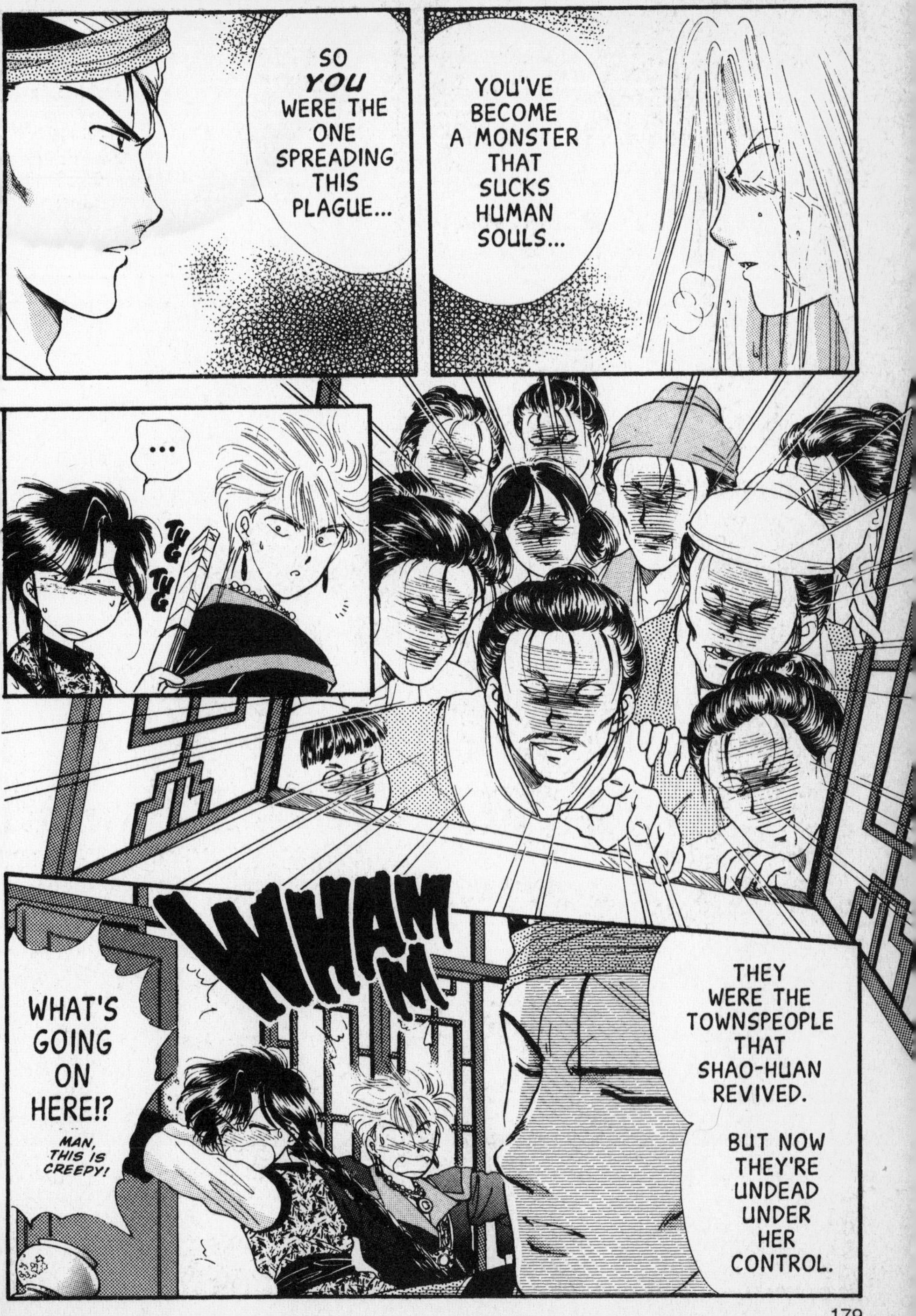
SO *YOU* WERE THE ONE SPREADING THIS PLAGUE...
YOU'VE BECOME A MONSTER THAT SUCKS HUMAN SOULS...
...
THG THG
WHAMM
WHAT'S GOING ON HERE!?
MAN, THIS IS CREEPY!
THEY WERE THE TOWNSPEOPLE THAT SHAO-HUAN REVIVED.
BUT NOW THEY'RE UNDEAD UNDER HER CONTROL.

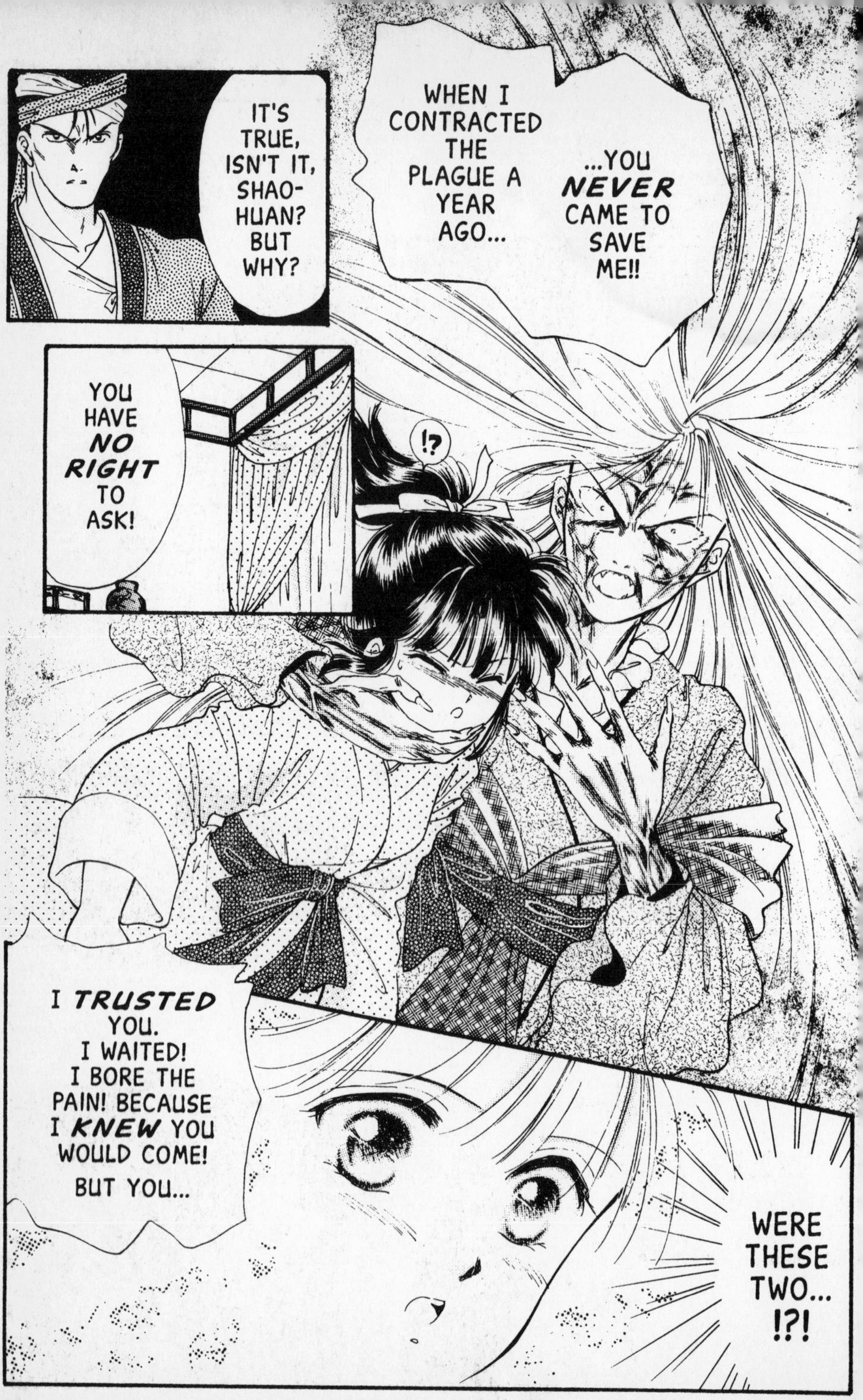
IT'S TRUE, ISN'T IT, SHAO-HUAN? BUT WHY?
WHEN I CONTRACTED THE PLAGUE A YEAR AGO...
...YOU NEVER CAME TO SAVE ME!!
YOU HAVE NO RIGHT TO ASK!
!?
I TRUSTED YOU. I WAITED! I BORE THE PAIN! BECAUSE I KNEW YOU WOULD COME! BUT YOU...
WERE THESE TWO... !?!

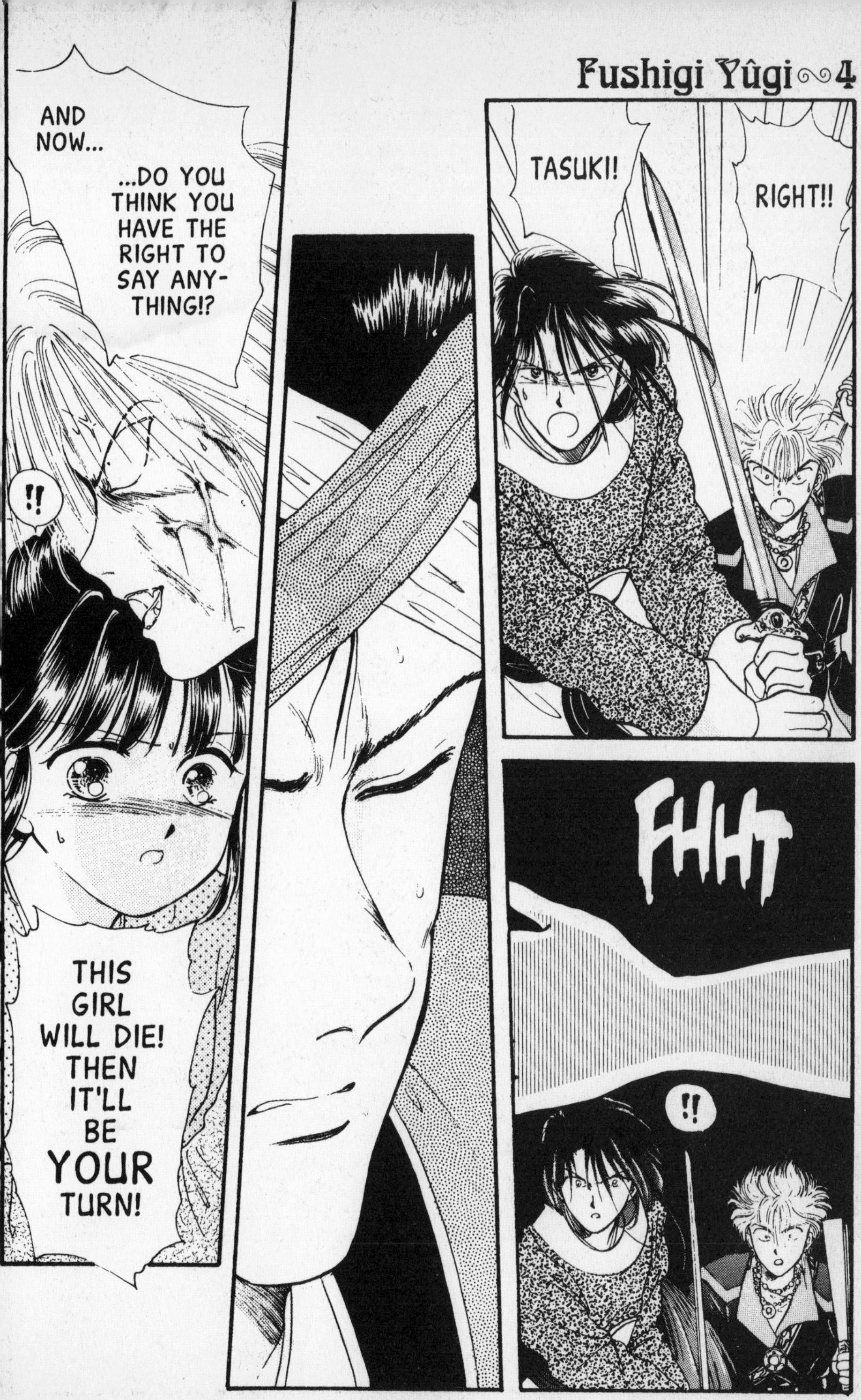
AND NOW...
...DO YOU THINK YOU HAVE THE RIGHT TO SAY ANY-THING!?
!!
THIS GIRL WILL DIE! THEN IT'LL BE YOUR TURN!
TASUKI!!
RIGHT!!
FHHT
!!

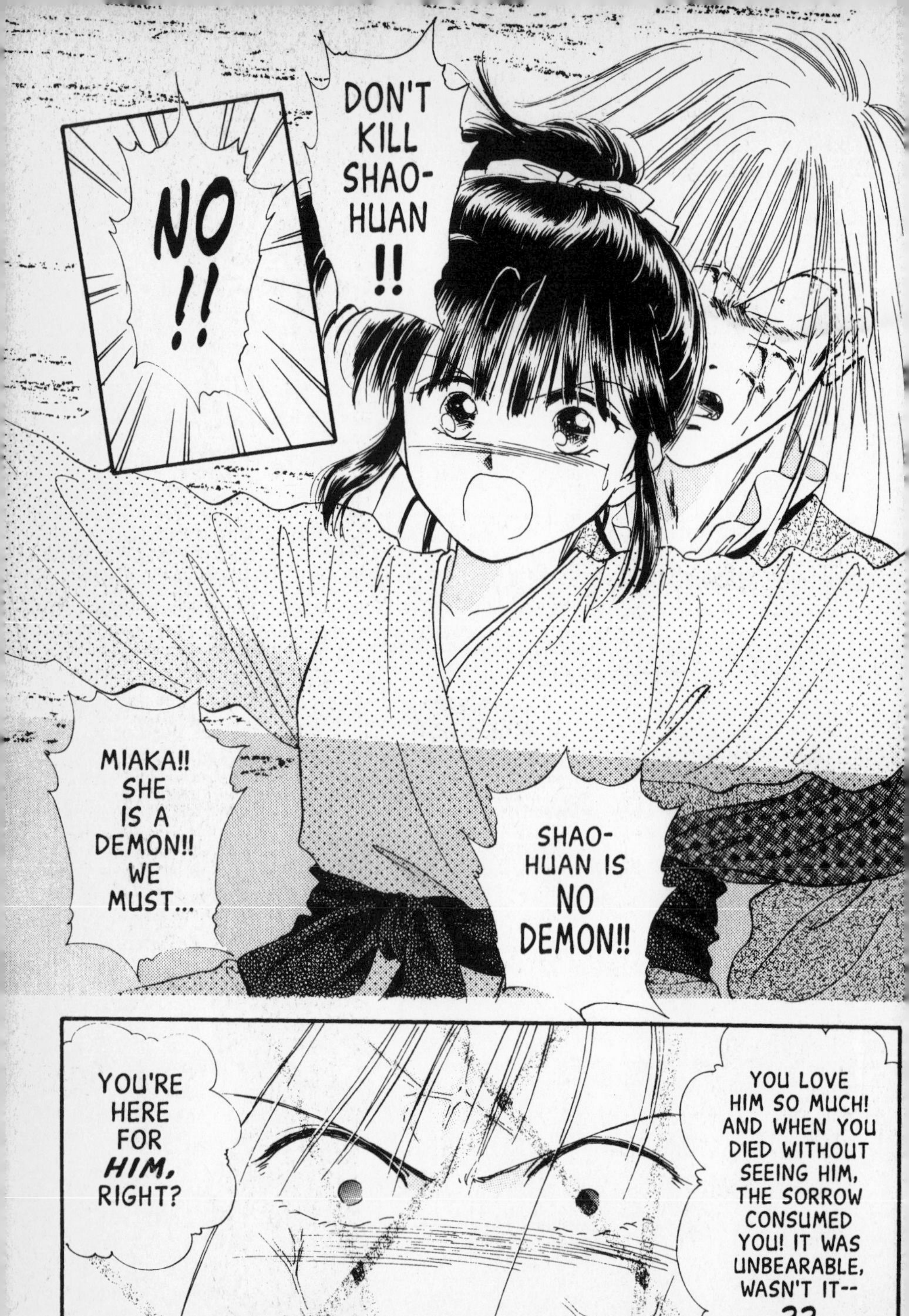
NO!!
DON'T KILL SHAO-HUAN!!
MIAKA!! SHE IS A DEMON!! WE MUST...
SHAO-HUAN IS NO DEMON!!
YOU'RE HERE FOR *HIM,* RIGHT?
YOU LOVE HIM SO MUCH! AND WHEN YOU DIED WITHOUT SEEING HIM, THE SORROW CONSUMED YOU! IT WAS UNBEARABLE, WASN'T IT--??

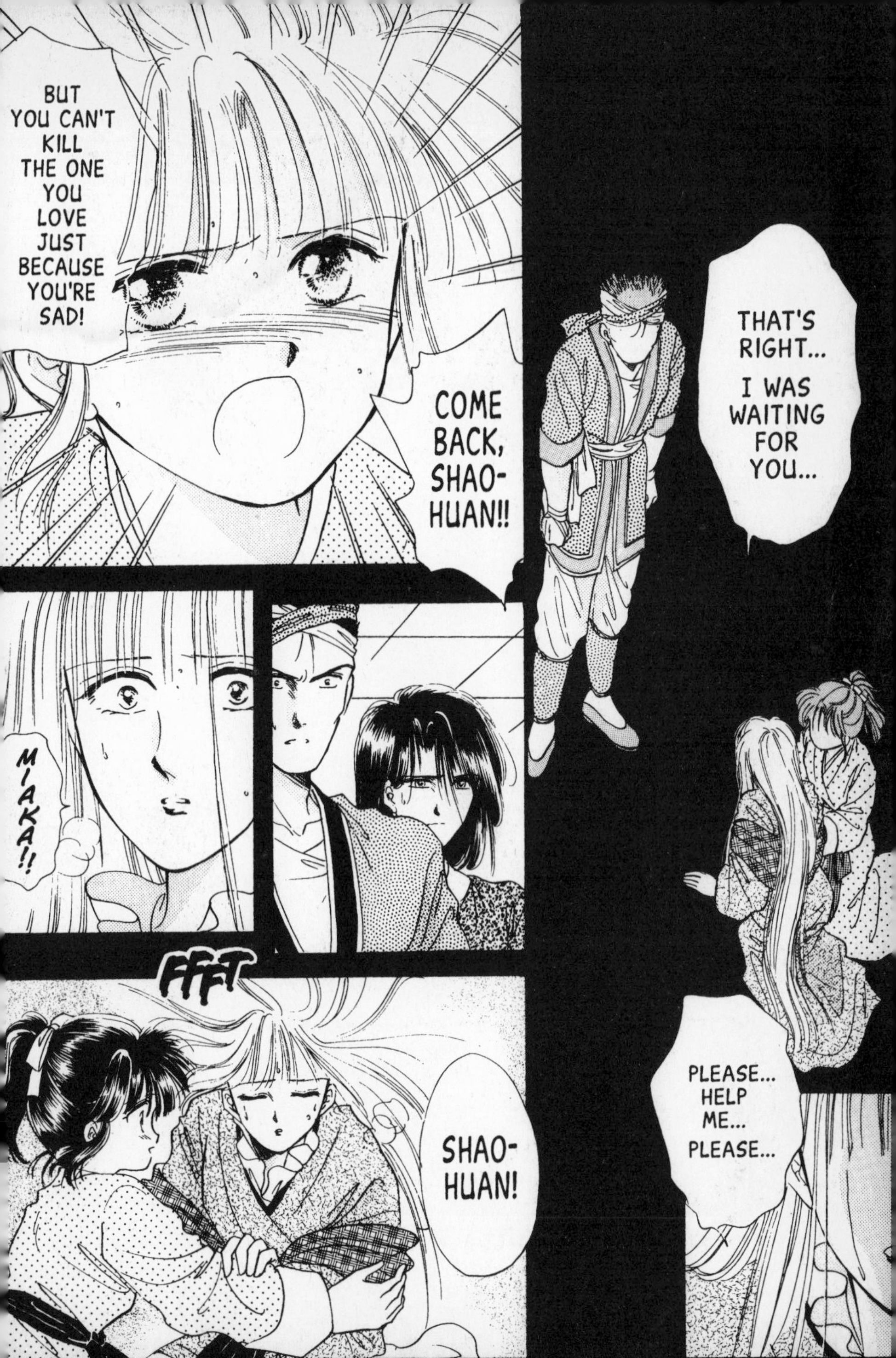
BUT YOU CAN'T KILL THE ONE YOU LOVE JUST BECAUSE YOU'RE SAD!
COME BACK, SHAO-HUAN!!
MIAKA!!
FFFT
SHAO-HUAN!
THAT'S RIGHT... I WAS WAITING FOR YOU...
PLEASE... HELP ME... PLEASE...

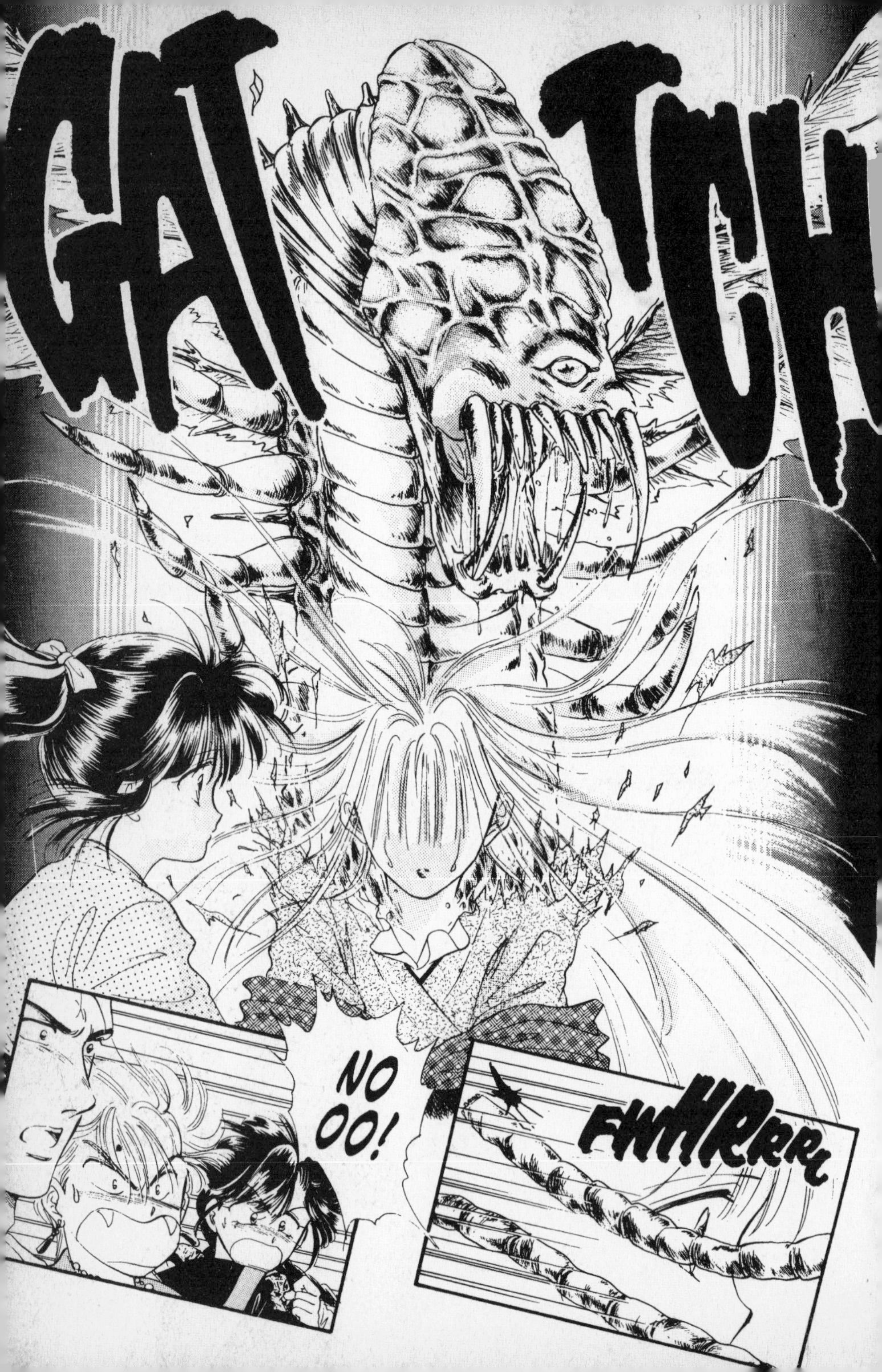
CATTCH
NOOO!
FWHRRRR

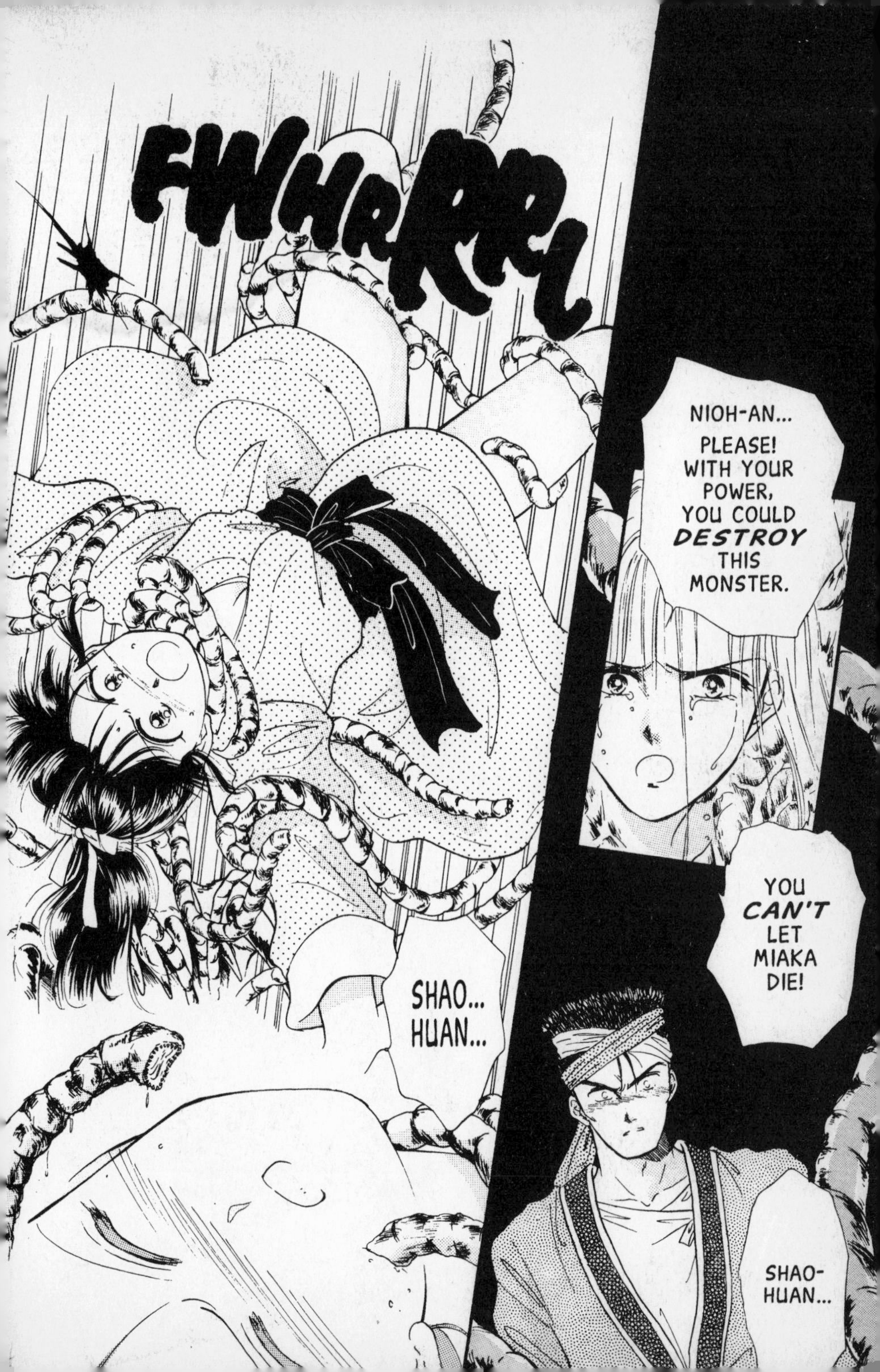
FWHRRRL
SHAO... HUAN...
NIOH-AN... PLEASE! WITH YOUR POWER, YOU COULD DESTROY THIS MONSTER.
YOU CAN'T LET MIAKA DIE!
SHAO-HUAN...

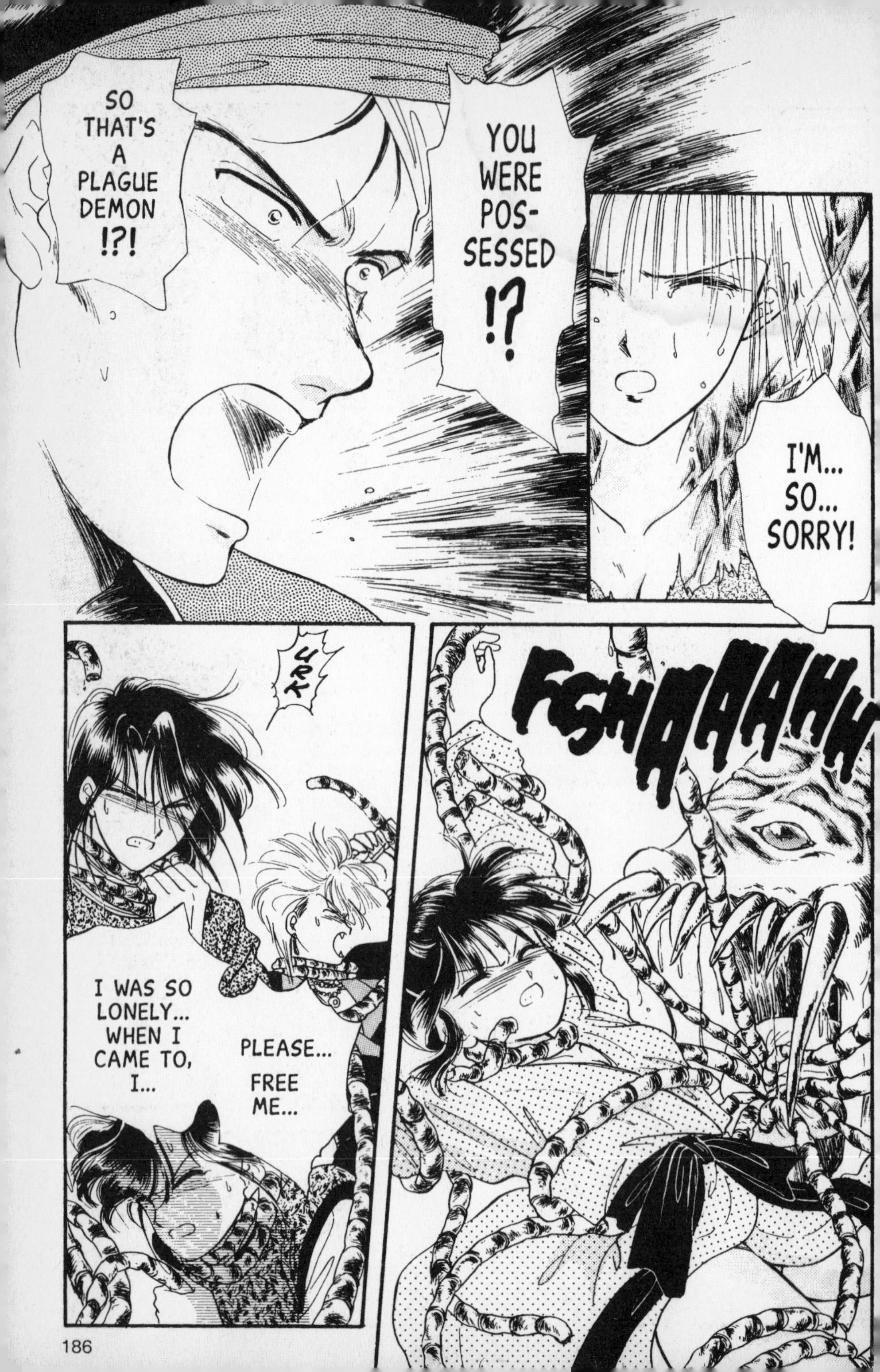
SO THAT'S A PLAGUE DEMON !?!
YOU WERE POS-SESSED !?
I'M... SO... SORRY!
URK
I WAS SO LONELY... WHEN I CAME TO, I...
PLEASE...
FREE ME...
FSHAAAAHH

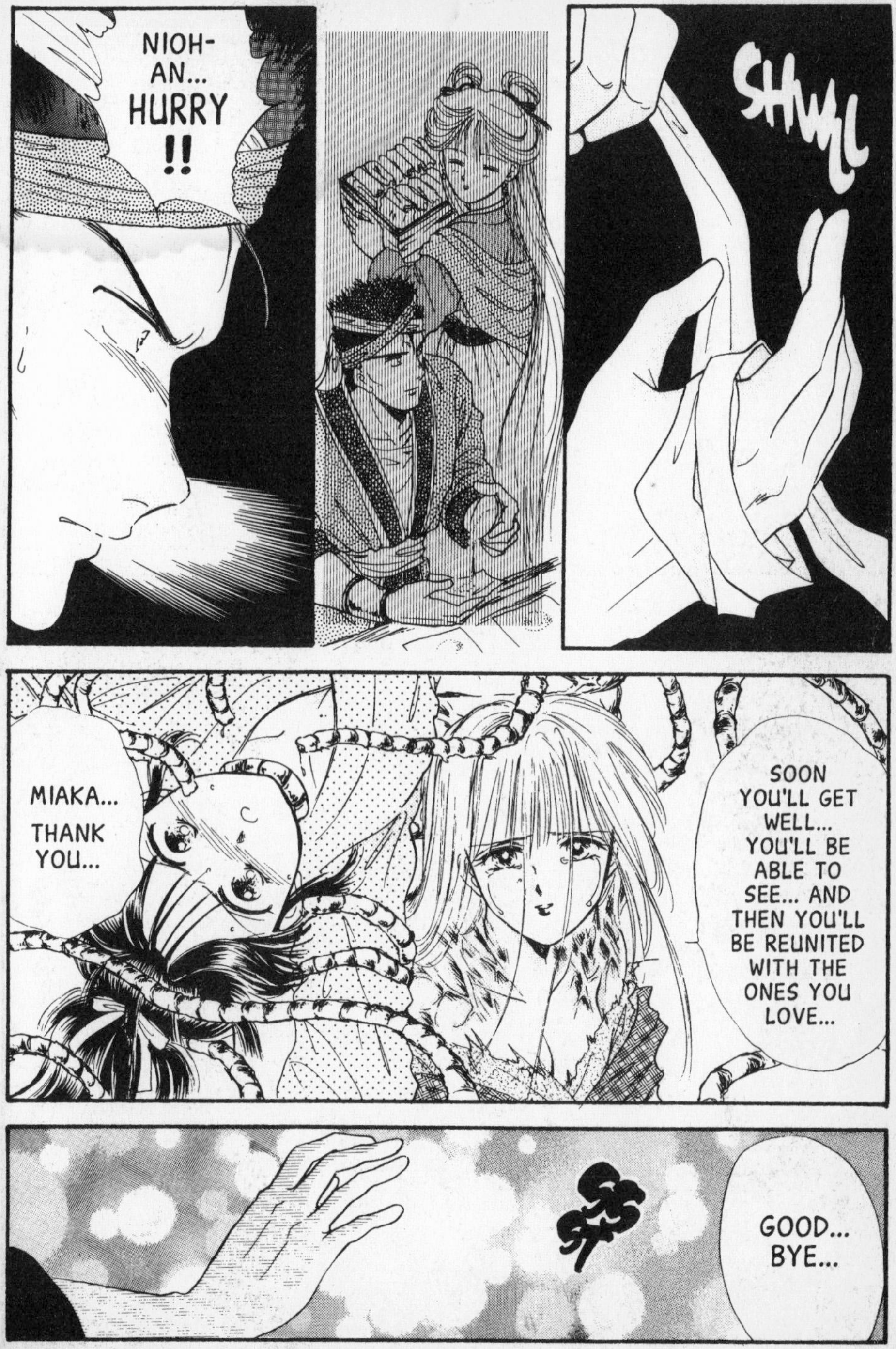
NIOH-AN... HURRY!!
SHWL
MIAKA... THANK YOU...
SOON YOU'LL GET WELL... YOU'LL BE ABLE TO SEE... AND THEN YOU'LL BE REUNITED WITH THE ONES YOU LOVE...
GOOD... BYE...

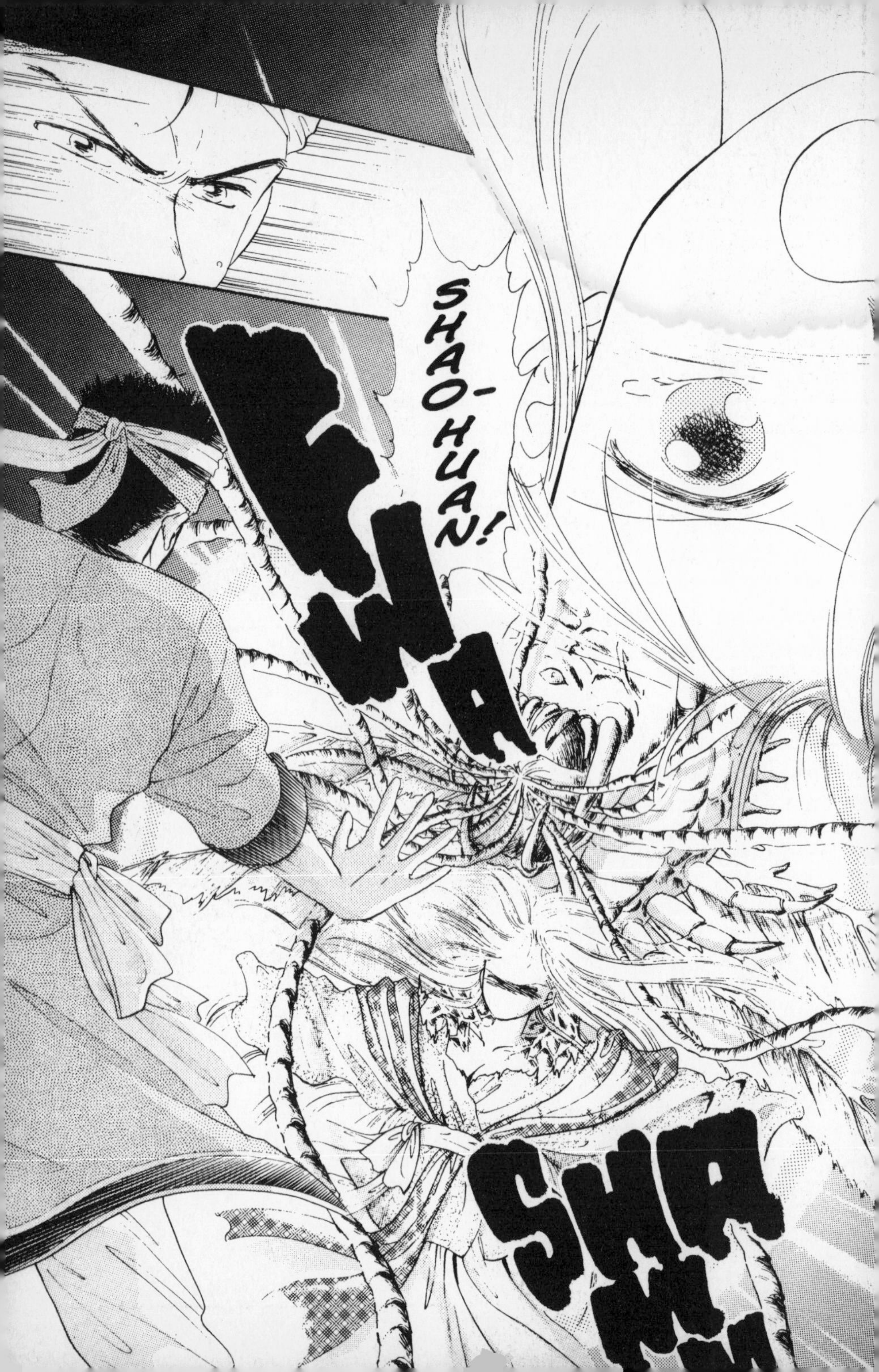
SHAO-HUAN!
SHA

I WANTED TO SEE YOU JUST ONE MORE TIME...

FSHH

THE WHOLE HOUSE WAS AN ILLU-SION!

MIAKA! ARE YOU ALL RIGHT ??

GROSS! THEY ALL TURNED INTO MUMMIES!!

TH' SPELL GOT BROKEN! AN' THAT'LL BE TH' END OF TH' PLAGUE!!

FARE-WELL, NIOH-AN...

MIAKA, CAN YOU SEE ME ??

.....

189

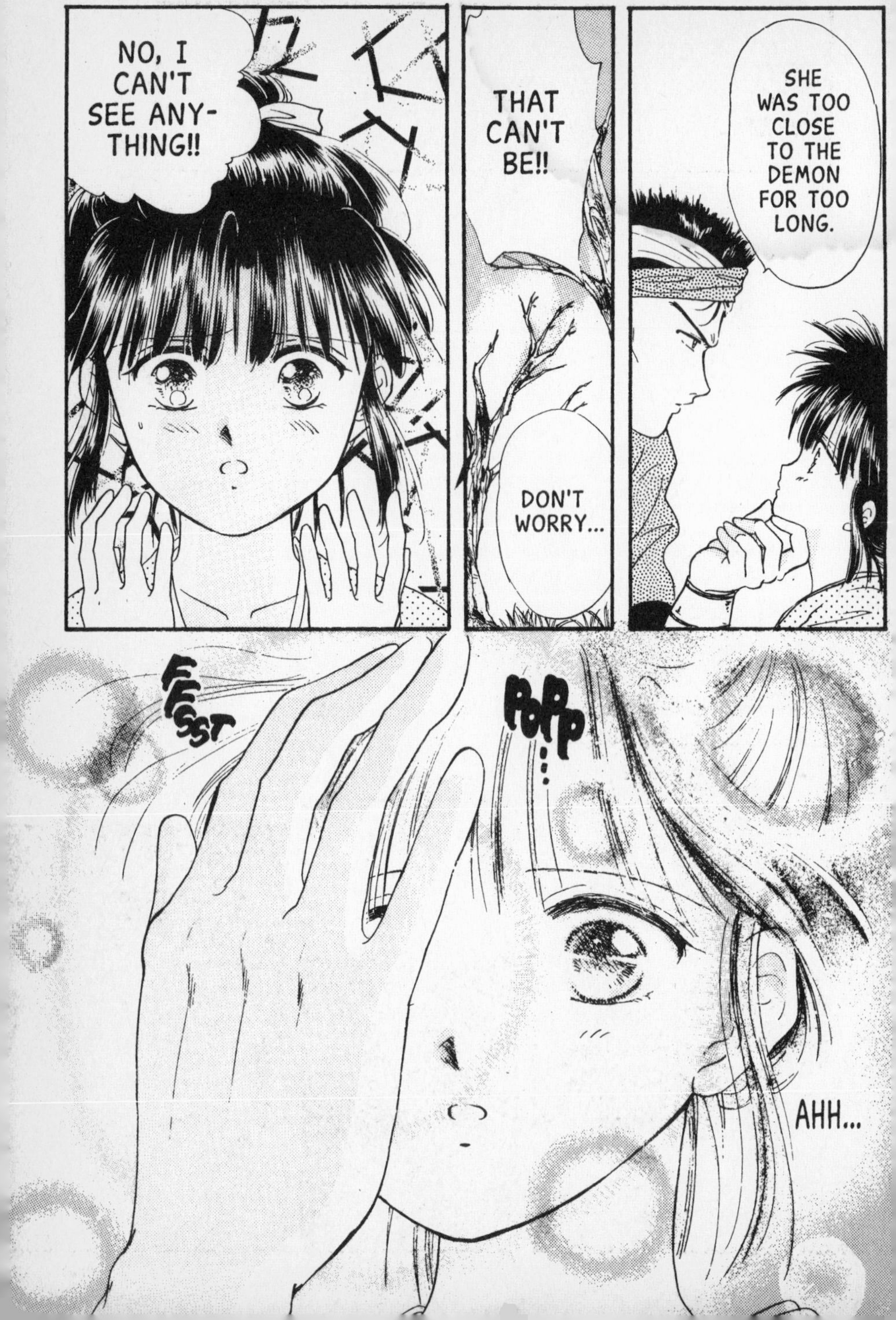
NO, I CAN'T SEE ANY-THING!!
THAT CAN'T BE!!
DON'T WORRY...
SHE WAS TOO CLOSE TO THE DEMON FOR TOO LONG.
FFSST
POPP...
AHH...

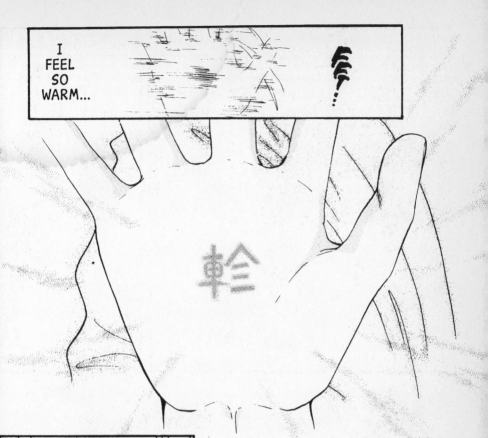

I FEEL SO WARM...

IT'S ONE OF SUZAKU'S CHARACTERS!!

GRABB

MIAKA! YOU CAN SEE!!

191

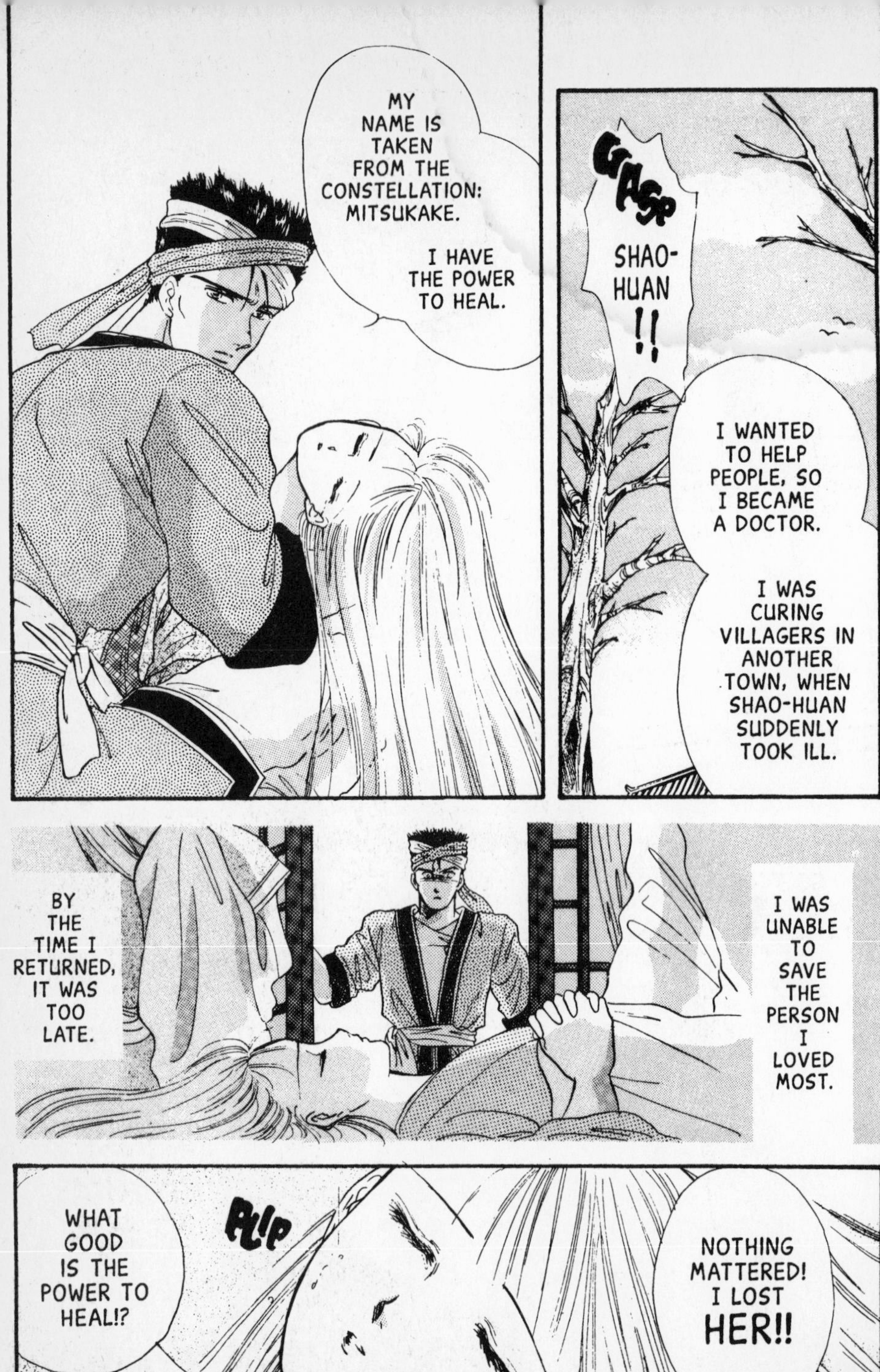
MY NAME IS TAKEN FROM THE CONSTELLATION: MITSUKAKE.
I HAVE THE POWER TO HEAL.
GASP
SHAO-HUAN !!
I WANTED TO HELP PEOPLE, SO I BECAME A DOCTOR.
I WAS CURING VILLAGERS IN ANOTHER TOWN, WHEN SHAO-HUAN SUDDENLY TOOK ILL.
BY THE TIME I RETURNED, IT WAS TOO LATE.
I WAS UNABLE TO SAVE THE PERSON I LOVED MOST.
WHAT GOOD IS THE POWER TO HEAL!?
PLIP
NOTHING MATTERED! I LOST HER!!

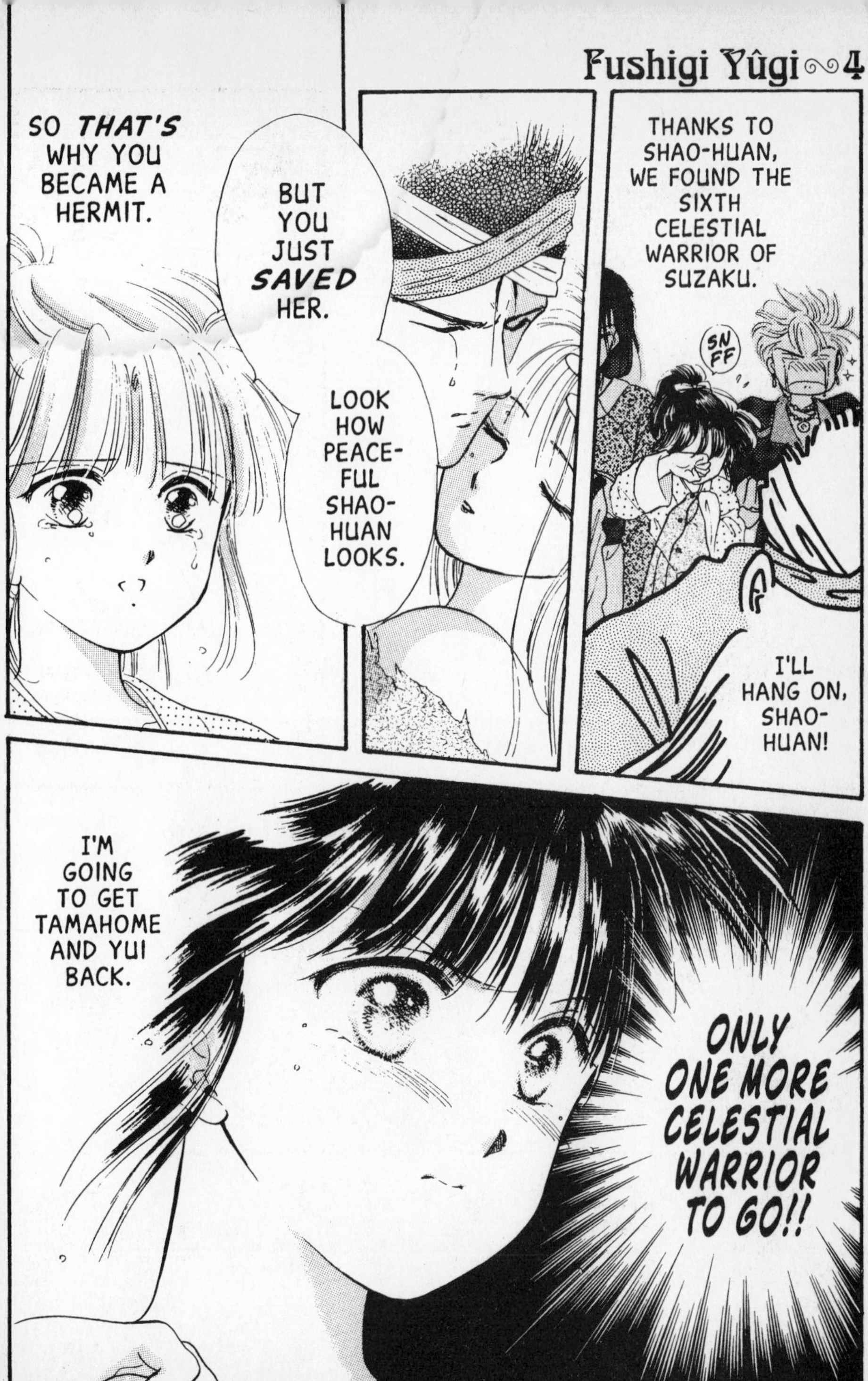
SO *THAT'S* WHY YOU BECAME A HERMIT.
BUT YOU JUST *SAVED* HER.
LOOK HOW PEACE-FUL SHAO-HUAN LOOKS.
THANKS TO SHAO-HUAN, WE FOUND THE SIXTH CELESTIAL WARRIOR OF SUZAKU.
SNFF
I'LL HANG ON, SHAO-HUAN!
I'M GOING TO GET TAMAHOME AND YUI BACK.
ONLY ONE MORE CELESTIAL WARRIOR TO GO!!

TO BE CONTINUED IN VOLUME 5: RIVAL

A CELESTIAL LEGEND GIVEN FORM!

CERES
Celestial Legend

By Yû Watase

From the acclaimed author of "Fushigi Yûgi" Yû Watase, one of the most anticipated anime series of the year! The supernatural thriller begins on the day of Aya and her twin brother Aki's 16th birthday, when their grandfather decides it's time to share a long guarded secret. The twins are summoned to the massive, mysterious Mikage House where they find thier extended family assembled and waiting. They are given a curious gift and in that instant their destiny begins to unfold... Both the video and the monthly comic unveil the secret of Aya and Ceres, the Celestial Legend

AVAILABLE MONTHLY IN COMICS, VIDEOS, AND DVDS!

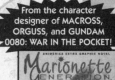

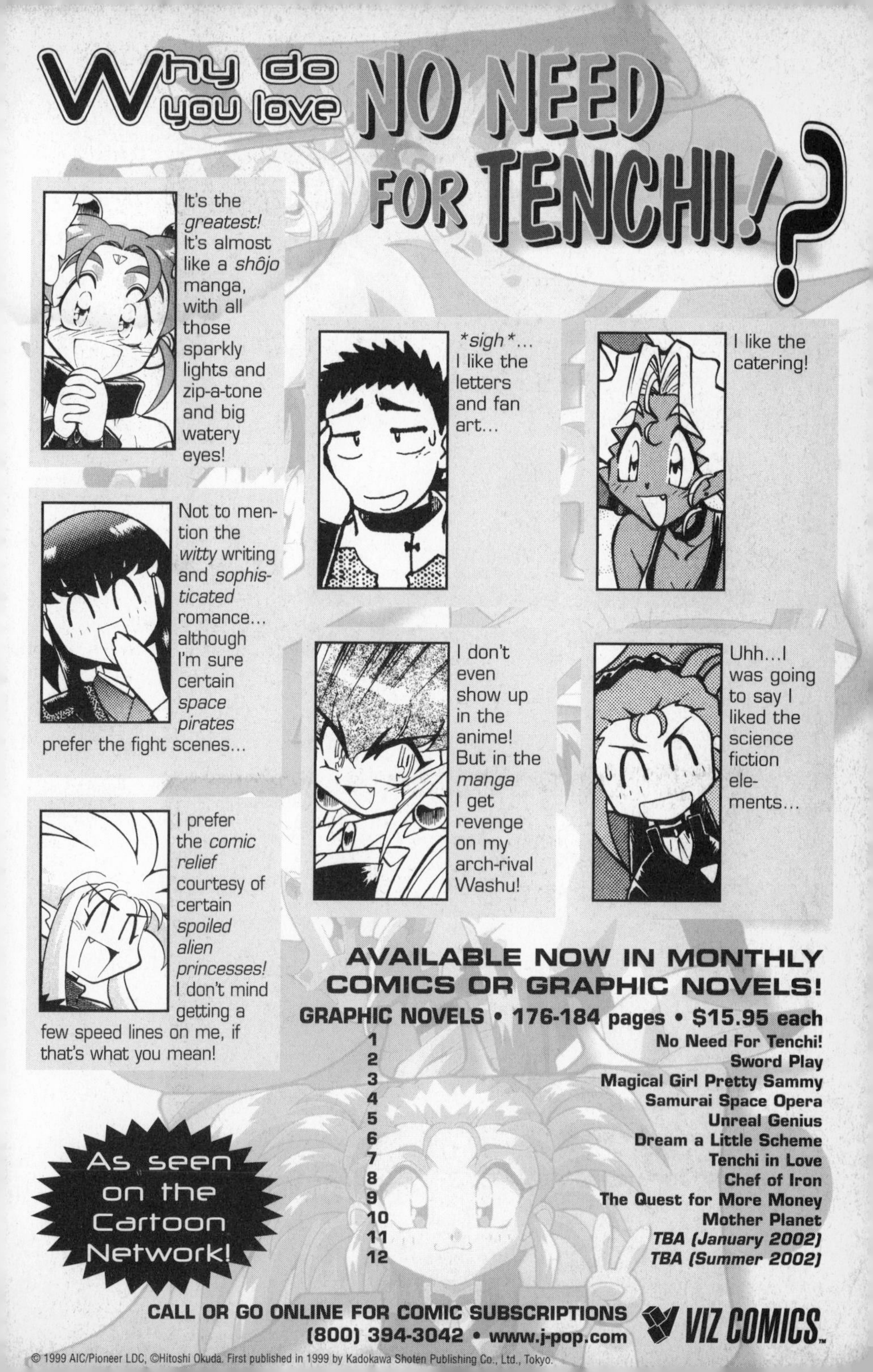
Why do you love NO NEED FOR TENCHI!?
It's the greatest! It's almost like a shôjo manga, with all those sparkly lights and zip-a-tone and big watery eyes!
sigh... I like the letters and fan art...
I like the catering!
Not to mention the witty writing and sophisticated romance... although I'm sure certain space pirates prefer the fight scenes...
I don't even show up in the anime! But in the manga I get revenge on my arch-rival Washu!
Uhh...I was going to say I liked the science fiction elements...
I prefer the comic relief courtesy of certain spoiled alien princesses! I don't mind getting a few speed lines on me, if that's what you mean!
AVAILABLE NOW IN MONTHLY COMICS OR GRAPHIC NOVELS!
GRAPHIC NOVELS • 176-184 pages • $15.95 each
1 No Need For Tenchi!
2 Sword Play
3 Magical Girl Pretty Sammy
4 Samurai Space Opera
5 Unreal Genius
6 Dream a Little Scheme
7 Tenchi in Love
8 Chef of Iron
9 The Quest for More Money
10 Mother Planet
11 TBA (January 2002)
12 TBA (Summer 2002)
As seen on the Cartoon Network!
CALL OR GO ONLINE FOR COMIC SUBSCRIPTIONS
(800) 394-3042 • www.j-pop.com
VIZ COMICS™
© 1999 AIC/Pioneer LDC, ©Hitoshi Okuda. First published in 1999 by Kadokawa Shoten Publishing Co., Ltd., Tokyo.

VIZ SHOP-BY-MAIL — recent releases & highlights

VIZ VIDEO

SANCTUARY: THE MOVIE (Live Action)	Sub $34.95
A CHINESE GHOST STORY: THE TSUI HARK ANIMATION	Eng $19.98/Sub $24.98/DVD $29.98
FATAL FURY	
THE BOX SET	Eng $54.95
GALAXY EXPRESS 999	
GALAXY EXPRESS 999	Eng $24.95/Sub $29.95
ADIEU GALAXY EXPRESS 999	Eng $24.95/Sub $29.95
GREY: DIGITAL TARGET	Eng $19.98/Sub $24.98
KEY THE METAL IDOL DVD	
AWAKENING (VOLS.1-3)	Bilingual $29.98
DREAMING (VOLS.4-6)	Bilingual $29.98
MAISON IKKOKU	
WELCOME TO MAISON IKKOKU	Eng $24.95/Sub $29.95
RONIN BLUES	Eng $24.95/Sub $29.95
SPRING WASABI	Eng $24.95/Sub $29.95
SOICHIRO'S SHADOW	Eng $24.95/Sub $29.95
PLAYING DOUBLES	Eng $24.95/Sub $29.95
LOVE-LOVE STORY	Eng $24.95/Sub $29.95
CALL ME CONFUSED	Eng $24.95/Sub $29.95
NO STRINGS ATTACHED	Eng $24.95/Sub $29.95
A WINTER'S YARN	Eng $24.95/Sub $29.95
HOME FOR THE HOLIDAY	Eng $24.95/Sub $29.95
KYOKO + SOICHIRO	Eng $24.95/Sub $29.95
SHE'S LEAVING HOME	Eng $24.95/Sub $29.95
MY BEST RIVAL'S WEDDING	Eng $24.95/Sub $29.95
THE FOLKS CAN'T HELP IT	Eng $24.95/Sub $29.95
ALL SWELL THAT ENDS (IN A WELL)	Eng $24.95/Sub $29.95
GODAI COME HOME	Eng $24.95/Sub $29.95
PIYO PIYO DIARIES	Eng $24.95/Sub $29.95
DATE FOR FIVE	Eng $24.95/Sub $29.95
DRESS YOU UP	Sub $28.95
PRESENT FROM THE PAST	Sub $28.95
HOT SPRINGS HOLIDAY	Sub $28.95
WISH UPON A FALL	Sub $28.95
ON THIN ICE	Sub $28.95
THE DAYS OF WINE AND FREELOADERS	Sub $28.95
WELCOME TO THE DOGHOUSE (DEC '00)	Sub $28.95
REQUIEM FOR SOICHIRO (JAN'01)	Sub $28.95
SCHOOLGIRL FANTASY (FEB'01)	Sub $28.95
MERMAID'S SCAR	Eng $19.95
NIGHT WARRIORS: DARKSTALKERS' REVENGE, THE ANIMATED SERIES	
VOL.1-4	Eng $19.95/Sub $24.95 ea.
DVD VOL. 1: ALPHA (CONTAINS VOLS. 1-2)	DVD $29.98
VOL. 2: OMEGA (CONTAINS VOLS. 3-4)	DVD $29.98
OGRE SLAYER 1 & 2	Eng $24.95 each
ONE-POUND GOSPEL	Sub $29.95
PLEASE SAVE MY EARTH DVD	Bilingual $29.98
POKéMON	
OUR HERO MEOWTH	VHS $14.98/DVD $24.98
THE FINAL BADGE	VHS $14.98/DVD $24.98
PO-Ké CORRAL	VHS $14.98/DVD $24.98
HANG TEN PIKACHU	VHS $14.98/DVD $24.98
SHOWTIME	VHS $14.98/DVD $24.98
INTO THE ARENA	VHS $14.98/DVD $24.98
RANMA 1/2	
DIGITAL DOJO BOX SET	$199.95
(All 18 episodes of first TV series plus bonus music disc!)	
ANYTHING-GOES MARTIAL ARTS BOX SET	$199.95
(All 22 episodes of second TV series plus bonus music CD!)	
OAV BOX SET (All 6 vols plus bonus music CD!)	$124.95
HARD BATTLE BOX SET (24 eps plus bonus music CD!)	$199.95
THE COLLECTOR'S EDITION: (Subtitled TV Series)	
VOLS. 1-6	$34.95 each
RANMA 1/2 OUTTA CONTROL	
GREAT EGGSPECTATIONS	Eng $24.95/Sub $28.95
PINKY PROMISED	Eng $24.95/Sub $28.95
YOU BET YOUR DOJO	Eng $24.95/Sub $28.95
EAT, DRINK, MAN-WHO-TURNS-INTO-WOMAN	Eng $24.95/Sub $28.95
RANMA 1/2 MARTIAL MAYHEM	
BATTLE: FOIE GRAS	Eng $24.95
SWIMMING WITH PSYCHOS	Eng $24.95
NIGHTMARE ON HAPPOSAI STREET	Eng $24.95
MY KAGEMUSHA, MYSELF (OCT '00)	Eng $24.95
BUNS OF STEEL	Sub $28.95
MARRY ME, AKANE (JAN'01)	Sub $28.95
RANMA 1/2 SEASON 6	
WHO DO? VOODOO (DEC '00)	Sub $28.95
VIDEO GIRL AI	
VOL. 1: I'M HERE FOR YOU	Eng $24.98/Sub $29.98
VOL. 2: PRESENT	Eng $24.98/Sub $29.98
VOL. 3: AI, LOVE & SADNESS	Eng $24.98/Sub $29.98

VIZ MUSIC

KEY THE METAL IDOL	
ORIGINAL CD SOUNDTRACK	$16.95
ORIGINAL CD SCORE	$16.95
RANMA 1/2	
OPENING SONGS COLLECTION	$16.95
CLOSING SONGS COLLECTION	$16.95
RESIDENT EVIL 2 ORIGINAL SOUNDTRACK	$16.95

VIZ GRAPHIC NOVELS

ADOLF	
A Tale of the Twentieth Century	hard $19.95/soft $16.95
An Exile in Japan	hard $19.95/soft $16.95
The Half-Aryan	hard $19.95/soft $16.95
Days of Infamy	hard $19.95/soft $16.95
1945 and All That Remains	hard $19.95/soft $16.95
ASHEN VICTOR	$14.95
BATTLE ANGEL ALITA	
FALLEN ANGEL	$15.95
ANGEL'S ASCENSION	$16.95
BIO-BOOSTER ARMOR GUYVER	
ARMAGEDDON	$15.95
CRYING FREEMAN	
PERFECT COLLECTION: THE KILLING RING	$19.95
PERFECT COLLECTION: ABDUCTION IN CHINATOWN	$17.95
DRAGON BALL	
VOL. 1-3	$14.95 each
VOL.4 (FEB '01)	$14.95
DRAGON BALL Z	
VOL.1-2	$14.95 each
VOL.3 (JAN '01)	$14.95
EAGLE: THE MAKING OF AN ASIAN-AMERICAN PRESIDENT	
BOOK 1, 2	$19.95
FUSHIGI YÛGI VOLS. 1-3	$15.95 each
VOL. 4 (FEB '01)	$15.95
GALAXY EXPRESS 999	
VOLS. 1-2	$16.95 each
VOL. 3	$17.95
INU-YASHA VOL. 1-7	$15.95 each
VOL. 8 (JAN '01)	$15.95
MAGICAL POKéMON JOURNEY:	
A PARTY WITH PIKACHU	$13.95
MAISON IKKOKU	
GAME, SET, MATCH	$16.95
WELCOME HOME	$16.95
MARIONETTE GENERATION (JAN '01)	$15.95
MOBILE SUIT GUNDAM 0079. VOL.2	$15.95 each
NAUSICAÄ OF THE VALLEY OF WIND	
PERFECT COLLECTION BOX SET	$69.95
NEON GENESIS EVANGELION VOL.1-4	$15.95 each
NEON GENESIS EVANGELION: SPECIAL COLLECTOR'S EDITION	

VOL. 1-4	$15.95 each
NO NEED FOR TENCHI!!	
TENCHI IN LOVE	$15.95
CHEF OF IRON	$15.95
THE QUEST FOR MORE MONEY (DEC '00)	$15.95
OGRE SLAYER VOL. 1-2	$15.95 each
POKéMON ADVENTURES	
VOL. 1	$13.95
VOL. 2: LEGENDARY POKéMON	$14.95
POKéMON GRAPHIC NOVELS	
THE ELECTRIC TALE OF PIKACHU	$12.95
POKéMON: PIKACHU SHOCKS BACK	$12.95
POKéMON: ELECTRIC PIKACHU BOOGALOO	$12.95
POKéMON: SURF'S UP, PIKACHU	$12.95
POKéMON THE FIRST MOVIE GRAPHIC NOVEL	$12.95
POKEMON TV ANIMATION COMICS VOL.1	$10.95
RANMA 1/2	
VOL. 1, 15	$16.95
VOLS. 2-16	$15.95 each
VOL. 17 (FEB '01)	$15.95
SANCTUARY	
VOLS. 7-9	$16.95 each
SILENT MöBIUS VOLS. 1, 2, 3, 4, 5	$16.95 each
STEAM DETECTIVES VOL. 1-3	$15.95 each
VIDEO GIRL AI VOLS. 1-2	$15.95 each
X/1999	
INTERMEZZO	$15.95
SERENADE	$15.95
DUET	$15.95

PULP GRAPHIC NOVELS

BAKUNE YOUNG	$16.95
BANANA FISH	
VOLS. 1, 2, 3	$15.95 each
BLACK AND WHITE VOLS. 1, 2, 3	$15.95 each
DANCE TILL TOMORROW VOLS. 1, 2, 3	$15.95 each
HEARTBROKEN ANGELS	$15.95
STRAIN	
VOL. 1	$15.95
VOL. 2-3	$15.95 each
VOL.4	$16.95
VOYEUR	$16.95
VOYEURS, INC. VOL. 1	$15.95
VOL. 2 (DEC '00)	$15.95

CADENCE BOOKS

ANIME INTERVIEWS: THE FIRST FIVE YEARS OF ANIMERICA, ANIME & MANGA MONTHLY	$19.95
DER MOND: THE ART OF YOSHIYUKI SADAMOTO	$29.95
FRESH PULP	$19.95
JAPAN EDGE: THE INSIDER'S GUIDE TO JAPANESE POPULAR SUBCULTURE	$19.95
JAPANESE PARADISE: EXQUISITE HOTELS AND INNS	$29.95
SECRET COMICS JAPAN	$19.95

POKéMON BOOKS

POKéMON TALES	
PIKACHU'S UNPARALLELED ADVENTURE (MOVIE SPECIAL 2)	$4.95
13: EEVEE'S WEATHER REPORT	$4.95
14: DIGLETT'S BIRTHDAY	$4.95
15: FIRST PRIZE FOR STARMIE	$4.95
16: SEEL TO THE RESCUE	$4.95
POKéMON TALES GIFT BOX 1 (INCLUDES VOL. 1-4 & MOVIE SPECIAL 1)	$19.95
POKéMON TALES GIFT BOX 2 (INCLUDES VOL. 5-8 & MOVIE SPECIAL 2)	$19.95
POKéMON ORIGAMI VOL. 1, 2	$8.95 each

LET'S FIND POKéMON! VOL. 1-3	$11.95 each
THE ART OF POKéMON THE FIRST MOVIE	$8.95
THE ART OF POKéMON THE MOVIE 2000	$8.95
POKéMON PAPER MASKS	$10.95
POKéMON STANDEES VOL.1-2	$14.95 each
POKéMON STICK N' PLAY BOOK	$11.95

PULP — SUBSCRIPTIONS (INCLUDES SHIPPING & HANDLING)

ONE YEAR (12 ISSUES) 5% off cover price!	US	$60.00
	CANADA & MEXICO	$70.00
	OTHER	$105.00

ANIMERICA — SUBSCRIPTIONS (INCLUDES SHIPPING & HANDLING)

ONE YEAR (12 ISSUES)	US	$50.00
	CANADA & MEXICO	$60.00
	OTHER	$90.00

ANIMERICA EXTRA — SUBSCRIPTIONS (INCLUDES SHIPPING & HANDLING)

ONE YEAR (12 ISSUES)	US	$50.00
	CANADA & MEXICO	$60.00
	OTHER	$90.00

MERCHANDISE (NORTH AMERICA ONLY)

MAISON IKKOKU T-SHIRT	
(L or XL, PLEASE SPECIFY)	$17.95
RANMA 1/2 MERCHANDISE	
RANMA 1/2 CAPPUCCINO MUG	$16.95
RANMA 1/2 CAP	$16.95
RANMA 1/2 P-CHAN WATCH	$29.95
RANMA 1/2 T-SHIRTS	
#4: RANMA 1/2 LOGO (specify: L or XL)	$17.95
GIRL-TYPE RANMA (specify: L or XL)	$16.95
BOY-TYPE RANMA (specify: L or XL)	$16.95
RYOGA HIBIKI "ANIME WORLD TOUR '99" (S, M, L, XL)	$17.95
STEAM DETECTIVES POSTER	$9.95
POKéMON 2001 POSTER CALENDAR	$12.95

**FOR A COMPLETE LISTING, CALL
1 (800) 394-3042
FOR A FREE CATALOG!**

OR *SHOP ONLINE @*
www.j-pop.com

2000 SPRING SUMMER CATALOG

Viz Shop-By-Mail 2000

(800) 394-3042
(415) 348-8936

ALSO AVAILABLE—GRAPHIC NOVELS, VIDEOS, MUSIC CD'S AND MERCHANDISE FROM